The Heron Legacy

The Heron Legacy

Leona Francombe

merle books
brussels

Published by
Merle Books Brussels
Belgium

First printing 2024

ISBN: 978-1-7371600-2-1 (Paperback)
ISBN: 978-1-7371600-3-8 (eBook)

Cover design:

Nicholas Maxson-Francombe
Art Director, Sandfall Interactive
Montpellier, France

www.leonafrancombe.com

Rien n'est laid dans la forêt parce que tout y est divin.

Nothing is ugly in the forest because everything there is divine.

—Jean-Luc Duvivier de Fortemps

The desire to be a pilgrim is deeply rooted in human nature.

—Sir Steven Runciman

PART ONE

The Pond

I

Forest...

At night it whispered to him from the frontiers of sleep where even dreams feared to go, and he would follow it there, to the places he'd known. On waking, a spicy note of pine sometimes lingered on his cheek, and as he strode to work on the hard pavement of New York City as he used to stride through the trees, it seemed he could feel soft, damp earth underfoot.

When everyone had left the office for the day and the great city glittered into splendor outside his window, he would take the few mementos of his boyhood from their drawer: a Roman coin and three pottery shards; a small rolled-up banner with the family coat of arms; a quartz crystal. He'd study these treasures as if for the first time, close his eyes and sigh, for at that moment the forest wrapped its silence around him like river mist. In these weightless arms, he could drift far from the alien world that had eaten at his soul for so long, and he could whisper truthfully, for indeed it seemed so real: *I am home!*

Charles Fontaine possessed a host of memory-ways for slipping into his past. His uncle's domain in the Belgian Ardennes was full of them: the steep forests where oak and yew had witnessed centuries of passages and knew Charles's especially well; and the alley of beeches leading to the pond where the herons fished. (He could walk *that* path in a blindfold.)

And Villa Antioch, of course.

His grandfather had constructed the fading, turreted retreat in the early 1900s in a particularly remote part of the forest and it still had no neighbors. From the terrace, you could look out across an unkempt meadow to the river, and beyond it, to the ruins of Blancheron Castle perched on their lonely ridge.

And then there was the river itself: that moody, unreliable Semois. The tight serpentine wound through sudden fogs and dizzying escarpments and folded epochs between its coils. History grew deep roots here. Its breath was still warm.

A stone bridge spanned the river near Villa Antioch, built by the Romans during their occupation of Gaul. According to the villa's current tenant, Charles's uncle, a horseman occasionally rode across the bridge at dusk. "It's your ancestor, lad: Stephen de la Fontaine!" Theodore liked to tell his wide-eyed nephew of an evening, when vapors blurred the ancient arches. "Depending on the weather, of course," he twinkled. "And how much Merlot you've had at supper."

Strangely, memory always seemed to guide Charles to a single boyhood afternoon. *How was it*, he wondered, *that seventeen years had not diminished its brightness?*

II

Nothing is as ancient as the forest, Charles. Except stones, of course. Not even time is as old as stones.

It was the last summer he would spend in the Ardennes before moving with his father to America. He'd been Charles de la Fontaine back then, a diffident, searching sixteen-year-old from Brussels, and the words had been those of his beloved uncle, Theodore de la Fontaine, professor of history at the *lycée* in Bouillon and local eccentric. Theodore had been wandering the Ardennes and clambering about its medieval vestiges since his own boyhood and knew a thing or two about ancientness.

"Uncle, wait!"

They'd crossed the stone bridge and started up the ridge via a near-vertical path. Autumn had already tainted the summer with morning brume and cold rains and the footing was slick.

"Do you feel it, lad?" Theodore called over his shoulder. "The twelfth century breathing on your neck?" His voice was uncharacteristically somber. They both knew this would be their last scramble up to the Blancheron ruins for a long time.

"Of course I feel it," Charles muttered, lagging behind. He always felt the past on his neck in his uncle's company.

"You'd better remember it, then," Theodore said. "You won't find anything like it in America." The battered leather satchel he carried on forest expeditions swung out from his shoulder and narrowly missed his nephew.

Charles peered up the steep, wooded ridge: a perfect natural defense of rock and trunk. No wonder his ancestor had chosen the spot for his castle. Trees took root in fissures and grew with ghastly deformities, and the rocks themselves, raw sculptures of schist and shale, seemed to have been tossed about by a sullen spirit. Maugis, perhaps, the enchanter of Ardennes lore. The notion filled Charles with foreboding.

Maugis was a shape-shifter; a ne'er-do-well. He could wrap himself in water...melt himself into mist. You never knew in what cave or pool he might be lurking.

Charles grasped a birch trunk and leaned out to watch the river glisten far below. *Stephen de la Fontaine had probably scrabbled up this very same shale nine centuries ago*, he thought. Then, with a frisson: *Someone else might have, too.*

"Maybe Duke Godfrey passed by here," Charles shouted ahead to his uncle, letting go of the birch to climb on. His boot let loose a volley of scree. Humidity clung to his chestnut curls and pressed them against his temples.

Theodore halted, breathing heavily. It always amazed Charles that his uncle could haul his heavy bulk up the ridge at all let alone wander for hours through the forest.

"Well, I don't know about that," Theodore said. "Bouillon Castle is over twenty kilometers away, after all. And Godfrey died in Jerusalem in 1100, remember—before Blancheron was even built. Stephen de la Fontaine didn't come back from the Holy Land until 1103, as you know."

"Yes, I know," Charles sighed. He'd already spent eight summers with Theodore and knew more about the medieval goings-on in this corner of Belgium than most post-graduate students. He'd taken to the subject with all the zeal his uncle possessed even if, at times, Theodore tended to repeat himself unduly.

Uncle never said much about Godfrey, though. Of all the figments that roamed these woods—fairies, gnomes, will-o'-the-wisps, witches—the presence of Godfrey of Bouillon was the most confounding.

There were many intriguing holes in his story, for one thing. For another, historians could never quite reconcile the fact that a leader of the First Crusade, who'd performed unspeakable acts with a sword that most scholars of medieval history could hardly have lifted, had also been remembered as a man who was modest, virtuous and kind. He'd been tall, fair and handsome, too, as it happened, so it was no wonder that he'd become an icon of chivalry. He'd powered popular imagination for centuries—and Charles's for all of his boyhood—until modern critics finally weighed in and declared the fair duke from the Ardennes a murdering thug.

Godfrey...Godefroid...Godefroy...Gottvart... Charles knew all the variations of the name. *The Duke of Lower Lorraine.* The nobleman haunted these woodlands even when no mention of him was made.

"Such an outsized historical figure for such a modest little realm!" Theodore liked to say. He never missed a chance to remind his nephew that technically, Godfrey was Belgian, not French. "Oh, all right, lad. He might have been born in Boulogne, it's true, which is in France. But he also might have been born in Baisy, which is now in Belgium. You decide."

Guiltily, with forbidden hero-worship, Charles would read late into the night about the medieval neighbor whose afterlife had turned out to be so troublesome. And what light work it was to cross nine centuries!

August 15, 1096. A Saturday. (Theodore was a mine of interesting tidbits.) Partly cloudy, with a slight breeze lifting the banners. The air reeked of dung and sweat. The scene played out clearly before Charles's eyes:

Godfrey, a descendant of Charlemagne himself, appeared at the gates of Bouillon Castle not on a sleek charger but on his sturdy *ardennais*, a horse described by Julius Caesar as rustic, hard and tireless. The duke seemed pale; distracted. He glanced back over his shoulder, memorizing, perhaps, the gray stone contours of his home. *Or was he looking for someone in the crowd?*

"What was he feeling that day, do you think?" Charles pressed his uncle, as it was he who'd taught him that history lived in such details. "Godfrey was leaving everything behind, wasn't he? His duchy...his beloved mother."

"Yes, you're right," said Theodore. "He probably wasn't feeling the exaltation of a pious Christian heading to Jerusalem, I can tell you that. Just think of all the noise and smell of departure! The terror of the unknown. Legend is rarely as glorious as it seems, lad. No, indeed. How would *you* feel before riding a horse through hostile territory for over four thousand kilometers? In truth, Godfrey probably slept badly the night before and woke up with indigestion."

Why did he never marry? Charles wondered. *Did he go to Jerusalem not planning to return?* Godfrey haunted history books with the same elusiveness that he haunted the woods around Villa Antioch, and thus the duke, whose castle brooded above the same river as Blancheron, kept Charles awake late into the evening. The boy would glance up from his books and hold his breath, wondering if he might have company in the shadows of the turret room where he lodged during the summer. Sometimes he would get out of bed and look down at the Roman bridge far below, considering that perhaps the horseman who clattered across the stones at twilight was not the ghost of his own ancestor at all, but of someone else.

III

The ruins appeared gradually, as if from a dream: here a shoulder of wall; there a broken archway. A chimney soared highest, but crumbled away at the top where ivy had engulfed it.

Charles ran his gaze up the jagged remnant. Something chilled his neck and he pulled up the collar of his oilskin. An uncanny hush draped the site.

"How far can we reach into the past, lad?" Theodore asked. His eyes flashed blue through the gloom of the pines. The unruly gray hair lent him a wizard's air. "Two centuries? Three? *Allez!* Let's try for nine!"

Normally it would have irritated Charles that his uncle still occasionally treated him like a child. But not now...not during this last summer together. His father would be taking him to America soon to start a new life, and with dread Charles awaited this terrible rupture.

"A great opportunity!" Hugues de la Fontaine had gushed to his son, and when he'd resisted, he'd targeted the boy's weakest point: "You can't possibly want Theodore's shabby life as a history professor, can you? No one would want it these days. I'll have my own law firm in the States. You'll go to law school (Yale or Harvard, hopefully), and become a partner. We'll be richer than you can imagine, Charles. You'll see..."

Charles drank in the castle ruins. *This is what I want*, he thought, his heart leaden. *To be like Uncle; to wander the Ardennes and dig up the past.*

He investigated the floor of what had once been the castle's main hall. Nettle, blackberry vines, ferns, milkweed... Nature had covered all human trace. It was tempting to imagine that it hadn't been Stephen de la Fontaine who'd inhabited this place, but someone wilder: Arduinna herself, perhaps, the Celtic goddess of woodlands, who'd taken her meals in this chamber with her retinue of stags, boars and foxes, and made her bed in the long grasses outside.

Charles cupped a toad in his hands, delighting in its softness. *The ermine of Arduinna's cloak.* A red berry glinted under a fern: the lady's ruby, dropped as she was retrieving her spoon.

The castle had been constructed from the shale of the ridge, countless thousands of stone wafers painstakingly laid on top of each other or wedged vertically to make lintels. Where mortar was scant, birds and spiders had moved in, feathering and spinning their boudoirs and traps.

A gap in the wall gazed blankly, its purpose obscure. A support for a wooden beam? A hideaway for valuables?

Charles caught his breath.

A crack in time?

He leaned in as close as he dared. The dampness was unbreathable. Something gleamed inside, then vanished.

"Touch any stone, lad," said Theodore, coming up behind him. "It will still feel warm from the hand that worked it."

What if time really did live in such cracks? Charles thought with a tremor. What if that gleam were the entrance to a corridor, and you could look down nine centuries to see things moving about at the end of it? A cloaked shoulder or quick, silent feet. The curve of a shield. A veiled woman. One image eclipsed all the others: the figure of Stephen de la Fontaine himself padding through this shadow play, pausing at the end of the corridor to look up.

Charles drew back. *Could Stephen see him across all those centuries?*

"Go on, reach inside," Theodore whispered. He'd gathered a bunch of the pale pink carnations that grew wild on the ridge. "*Go on*, lad! History lives in there. You'll be the first to touch that stone since the builder himself, I guarantee you. A medieval handshake, as it were!"

Charles closed his eyes and reached into the gap.

Downy threads brushed the back of his hand. A nut casing scraped against his palm. Nine centuries of damp gave off a chill beyond words.

Theodore pushed him playfully and his hand plunged deeper into the opening. Charles gasped: the stone had a trace of warmth. *Had he imagined it?* His heart pounded.

He turned around:

Theodore was gone.

"Uncle?"

Charles picked his way through the nettles to a broken edge of wall and peered across the ridge. Here and there, castle foundations bulged up under the bracken and grasses and it was difficult to tell which hillocks were natural, and which man-made.

"Uncle!" he shouted. A magpie lifted from the pines with an angry *chak-chak-chak*. Humidity hung over the empty vista like an exhale.

Charles turned back to the castle.

It was then that he saw her.

IV

O f all his memories of Blancheron, this one was the most illusory. He would remember her as an artist might have painted her, in failing light, his brush trembling. Later he would doubt the accuracy of his portrayal: tall and wraith-like; skin lit from some inner source; an odd detachment to her demeanor. And that long cape of handsome dark-green wool with a hood she wasn't wearing just then, a detail impossible to forget. *For how could anyone have forgotten her hair?* The dark cloud framed her face and seemed of an unknown substance: something to do with nocturnal ethers, perhaps, that gleamed only by starlight.

"*Bonjour,*" said Charles. Not loudly enough, apparently, because she didn't return the greeting.

She was standing in the castle's main hall where Charles had just been, knee-deep in ferns. *Where had she entered? How long had she been there?*

She emerged from the ruins and took a few steps toward him.

"*Bonjour,*" she said. Her voice had a rich, viola harmonic.

Charles guessed that the girl was more or less his own age, although she had a queenly bearing for someone so young, as if she'd been born with complete sovereignty over the ridge—if not over all the forests around it—and her age was of no consequence. He could see her face now: an exquisite oval infused with the very stillness of the place. Her eyes held various shades of green and hazel and were flecked like the forest floor on a summer's day. Dry leaves clung to the hem of her cape, and in a delicate white hand she held a walking stick.

"Have we met before?" the girl asked. There was recognition in her eyes.

"I...I don't think so," Charles faltered, avoiding her gaze. He tried, but failed, to remember this girl from his trips into Rêve-sur-Semois, the closest village to his uncle's house. He glanced at her feet: she was wearing solid hiking boots and thick gray trousers which, along with the woolen cape and walking stick, indicated someone familiar with local weather in August.

Charles gathered his thoughts, shreds though they were. He was intimate with the weirdness of the Ardennes—a land of margins; of interfaces between vertical forests and sweeping valleys...between this world and the next. *Which world had she come from?*

"I've seen you at the pond," said the girl. An errant breeze lifted the edge of her cape and ruffled her hair. "Do you go there often?"

"Oh, yes!" Charles blushed. The walk to the pond down the alley of beeches was one of his favorites. The area was technically on de la Fontaine property, but walkers were generally tolerated.

"Do you know the stone where the herons fish?" the girl asked.

"Of course!"

"You know about the spring, then," she said.

Charles hesitated. "How do *you* know about it?" he asked, for hardly anyone did. The rocks from which spilled the coldest, purest water one could imagine were a steep climb up from the pond through dense overgrowth. In pagan times, the spring had been considered sacred. *Had she followed him there?*

"The spring is part of the legend, of course!" She smiled: a brief dazzle.

He stared at her. "You know the story of the White Heron, then," he said.

"Well, just the outlines. There's more to it, I think," came her queer response.

"Stephen de la Fontaine was my ancestor, you know," Charles offered. He stooped slightly, self-conscious of his height, and of the shapeless oilskin he'd borrowed from Theodore.

"Yes," said the girl. This information did not seem new to her. Her face grew more luminous as she added: "You look like you belong here."

"*Charles!*" Theodore was gesturing from across the bracken.

Charles signaled to him curtly and turned back:

The girl had vanished.

V

Charles said nothing to his uncle about the encounter. They settled on their favorite spot at the far end of the ridge—a patch of dry ground sheltered by two prehistoric menhirs—and fell into companionable silence.

The mottled, tilting rocks overlooked a precipitous drop to the valley below and were known to locals by their medieval name, *La Porte du Chevalier*, although during this particular summer, Theodore referred to them in English—the Knight's Gate—in a nod to Charles's impending departure. Nearby, beneath a stand of pines, a long earthen shoulder slept under its quilt of carnations.

"Sylvie is her name," Theodore said at length, gazing out over the panorama of fields and forests and probably, given his propensities, a large swathe of time as well.

Charles stared at him. It wasn't unusual for his uncle to guess his thoughts. This time, either Theodore had seen the girl from the far end of the ridge or, as Charles was fearing he might have done himself, he'd conjured her.

"Sylvie..." whispered Charles. "I didn't imagine her, then."

Theodore laughed. "It sometimes seems like she's imagined, I'll grant you that. Her family name is Longfaye."

"Longfaye... An Ardennes name, isn't it?"

"Yes. A very old one. Sylvana is her full name."

"Sylvana..." Charles repeated each syllable as if it were a revelation. "You know her, then!" he breathed, for if anyone could know such a woodland vision, surely it would be Uncle.

Theodore continued staring out at the vista. His profile had the hazy aura of a tapestry. "I cross paths with her in the forest from time to time," he said. Then, unconvincingly: "That's all I know." He wandered off to gather a few more carnations from the earth mound, then returned to Charles.

Their silence had become charged; unresolved. There was enough space on the dry ground between them for the leather satchel and carnations as well as for that less tangible thing: the curious presence of the past that Theodore carried about with him everywhere.

"I'm surprised you haven't run into Sylvie yourself, Charles, with all your rambling," Theodore said, as if he owed his nephew a few more crumbs on the subject.

Charles breathed in the perfume of the ridge and said nothing. Decaying nettle...peaty earth...spicy carnation: the dense potpourri of approaching autumn. Melancholy tainted the air—that lingering, late-summer ache.

Maybe it wasn't so surprising that he hadn't seen the girl during all the summers he'd spent at Villa Antioch. Indeed, perhaps the surprising thing was that he'd seen her at all. What had she meant, anyway, about him belonging here? And what kind of perverse joke of Fate had put this divine creature into his path just before that path was about to lead him away...probably forever?

Theodore rummaged through his satchel and produced a bar of chocolate that he broke in half and shared with his nephew.

"She said something about the heron legend," Charles blurted, taking the chocolate. "That it's connected to the sacred spring somehow."

"Ah, yes," Theodore said. "The White Heron."

"Why is she so interested?" Charles pressed him.

"I'm not sure. It's the oldest legend around here." Theodore thought for a moment, then smiled. "Maybe because she seems to live in such a world herself."

"Hmm." Charles munched his chocolate, feeling grateful for this bit of information. He considered what his uncle had told him just a few weeks ago when they'd been sitting on this very spot: that there was a magic realm caught in the arc between cloud and Earth, what Theodore called "the world between worlds", of echoes, rustling, whispers, wind: an invisible world as real as the one we could see. *Was that what he'd meant?* Charles wondered. That Sylvana inhabited *that* world?

There's more to it, I think...

Charles turned to his uncle. "Do you teach the heron story in your history class at the *lycée*?" he asked. Envy twisted in his stomach. He would have given anything to have been a student in Theodore's class. As it was, he spent the school year in Brussels, where his father had enrolled him at the pretentious International Academy from an early age.

"I usually just teach the basic outlines," Theodore said, getting up to go. With his jutting hair and hooded rain gear, he could have been a soothsayer from a time when Blancheron Castle had actually been operational. "You know: the nobleman and the heron."

Charles knew the outlines, of course. He'd practically been weaned on them. Guide books sold in Rêve-sur-Semois recounted the following:

A local nobleman from the latter part of the eleventh century, Stephen de la Fontaine, left for Jerusalem on the First Crusade with the army of Godfrey of Bouillon. Before leaving, he fell in love with a pious local girl, Arda. She was the daughter of a poor potter in the village and died during Stephen's absence.

When he returned, Arda's death plunged Stephen into despair, but soon he learned that the girl had been responsible for several miracles in the village while he was gone. These were attributed to her extreme piety and saintly qualities. Though she was never formally beatified, the local parish of Rêve-sur-Semois has always considered her their local saint.

Still burning with the religious fervor of his journey to the Holy Land, Stephen drew strength from Arda's miracles. He became a knight of some stature and built Blancheron Castle. According to popular belief, Arda was transfigured into a white heron so that she could always be close to Stephen. The bird can sometimes still be spotted in the vicinity of the pond near present-day Villa Antioch.

The story dated from the early twelfth century, which would have made it one of the earliest *chansons de geste*, or "songs of deeds": medieval epic poems in Old French recounting the heroic exploits of knights and warriors during the time of the Crusades.

Before his death, Charles's grandfather, Guy de la Fontaine, had hinted there was a twelfth-century parchment in the archives of the *Bibliothèque de l'Histoire Européenne* in Brussels that had something to do with the legend, but despite friendly overtures to the library's Head of Manuscripts, Theodore had never managed to track down any written record of the heron legend. Serious historians usually dismissed it as folklore.

VI

In his waning days in the Ardennes, Charles walked, and walked, alone and in turmoil. He had no itinerary; no particular destination. His thoughts roiled and collided and led him astray. He was oblivious to the wild boar, a dangerous animal when startled; and though stags were to be avoided at all costs, he half-welcomed a fatal encounter.

His sadness seemed as deep as the forests he was wandering, and no matter how far he went, or for how many hours, he could find no way out of his sorrow. *Disappear into the forest, lad, and you'll return changed.* Charles took Theodore's words to heart, but to his chagrin, they were losing their potency, as if he'd already left this place without changing at all and absence had begun its slow, inevitable erasing.

At times he would stop at a particular spot in surprise, not sure how he'd gotten there. When he found himself in the beech alley he turned back, because the trees themselves, that had always spoken to him in their own singular tongue, had said nothing. He scrambled up forested slopes and slithered down the other side to the river, seeking comfort in the shallows. But though the water seemed tranquil, and was even fordable in places with a decent pair of boots, Charles remembered what Theodore had warned: the Semois had an unreliable character, and even on a high summer day you could find yourself wading in deep, cold currents where you couldn't see the bottom, and weeds streamed like a dead woman's hair. No wonder that only enchanters and seeresses could read the water's messages.

Charles couldn't admit to himself that he was not so much bidding farewell to these beloved forests as he was searching every corner of them for the person he'd come across on the ridge. *Sylvana.* There'd been no sign of her. *Where was she?* After endless hours of wandering, he even toyed with the notion that in spite of Theodore's evidence to the contrary—that one occasionally came across Sylvana in the woods—she might well have disappeared into that world between worlds.

There was one more place Charles hadn't tried.

In despair, he visited the great oak. It was what most despairing locals used to do, after all. Before the evangelists came, that is; before they imposed their edicts and penitentials and demonized all reverence for Nature.

The tree wasn't easy to find. It had allegedly witnessed pilgrims depart for the Holy Land so one would have thought that a path to it would have been kept open. But instead, access was almost impossible. The oak could only be reached by navigating fallen logs and thorny scrub until a most unexpected clearing materialized. At its center stood a single tree.

The trunk was rent down the middle where lightning had struck it. Ivy hung like torn clothing. Giant baubles of mistletoe clustered in the higher branches, and from the tree's hollow center issued the rich, mushroom odor of rot. None of this, however, discouraged life from taking hold wherever it could. Leaves still covered the crown and were even beginning to turn ochre, as if to say that after almost a thousand years autumns, there was no reason to miss one now.

This was the matriarch of the woodland: a divine being, according to ancient custom. It had been listed by local authorities as an *arbre remarquable:* an exceptional tree. "I should charge admission to see it!" Theodore joked, for technically, the tree stood on his property. But he was glad that the woods had closed in around the oak. He feared that some village delinquent would try to chop it down, or light a fire inside the hollow where generations of Earth-worshippers had tucked offerings of bread, salt, herbs and grain.

Charles placed a hand on the deeply ridged bark. He gazed up. "Have you seen her?" he said under his breath. It felt oddly comforting, talking to this tree. "Do you know where she is?"

He sank down and leaned against the trunk. It seemed that he could actually feel the oak's life force against his back—a distant, leviathan pulse, part organic to the tree, and part to Charles. His spirit revived. "People have been finding wisdom in trees for millennia," Theodore had told him. "Keep still and listen. You'll understand. But you must *listen*!

So now Charles listened.

Wind rasped in the mistletoe. A blackbird scolded from the edge of the clearing. He closed his eyes, and in the whispering ocean of leaves he imagined vaguer sounds: shuffling movements; oxen grunting; the crunch of beechnuts under wooden clogs.

The poor of this region had left to join the Peasant's Crusade in 1096, several months before the princely armies had mustered. Men, women and children, their stories of extreme hardship largely untold. Theodore had told them to Charles, however: "Floods and pestilence in 1094. Drought and famine in 1095. No wonder people wanted to leave Europe, lad! Do you know what ergotism was? *No?* Oh, my, but it was grim! Vomiting. Convulsions. Gangrene in the fingers and toes. Caused by eating moldy rye, you know."

Pilgrims would have stopped at the oak on their way past. It had been young and vital then. Maybe they'd left an offering, or laid a hand on the trunk where Charles was resting his nine centuries later. They would have paid a visit to the spring, too, and left something enduring there—a piece of horn, or a stone—even though such offerings had been expressly forbidden in the penitentials.

The peasants themselves had embraced the pope's zealous plea to walk all the way to Jerusalem and help rout the infidel from the Holy Sepulcher. *Deus vult!* God wills it! But still... *Which god had willed it, anyway?* Not one of the local goddesses: that much was certain. Better to leave their respects at the waters and trees as they always had, just to be sure...just in case they never returned to the land of their ancestors. The clergy would threaten them with damnation, of course. But old ways were not so easily snuffed out.

The spring.

The notion welled up in Charles like the waters themselves.

He got to his feet, energized.

I'll go there tomorrow! There's enough time before my train. It's my last chance to find her.

VII

Charles entered Theodore's study that evening as if it had been any other visit to the sanctum. But with rising panic he realized that this would be the last one—that in fact he was a refugee on the eve of departure, committing everything he loved to memory.

He stood in the middle of the room and drank in all that was dear: the wall of moldering books...the leather sofa where Theodore stretched out for his naps...his cedarwood cologne lacing the smell of mildew.

Charles approached the desk. The oak behemoth looked sturdy enough to sail through time, which was exactly what Charles felt the two of them had been doing all summer. The desk faced French doors giving onto the terrace and was choked with papers. On one pile sat an ivory olifant: a priceless twelfth-century hunting horn that Charles was permitted to blow from time to time; on another, a cobblestone from the old Roman road. A chair of cracked bordeaux leather let out a long, meditative croak whenever its occupant leaned back too far, like frogs in the river shallows.

At night—Charles's favorite time for studying—the dark-green banker's lamp created a sort of moonlit glade. There was a candle on a brass stand that Theodore also lit for his nephew's evening studies. (*Puts you in the right century, lad!*) Enthralled, the boy would watch the flame shimmy in the villa's drafts, throwing humanoid shapes across the walls and making the shadows dance. *Whose shadows?* Charles always wondered, as they seemed to have no tangible provenance.

A wooden stool sat at a distance that wouldn't disturb the pondering occupant of the leather chair. How many hours Charles had spent on that meager perch! Here he'd tackled the original Latin of Ralph of Caen's *Gesta Tancredi*, a primary source of the First Crusade, and cataloged whatever happened to be lying on Theodore's desk that day: a rusted horseshoe nail; a chipped tile; a fossil—marvels beyond measure. He'd hardly noticed his sore hips, for what was the discomfort of a stool compared to the worlds he'd encountered on it? Ancient history; Latin poetry; Homer; *The Da Vinci Code* (*Mustn't be snobbish about our reading, Charles!*). The pupil's fortitude had been as unflinching as his backside.

Charles stood next to the leather chair now and imagined Theodore as he wanted to remember him: gaze searching, pen lifted like a magic wand as he commanded not only the unruly tide of papers, but the entire vista beyond the window as well. The Roman bridge was visible from the study, and many were the times that Charles had lingered at the desk, hoping—dreading—to hear the clatter of the horse.

"Charles?" Theodore shuffled in and stood beside his nephew. "Shall we eat on the terrace tonight?"

For a moment they remained side by side as twilight slunk into the river-kingdom, carrying with it the inevitable.

"Sixteen," Theodore mused between mouthfuls of *croque monsieur*. He wasn't much of a cook, grilled cheese with ham being one of the few things he could manage. "A good age for adventuring, I'd say." He'd been trying all evening to put a positive spin on Charles's departure. "Come to think of it, lad, you're about the age Godfrey was when he inherited Bouillon Castle from his uncle in 1076."

This brought little comfort to Charles, who ate in silence.

"He was tall and fair like you, too," Theodore persisted.

Charles had no desire to be compared to his boyhood hero just then.

"Oh, Charles," sighed Theodore. "Hugues only wants the best for you. America will open many doors." He almost managed to sound convincing.

More silence.

Charles had no interest in doors; he didn't even particularly want what was best for him. He slumped at the terrace table and stared glumly across the river at the ridge, now just a black, pine-notched mass against an indigo sky.

All around the villa lay vast tracts of forest. *Couldn't he just vanish into them...just melt away?* No one would ever find him there. They might not even miss him. Isn't that what people had been doing since the dawn of the forest? Disappearing? Of course these days, there were mobile phones, and satellites. Maybe it wasn't so easy to disappear anymore. *How did Sylvana manage it?* Charles thought with admiration. She seemed to possess perfect synergy with the natural world, coming and going as she pleased. Imperceptibly, too. *How long did she stay out in the wild, anyway?* He bit his lip. The disappointment of not being able to find her was taking on grim finality.

"The Ardennes Forest was immense once," Theodore said, watching his nephew study the view.

Charles smiled through his misery. Theodore's impromptu lectures were not always welcome, but tonight, at these lonely crossroads, he was happy to listen.

"It's not like what you see now," Theodore went on. "The Romans called it *Arduenna silva*, or "wooded heights". It stretched right across southern Belgium into Luxembourg, France and even Germany." Then, as if he'd perceived Charles's desperation: "The Ardennes could conceal anything or anyone—sometimes forever. Saints, wise women, hermits, thieves...you name it." Theodore chuckled. "I'm not sure that sixteen-year-olds from Brussels are on that list, though!"

Charles reddened and looked away. It was difficult to keep anything from his uncle.

"I'll get the chocolate, shall I?" said Theodore quietly. He collected their plates from the little iron table and shambled across the terrace to the kitchen door. An infusion of peppery nutmeg floated out on the evening air from the wild carnations he kept in the kitchen.

Charles sipped the wine Theodore had diluted for him and set the glass down on the Delft tiles of the tabletop. The high chink against ceramic reminded him of the loose shale on the Blancheron ridge, surprisingly tuneful as it scattered under one's feet. *Remember this sound,* he told himself, and gently set the glass down again so that he would. It was here, at this table, that he'd learned the meaning of Blancheron: literally *blanc héron*, or "white heron". He'd never thought of the word that way until Theodore had pointed it out.

Sometimes we just can't see the obvious, lad.

VIII

Theodore shambled back from the kitchen with a plate on which he'd arranged the coffee cream chocolates that were Charles's favorites, and the dark raspberry hearts that were his own.

"The Americans are not known for their chocolate," he said, shaking his head. "So eat as much as you can before you leave, *d'accord?*"

Charles munched and meditated. "Uncle, did Grandfather really walk from Antioch to Jerusalem?" he asked.

Theodore grinned. "Yes, indeed! Almost seven hundred kilometers. He just packed up and left without telling anyone. He was wearing a hauberk, too."

"A what?"

"Chain mail, reaching to the thigh. It could weigh up to 40 kilos. We used to have one lying around the house somewhere but Father sold it years ago.

"Gosh."

"He came home covered in sores. Oh, your grandmother was livid! He was a strange one, Guy de la Fontaine."

"What was he like?" Charles asked, awestruck.

"Ah, it's a pity he died before you could know him," said Theodore. "Your grandfather was gruff, stubborn and rude. A brilliant scholar, but few could get along with him. His—well, *original*—ideas made him lose a lectureship at Cambridge. Sometimes I think your grandfather wanted to shut himself into a fortress like the ancient city of Antioch, and that's why he lived in this God-forsaken place and gave the house its name." Theodore waved a hand to indicate the lonely, leaking pile. "A psychological fortress, that is," he laughed. "Godfrey and his army could have broken into this house in minutes."

The mention of the duke left Charles oddly cold. *Was the chill part of this bleak farewell?* "And what about Aunt Ida?" he asked with an ache. Along with his uncle, the gentle, wise Ida was the person he'd miss the most.

"You know what Ida's like, Charles," said Theodore. "She inherited the family dreaminess." He guffawed. "I can hear your father now: 'Ida's head's in the clouds, just like yours, Theo. Such a useless place to spend one's time.'" He gave Charles a piercing look. "He said the same about you, by the way."

"Yes, I remember," Charles said. He also remembered his uncle's comment: *Never mind, lad. It's a compliment, really. The clouds harbor many revelations. Your ancestors knew this well. Your father's just too obtuse to realize it.*

"Did Ida know something about Arda?" Charles asked.

"Oh, she was obsessed with Arda when we were growing up!" said Theodore.

"Really?" Charles's eyes widened.

"She always wanted to change the name of this house to 'Villa Arda' in honor of the heron legend," Theodore said, "but there was never a family consensus. She was convinced that the story was chiefly about the female character, not about Stephen de la Fontaine at all. She's sure that the tourist version is incomplete."

Charles tingled at the thought. The vision of Sylvana Longfaye knee-deep in ferns surfaced clearly. *There's more to it, I think...*

"Ida was always looking for the women lost to history," Theodore went on. "Grandfather was rather, to put it kindly, *dogmatic* about his views. He never liked alternative or politically correct interpretations— of the Crusades, especially. He thought Godfrey was a great hero, *point final*. But Ida didn't take to male icons like Godfrey and Stephen. She felt there was something missing from their stories."

"Did she find out anything more about Arda?" Charles asked.

"There's virtually no record of individual village women from the time of the First Crusade. Only some information about noblewomen. But compared to male histories, even that is scant."

"So Ida looked for traces of Arda in folklore, then," Charles offered.

"Yes."

"The name comes from Arduinna, the pagan goddess, doesn't it?"

"Of course!" Theodore motioned for Charles to take another chocolate.

"But Arda was a Christian woman, wasn't she?" Charles pressed him. "She worked miracles while Stephen was on Crusade."

Theodore gave his nephew a piercing look. "That's the tourist version, lad," he said. "And the Church's, which hasn't changed in a thousand years."

Charles stared at his uncle. "What's the other version, then?"

Theodore fell silent. Then, with a grave tone: "In fact, Arda was a wise woman, Charles. A seeress. A diviner. In the eleventh century, such pursuits were considered heretical. Deadly, even. There could be no such thing as female spiritual power in patriarchal dogma. Women like Arda were on a collision course with the clergy."

"So they lived in hiding..."

"Yes. But it hadn't always been like that. You know, Charles, there was a time in history when 'witch' was synonymous with 'healer'; 'knower'. And yet the Church hounded such women mercilessly; forever tarnished their position of honor in ancient societies. These days, if we think of witches at all, it's as old women with warts on their noses riding broomsticks at Halloween!"

"Gosh," said Charles. "So Arda was...*pagan*." The word emerged uneasily.

Theodore grinned. "You say it as if she'd been of the devil! And in fact, that's what we've been brainwashed to think. Arda practiced the old religion of revering Nature, if that's what you mean by 'pagan.'" Theodore nursed his Merlot. After a pause he said, "Actually, *paganus* was Latin for 'country-dweller'. Unfortunately, the word has taken on much baggage since then."

Theodore gestured grandly toward the twilight beauty beyond the terrace. Dusk, breathless, hung between day and night. Awe swelled through the wild sanctuary. "How can any religion demonize this?" he whispered.

Charles stared into the gloaming. His visit to the old oak that afternoon had shaken his spirit in a way no visit had done before. This time, it had been clear that a deep, abiding energy lived within the tree: a force that would accompany the oak's pungent remains back to the

Earth, where new life would emerge from the same material. In spite of his sorrow at leaving this place, hope surged in Charles at the thought of that tree and its resurrection.

"The Church had absolute power over medieval Europe," Theodore said. "Heresy was punishable by death. Sin and damnation shadowed every soul, all day, every day. Which is why women like Arda and their folk wisdom were essentially cut out of the historical narrative."

"So the story about her piety...her miracles..."

"All Christianized," said Theodore. "Ironically, that was how pagan vestiges survived at all: in Christian documents. Scribbled in the margins. Woven into illustrations. Ida believes that Arda *did* perform miracles as a healer and seeress, just not in a Christian context."

"So *that's* why she wasn't beatified!" Charles exclaimed.

"Well, the ladies of the parish would beg to differ!" said Theodore. "The church of Saint Arda in Rêve is named after her, of course."

"But what about her lover?" Charles demanded. "Our ancestor, Stephen?"

"What about him?"

"Well, he answered the call to go on Crusade!" Charles said, growing impatient. "To liberate the tomb of Christ from the infidel and have his sins absolved. They were all yelling *Deus vult!* heading off to Jerusalem, weren't they? *God wills it.* You taught me that, Uncle!"

"And your point is?"

"Well, how could Stephen have fallen in love with a pagan after he'd taken the Cross?"

Theodore smiled his most enigmatic smile. "A loose end in the tale, wouldn't you say?" He grew serious. "Stephen couldn't have admitted his love for Arda to anyone, of course. He was in the retinue of a man renowned for his piety: Godfrey of Bouillon. As for Arda herself, well... Christianity and paganism existed side-by-side for several centuries, it's true. But really, they were more on a collision course."

"Arda lived around here somewhere, didn't she?" Charles said. He studied the darkness thickening over the river.

"Yes."

"She must have hidden in a place where the clerics couldn't find her. Maybe in a hermit's cell. There're traces of them in these woods, aren't there?"

"True," said Theodore. "But the common people still would have sought her out. The old ways worked for them. The knowledge of herbs. The reverence for Nature. They consulted wise women in spite of the Church's interdictions. I think Arda would have received them near the spring somewhere. Maybe in a cave."

Charles stared into the gloaming. Here and there the river gave off a fish-scale gleam, as if rolling onto its belly. The pines on the ridge sharpened against the evening sky.

"Where is this cave?" he asked.

"I've never been able to find it."

A chill filtered up from the meadow onto the terrace.

"Uncle, what happened to her?"

IX

Theodore got up abruptly and headed to the French doors of the study. "I'll be right back," he said.

He reappeared bearing a large brown envelope with Charles's name on it. This he set on the tiled table and without a word returned to his seat.

Charles sat very still. He didn't touch the envelope.

Theodore glanced at the ridge. His blue eyes had taken on the deep indigo hue of the sky. At last he said: "A few weeks ago, I came across this envelope in a pile of papers your grandfather had left on the stairs."

"Oh?" Charles mouthed.

"It's his translation of the heron legend."

Charles sat very still. His hands went cold. "You mean the manuscript Grandfather said was in the Library of European History?" he gasped. "The *chanson de geste* about Stephen?" His chronic sadness evaporated.

"Well, I think so."

"What do you mean?"

"You'll see when you read it." Theodore pushed the envelope closer to Charles. "I want you to have it…to read it once you've left here. All the papers at Antioch will be yours eventually anyway. The family has no other heirs."

There was uncharacteristic finality in Theodore's tone. Normally he would have been bubbling about such a find.

"The manuscript was originally kept at the abbey of Valdoré—now in ruins, of course," he said. "Then it was passed to a private library, and from collector to collector. It's one of the oldest such manuscripts known—from 1120 or so. Only three *chansons de geste* are older."

Theodore's tone lightened and he flashed an impish smile. "Now, Charles…" It was how he always began one of his little quizzes, which he could spring on his nephew at any moment, on any subject.

"Oh, Uncle, not now!" Charles groaned, all the while relishing the challenge. He pulled himself up straight and said: "*The Song of Roland*, *The Song of William* and *Gormont and Isembart* are older."

"Excellent!" Theodore enthused. "Stephen de la Fontaine himself might have even laid eyes on the manuscript." His demeanor sharpened. "The text recounts some very unusual events. It's hard to believe there's any truth to them."

"But most *chansons de geste* embellished the truth, didn't they?" said Charles. "You said yourself that they were written to appeal to a popular audience." He placed a hand on the envelope and noticed that it was sealed.

"That's true," said Theodore. "And your grandfather knew how to embellish, believe me! Just like the best troubadours. But this is another sort of story altogether."

Charles watched his uncle, expectant.

"You see, Charles," Theodore continued, "what's recounted in this envelope is really a feminine story. About the pagan sage, Arda. Not about Saint Arda of local lore. It's not so much an account of the Crusades, like other *chansons de geste*—or like any other bellicose bit of history your grandfather might have preferred. Rather, it's an account of events *afterwards*."

"Maybe Grandfather became more of a feminist when he found that manuscript!" Charles said.

Theodore chuckled. "That would have been a stretch, I think! I just wish that I'd been able to track down the original. It was probably misfiled somewhere. Your grandfather's translation is in prose, by the way. He usually worked with a bottle of Côtes du Rhône on his desk, revising what he'd translated at the library, so I'm not sure he would have been able to duplicate the quatrains of medieval French verse even if he'd wanted to." Theodore winked. "He drank most of a bottle every evening."

They smiled at each other.

"Oh, by the way," Theodore added. "Don't let anyone read what's in the envelope—especially your father. He'll just give you a hard time about it. Not even Ida. Keep it to yourself for now, lad. That is, until we can verify its authenticity." Theodore gestured to the plate on the table. "And that last chocolate is for you!"

Charles took the raspberry heart—a truly selfless offer on the part of his uncle. He surveyed the forest across the river, just ink on dark-blue paper now, and wondered what a white bird might look like flying past it.

"Have you ever seen the white heron, Uncle?" Charles asked, suddenly not sure he wanted to know the answer. *How much truth was there in those old stories, anyway?* For his part, he'd never really wanted to know the truth about the horseman on the bridge. To know it might have endangered the myth. And how much more intriguing myth was compared to reality! (Never mind that on more than one occasion, Charles was sure that he actually did hear the clip of hoof against stone.)

Theodore got up and wandered over to the terrace railing. His silhouette was pleasingly lumpen in the failing light. After a few moments he said:

"Charles, stories like the White Heron live in these trees...in the water and stones. Not only in the past. But *now*."

"Yes, I know," Charles said, not entirely sure that he did. "But have you ever seen it?"

Theodore sighed. "One day a few winters ago, I saw something at the pond that I thought was a large white bird," he said. "But it had snowed: it might have been snow falling from a pine branch. I couldn't be sure."

"It could have been a white heron, though," Charles pressed him.

"Yes. It could have been..."

"Did you go back to look for it?"

Theodore sighed again and drifted back to the table. "Sometimes I feel as if I've been looking for it all my life."

Charles studied his uncle as if he were going to draw him: the broad face, furrowed and proud; the schoolboy hair straggling over his ears and forehead; and that elusive thing: the incorrigible whimsy. At that moment, if someone had asked Charles what America signified to him, the only thing he would have been able to say was that it meant the absence of Theodore.

"Never forget," said Theodore, addressing more the forest than his young acolyte. "A story like the White Heron—any story from the past—offers you a thread. You must grasp that thread and pull it. Eventually, what comes to the surface is a revelation no one can ever predict...or even imagine. You must then weave that thread into your own life somehow." He turned to his nephew. "The past is alive, Charles. In *you*."

X

"The bus leaves in two hours, lad! There's no time to go to the spring!" There'd been so much to do—so many things to gather up from all those summers spent with Theodore. Books, of course. And the treasures from their forest walks: a second-century silver coin from the reign of Marcus Aurelius; a corner of Roman tile with the potter's finger mark still on it; wafers of shale from the Blancheron ridge and a medieval horse shoe, all of which Charles intended to take with him to America if his father didn't wonder why his luggage was so heavy.

And then there was the gonfalon: the banner with the family coat of arms that Charles hung out every day from the turret room of Villa Antioch, and took in every evening. "It's yours now," his uncle said solemnly, handing him the banner, and with ceremony Charles rolled it up and tucked it into his duffel bag. Soon Theodore would drive him to Bouillon for the bus to Libramont, where he'd catch the train to Brussels.

"I'm packed, Uncle!" Charles called from the front door. "I'll be back soon."

He crossed the drive at a sprint and hurried down the alley of beeches. The day was cool and still, the sky a monochrome gray. Though the calendar read August it was a Belgian August, and he'd dressed in a handsome woolen jacket and corduroy trousers as if it were October...as if, indeed, this might be a special occasion.

The alley was a vestige of the old Roman road that had traversed the forest two millennia ago, and here and there an original paving stone poked from its burial place. The ground rose steeply on one side of the alley, crowded with gray beech trunks and interlocked roots where last year's amber leaves still lay caught in the lacing.

Heaviness trailed Charles as he walked between the beeches. *How could he be so certain she'd be at the spring?* Doubt lingered from his evening with Theodore: something to do with things unfinished...with the mystery of Arda, and the glimpse of the white bird that had never returned.

Charles knew how to tune his ears to the forest's acoustic: the stirring of wind and creatures that many city people couldn't perceive in what they assumed to be silence. But now he ignored them. A gray heron passed overhead, its elegant legs stretched out in flight, a sight he'd normally stop to admire but didn't even notice. He was deaf to the wrens fluting in the canopy; to the hoarse alarm of a rook.

A single majestic pine marked the turn-off to the spring and Charles plunged into the overgrowth. He picked his way through brambles and ferns to a steep rise that reared suddenly, Ardennes-fashion, in a tumble of rock and lush greens. Notes of trickling water purled even before the spring itself was visible.

Charles halted. He listened for the note he'd always loved: a pitch with singular resonance, repeating every five seconds or so. It was a prehistoric sound, Theodore said. As old as the Earth herself. The note carried a hint of music in its purling, caught ages ago, Charles liked to think, from a pilgrim's stray tune.

He clambered up a rise of loose shale to a small natural platform cushioned with moss and decaying leaves. It was curious that the spot had never been Christianized like so many others in the Ardennes. No pipe had been installed to direct the water, or iron railing where pilgrims could tie their offerings. There was no crucifix or Virgin Mary. The spring of the eponymous de la Fontaine family was a simple cleft in a rock from which water poured into a mossy basin and drained mysteriously away.

Charles knelt before the basin and cupped his hands. The water was intensely cold, gem-pure, and pooled thick in his palms like liquid crystal. His knees sank into the soft moss as if it were a prie-dieu, and as always thought about who had knelt on this very spot a thousand years before him and also left their imprint in the moss. *Had they been as troubled as he? Had they found comfort here, in the vital essence of water?*

He dried his face on his sleeve and looked around for a sign—a depression in the weeds, or dislodged shale—anything that might have indicated a presence. But with resignation he realized he was alone. He skittered back down the rise and checked his watch: there was still time to take the long way back via the pond.

The oval of water opened in the trees without warning: a glistening mirage of branch, air and sky. A broad, flat rock protruded from the pond and was an easy leap from the bank. It was here that Charles used to sit with his uncle of a summer's night to watch the meteor showers; here where on drowsy afternoons, the herons stood for hours gazing into the watery mirror, as still as oracles.

Charles stopped on the grassy bank and peered into the water. Tree and sky were reflected so clearly that as a boy, he'd imagined their water incarnation was as real as their earthly one—so real, in fact, that a swimmer diving beneath the surface would have come upon an entire submerged forest full of light and life.

At first he didn't see the slim object lying on the rock.

He moved closer: a walking stick.

XI

Charles glanced around. The pond was windless, its glassy surface dark. A rook muttered unseen in the pines. Watchfulness weighed on the air.

He picked up the stick with some hesitation, as if it were forbidden to do so. The shaft was of swirled, polished wood, and the ebony handle had a beautiful curve that fitted so well under the hand, he found himself clasping it out of sheer pleasure.

"I was wondering where I'd left that!"

He whirled around. The voice had the same harmonic as the spring. Sylvana was smiling at him from the bank.

Charles caught his breath. Once again, she was standing in a bed of ferns. Indeed, it was beginning to seem that it was her natural habitat. She was wearing a white shirt with the sleeves rolled up. The green woolen cape was draped over her arm, as the day had become warm and close. She resembled a woodland goddess on her day off.

Charles trembled with confusion. He leapt from the rock to the bank and handed Sylvana her stick.

"Ah, my distaff!" she laughed. At his consternation, she explained. "You know: the stick on which wool was wound before it was spun. Once upon a time, it was a consecrated tool." Sylvana held up the walking stick to demonstrate with invisible yarn. "There were three periods of time: the past, which was spun and wound on the spindle; the present, which was the passage of the thread through the fingers; and the unspun wool on the distaff symbolized the future."

Charles stared at her. This was quite another being from the one he'd encountered at the Blancheron ruins: more teenage girl than remote pagan queen. There was a wry turn to her mouth, as if he amused her. The unexpected warmth of the day suddenly felt suffocating and he took off his woolen jacket.

"I've been to the spring for a drink," Sylvana said. "Did you have one already?"

"Yes," said Charles, disarmed. *Had she been watching him from one of her lairs?* It hadn't escaped his attention that her thick mass of hair was dripping at the ends where she'd leaned into the water.

"I'm leaving tomorrow, you know," he blurted. It was not what he'd imagined saying in this situation—something on the order of: *I haven't been able to forget our meeting on the ridge.* Or maybe: *I was afraid I'd never see you again.* That other observation that had occurred to him—the one that troubled his sleep—he could never divulge: *I wasn't sure whether you were real or not.*

"Tomorrow?" she said. The green eyes darkened; the wryness vanished.

"To Brussels," he explained. "I live there with my father."

"Oh." Sylvana seemed to be waiting for more. It was the sort of pause that expects to be filled imminently: the pause before a hawk dives...before music begins.

Charles didn't take the cue, however. He couldn't bring himself to tell her that he would be going much farther than Brussels, probably permanently.

"You should always go to the spring before a big departure," she said. "It helps you find the balance between who you are now, and who you'll be when you come home."

Charles nodded and looked away. Once again he'd heard a viola tone in her words, so similar, he realized now, to the voice of the spring. But it was the wisdom far beyond her years that befuddled him. Somehow she'd perceived that he'd be gone for a long time.

Home. It was an odd term for someone to use just then, Charles thought. Maybe because he didn't have a clue what it meant anymore. *Brussels? Blancheron?* And where would home be once he'd left here?

Sylvana leapt across the short stretch of water to the herons' stone and beckoned Charles to join her. This he did, leaving his jacket on the bank. He sat down next to her, relieved that the rock was wide enough to accommodate a diffident sixteen-year-old in the presence of an enchanting young woman. He was further relieved when she placed her cape and walking stick between them.

"I'm Charles, by the way," he said.

Her gaze was solemn and level. "I'm Sylvana."

Charles glanced down, unable to admit that he already knew something about her. "Do you prefer Sylvie?" he asked.

"No," she snapped.

Charles smiled, remembering how casually Theodore had used the nickname she obviously hated.

"Do you spend a lot of time in the forest?" he asked blandly. The girl was not as easy to talk to as she'd been in his many imagined encounters.

"It's where I feel at home," she answered. "Like you."

"But how did you know?" he stammered.

Her gaze moved from Charles to the far side of the pond. Haze hung over the water. Beneath it, the surface resembled unpolished ebony more than it did a mirror. The portal to that netherworld was closed.

Charles regarded Sylvana openly. *Might she be as unhappy as he was,* he thought, *and that was the reason she came to the forest?* Her luminous profile seemed infused with harmony and he couldn't imagine she was unhappy. Maybe Sylvana wasn't so much escaping to the woods in despair as she was embracing them in a sort of homecoming. The thought brought a lightness to Charles, as if he, too, had sensed that harmony, and his departure could be tolerated now that his true home had been established.

"This is what ancient people called a peace-spot," Sylvana said, turning to her companion and holding his gaze without wavering. She sat with the poise of a dancer.

Charles let out a nervous laugh. "That sounds like something my Uncle Theodore would say!" he said.

Sylvana's eyes grew wide. "Theodore de la Fontaine is your uncle?" she exclaimed.

"Well, yes," said Charles. "He lives at Villa Antioch and teaches at..."

"Yes, I know!" she jumped in. "I take his history class."

Charles gaped at her. "You're his *student*?" His stomach churned with a curious torment, part resentment that he hadn't been able to attend the *lycée* in Bouillon himself, and part anger that his uncle had said nothing about Sylvana being in his class. *Why hadn't he mentioned this on their last visit to the ridge?*

"Your uncle's a wonderful teacher," Sylvana said, adding to Charles's bitterness. "I've learned so much about history...about how it lives alongside us."

Charles said nothing. Suddenly he wished that he'd left already—that he'd torn himself away from Blancheron in one, painful jerk instead of this long, searing tug.

"Peace-spots used to be places with sacred energy," Sylvana went on. If she'd perceived Charles's discomfort, she ignored it. "Groves, springs, ponds...they were all revered."

Charles calmed somewhat, happy that he'd already learned these things from his uncle—maybe long before Sylvana had.

"Yes, I know," he said neutrally.

"There's a stillness here," she said. "You know this, Charles. You have the sensitivity to perceive it: the stillness of the heron."

Suddenly the conversation started down a path Charles could not see clearly. It was a beautiful image, to be sure: the stately bird...the deep calm of the pond caught in its bearing. But Sylvana clearly had more to say on the subject and Charles wondered if he could hold up his end of the conversation.

She said: "I think that the woman from the legend had that stillness, too."

He stared at her. "Arda?"

"Do you ever wonder about her?" she asked.

"Yes, I do!" he said. "According to the legend, she was transformed into a heron."

"Indeed," Sylvana said. "A white one." She made a sweeping gesture that encompassed the entire pond, her delicate hand like a wing.

Unease filled Charles. *How could anyone be sure that a white heron was a pious girl transfigured, and not the shape-shifter Maugis?*

"Something else happened here, as well," Sylvana said. "Sometimes peace-spots are places that have witnessed remarkable events." She hesitated. "Terrible ones."

Charles glanced away, unnerved by Sylvana's riddles. He thought he knew all the pond's moods, but not this one: a collective holding of breath, as if something monumental had, indeed, happened here.

"So you think there's unfinished history here," Charles said.

"Oh, yes! Arda's history. I think that she lived near here somewhere. That she used to sit on this very rock."

Charles drew himself up. During all the times that he'd sat on this rock with Theodore, his uncle had never mentioned that nine centuries before them, Arda might have been sitting on it, too.

"Uncle said she would have hidden in the forest to escape punishment by the Church," he said. "Maybe in a cave."

"Or maybe she transformed herself into a heron so they wouldn't find her!" Sylvana laughed: a brief, clear bell-pitch. "Did you know that Arda was a musician?" she asked, the laughter gone.

Charles dipped his fingers in the pond to conceal his surprise. He hadn't learned this detail. "A musician..." he echoed.

"It's just something I heard in local lore. But it's interesting, *n'est-ce pas?*

"It certainly is." Charles placed a cool palm on the warm rock. "Do you think that her being a musician had something to do with what happened to her?" he asked.

"Yes," Sylvana said without hesitation.

Charles considered his Aunt Ida's fascination with Arda. Ironically in this country of mystical women, the thought made Sylvana seem utterly real. The notion that she inhabited that "world between worlds" was suddenly ludicrous. So real was she that she made everything that had ever happened in this forest, then and now, seem totally believable. Probable, even. *Arda. Stephen.* If one searched long enough, Charles thought, physical evidence of their existence would surely surface. The only impediment was his departure. He would never have a chance to search for these things now.

Sylvana stood up and gathered her coat and walking stick. She leaned to pluck a leaf from Charles's curls before saying: "You are straight and true, Charles de la Fontaine. You're not like anyone I've ever met."

Charles struggled to his feet, flummoxed as much by the comment as by the removal of the leaf.

"You're not coming back, then," Sylvana said. Her eyes had become miniature forest pools.

Despair overcame Charles.

Sylvana reached into the pocket of her trousers and pulled out a small, luminous object. She reached for Charles's hand and gently turned it over.

He stared at the quartz crystal she'd placed on his palm. The facets of the hexagon flashed in sequence as he tilted his hand. Inside the crystal glinted a tiny forest of feathery threads. Charles peered closer: the luminous essence of a forest did, in fact, seem to have been captured there.

"You might need this where you're going," Sylvana said. "I found it on the ridge."

People had cherished such objects long ago, Charles knew. Animal teeth, amber, horns, stones—all possessed concentrated matter and therefore, healing properties. Quartz was especially charged with vital energy.

Sylvana leapt back to the bank before Charles could react. She turned, and lifting her stick said: "Goodbye, my woodland friend. Good luck Outre-mer...whichever sea it is that you'll be crossing."

Charles gaped. *Outre-mer*...a term used since the tenth century to mean "the lands beyond the sea." *Had she learned it from Theodore?* He could still hear his childish voice droning out the answer to one of his uncle's quizzes: "The County of Edessa, the Principality of Antioch, the County of Tripoli and the Kingdom of Jerusalem." What Sylvana wouldn't have known was that instead of the ancient Middle East, his own personal "Outre-mer" would be the state of Connecticut.

Charles lifted his hand to wave good-bye, but the girl had already disappeared into the trees. It was a vanishing that would still confound him years later, for something of Sylvana had remained in the haze over the pond: a light, like the will-o'-the-wisps one sometimes sees above a marsh, only this one seemed brighter and steadier, and no one would have been able to explain scientifically how Charles, awash with questions about this person, managed to carry the illumination away with him.

He made his way back to the villa through a gloomy pinewood. It was a path he'd once taken with Theodore on an afternoon of heat and rolling thunder. He recalled the smell of resin sticking to the air, and his uncle hurrying ahead of him through the crowding pines. "He could be anywhere, lad," Theodore had laughed over his shoulder, meaning, Charles knew, the ghost of Godfrey, and a thrill had raced across his skin at the thought.

Until now, the most enthralling spirit to have roamed this haunted land had been Godfrey of Bouillon.

Charles tightened his grip on the crystal.

Until now.

XII

Charles said good-bye to his uncle at the bus stop in Bouillon with the promise that they would see each other in Brussels in a few weeks' time, just before he left for America.

He'd barely settled into his seat on the train from Libramont when he took Theodore's envelope from his backpack and unsealed it. A short note in French was fixed to the document with a paperclip. Everything had been typed by his grandfather on a manual typewriter.

To whom it may concern:

This is my version of the White Heron legend, translated from the Old French into modern prose. The original is in the Biblothèque de l'Histoire Européenne in Brussels. I've taken some liberties with the text to make it more readable. This I admit freely. Punctuation has been used for clarity, not authenticity. There were several illegible passages in the manuscript. I guessed at these in my own way. This alone would have cost me my lectureship at Cambridge! However, I don't write fiction. The singular plot is not something I could have made up. Do with it what you will. Only history will be the judge.
G. de la F.

Grandfather obviously had had little patience for letter-writing, Charles mused. Just as well, too. For he couldn't have waited a moment longer.

1085 AD, or thereabouts. Early autumn. About four in the afternoon. The forest was brushed with gold when a young nobleman and his squire went hunting for wild boar.

They passed over an old stone bridge into deep woodland. The days were still warm, but nights had been chilly enough to move along the acorn harvest. The riders fell silent. They'd come across that premier acorn-lover before, the wild boar, and knew he was far more dangerous than his tastes suggested. One had to be careful.

At once something rent the peace of the forest: a sound that would change both men's lives forever. They pulled up their horses. The sound was a sort of wail laced with yearning that lasted as long as one could hold a breath. Not human, exactly. Or angelic, for that matter. But a soul trapped somewhere between the two.

The men dismounted and listened. The sound had stopped. There were only the oaks shivering overhead. At once the wail began again and the hunters were determined to find its source. The woods were impassable on horseback so they would have to proceed on foot.

Their cloaks caught on nettles and blackberry vines and their peaked shoes got wedged between roots. Whenever the sound stopped, it seemed they were making the noise of two blundering oxen. So it was indeed remarkable that when the trees suddenly opened to reveal a large pond, the girl didn't appear to have heard them.

She was sitting on a flat rock on the pond's deep-green mirror. Her hair was cut short like a boy's and was so dark that her skin, though with a pearly glow, seemed like a dead person's. She wore a simple gray shift of rough weave. Her feet were bare.

It was evident at once why she hadn't heard the intruders: in her lap sat a curious object the size of an infant to which she was giving her full attention. The thing was made of blond wood and fashioned in the shape of a teardrop. Two semi-circular holes stared like eyes from near the bottom of the tear, and three strings spanned the long neck and body. Even the young squire could tell it was a musical instrument. But it was quite unlike the lutes or viols he'd seen played on the village square, or in the greasy confines of the castle hall after supper.

In her right hand the girl held a bow. Tilting her head tenderly toward the object, she began to draw this over the strings.

"It's Arda," whispered the squire, Stephen. "You know: the girl they call Maugis's daughter." He glanced up. "Monseigneur?"

But his master appeared to have momentarily stepped from this world. His expression was turned inward. In one of those tricks of nature, a shaft of autumn light slanted through the beeches and transfigured him, and a most unusual chestnut color blushed in his hair and beard.

The nobleman, Henri of Rêve, had heard of this forest girl; he'd also heard all the explanations for her strangeness: that she was a witch...or at the very least, had been fathered by Maugis, the Ardennes enchanter; that she was simple-minded and barren and spoke an unknown tongue; that she was a pagan and followed the old religion of the woods. This last claim disturbed the pious Christian most of all. Until now, that is...until the pull of her presence disturbed him even more.

He ignored his squire and stepped closer to the pond, keeping behind the thick trunk of an ash. Amidst all the vicious gossip no one had ever mentioned that Arda was a musician.

The instrument was a Byzantine lyra that somehow, by some unknown emissary, had come to northern Europe. A pilgrim could have brought it home through Bulgaria, or northwards from Iberia. The young men knew only that the instrument spoke in perfect unison with the forest.

They remained hidden for some time, listening to the lyra throb and sigh, and to the girl sing aching melodies that echoed it. The two sounds were so similar that it wouldn't have been at all surprising if the girl had laid the instrument aside and it continued to sing with her voice. There was something intimate about what they were witnessing and the men, chivalrous to a fault, regretted their intrusion. They turned to go.

At once a figure emerged from the ferns.

The squire grabbed his master's elbow—a bold gesture—and pulled him back behind the ash. The imposter was thick-set and swarthy. There was an alertness about him, a stealth that made him seem more animal than human. He'd crept from the undergrowth as a beast would have, reluctantly, ever ready to plunge back into it.

The nobleman clutched his dagger but at once loosened his grip: the little man had approached the girl quite peaceably. He leapt from the bank to the rock. Soon the two of them were sitting side by side. What an extraordinary turn of events! There was no doubt about it: harmony coursed between them, though their fascination was more with the lyra than with each other. Indeed, they took turns playing, and their music described something unknowable. The long notes lingered and seemed animate. The stags called at night with similar wild beauty.

The dark-skinned man had an earnest, heavy brow and was broad and proud. His hair was black as coal. He'd probably migrated north looking for work.

"It's the jongleur from Bouillon, Monseigneur," whispered Stephen. "Rodolfo." He'd seen this itinerant musician from Moorish Spain before, in the smoky, fetid hall of Bouillon Castle. Stephen often found himself at the castle for dinner, as his master was part of the retinue of Godfrey of Bouillon, Duke of Lower Lotharingia. Rodolfo had sung to Godfrey's diners and played the viol in a pensive and serious manner. Afterwards, he'd curled up in a corner on the rushes and fallen asleep. Jongleurs had an unsavory reputation as thieves and opportunists and people kept their distance.

Was the little man Arda's protector? Her muse? Her lover? These questions plagued the two onlookers, for they'd both fallen instantly under her spell, although the squire, hailing from a good family and hoping to become a knight himself one day, would never have admitted such a weakness to his master.

The two men made their way back through the undergrowth to their horses. They abandoned the hunt, each lost in his own thoughts. Neither ever mentioned the incident again.

Arda...

The men knew better than to believe, as local peasants did, that she had been fathered by an enchanter. Local knowledge assured them that her mother was dead and her father none other than the scar-faced potter who lived and worked in the outermost hut of Rêve-sur-Semois.

Arduinna...

The Celtic goddess of the Ardennes. The men had some education; they knew the ancient ways of these lands. Still, the name seemed dangerously close to the girl's. This sat uneasily with the two Christians. Had Arda been named something else at birth, and on exhibiting a troubling intimacy with Nature, acquired her nickname?

When she was sixteen, Arda caught the eye of Walderic, a powerful and corrupt bishop at the abbey of Valdoré. He had considerable holdings in the Ardennes—some of which were disputed by local aristocrats, including the Duke of Lower Lotharingia. One evening, Walderic's henchmen entered the potter's hut in Rêve-sur-Semois and abducted his daughter. She knew it was useless to resist. She asked only that she be allowed to take the lyra with her.

Arda was forced into servitude at the bishop's residence at the abbey. He had saved all the greatest luxury for himself, with sumptuous wall hangings in his apartments, golden goblets and fine silks, and holy statues on display more for their jeweled opulence than any spiritual efficacy. His own personal cross had been made especially for him from a cedar of Lebanon.

Walderic lusted after Arda, of course.

Charles looked up from the page with a smile and watched the fields and red-tiled roofs whisk past his InterCity train. Grandfather's fingerprints were all over that last comment, surely! It made him wonder how much more of the story had been embellished. After all, Guy de la Fontaine had readily admitted to it himself.

Charles smoothed his hand over his grandfather's text. *Had Arda and Rodolfo been sitting on the very rock that he and Sylvana had shared just that morning?*

He plunged back into their world.

XIII

The girl's attachment to the forest troubled the bishop. On dark nights, alone with his mead, he considered that she might, indeed, be Maugis's daughter. The thought terrified him. In despair he found himself wondering about his own religion. How could the teachings of someone who had lived a thousand years ago—and four thousand kilometers away—ever get a foothold in a heathen wilderness like the Ardennes?

Walderic knew the old pagan beliefs still lingered. But where? The bishop suspected each grove and spring...every cluster of stones that blocked his path. He avoided empty crossroads, where everyone knew the devious Hecate lay in wait. And of course, nights of the full moon found him safely indoors. He couldn't prove Arda's role in all of this. But then, he didn't have to. He was a high church official and she a serf. Whenever he desired, he could have her burnt alive for heresy.

Walderic carried around a little silver reliquary with the toenail of St. Simeon, the fourth-century ascetic who'd lived atop a pillar near Antioch for thirty-seven years, and to this relic he prayed most fervently. Arda's music was of the devil, he decided, and forbade her to play the lyra. She took to spinning and weaving, therefore, perhaps an even greater irritant, for weaving women in the village were also seeresses, who healed and gave council. The penitentials discouraged people communing with them.

Even though Walderic said Mass daily, prayed to the sacred toenail and clung to the power invested in his bejeweled cincture, staff and huge sapphire ring, he felt himself slipping into Arda's grip. He even considered that St. Simeon might, in fact, be punishing him, as the toenail had been smuggled illicitly out of Constantinople. And there was more: Walderic sensed some sort of vibrant spirit in the girl, forest-fueled and strictly speaking, unholy. But it was far more vital than any conviction he himself possessed. This spirit of hers was busy whittling a crack in the battlement against sin that the bishop had so carefully built around himself and tended day and night.

Walderic put his jewels away and shunned all opulence; he banned from his bed the little scullery maid he had once thought alluring; he even considered purifying himself by giving up his position altogether and joining the monks at a more obscure abbey. But still he could not wrest himself from Arda's spell.

Finally he let her go. For her part, Arda knew she would never again be safe from Walderic and his men. No sooner had she returned home than she kissed her father goodbye for the last time, took the cracked bowl he offered her, tied a hunting knife and a few crusts of bread into her dead mother's shawl and sought refuge in a cave beyond the spring. There, terrified that Walderic might pursue her again, she cloaked herself not in invisibility, as those who claimed she was Maugis's daughter believed, but in the only protection she knew: her melodies.

About a month after the nobleman and his squire had chanced upon Arda, the call resounded across Europe to free the Holy City from the infidel. Henri of Rêve took the Cross and became a knigh. He received the traditional symbols of the pilgrim—the staff and the purse—and threw himself into preparations for Crusade. It was a time of great alms-giving: soul and conscience needed to be purified. Armed pilgrimage would ease the way to the Last Judgment, people were told. All sins would be forgiven.

Every Frankish knight confessed his sins before leaving for Jerusalem. The grueling trip itself would serve as their penance. Unfortunately, the knight who'd fallen in love with Arda was obliged to make his confession to none other than Bishop Walderic.

Walderic's infatuation with Arda was common gossip, so of course Henri couldn't confess his sin of falling in love with her himself. The bishop was a jealous, vengeful soul. Oh, the knight would have welcomed a confession! He was as concerned about the fires of hell as the next Christian. And that mysterious dark-haired girl commandeered his every thought. The voice of her lyra couldn't be subdued, either, so that he was forced to spend many long, sleepless nights listening to the sound echo through his soul and cling to him at dawn. Never before had he been moved to such exquisite discomfort. Moving him to even greater discomfort was the knowledge that according to local hearsay, the lyra had been a gift from Rodolfo. What deeper expression of love could there be?

And so this strong, comely warrior, who consorted with bishops and kings and normally would have been seeking marriage into a family whose estates he could join to his own, could think only of the forest girl. He even wondered if her peaceful oneness with the trees...with the waters and stones and high places...made more sense than the holy war he was about to embark on. What was holy about killing, anyway? One had to hate in order to kill. Hadn't the Savior preached love? An intolerable conflict tore at him, pitting the oath he'd sworn to protect the Christian faith against his obsession with a wild unbeliever. And naturally he couldn't bear the thought of her in the arms of that stocky little forest man.

In July, 1096, just a month before his departure to the East, he paid another visit to the pond.

It was dawn. The knight was alone. He listened for the lyra but the woods were silent. It had rained all night, and by the time he'd reached the pond a gauzy mist was lifting from its surface.

He spotted Arda at once. She was sitting on the flat stone where the herons fished, her instrument beside her. She was gazing into the water with abiding calm...the calm of a chapel, thought Henri. He'd heard that such seeresses gazed into water to find their knowledge. And he also knew that church teaching forbad sitting out in natural sanctuaries. He could hear the words of his confessor: "Hast thou come to any other place to pray other than a church or other religious place which thy bishop or thy priest showed thee?"

He could not lie and say that he hadn't. And so he'd said nothing, which was itself a lie.

He approached: the girl had been weeping. Her smile astonished him, therefore. It was as if she'd been waiting for his arrival to cure her sorrow. Boldly, she took his hand, snatched up her lyra and led him up through steep forest to a high place overlooking the river. It was a sacred spot, she told him. They sheltered between two stone pillars, and there she played and sang for him.

She'd been weeping because Rodolfo had gone...simply vanished. She suspected he'd been ambushed by Walderic's men on the pretext of poaching, though Walderic hardly needed an excuse to abuse an inconvenient jongleur. Arda didn't know if he was alive or dead. Punishments varied for poachers: they could be flogged, or hung. Castrated, even. All she knew was that her forest protector was gone. Might her noble admirer be able to find out where he was?

But Henri was about to embark on an epic journey—perhaps forever. He had come to say good-bye, not to track down Arda's jongleur. Did she love him? He could not ask. But he could, and did, declare his own love that day. For he knew already that no matter how pious his preparations for pilgrimage might be, no religion would ever touch his spirit more deeply than this forest girl.

Henri left for the Holy Land with an army of ten thousand. Stephen was promoted to "squire of the body"—the most coveted rank and closest to his lordship, helping him dress, caring for his weapons and armor, never leaving his side in battle. In such closeness the squire could tell that deep in his soul, his master suffered most cruelly.

XIV

About a year after the Frankish armies conquered Jerusalem, the knight from the Ardennes fell gravely ill. In his final hours, four of his companions were with him: some took his feet onto their laps; others supported his head. Some indeed were weeping over him with very great grief and lamentation, because they were very afraid of being forsaken in this long exile.

The knight asked his companions to leave, just for a moment, and he summoned his squire to his side.

"Take this, I beg you," he said, softly, so the others couldn't hear. He handed Stephen a small olive wood box and bronze key. "Go home, please. Give the box to Arda. You remember her, I think. The girl in the forest. Who played the lyra." The knight had never learned of his squire's own love for her.

Stephen nodded. He took the box and key and turned his back briefly to his master, unable to control his tears. It had been four years since they'd left the Ardennes for Outre-mer...four years since either of them had known the soft, fragrant embrace of their native forest.

"You must give it to her in person," gasped the knight, faint with pain. He labored on for another few minutes, explaining about the cave beyond the spring where Arda might be hiding. "If you cannot find her, then covet the box yourself, and hide the key in a separate place. And please..." Henri closed his eyes, spent.

The squire took his master's hand and felt the muscles ceding their strength. It seemed inconceivable that this same arm had wielded the iron sword of a warrior.

"Please," Henri whispered. "Tell her that I swear before God she will find me again, no matter who her own god may be."

Stephen fully intended to do everything that had been asked of him. He was about to become a knight himself: the oath of loyalty he would swear was immutable. He would gladly have accepted death rather than leave his master's wishes unfulfilled. But alas, he could not fulfill them. For by the time he finally returned home to the Ardennes, Arda was dead.

Stephen searched in vain for a trace of her fate. He visited the cramped, dust-choked potter's hut where Arda's father was ignorant of her death. He scoured the village for clues, and though the inhabitants stared in awe at the returning pilgrim, their expressions went blank at the mention of Arda. Finally, he made the trek into the forest.

It was mid-summer. Vegetation had erased the path he remembered. It took him an hour to find the pond and several more to locate the spring. He searched fissures and hollows for a cave. At last he came across it, and there he confronted the jongleur.

Rodolfo was unrecognizable now. Indeed, at first the squire thought he'd startled a wild beast and unsheathed his dagger. Even in the lightless cavern he could detect that the man was filthy, desperate. The stench was worse than a summer cesspool. Fear clutched at the squire: in a terrible moment he considered that perhaps this vagrant—this savage—was something else. Not beast, or human, but that other thing, spawned in these woods eons ago and liable to appear at any moment. Maybe in a cave.

At once a clear, rich baritone rang through the cavern: "Who sent you?"

Stephen froze. The sound was refined. Pleasing. It didn't belong in this reeking hole, and in a suspended moment he remembered the same sound in the hall of Bouillon Castle where Rodolfo had entertained the duke's guests. Stephen's breathing slowed; his mind cleared. This had been Arda's refuge, after all. And this man had been her protector.

"You know who sent me," the squire whispered. The cave echoed with a snake's hiss. Surely Rodolfo knew about Arda's love for the nobleman.

"What happened to her?" said Stephen, loudly now. The echo responded in kind. "Was she ill?" His heart bore the grief of two men. He fingered the olive wood box, sewn securely into a fold of his surcoat.

Rodolfo moaned. He slunk backwards with his forest tread. There was enough light in the gloom to catch the terror in his eye and a moist, feverish lip. "They say I did it," he anguished. "Oh, you're a good man, sir! I know you are. They'll believe you if you say I never could have harmed her."

The squire's blood congealed. "Someone harmed her?"

Rodolfo rocked on the balls of his feet, as if gathering whatever energy remained in him for flight. "I buried her myself," he said. Then he exploded past the squire and out of the cave, where the forest swallowed him whole.

XV

The train slowed. Charles pressed his head against the window, his eyes half-closed. It was not the outskirts of Brussels he perceived slipping by but shadow-images, of dripping ferns...of shimmering water. The *chanson de geste* had been written anonymously over nine centuries ago. But thanks to Grandfather's liberal embroidery, Charles held a loose piece of weave in his grasp, freshly colored with the hues of the pond and woodland that he'd visited only hours ago. He reached into his coat pocket and his fingers curled around the quartz crystal Sylvana had given him. The cool, sharp facets spurred him into the present. The meeting at the pond had been real...*she* had been real.

He turned back to the text.

After his encounter with Rodolfo, the squire would return often to that part of the forest to honor the memory of his master, whom he had laid to rest in the hot dust of the Kingdom of Jerusalem, but also to appease his own unfulfilled longing for Arda. Though Rodolfo never divulged where he had buried her, the squire was certain she must be lying somewhere near the pond. He thought he might steal a few moments in her company if he lingered there.

Stephen wasn't alone. There were many visitors. Locals told him that Arda's music used to lure passersby into the woods. At the same time, it had kept Walderic and his men away, fearful of its magic. Connections had been made: those who heard the sound of the lyra escaped sickness; their crops flourished; their loved ones returned safely from pilgrimage. After Arda's death, the flat rock on the pond's deep-green mirror became a sort of shrine.

One twilight, alone at the water's edge, Stephen had a vision: he saw a pure white heron standing on the rock. He was amazed. Gray herons were common. But no one he knew had ever seen a white one. There was a singular aspect to the bird: a profound calm. Stephen felt overcome by a peace he'd never known before. He could only conclude that the bird must have been Arda herself, exquisitely transfigured.

He watched the bird until twilight fell and the pool released its breath...until he couldn't be sure whether the bird had flown away, or dissolved into mist.

Stephen de la Fontaine was a man of some importance now. A knight. A respected noble. He had means and influence. His family already owned land near Bouillon. It was expected that he would take over those holdings as seigneur and expand his parents' manor into a fine seat for future generations.

The white bird changed all that. Stephen found himself slipping away from estate business whenever he could, inventing a reason for his absence, making the long ride alone to the forest pool where he would crouch for hours in the ferns, waiting for the bird to appear. He listened for stray notes of Arda's lyra on the wind. From a simple wooden object she had coaxed a tiny piece of the universe. The echo must be lingering somewhere. Should a true Christian acknowledge such grace outside his faith? With a jolt Stephen realized that his beloved master, that nobleman of knightly virtue asleep forever in Outre-mer, must have asked himself the same question countless times.

He never saw the heron again.

What did life hold for Stephen now, with his master dead and the woman they both loved gone? He searched the heavens for a sign.

And he found one.

A star wondrous to behold, visible across the world, trailed behind it a beam of light of exceeding brightness, thick as a pillar. Such a thing was always a sign. Stephen made a generous donation to Valdoré and in return, the abbey gave him title to the ridge and forests near the pond. Then, on the most inaccessible part of the ridge, he set out to build a castle that he would call Blancheron.

"Blanc héron," Charles said to himself as he tucked the translation back into its envelope. "White heron." His own child's voice was cloying in his ear: *But Uncle, color adjectives usually come after the noun, don't they? So shouldn't it be "héron blanc"?* The youthful diligence made him cringe. *Not necessarily in Old French, lad,* Theodore had said. Then, cryptically: *And anyway, the two words together mask their meaning nicely, don't you think?*

The train pulled into Brussels Luxembourg station. Charles took his duffel bag down from the overhead rack and thought of the gonfalon rolled up inside. Now he understood why the family coat of arms was blazoned with a lyra and a heron.

XVI

Hugues de la Fontaine embraced the idea of going west as fervently as his crusading forebear, Stephen, had headed east. Only the source of their zealotry differed: money for one; God for the other. The biggest challenge for Hugues—greater, perhaps, than Stephen's riding off to Jerusalem to confront the infidel—had been convincing his teenaged son to leave his native country and everything he held dear. This feat he accomplished using the most-used weapon in his arsenal: subterfuge.

As far as Charles understood, they were moving to America for a few years only, and though the time would weigh heavily, at least they'd be returning to Belgium in the near future. Hugues saw no reason to upset the boy with the truth: that he had no intention of ever returning. *It will be a good chance for Charles to learn English for a year or two*, and *Working in an American law office will help me set up my own international firm in Brussels* were some of the artful guises Hugues circulated among his sycophants, and tossed like crumbs to his siblings, Ida and Theodore. Thus he was able to render almost painless the brutal, single-stroke amputation of Charles's universe.

"I hope you're not dragging all that to the States," Hugues muttered as Charles hefted his duffel bag into the trunk of his father's Mercedes SUV. "What do you have in there, *nom de Dieu?*"

"Oh, just some books," Charles said, avoiding his father's eye and bracing himself for the inevitable: the little snigger of sarcasm that could always make Charles flinch.

"More of Theo's useless tomes, no doubt," Hugues said, the snigger on cue. It was often followed, as it was now, by a curious, curling smile, a hopeful sign until one realized that it was directed inward, at some private joke.

They rode home in silence through the dense, cobbled streets Charles so loved. Soon the majestic centenarian townhouses gave way to the Ixelles ponds and Abbaye de la Cambre, a dreamy slice of history captured in perpetual slow motion. Hugues skirted these beauties without seeing them and gained the airy boulevard near the university, where he owned a penthouse.

He'd shared this lodging with Charles since his son's birth. Female presence in the place did exist, but only in the form of domestic workers, nannies, and the ladies Hugues occasionally invited home for "dinner"—a meal generally taken in his bedroom. No maternal soul had ever crossed the threshold.

As for Charles's mother, she'd been just a passing fancy—a bored German-American whom Hugues had met by chance at À la Mort Subite, one of the tourist bars in Brussels, and who must have regretted that she'd been too drunk to care about where the humorless lawyer had taken her afterwards, or what he'd asked her to do.

For his part, Hugues hadn't been at all troubled that the woman he'd seduced had been neither rich nor beautiful; he hadn't even fretted much when she'd become pregnant and abandoned Charles at birth. For during the short time she'd stayed in Belgium, Charles's mother had married the father of her child, and thus Hugues managed to get his hands on the greatest gift he could imagine—greater, even, than a son: an American passport.

The penthouse salon faced the airy boulevard and a large sweep of the Bois de la Cambre park. On the vast and inhospitable terrace, massive pots of gray ceramic had been placed at regular intervals and planted with identical ball-shaped hedges that bore no resemblance to anything seen in nature.

Light filled the room in a flat, hygienic way. The furniture had been chosen not to welcome but to impress: a huge sofa of beige leather on which the sitter slithered around in discomfort, and several matching armchairs. An abstract mural dominated the space, a gift from a foreign client in exchange for legal services. Charles detested its size and vulgar pretention, though he'd never dared to ask what, exactly, those services might have been.

"Father," Charles said, with a higher pitch than he'd expected. They were standing on opposite sides of the cold expanse. "I can't leave. I'm sorry. I just can't." He'd rehearsed these words many times, but only now did he summon the courage to utter them.

Hugues de la Fontaine was a block of a man, heavy-footed and balding, with dark, suspicious eyes and fleshy hands without a blemish. Coldness filtered out from his refrigerated interior along with an odd ferric smell. No one would ever have guessed that the fair and elegant Charles was related to him. *You must be more like your mother, thank heavens!* was all Theodore had ever said on the subject.

"Theo has filled your head with medieval nonsense again, I see," said Hugues. He was standing at the wall of windows, where his back-lit figure loomed large. "It's all arranged, Charles. The move. Your school. Everything. I've found a buyer for the penthouse. You must leave your life here behind you."

Charles squared his shoulders and shifted his gaze from the pots on the terrace to his father.

"Uncle Theo said that I can live with him," he lied. Desperation rose in this throat. "I can finish the *lycée* at Bouillon and then go to the ULB." He was referring to the local university, the excellent *Université Libre de Bruxelles*.

Hugues took a few steps toward the center of the room, where the air became instantly dense and leaden. Control sat at his core, heavy with its own gravity. Though Hugues rarely raised his voice at Charles or punished him overtly, his son was caught, like so many others, by the pull of that force. As he faced his father now, the boy felt as the crusading princes must have done nearly a thousand years ago during their audience with Alexius Comnenus, when they'd come to pay homage to the Byzantine emperor.

"You will do no such thing," Hugues intoned. "I've already paid your tuition in Connecticut. You must get ready to leave." There was sometimes a brief hesitation before Hugues spoke, during which Charles could never guess whether his father was preparing the force of his verdict, or on rare occasions, summoning a shred of kindness.

"But my life is here, studying history," Charles pleaded. "And in the forest," he added, all hope gone. His cheeks flamed; his eyes glittered as if with fever. In his distress he turned his attention back to the terrace, where his mind, in emergency mode, replaced his father's topiary mausoleum with another vision entirely: a tall young woman knee-deep in ferns.

"Your life will be in America, *point final*," countered Hugues with an iron-tipped parry. There would be no shred of kindness today. "Belgium is a dead-end." He wavered. "For both of us."

Charles's time in the forest had honed his perceptions well enough that he'd understood perfectly the waver in Hugues's remark: his father had meant, of course, that Belgium was a dead-end for *himself.* Charles knew better than to argue. But his blood rushed wondering why his father's life had come to a halt here. What laws had he transgressed? He blanched. *Had he harmed anyone?* As he held Hugues's stare for longer than usual, Charles could see doubt lurking in the dark eyes, along with the realization that if his father wanted to continue lying to his son, he'd have to resort to more skillful subterfuge.

Charles slammed the door of his room, curled up on his bed and telephoned Theodore. He felt greatly diminished, from the budding young man he was to the small boy who'd curled up on this bed in the same fashion countless times, usually for the same reason: to escape his father.

Theodore always took his time answering...if he answered at all. He had no mobile phone, so it was impossible to reach him in the forest. If he happened to be at home, Villa Antioch had many inconvenient hallways and stairs. Charles could imagine the telephone ringing on the table in the front hall, six, seven, eight times or more, shrill in the high-ceilinged space. He wondered from which door or corridor his uncle would finally emerge.

"*Oui?*" came the voice on the other end after ten rings. "Ah, Charles! I'm glad you called. I'll be coming up to Ida's next Friday, the day before you leave." Theodore chuckled. "Just in time for the pleasures of the monthly family coffee."

Charles squeezed his eyes shut. Tears burned at his uncle's sarcasm—at the prospect of what would, in fact, be the last of those deadly coffees.

"Uncle, I read the translation," he said, sitting up on the bed and banishing his tears.

"Oh, good! Maybe we can discuss it when I come."

"I have so many questions!" Charles said. "What happened to Rodolfo? Where did he bury Arda? Where is her cave? Oh, Uncle, it's amazing that you found Grandfather's translation!" In his fractured state he almost forgot to ask the most important question of all:

"Why didn't you tell me that Sylvana Longfaye was your student?"

"Oh, didn't I?" Theodore said vaguely. "I must have forgotten."

The same sour envy twisted in Charles's stomach. "Did you tell her that Arda was a musician?" he pressed. He had to muster the courage to add: "In your class?" For if Theodore answered "yes", then the girl had simply learned about local folklore at school with all the other teenagers from Bouillon. But if not—if Theodore said "no"... Well, that could mean only one thing: that she'd ventured into the place that had no rival in Charles's universe—the place where he alone had special privileges: Theodore's study. Even someone as beguiling as Sylvana had no right to those honors.

"Yes, in class," Theodore said, and Charles slumped in relief. "Listen, lad..." The beloved voice had become sober. "I didn't think it would be easy for you...you know...beginning such a friendship so soon before your departure. I mean..."

"You mean, she's extraordinary," Charles prompted him. The words had appeared of their own accord.

Theodore hesitated. "*Exactement.* I'm sorry, Charles, truly I am. I should have told you more about her. You're a young man now."

Silence ensued. Then, with as much solemnity as he could muster, Charles announced: "Uncle, I've decided that I want to get my Ph.D. in medieval studies and use the heron manuscript for my dissertation."

More silence, which Theodore broke with: "The original manuscript appears to be lost, lad."

"But you said you were in touch with the Head of Manuscripts at the Library of European History!"

"Yes, I was. But the directorate has changed since your grandfather's time. The current head instituted a major reorganization. The MS was probably mislaid." Theodore paused. "Charles, listen to me: you must obey your father...you must do what he wants, at least until you're older. The day will come when you'll be able to stand up to him."

Charles shrank. He'd never heard fear in his uncle's tone before. "But I...I..."

"He's *escaping* to America, lad. Not going there to better himself." He faltered. "Or to better you, for that matter."

"Uncle..."

"Please, just do what he asks," Theodore snapped. His tone was unrecognizable now. "I can't emphasize this strongly enough, Charles. Your father is a dangerous man."

XVII

Memories of a childhood abruptly severed would flit like damaged butterflies for years to come. Most of the time, they shunned the light, too weakened from their trauma. But occasionally, a recollection would turn a wing and arrest Charles with a sudden, vibrant image: Theodore sitting in his study, pen poised; the statue of Godfrey de Bouillon astride his charger on the Place Royale; the monthly family Mass at the Church of the Minimes (out of courtesy to the priest, who'd baptized all three de la Fontaine siblings as well as Charles himself) and glutinous lunch that followed, the whole affair best described as a sort of collective embalming.

And that farewell coffee at Ida's.

A fairy queen.

That was how he'd always thought of her.

White house...gossamer dress...moonlit hair.

Coffee at Ida's floated on dualities: kindness and insult; nuance and vulgarity. The Manichean ritual even had its own witch (in the original, beneficent sense of the word): Ida herself.

In naming his daughter after Godfrey's mystical mother, Ida of Lorraine, Guy de la Fontaine had either been a seer himself, or very lucky with his choice of names. Because his own Ida had turned out to be a woman who, like her namesake, trailed ephemera: wisps of philosophy; threads of discreet wisdom. Whenever he visited, Charles followed in the wake of his aunt's remarks and meditations, hoping to grasp one of those trailing delights.

Ida de la Fontaine's ex-husband had left her a Brussels villa that defied logic for a crowded city, completely invisible at the end of a long, hedge-lined alley. A weeping beech obscured most of the roof and façade, and pines pressed darkly against the back wall. One moment you were on a busy urban street, and the next, in the hideaway of an enchantress.

Charles had never noticed the gradual fraying of Ida's universe. Children rarely see such things, finding wonders in what adults considered shabbiness. To him, her curtains weren't faded but of palest mints and pinks; the lacey *voiles* were white and sheer, when in reality they'd gone gray and the hems sagged. A creamy leather sofa—one of the few pieces of furniture in the salon—slouched under the front window and was covered with a network of cracks that Charles had always thought were meant to be a sort of map of the world. On the opposite side of the salon, marooned on a honey-blond floor, a grand piano stood before a picture window at which brooded those pine trees. To an impressionable child sitting on the sofa, the general effect was of looking across a sun-lit meadow toward a haunted forest, with a large, three-legged beast standing in the way.

Ida's windows were lofty, and even through their crust of dirt they admitted an extravagant amount of light for northern Europe. Charles would muse later that perhaps it was Ida herself who provided the illumination in the room. She was always dressed in a loose, gauzy shift, her silver-blond hair spilling to her waist in a gleaming stream, her skin lit from within. Her eyes were often half-closed, as if to indicate that she herself didn't usually live in this bright living room, but in dimmer reaches of the villa.

The final Sunday unfolded like all the others.

The four de la Fontaines sat in a row on the leather sofa, staring straight ahead of them. Ida perched on one end, her delicate wrists poised over a china coffee pot set on a table made from an old tree trunk.

Ida's head's in the clouds... His father's words crossed Charles's mind as he helped his aunt pass the cups. He drank in her soft form— the weightlessness with which she occupied her niche in the world; he reveled in the notion that his father's jab had been anything but an insult.

"You must be looking forward to your foreign adventure, Charles," Ida said without enthusiasm. She passed her nephew the plate of Speculoos biscuits he so loved.

"I guess so," he mumbled, pressing closer to his uncle on the sofa. The pleasant ursine weight of Theodore on one side counterbalanced the unyielding mass of his father on the other.

Your father is a dangerous man.

It was strange how Theodore's words had not really shocked Charles. Or maybe, in his grief, he'd been too numb to absorb them. But though the words hadn't shocked him, his uncle's urgent tone certainly had, and now, sandwiched between the two men, Charles felt the tired cliché of good and evil taking on new life.

"There are excellent universities in America, cheri," Ida continued, warming slightly. "Many have programs in the subjects you love. You'll see."

"He's going to study law," said Hugues.

Charles couldn't see his father's expression but could imagine it perfectly: the impatience in the cool, dark eyes—impatience to be rid of this place and all the people in it...of what he'd always called a toothless, irrelevant existence.

Theodore dipped a biscuit in his coffee and made a pretense at civility. "Does the school in Connecticut have a decent history program?" he asked.

"It's renowned for math and science, thank heavens," Hugues answered.

"Charles is very strong in Latin. You should make sure he keeps it up."

"Only if he intends to go to medical school. Otherwise, it's useless."

These parries and ripostes seemed harmless enough. But the epées were sharp, and had long since left scars in both men.

"You'll let him come back to Blancheron for his holidays, then?" Theodore asked with false pleasantry.

Charles sat up, electrified by this prospect. He might be back in a few months' time! For Christmas, perhaps. Or the Carnival break in February.

"I doubt it," growled Hugues. "His studies will be too demanding."

The atmosphere took on its usual barbed chill and Charles escaped it as he always had, by counting the rings in the tree-trunk table.

After many attempts during many coffees, he'd finally come up with an age for this sad object: one hundred and fifty years, more or less. He considered what it must have been like to take an axe or a saw and kill a living thing of that age. The oak at Blancheron was perhaps six times as old as this trunk and still breathing thanks to the reverence of local people. *But for how long?* Charles looked over at the pine grove beyond the piano. *Will I lose my reverence for the forest, too?* he anguished.

Ida stood up and gathered the coffee things. This had always been Charles's cue to follow her to the kitchen with the tray and he relished the task now. He'd have his aunt to himself for a few final moments while the men sparred in the salon.

The kitchen was dominated by a broad scrubbed table with nicks and hollows, a huge iron stove, and the ever-vigilant pines at the window.

"Aunt Ida," Charles began. He set the coffee tray on the table and pulled out a chair. He found himself caught between desolation and curiosity. His departure from Ida's gauzy realm was imminent. But she had a way of pulling him out of himself. She'd always answered his questions, and before he left for America he was determined to ask her about the woman who so fascinated her: *Arda.* He would have to do this while honoring his promise to Theodore to keep the translation to himself.

"Arda…" Ida whispered, drifting around the kitchen. Her filmy wrap stirred at her slightest movement. "Yes, I've always been fascinated by her. Mainly by history's conflict with her: whether to treat her as the pagan healer she was. Or as a saint, which is what the people in Rêve consider her. Alas, there's so little information."

She clearly doesn't know about the translation, Charles thought, and looked away lest his aunt detect he was hiding something.

"She's still present around the village, though," Ida said.

Charles gave her his full attention.

"You know the ancient yew tree next to the church in Rêve?"

He nodded.

"It's older than the church, which dates from 1059—the year before Godfrey was born."

"Yes, I knew that," Charles said. "But what does that have to do with Arda?" His mind wandered momentarily to the young Godfrey and the visits he might have made to the church in Rêve on his travels through the forests. He would have seen the yew in its infancy...maybe even paused beneath it.

"At some point," Ida went on, "the church was dedicated to St. Arda by the early Christian proselytizers.

"A pagan saint, then," said Charles.

"Yes. She would have venerated that yew like other locals. It occupies pre-Christian holy ground, so certainly the church was built next to it to entice people to worship the new god in the same spot." Ida paused. "And, in my opinion, to trick them into thinking that Arda was in fact a Christian."

"Oh..."

"Yes. A perfect example of imposed reverence pushing out ancient ways, don't you think, cheri?"

"I guess so," Charles said. He thought for a moment. "The tree was Arda's witness, then," he offered. "And maybe Godfrey's."

Ida smiled. "If you believe such powers of Nature, yes," she said. "Your uncle does. He's a historian, of course. But he understands the deep connection of his ancestors to the forest."

Ida continued to float through her kitchen. "Have you heard of St. Walfroy?" she asked.

"Yes!" exclaimed Charles. "In the 6th century he smashed a statue of Diana in the Ardennes into dust. Then he put up a pillar on the same spot and lived on it barefoot."

"Well, well!" Ida exclaimed. She passed by the table to ruffle Charles's curls. "My sweet knight," she murmured. "Just the sort of 'useless' knowledge your father loathes! Poor Walfroy. The evangelists who roamed the Ardennes after the Romans left had a hard time of it. They'd found themselves in a land of female nature mysticism. Oh, how that terrified them! It was much easier to smash statues and sit on pillars than it was to suppress water or moonlight, I assure you."

"Uncle included Walfroy in one of his quizzes," Charles said.

"Ah, dear Theo and his quizzes," Ida sighed indulgently. "But he knew what he was doing, your uncle. A tidbit like that makes the past come alive." She paused. "And if it's alive, it speaks."

Charles nodded. The concept was pure Theodore.

"Auntie?" he said quietly.

She stopped pacing. "Yes?"

"Did you ever experience anything...well...*extraordinary* near the pond at Antioch?"

Ida wandered to the window and studied the pines. She gathered her wrap around her and said: "Yes, I did. And not that long ago."

"A bird?" Charles prompted her.

Ida came back to the table. "Not the bird that you think," she said.

"Not the heron?"

"No."

Ida settled back on her chair, vaguely avian herself.

"It was a swan," she said.

Charles held his breath. "*Really?* At the pond?"

"Yes. Swimming near the big flat rock."

"But they never visit the pond! The closest they get are the shallows near Rêve."

"I know. That's why it seemed like..." Ida hesitated.

"Like what?"

Ida reached over and squeezed Charles's hand. "A messenger," she said.

Charles couldn't suppress a smile. *Her head's in the clouds...* Ida, however, did not smile back. A spell filtered into the kitchen and Charles thought of Sylvana sitting on the stone in the pond, telling him that something remarkable—something *terrible*—had happened there.

It was Ida who broke the spell: "I was wondering if the swan was pulling a boat," she teased. "There was some mist. I couldn't see things that clearly."

"The Swan Knight, you mean," Charles quipped.

"Of course!"

Charles knew the tale intimately. It was part of the lore of Godfrey of Bouillon: that he was descended from the mysterious knight in a swan-drawn boat who'd come to rescue a lady, his only condition being that no one should ever know his name.

But Ida's jest withered. She hadn't recounted the incident just to pass the time, Charles knew. There'd been an edge to her tone.

"I'm sure that Theo must have told you about white animals," she said. "That to our ancestors, they were keepers of wisdom...they *knew* things." She got up and moved to the door. "That swan was carrying a secret, Charles. Maybe you'll figure it out some day."

Ida said no more. Charles hurried over to embrace his aunt before they rejoined the men in the salon. He was already taller than she and had to incline to kiss her cheek. It would be their last tête-à-tête before his departure. He took a long, deep breath of her orange blossom scent, hoping with an ache that he would remember it.

XVIII

They met up later, Theodore and Charles, at the site where so many of their explorations had begun: the statue of Godfrey of Bouillon on the Place Royale. It seemed a fitting place to say good-bye.

Charles was only eight years old when he'd first visited the bronze horseman. He remembered the driving rain; the sour, metallic smell. He'd clung to Theodore's hand so tightly that perspiration had fused their palms together. How reckless it had been—how daring—to stand beneath the hooves of that charger! The horse's eyes bulged. His nostrils flared. The raised hoof could have crushed anyone or anything caught beneath it.

It's a romantic rendition from 1848, Theodore had told the boy. *Godfrey probably looked nothing like that. And his battle charger was a good deal smaller and bulkier.* This information had comforted his nephew somewhat, as Godfrey's bronze mount looked alarmingly like the horse portrayed in his book of Ardennes myths: Bayard, Maugis's magic steed, who could jump across rivers and valleys in a single bound and would not have taken kindly to being welded to a plinth in the middle of the Place Royale.

Godfrey probably didn't even have *a horse by the time he got to Jerusalem, lad. Most of them died along the way. And the crown he's wearing is all wrong. After the sack of Jerusalem, he refused the title of king. He opted for* Advocatus Sancti Sepulchri *instead. Advocate of the Holy Sepulcher. You see, Charles, he didn't want to wear a crown of gold in the place where Christ had worn a crown of thorns.*

They stood there now, the young man and the ageing one, not holding hands or admiring the statue but staring resignedly down the hill toward the filigree tower of the Grand'Place. As if in solidarity, the weather mimicked their very first visit with a persistent, chilly rain slanting down the boulevard.

"Uncle, did you know that Henri of Rêve had joined Godfrey's army?" Charles asked after a tram rumbled past. They were standing directly in front of the pedestal—a precarious place to get to, as one had to cross the traffic thundering at random around the square.

"The first I knew of Henri of Rêve was from your grandfather's translation," said Theodore. He shifted the strap of his satchel from one shoulder to the other. "It makes sense, since Stephen de la Fontaine was also local and from a good family. Henri would have engaged such a youth as his squire."

"It's incredible that one of our relatives was in Godfrey's retinue!" Charles said. To his chagrin, the high notes of a boy had crept into his voice.

"Yes!" Theodore exclaimed. His face brightened. "Stephen was just a squire then, so perhaps he wouldn't have gotten very close to Godfrey and the other lords. But he would have laid eyes on him, certainly." Theodore winked at his nephew. "And he would have recognized that Godfrey embodied the code of chivalry. Now, Charles..."

"Oh, Uncle..."

"Come, now! You know that I can never pass up the opportunity for a quiz."

"Oh, all right. The code of chivalry was: courage, military prowess, honor, loyalty, justice, good manners, kindness and respect."

"Not a bad example to follow, wouldn't you say?" said Theodore. "Minus the military prowess, perhaps." He gestured up at the horseman. "Godfrey embodied those qualities. Not just in myth, but by all accounts, in person. And don't forget that the tenets of chivalry helped to shape the values of our own culture."

Charles looked mutely across the square. He recalled Uncle's other words about this horseman:

The trouble with Godfrey, lad, is that he engaged in holy war. That doesn't sit very well with people these days. Funny, isn't it, that they should single out this particular knight to condemn? Because people still fight over religion. They still pillage and murder all over the place. Which is heinous whoever's doing it, of course. But there's always an excuse, isn't there? These days, the excuse for bloodshed most often seems to be "self-defense". In Godfrey's time, the combatants were "soldiers of God" fulfilling the highest aim they could imagine: to liberate the tomb of Christ from the infidel.

Charles looked up at the statue now. He secretly thrilled at the notion that his ancestor would have laid eyes on this legend...this inscrutable myth. If he were standing where Charles was just then, Stephen de la Fontaine would have recalled firsthand the smell of Godfrey's horse; the crick of the saddle and dull sheen of chain mail. He would have remembered the living gaze in those hollow metal holes. But now the proud warrior seemed inert, as if he'd never taken a breath of life at all let alone commanded one of the most rash and perilous enterprises in history.

Doubt filtered into Charles's observations. It was not the feeling he thought he would be having saying good-bye to this companion of a lonely childhood.

"What else struck you about your grandfather's translation?" Theodore asked.

"Well, I wondered who Rodolfo was," his nephew answered. "I mean, was he Arda's, um...lover?"

"That's not clear."

"What happened to him?"

"Caught poaching by Walderic's men, most probably. He was a foreigner, remember. And a *jongleur*. He would have been at the bottom of the social order, living off whatever he could get his hands on."

"And what about the olive wood box?" Charles asked. The traffic had quietened suddenly, and in the lull it seemed that not only Theodore and Godfrey but all the classical façades lining the square had leaned in to hear the answer.

"Ah, the box," said Theodore.

"Where is it, do you think?"

"Stephen must have kept it, of course. He made a promise to his dying master, Henri, and a promise was a promise back then. But after nine hundred years, it's not surprising that the box lost its way somewhere."

"What was in it, do you suppose?" Charles said. A tremor stirred in his chest, as it always did at the mention of ancient objects. "Treasure from the Holy Land?"

"That's a tall tale, I'm afraid, lad. Knights didn't generally bring home riches. On the contrary. Armed pilgrimage was risky; cripplingly expensive. Most nobles were reduced to penury. Oh, there was wanton looting and pillaging during the campaign, it's true. But most of them limped back home to Europe without a penny. Their 'booty' consisted mainly of holy relics: bones, hair, teeth, you name it. Or palm fronds, the symbol of pilgrimage."

"Or toenails," Charles said, reminding his uncle of Bishop Walderic's relic.

"Or toenails!"

Theodore regarded Charles. The blue of his eyes pierced the misty rain. "I doubt there were any toenails in Stephen's box," he said. "But consider this, lad: nothing is more compelling than a physical trace of the past, is it? Just imagine if you could actually *touch* something that had been Godfrey's: a nail from his horse's shoe; a piece of his chain mail. Even a claw from the bear that attacked him in Anatolia."

"That's why I want to study history, Uncle!"

"You'll have to confront your father on that one," said Theodore, shaking his head. "And I don't envy you there."

Charles watched his uncle wander off around the base of the statue. The very idea of confronting his father emptied his spirit. He breathed in the sour smell that clung to the statue when it rained and studied the pottering form of his uncle. *When would they see each other again?*

Theodore wandered back to Charles. "There's a missing piece in Godfrey's story," he said cryptically. "Some reason why this mysterious duke caught history's imagination. Oh, I almost forgot!" He patted the satchel at his hip. "I have something for you, but let's get out of the rain first." He seized Charles's arm, and together they dodged the traffic to shelter under the great portico of the church of Saint Jacques-sur-Coudenberg.

Theodore pulled a book from his satchel and handed it to his nephew.

Charles gaped at the slim volume. "Ralph of Caen's *Gesta Tancredi*," he cried. "And in English! Oh, Uncle...*The Deeds of Tancred*. Thank you!" He smoothed the handsome, silky white cover with his fingertips. In one corner, a tiny knight reared on his charger and brandished a sword.

"You'll appreciate it more in English," Theodore said, his eyes moist. "It's the least known of the crusade chronicles but more riveting than a thriller!"

Charles pressed the book against his chest. Ralph of Caen had been a Norman chaplain with Bohemond of Taranto, one of the crusading princes. The exploits of Bohemond's nephew, Tancred, who ruled the Principality of Antioch from 1108 to 1112 and whom Ralph also served, were the subject of his chronicle.

"Uncle," Charles said. "What did you mean just now about a missing piece?"

"What I meant was, there's more information about Godfrey in the Library of European History. I'm sure of it."

Charles stared at his uncle. A few curls escaped his hood and the rain weighed them down with plump beads.

"I'll keep looking while you're in America," Theodore added. "I promise. In the meantime, remember this: the importance of *your* past, and the importance of *the* past, are one and the same thing." He held Charles's face between his thick weathered hands. The boy was weeping now.

"Charles d'Outre-mer," his uncle said solemnly. "Heroes summon *us*. There's nothing we can do about it. So take the good qualities we know the enigma over there possessed." He gestured to the bronze horseman. "Take his wisdom and will...take his humility and loyalty and seize your endeavor, whatever it might be. And for heaven's sake, persevere to the end of it!"

PART TWO

Metamorphosis

XIX

Hugues de la Fontaine worked without respite to erase his past. He dropped the "ues" and "de la" from his name and became simply Hugh Fontaine, American lawyer. He also legally changed Charles's name without consulting the boy and confiscated his smart phone, giving him only a basic mobile for local calls.

The new, Americanized Hugh chose southern Connecticut for their home. Playing his European card, he oiled his way into meetings with famous Yale law professors, not only for his own aggrandizement, but also because he'd set Charles's course with law school as its destination. New York City was not far away, with all the bounty that Europeans of Hugues's class expected to find there, and in short order Hugh Fontaine, a bona fide citizen, set up his law office near Grand Central Station.

Guy de la Fontaine had designated Hugh as the sole heir of the Blancheron estate. This comprised Villa Antioch, the castle ruins, lands on both sides of the river and a bank account with which to pay taxes and upkeep. The fact that Theodore was the only sibling who'd ever actually wanted to live there had suited his older brother perfectly—

especially now. For while Hugh and Charles were amassing their fortune abroad, Theodore could run the profitless pile into the ground if he wanted to. This would doubtless occur in any case, for before leaving Brussels, Hugh emptied the account he'd inherited from his father to keep up Blancheron and paid cash for a large mock-colonial in trendy Fairfield County. He discarded his Belgian telephone and closed his social media accounts so that no one from his old life would be able to reach him...not even Theodore, who now had only his teacher's salary to keep up the crumbling estate.

The Fontaine colonial was smaller than Hugh would have liked, and positioned as it was just off a hectic road, less expensive than he cared to admit. But its purchase was a triumph and he glowed with entitlement. The house came with an acre of land and large pine trees on the property lines that shielded it from its neighbors.

The newly-minted Fontaines had no experience of this unrooted, neither-country-nor-city world. In summer, plenty of greenery created the illusion of the country and wild animals occasionally strayed in. Birds flocked to feeders and birdbaths. Deer still followed ancient trails across sterile lawns. There was even an occasional coyote, mainly on rubbish days. Yet smells and sounds always betrayed the human hand: steaks blackening on the grill; the lawnmower's nasal roar; the pock of a basketball and its jarring thud against the hoop.

For Charles, it was a land of pretense and excess. Things seemed too large for their intended purpose here. And the purpose itself— barbecuing, for instance—seemed too shallow to be so exalted. A vapid sameness clung to everything, along with the frank admission that in all this newness, the past and its mysteries would have trouble getting any toehold.

For Hugh, it was a place to bury his past and get rich.

Just months after their arrival, he successfully defended his first client, a crooked real estate developer who'd paid with banknotes stuffed into a gym bag. Hugh had thought nothing of it. He was not a man prone to reflection—acquisition being his preferred activity—so looking inward at the state of his ethics was not something he indulged in. Sentiment was likewise shunned. He'd learned to bury his feelings decades ago at the *lycée* in Bouillon, where his gentler siblings had had the protection of their teacher, but his own natural scrappiness had set the bullies in merciless pursuit. America promised him justice at last. If she had taught him anything in the short time he'd been there, it was that money alone could get him everything he needed: for status and leverage, but also for the settling of scores. And so Hugh pledged all his allegiance to this god.

And Charles...Charles Fontaine now.

Outwardly, he'd taken like a sapling to his new soil. He'd turned seventeen in October and was already taller than his father, with a quiet elegance no one would ever have attributed to Hugh Fontaine. An academic stoop was nascent in the boy, along with myopia. As Hugh's thinning hair retreated to its last redoubt, Charles's chestnut-blond curls burgeoned and filled his father with envy.

No one could have guessed that beneath the young man's calm lay a seething inner life. Or that he continued to live in two worlds, even if he himself was unaware of this. Unrest invaded his sleep; it frayed his nerves and marred his studies. The sapling might have taken well to its new soil, but its roots had been damaged. On weekends, home from his boarding school, Charles wandered through the Fairfield house when his father wasn't there, and when he was, wandered the byways of suburbia instead, alone, adrift, returning from his chilly exile just as lost as when he'd left, hoping only that his father might have gone out in the meantime.

You must do what he wants.

Charles lived to the rhythm of his uncle's warning. He dared not do otherwise. For though he possessed Theodore's razor senses—he could glean much from turning over not only banal-looking stones and dry leaves but layers of a person's character as well—he could not, even with this talent, fathom his father.

He'd guessed, of course, that Hugh was in some sort of deep trouble. Financial, legal, criminal...it mattered little to Charles what sort it was, only that his father left him alone. The image of the wily emperor Alexius seemed ever-present, scheming amidst his silks and gold and gems. What an irony that Hugh, who detested history, would have found himself perfectly at home in twelfth-century Constantinople!

The Frankish armies had been obliged to mollify and flatter Alexius; negotiate and barter in order to cross the Bosporus and head south to Jerusalem. "The yoke of homage", Ralph of Caen had called it. Alexius hadn't been menacing, exactly. At times he could even be pleasant, like Hugh Fontaine. But there'd been something genteelly sinister about him as well, also like Hugh. Quietly ominous. *The yoke of homage...* The term had weathered nine centuries rather well, Charles thought. After all, he was wearing one himself.

He knew better than to ask his father for a proper phone—or even to inquire whether there'd been any news from Theodore or Ida. He was sure that his computer was being closely monitored. Not that it would have made any difference: neither Ida nor Theodore used email. Clearly, Hugh had not only closed the book on his siblings but thrown it away as well. With foreboding, Charles realized that this had been his father's intention all along.

They were facing each other across the granite-topped island in the kitchen when Charles said, as forcefully as he dared:

"I would like to be in touch with my uncle, Father." He'd broken house rules and said this in French.

"Write to him, then," came the reply in English, a clever challenge, as they both knew that the post office in Rêve-sur-Semois regularly mislaid mail destined for Villa Antioch.

"I'll write to Aunt Ida instead," Charles retorted, persisting in French. "Letters will reach her all right."

Hugh had just made espresso, a smell that always lured memories of Ida. It seemed that Charles could even make out her form hovering near the coffee machine, impossibly gauzy against the backdrop of steel and granite. He thought of their parting; of breathing in the scent of orange blossom as she'd whispered against his cheek: "You will love America, Charles. New shores. New friends. Just don't forget where you came from, my sweet knight, *d'accord?* Your story began here, in Belgium. Like our own Stephen."

Hugh put his cup on the counter in a studied manner. This was followed by the hesitation that could have gone in any direction. "Put Belgium behind you, Charles," he said. His voice was low and intense and had greater effect than a loaded pistol. "And we're in America now. We'll speak English from now on."

Charles watched his father as the edict was delivered. Once again, he'd waited in vain for that hesitation to produce what he'd always hoped lay hidden in his father: some remnant of a better self.

"*Je ne veux pas oublier mon français*," Charles said defiantly. "I don't want to forget my French."

Hugh's silence charged the air. Slowly, heavily, he turned his back, indicating the end of the conversation.

You must obey your father.

Theodore's warning lurked in the silence.

"*Je ne veux pas oublier mon français!*" Charles dared again, buoyed by this act of rebellion. He left the kitchen before his father could respond and made the long trek back to his room.

His heart felt bruised, as if a surgeon, peering inside him, would actually have found a blackened organ. Charles rounded his shoulders even more than usual as if to protect this sorry, shriveled thing from further damage.

He passed the colossal dining table, large enough to seat all of Alexius's entourage, and hurried through the opulent reception room already stuffed with Hugh's antiques: gilded chairs and brocade sofas that neither of them used. With relief Charles arrived at his door and closed it on the rest of the house.

His room was small, but its simplicity was a balm after his father's excess. His desk looked out over the front yard and was a fruitful place for study. Books in their dozens lined the walls. Sometimes he would just lie on his bed and gaze at these trusted friends: Ralph of Caen, of course, Theodore's precious gift; new writings about medieval Europe; Horace and Marcus Aurelius and Herodotus, all gazing back at him with their avuncular smiles; guidebooks about Ardennes legends and ancient places.

Charles looked out the window at the ochres and russets of his first American autumn. There was a hint of the Ardennes about the vista, he decided. He sighed, and followed nostalgia where she inevitably took him: to the drawer of his desk.

He opened it now and pulled out his precious relics: the quartz crystal and medieval horseshoe; the piece of Roman tile with a finger mark (*Now you can* really *touch the past, lad!*); wafers of shale from the ridge; the family gonfalon. The treasures seemed lost, somehow, as if they, too, had found no home here, and Charles realized that they'd been as brutally dislodged as he.

He picked up the items in turn and like an amnesiac tried to remember the circumstances around each one. This shocked him most of all: the misting-up of memory, even at the age of seventeen. He could summon the drenching rain in the clearing where he and Theodore had found the Roman tile, but not the amazement on his uncle's face; he recalled digging on the riverbank near Villa Antioch, but not the jump in his belly when the horseshoe had poked from the mud. Maybe this was simply self-protection: his spirit draping him in softness until he'd healed from the bruises of loss, like covering an ailing tree in winter.

The only object that memory had not blurred was the quartz crystal. Here his mind shone like the sky after a tempest. *Sylvana...* Her willowy form stood straight and clear before him and it took no effort at all to conjure her cloud of dark hair and changeable green eyes...to feel her reach for his hand, and the coolness of the crystal when she'd laid it on his hot palm. With ease he imagined her in her natural habitat: the pond and its woodland, and the brooding, overgrown ruins on the ridge, for it was his own natural habitat, as well.

XX

Hugh's property was so new that construction debris and rain-filled craters still littered the empty lot behind the garage. Hidden from the main house, it was to this wasteland that Charles retreated on weekends and school holidays. He hung the family gonfalon with the lyra and heron from the back of the garage, where his father wouldn't notice it, thus laying formal claim to his kingdom.

A few pines had escaped the bulldozers along with a spindly oak, more than enough for an enterprising dreamer to construct a forest. There was also medieval bounty to be found here if one's imagination was especially keen (this was still modern Connecticut). Bent nails might have been used to attach a layer of leather to a wooden shield; a canvas sack was probably what a surcoat would have felt like after nine hundred years behind someone's garage. *We must have physical contact with the past to understand it.* Theodore's words followed Charles everywhere. *Would you prefer to read a boring biography of Godfrey, or touch his rusted spurs?*

When it rained, one of the craters overflowed to become a miniature forest pool and Charles would lean over it, teasing from the water his vanished world. At twilight, the lamp on the garage reflected in the puddle like a face staring back at him—a luminous oval like Sylvana's, as unreadable as hers. From a pine bough overhead, the water shaped the lyra's dark curve. Now and then, the surface of the pool wrinkled from some distant tremor, and for a few seconds Charles could hear the heavy tread of a horse in the woods around the villa. Once he even saw a flash of white in the water and imagined Arda's heron, but it was only the evening shuttle from Boston to LaGuardia passing overhead, its wingtip mirrored in the pool.

It doesn't matter where you find yourself, lad. If you're a true historian, the centuries will pull away like the tide and leave treasures as fresh as when they were dropped.

Charles wandered about his new-found kingdom, hope still stirring. *Maybe I really* am *a true historian!* he thought. *Because even here I'm finding treasures.*

He would sit on the dry pine needles behind the garage, lean against the clapboard siding and people his tiny universe with the books he took outside with him. There was always plenty of company: history was a crowded forum. Grandfather's translation of the heron legend was usually tucked between the volumes, Arda, Henri, Stephen and Rodolfo all having made the trip to Connecticut more or less intact. Odysseus would drop by now and then and spirit Charles off for an adventure. There was Latin to keep up with, too, and the gentle Horace to help him with this struggle.

One cold Thanksgiving eve, his first spent in America, Charles took Theodore's gift behind the garage: *The Deeds of Tancred.* He sat down on his usual spot and for a while simply held the book in his lap. The back of the garage faced west, and the siding felt warm against his shoulders in the setting sun.

Charles closed his eyes and transported himself to his native land. It took no effort at all to turn the odor of pine into Theodore's cedarwood cologne. He could imagine his uncle's blue eyes glinting with the latest historical quiz. He listened to the chink of their glasses against the tiled table as they sat on the terrace and watched twilight creep in. Among the many things Theodore had taught him was that the past was a constant and faithful companion. One could always escape into its company. It never lacked for exciting diversions and life lessons. And it never, ever judged you.

He opened the book to a passage about Antioch that he knew well:

...Rivers and mountains ran along its flanks. The city was even joined to the flank of the mountain, although it was inhospitable, with walls reaching up to its summit and a citadel built there as well. Its western edge was a short distance from the river. In the east, a stagnant marsh strengthened the double walls.

December, 1097. The crusaders had crossed the Bosporus and made a fragile alliance with Emperor Alexius in Constantinople. Now they were camped outside the walls of Antioch, a city without which they could not advance to Jerusalem. With the Mediterranean to Antioch's west, supply ships could come to the aid of the crusaders. Nevertheless, the city seemed impregnable. Turks would descend from their mountain stronghold to attack with bows, swiftly retreating with their light arms. The Franks, heavily burdened, could not make the steep ascent to chase after them.

They would languish there for eight months. All winter long, death and hunger stalked the crusaders' camp. Rain and cold rivaled anything they'd known in the West. Neither tent nor hut could withstand the raging winds. Most of the horses died. People ate thistles; they picked grain from manure. Nobles endured all this side by side with the poor, and like them wondered what portents lay in the bizarre movements of heaven and earth: the blood-red skies...the trembling ground...shifts in the wind, and warriors clashing in the clouds.

"What did it all mean, Uncle?" Charles had asked many times.

"Well, it meant that something was about to happen," came the usual response. (A bit of an evasion, thought Charles, as something was always about to happen to the crusaders.) "Something big," Theodore added, which made more sense, especially as the siege of Antioch was imminent.

In fact, at about the time that amazing portents were appearing in heaven and Earth, history turned on a single shadowy figure: Firuz, a disgruntled Armenian camped inside the battlements of Antioch, who fell for Prince Bohemond's generous bribe and dropped a rope ladder over the wall.

"I always had the impression that had it not been for Firuz's betrayal," Theodore said, "everyone would have gone home. They were simply at the end of their tether. And that would have meant the end of the crusade. No Antioch...no Jerusalem."

"History might have been better off," Charles offered.

"Maybe."

"Jerusalem wouldn't have been running with blood."

"Not on that occasion, anyway. There would be plenty of others, of course."

"But then the crusaders got stuck inside Antioch," Charles reminded his uncle.

"Yes."

"And there was that business of the Holy Lance, wasn't there? The weapon that pierced Christ's side. They dug up a fragment of it under the basilica."

"If you believe it, yes."

"They found strength in this, didn't they?"

"The chroniclers thought so," said Theodore. And then: "Those with broad minds are tempted to venture into that world between worlds, Charles, where answers can sometimes be found. But it's a treacherous locale for modern scholars, believe me."

Charles turned from memory back to his book.

After the discovery of the Holy Lance, a small number of crusaders set out to a river crossing to attack a much larger contingent of Turks commanded by the fearsome Kerbogha. Most of the horses had perished, so the Frankish commanders were reduced to riding asses or fighting on foot. The crusaders employed the ruse of concealing themselves behind a hill and attaching a banner to each spear, as if the hill hid as many units as there were banners.

Dust rose up, arms rang, hooves stomped, shields clanged, eyes were blinded, ears were deafened, and they overwhelmed the hearts of their enemies... It is marvelous to tell and hard to believe, but that great multitude turned in retreat.

Charles's pulse quickened. *How could his fellows at boarding school prefer video games to this?* His blood rushed at the thought of his own ancestor caught up in the melee. As squire of the body, Stephen de la Fontaine would have followed Henri of Rêve into battle and never left his side.

Charles pulled out his grandfather's translation of the legend—a gesture he'd done so many times that the envelope sagged like worn calfskin. Once again, he zeroed in on the meagre scraps in the *chanson de geste* about Henri of Rêve and his squire. The battle scenes in the manuscript were almost non-existent. But there were enough emotional scraps to leave one begging for more.

Stephen was promoted to "squire of the body"—the most coveted rank, and the one closest to his lordship, helping him dress, caring for his weapons and armor, never leaving his side in battle. In such closeness, the squire could tell that deep in his soul, his master suffered most cruelly.

Had the two men consoled themselves with thoughts of Arda? Charles mused. That sibyl of the woodland...that pagan seeress they both adored?

As he lay dying, Henri had summoned Stephen with instructions for the olive wood box:

"Go home, please. Give the box to Arda. You remember her, I think. The girl in the forest. Who played the lyra." The knight had never learned of his squire's own love for her.

Stephen nodded. He took the box and key and turned his back briefly to his master, unable to control his tears. It had been four years since they'd left the Ardennes for Outre-mer...four years since either of them had known the soft, fragrant embrace of their native forest.

Throughout all the deafening mayhem and slaughter, had the men preserved a few molecules of Arda's forest peace?

"Do you think that humanity has learned anything since 1097, lad?" Theodore's favorite question had reached the Connecticut garage. "No."

"Well, maybe it's we historians who have to enlighten them, don't you think? Because if not us, then who?"

Charles closed *The Deeds of Tancred*, tucked the translation back into its pages and smiled.

We historians...

XXI

"What are you reading?"

A woman was standing at the chain link fence marking the Fontaines' rear property line. She wore a fuchsia track suit that ballooned around her ample girth. Her hair, of a copper color not found in nature, ballooned in similar fashion around a broad, pendulous face.

Charles looked up from his book. The woman must have come from the modest, single-story brick house some distance across a scrubby yard.

"Ralph of Caen's account of the First Crusade," Charles said, realizing what this must have sounded like to such a person (or to any person, for that matter). "It's about Tancred," he said, beginning to founder. "He was Bohemond's nephew..."

He got up, dusted off his corduroys and handsome navy pea coat and approached the fence. He noticed that the woman's yard was covered with a medley of ochre leaves, like the wallpaper in Villa Antioch. A tinkling of wind chimes issued from the direction of her house.

"Oh!" said the woman. The single word sparkled with interest, and Charles rued his initial assessment.

"I'm Charles Fontaine," he said.

"Yes, I know." The broad face beamed. Curiosity shone in the vibrant grey eyes. "People talk around here," she said, and let out a grand, artless laugh. "I'm Grace Holmes, by the way." She handed a foil package over the fence. "Cookies for Thanksgiving...in case you get hungry while you're reading. I notice you do quite a lot of it." At Charles's confusion she added: "I can see you from my kitchen window."

"Thank you, Mrs. Holmes," Charles mumbled, unnerved that the woman had been watching him. He glanced down: she was wearing cheap crimson slippers with no socks. Her ankles gleamed in the failing light like cod filets.

Grace tilted her head to one side. "So...the First Crusade. A lot of knights in armor, I guess."

Charles cringed at the depiction. Then he remembered that most people living in the twenty-first century had only rudimentary knowledge of the twelfth—if they had any at all.

"One of those knights was my ancestor," he blurted.

Grace froze. She briefly became a fuchsia garden statue before shaking out of it. "You don't say?" she breathed.

"Yes! His name was Stephen de la Fontaine."

"Oh...is that your French name?"

"Well...Belgian."

"He was a knight, then, your Stephen."

"Yes. But he started out as a squire, to a nobleman from the Ardennes: Henri, Count of Rêve-sur-Semois."

"Oh, my." Grace gaped at him. "I just love your accent, Charlie!"

Charles stared back. No one had complimented him since he'd come to America. No one had called him that, either.

"They were in the entourage of Godfrey of Bouillon," he said, "one of the leaders of the First Crusade. He was very famous. Maybe you've heard of him?"

"Oh, I don't think so." Grace blushed, adding yet another shade to the fuchsia-and-red medley. "Did Stephen know him?" she asked.

A frisson passed over Charles. Godfrey was unknowable...beyond reach. It was as if Grace had shone a light on his hero and revealed traits no one had ever seen: a few white hairs in his beard...a cut on his hand from a spur...creases at the corners of his eyes when he laughed and a sun-burnt nose.

"Maybe they passed each other in one of the camps," Charles said off-handedly. "But Stephen was only a squire, and Godfrey a duke. Actually, he's often referred to as a prince."

"A squire is like a servant, right?"

"Yes."

"To Count Henri." She made a brave attempt pronouncing it "on'ree".

"Yes."

"So Henri and Godfrey were probably pals."

Charles said nothing. *In fact, they probably were*, he thought.

"Could you tell me more, Charlie?" Grace asked. She pushed some dry leaves around with the toe of her slipper. "I don't know any knights or squires. There aren't many around Connecticut these days."

Charles pulled himself out of his stoop and smiled at Grace. He cleared his throat and shuffled his feet.

And he told her more.

He began with Theodore and their history lessons. Then he traced the loops of the Semois River in the air over the fence and talked about the steep forests guarding Blancheron. As Grace didn't seem in any hurry, he indulged her with the smell of moss on the castle ruins, and the way it grew shaggy like hide on the old oaks. He mentioned the proximity of Bouillon castle and the fact that Godfrey himself had probably hunted in the forests around Blancheron. Something about the way Grace drank in his story made everything he was recounting seem so alive.

Before he knew it, Charles had told her just about everything that had been locked in his heart clamoring to get out. The November sun was slanting through the chain link fence, and the temperature had dropped considerably, but Grace showed no signs of impatience. Clouds began to gather and snow looked imminent and still she stood there, shivering in her track suit, listening. Her silhouette had taken on a pleasing pineapple shape against the western sky.

He didn't mention the heron legend, however. Or Arda. Or the fact that his own grandfather had made a translation of the *chanson de geste*. He'd vowed to respect Theodore's wishes to keep it to himself.

"You loved it there, didn't you, Charlie?" Grace said after a pause. She leaned over the fence and squeezed his arm.

"It's...it was...*home*," he said.

"You know, you have a look in your eyes," Grace said. "Like you see what other people can't see. Like you can see the past or something. Is that what historians do?"

Charles couldn't answer her. *What was she talking about?* Whatever it was seemed like a good thing. If you can see the past, then presumably you can touch it, too. The idea (a typically Theodorean notion) had suffered cruelly from Charles's move to America, and yet now, for the first time since his arrival, he felt it shake to life through this most unlikely intermediary.

"Do you think that Godfrey still haunts those forests around your uncle's place?" Grace asked. Against the backdrop of the setting sun the friendly, pendulous face seemed suddenly remote.

"Why do you ask?" Charles said with some alarm.

"Because he still haunts you!"

Charles digested this comment. "I...I'm not sure what you mean, Mrs. Holmes," he said at length.

She touched his arm again. "You talk about Godfrey with even more passion than you talk about your ancestor Stephen," she said.

This remark confused Charles. He looked over Grace's shoulder toward her little house. A family of plastic ducks dotted the crabgrass near her porch and glowed eerily in the twilight. The effect disoriented him, as did most things about this place.

Grace was right...and not only about Godfrey. People from his past did, indeed, haunt him. They'd catch the light briefly whenever he looked them in the face but soon slip away, leaving him alone again in his rootlessness. Nothing seemed real here, or authentic. Nothing seemed connected to anything else: no past, no future, just a bland, manufactured present. Only Grace Holmes seemed authentic at that moment. In her company Charles felt untethered, buoyant, as if she could help him float back to his native soil if he wanted to. And oh, how dearly he wanted to!

"There's such a mystery about Godfrey," Charles said. "I mean..." He faltered. "He haunts *history*, Mrs. Holmes. Not just the forests of the Ardennes."

He went on to describe Godfrey's elusive myth through the centuries: the swan-drawn boat in Lohengrin; appearances in *The Divine Comedy* and Händel's opera *Rinaldo*: shiny clues that more often than not were fool's gold.

As Grace seemed eager for more, Charles told her how in Asia Minor, Godfrey ventured into the hills to go hunting and came across a peasant being attacked by a bear. The duke heroically intervened, but the bear hooked its claws into his tunic and pulled him from his horse.

"He saved the peasant," Charles said. "And killed the bear. But his sword got tangled in his legs during the struggle and cut an artery. He almost bled to death, Mrs. Holmes! He was ill for many weeks afterwards."

"Golly!" breathed Grace. And in the next breath: "But he must have killed so many people, too."

"Yes." Charles hesitated. "He even cut an enemy soldier in half with his sword."

"You don't say!"

"The bottom half rode away on the horse."

Charles regarded Grace askance, as if this last detail might have proven too much for her. She seemed unfazed, however, so he added: "Our time is pretty violent too, isn't it, Mrs. Holmes? It's just that the enemies and weapons have changed. I don't know why people are so self-righteous about criticizing medieval times."

"Yes, this is a violent age," Grace said sadly. "Sickening, really. No one learns any lessons."

It's we historians who have to enlighten them, don't you think?

Charles looked at Grace, as if she'd heard Theodore's words, too.

"So…" she began. "Was your Godfrey a hero or a murderer?"

Charles opened the book he was holding and found the passage he was looking for. "This is how Ralph of Caen described him," he said:

His nobility was marked by many virtues, both secular and divine. These included charity to the poor, mercy to wrongdoers, humility, clemency, sobriety, justice and chastity. In fact, the duke demonstrated more of the qualities of a monk than he did of a soldier. However, he was not less experienced in secular virtues. He knew how to wage war, to arrange a line of battle and to find glory in arms. As a youth, he was first or among the first in learning to kill the enemy. Thus, as the son of a fighting count and a most religious countess, even when he had been observed by a rival he deserved to hear: "in his eagerness for war look to the father, in his cultivation of God behold the mother".

Charles closed the book and looked up. A final ray of sun teased a bright chestnut color from his curls before ceding to snow clouds.

"Hmm," Grace muttered again. "He sounds like a hero *and* a murderer." She reached over the fence for the book and flipped through it. "Most heroes are, though, aren't they?"

"Well, Godfrey was known as one of the *Neuf Preux*," said Charles.

"One of the what?"

"The Nine Worthies: nine historical personages who embodied the perfect ideal of chivalry—at least as the Middle Ages understood it. There were three good pagans: Hector, Alexander the Great and Julius Caesar; three good Jews: Joshua, David and Judas Maccabeus; and three good Christians: King Arthur, Charlemagne and Godfrey of Bouillon." Charles hesitated. "Most of them killed people, Mrs. Holmes. You're right."

"Well, well," said Grace. "No women on the list, I guess."

Charles searched her expression for anything deeper than playfulness but it was getting too dark.

"There should have been," she added, with the gravity he'd been looking for.

Charles thought of Arda: of the wise women without name or number who'd been seeresses and healers as she had been, surely as worthy as any of the bellicose men on that list, and maybe more so.

"Did Godfrey marry a beautiful princess in the end?" Grace asked.

"He never married," Charles said.

"Really?" Grace tilted her head, intrigued.

"It's very odd, Mrs. Holmes. Truly. At the time, it would have been unthinkable for such a lord not to find a suitable wife."

"Well, then," she mulled. "Maybe he found an unsuitable one, and couldn't marry her. Maybe he left her behind."

Charles fell silent. He'd never thought of that.

"Did you leave anyone behind, Charlie?" Grace asked.

Charles flushed and stared at his loafers. Her question had stirred the phantom company sequestered deep within and one of them rose up briefly: *Sylvana.*

Grace perceived this at once. "Ah," she chimed. "There is someone!"

Charles continued to study his shoes. "Maybe," he said, growing hot in the chilly twilight. Suddenly the very notion of Sylvana being "someone", in Grace's parlance, seemed outrageous to him—an impossibility that even science could have proven, and handily at that, like proving that oil will never mix with water.

He pushed some pine needles together with the toe of his loafer. *And what was Sylvana to him, anyway?* A person standing in the ferns...a stranger whose only tangible evidence was a piece of quartz he kept hidden in a drawer.

"I'm sorry, Charlie," Grace said. "It's none of my business." She stepped away from the fence as if preparing to go home. She was still holding Ralph of Caen. "But if you ever want to talk about it, I'm here for you."

"*Sharl'!*"

Hugh's voice carried all the way to the back lot.

Charles turned to see his father advancing with heavy purpose.

"*Sharl'!*" Hugh bellowed again. He still pronounced his son's name in the French manner even though he'd outlawed the language.

He stopped several paces from the tête-à-tête at the fence. "Come inside!" he commanded. "Did you forget that we're going to Manhattan for Thanksgiving dinner at my new partner's place? I want to speak with you beforehand. It's going to snow. We should get to the city before the roads get too bad."

Hugh stood with his feet planted, weighing down the twilight. He ignored Grace entirely.

"I'm coming, Father," Charles said. He turned back to Grace.

She leaned close over the fence as she handed Ralph of Caen back to him. "Come and see me whenever you want, Charlie," she whispered.

"Mrs. Holmes," he whispered back.

"Yes?"

Charles balked. Confusion overcame him. He hardly knew this woman, and yet it seemed completely natural to ask her: "Could I give my uncle your address to write to? My father is...well..."

Grace smiled. "Of course! I understand," she said under her breath. Hurriedly, aware that Hugh was still standing not far away, she told her address to Charles and made sure he memorized it. "You'll find your endeavor, Charlie," Grace added. "Just don't give up until you do. Happy Thanksgiving!"

She walked away across her scrubby yard.

Charles remained at the fence with his back to his father. It didn't feel coincidental, somehow, Grace Holmes giving voice to a word he'd always considered to be Theodore's: *Endeavor*. It wouldn't have surprised him to have seen his uncle standing at the fence just then, eyes shining at the impromptu history lesson Charles had just given— and to such an unlikely pupil, too.

His heart grew heavy at the sight of Grace retreating, as if she were taking with her all the relevance of the life he'd just been describing so passionately...as if she were the only person in this new-fangled land who understood him.

When he turned around, Hugh was gone.

It had started to snow.

XXII

The audience took place in Hugh's salon. The room was crowded with antiques he'd bought at auction, all shouting expense and a certain funerary pomp. Their pretension fitted the room perfectly, as its very size was an exercise in bad taste and demanded similar furnishings. Drapes of shimmery damask were fastened back with gold tassels. The marble fireplace boasted handsome brass andirons in the shape of griffins. The mantelpiece was covered with Victorian ceramics along with an ornate Rococo clock. The fire was lit only for visitors who might eventually prove themselves to be useful. It was never lit for discussions with Charles.

Hugh was already running his own law firm in New York City and had rented a three-bedroom apartment in the fashionable East Village, so the Fairfield house was more for show than anything else. It was in New York that he had the most success oiling his way upward. He occasionally tried to drag Charles along to corporate functions and opera premieres, but the weight was considerable and he eventually gave up.

"What were you doing with that stupid cow?" Hugh asked as they took their seats in the salon. They were facing each other on opposing sofas like travelers in a waiting room.

"Are you referring to Mrs. Holmes, Father?" Charles said. He blew on his hands to ward off the sepulchral chill.

"She's probably a gold-digger. Stay clear of her."

Charles smiled inwardly. How extraordinary, he thought, that despite her humble circumstances, Grace Holmes seemed far too lofty a person to dig for Hugh's gold.

"I want you to speak to Michael about interning with the firm next summer," Hugh went on, dismissing Grace entirely.

Charles loathed his father's new partner, the perspiring, over-eager Michael Milligan. He extended his long legs over the Oriental carpet, stared at his feet and muttered:

"I'm going to see Theodore next summer before college."

"Impossible!" Hugh snapped. "It's not too early to think about law school." Irritation rose in his voice. "You'll be taking over the firm eventually. You need an internship. What will you be taking at Yale next year, by the way?"

Charles could hardly tell his father that among the courses he'd planned to take were advanced Latin, Forgotten Women of Medieval Europe, and Beowulf and the Northern Heroic Tradition. He did muster the courage to say:

"I want to be a historian, Father."

Charles glanced up. Hugh was sitting with his back to the window, his graying hair indistinguishable from the gathering storm. His face was also ill-defined, though his eyes reflected an uncanny illumination. Charles recalled the words of Emperor Alexius's biographer, his own daughter, Anna Comnena: *The grim flash of his eyes as he sat on the throne...*

"Your uncle's fingerprints are all over this," Hugh said. Then he delivered a short lecture on the American Dream, as he often did, intoning that Charles should be grateful he'd been brought to these shores.

"How many young people around the world would leap at this chance?" Hugh said. "And here you are, actually *living* the Dream— going to an expensive prep school where you can meet the right kinds of people. Going to Yale. Having a guaranteed job at my law firm in New York City. Instead, all you want to do is to lose yourself in anachronism. Just like your useless relatives."

Charles waited for the derisive snigger and sure enough, it didn't fail.

He answered his father the only way he could think of, with Theodore's favorite advice from the code of chivalry:

"Despise pecuniary reward," he said quietly.

"What the hell are you talking about?" barked Hugh.

"Father, I don't care about the American Dream," Charles explained, his voice barely audible. He felt as if he'd uttered the most egregious blasphemy. *How could anyone not care about getting rich?* He bit his lip, and stared beyond his father at the encroaching snow. The air had thickened to a whiteout. Passing cars crept along like dream-farers. The gauziness heartened him: it reminded him of Ida.

"I'm looking into a little red sports coupe for your graduation," Hugh bulldozed on. A trace of generosity actually warmed his words. "You'll be driving a lot between New Haven and the firm. Of course, it all depends on how seriously you prepare for law school."

"Thank you," Charles said. He hated sports cars. He half-expected lackeys to appear from behind his father's shimmery drapes bearing the gifts with which Alexius had sweetened the Western princes' capitulation. They'd acquired a mound of gold and silver from the emperor's imperial treasury for the oath they'd sworn, along with splendid purple silks and fine horses.

"I can earn my own money to go to Blancheron next summer," Charles said.

"How can you possibly waste another summer in the Ardennes at this point in your life?" Hugh said, incredulous. "You should be looking ahead to your future, not behind you." He added, not without kindness: "I only want what's best for you."

Charles stood his ground. "The history of our family is important, Father!" he said.

Hugh guffawed; he tensed a pale hand on his knee. *Again the grim flash.* "I suppose that my brother filled your head with ridiculous stories of herons and mystics," he said.

"Yes!" Charles exclaimed. He'd noticed his father's smug smile but managed to ignore it. "You know the story, then: that our own ancestor, Stephen de la Fontaine, was squire to Henri of Rêve and came back from Jerusalem to build Blancheron."

Hugh showed no interest in this information. He checked something on his mobile phone while saying: "Your grandfather tried to indoctrinate me, too. Thank God I had the gumption to escape it." He put his phone away and narrowed his regard on Charles. "Did your uncle never tell you the truth about our Blancheron neighbor with whom Stephen and Henri went on crusade?" he condescended. "He was hardly a paragon of virtue, old Godfrey. Did Theodore tell you how on their way, the crusaders extorted money from Jews in Germany in exchange for their safety and massacred them anyway? Or about the atrocities they committed in Antioch and Jerusalem?"

Charles watched tiny flecks of snow patter at the window like fingertips seeking a way in. The whiteout was complete.

"I know about those things, yes," he said, his voice drone-like. "You seem to forget, Father, that atrocities and extortion are alive and well in our own century." He paused. "Chroniclers of the time were unanimous in their judgment of Godfrey as an upright and pious man."

Hugh ignored the comments. "Do you know how my brother lost his teaching job?" he said.

Charles hesitated. "I thought he retired early to spend more time with research."

"Bullshit!" Hugh exclaimed, relishing the local patois. "Theodore was forced to take early retirement because of his habit of leaving the school premises with an entire class of students without anyone's permission, digging in the local forest and coming back with kilos of stones. Wouldn't that worry you, if you were a school principal?"

Charles suppressed a smile. "That sounds like Uncle," he said. "He's convinced that stones have stories to tell, if you know how to listen." Theodore's words seemed to be offering a lifeline and Charles repeated them now: "Stories like the White Heron live in the trees...in the water and stones. And not only in the past. But *now*."

Hugh grew very still. The dark eyes glistened. "With your intellect you intend to listen to *stones?*"

Charles squared his shoulders and met his father's gaze. "Theodore was the best teacher I ever had," he retorted, his voice breaking.

For a moment Charles regretted the outburst, for although the half-light had darkened sufficiently to almost entirely conceal his father's aspect, Hugh shifted uncomfortably on the sofa, as if a projectile had grazed him. Charles could feel Hugh's gaze through the gloom as he riposted:

"What did he teach you besides irrelevance?"

XXIII

It was snowing too hard to drive into the city for Thanksgiving dinner. A fluffy, dream-like universe had replaced the Fontaine neighborhood, transforming barbecues, rubbish bins, decks and cars into domed fairy-things. All points of reference had disappeared. One might miss a step and vanish forever under the drifts. Sound existed only as close-ups: the Velcro of a parka; the squeak of a boot; a laugh. Otherwise, the airwaves had gone silent, the sky come to ground. The only people on the road were those addled by the lure of roast turkey and pumpkin pie, or those who were lost.

Lost...

The two Fontaines shared frozen dinners at the twelve-seater table in the dining room without exchanging a word.

Lost...

Charles bid his father good-night early, feigning tiredness. He climbed the plush, carpeted stairs to bed, and in their silence he could hear the cricks of the old staircase at Villa Antioch. He brushed his fingertips against the surgical white walls: somewhere in his nerve endings there remained the knobby texture of the villa's wallpaper.

As the snowstorm spread its cloak over the night, Charles finally sat down at his desk and wrote a letter to Theodore.

He could have found a way to communicate with his uncle much earlier than this, Hugh's edicts notwithstanding. But he'd simply lacked the courage. He'd been adrift; a wayfarer ill with buried longing. Tonight, at last, he summoned the nerve to confront all that—to acknowledge the curious stirring he'd felt after his encounter with Grace Holmes, proof that a few glowing embers remained of the passion Theodore had once kindled. Outside, under a forest sky, such embers would be cold by morning. But in the deepest reaches of a young man like Charles, somehow, through chance or miracle, they'd kept warm.

It was well past midnight by the time he'd folded the six sheets of paper on which he'd spilled his heart, tucked them into an envelope and addressed it to: *Prof. Theodore de la Fontaine, Villa Antioch, Rêve-sur-Semois, Belgium.* On the back of the envelope, he wrote the address Grace had whispered to him over the fence. If the post office in Rêve was as negligent as he suspected, at least the letter would be returned to her. But if it did reach Theodore, he would know where to write to his nephew.

Charles stretched out on his bed fully clothed. The snow had turned icy, and sounded like a wire brush against the window.

Forest...

He said the word aloud in English. The French word—*forêt*—had sadly lost its "s", the letter that best described the wind, and rushing water, and rasp of dry leaves as animals shuffled by. Charles whispered the word several times, letting the "s" freshen his tongue. Uttering a word aloud always made it seem real. Potent. Sometimes other senses were awakened, and one could smell the rich decay on the riverbank, or feel the liquid crystal of spring water on the tongue. This time, the word swept him right back to his leafy beginnings.

Nothing is as ancient as the forest, Charles.

He slept.

The dream began with a white bird. Not so much the bird itself, but its preternatural color. And that other thing: the stillness in the air. *Sylvana?* Charles murmured. For it was she who'd slipped into the dream's undercurrent; she who'd uttered those words: *Sometimes peace-spots are places that witnessed terrible events.*

Charles approached the pond: the bird was idling in the water near the rock. It seemed to have been gazing for centuries into the glassy mirror, looking for a way in, and indeed, should a gap have opened up, the bird would have slipped down into it, never to return.

Charles inched closer, trembling, fearful that he, too, might be lured into the watery netherworld.

White animals were keepers of wisdom...they knew things.

Something disturbed the bird: a shudder deep in the earth. *So heavy...so weary...*

A hoof clipped against stone.

The bird didn't shy from the sound. Instead, a rolling mist crossed the water with stealth and enveloped it. The creature disappeared before Charles's eyes.

He felt the shudder again, resonant this time.

Closer.

He cried out, and plunged through the ferns in a direction he hadn't chosen himself. It was the dream that had chosen it for him. There was no alternative but to blunder ahead, breathless and afraid.

He found a way up the ridge between the rock carcasses...past the twisted trunks and dreadful, yawning fissures. There was no merry chink of shale underfoot. No Theodore climbing ahead, satchel swinging from his shoulder.

Charles was alone.

Was this really the place he'd loved...that he'd considered his home?

He arrived at where the castle ruins should have been, but the forest had swallowed them. Nothing remained of Blancheron now. *Had it ever existed?* The meadow lay before him, but not a single landmark was familiar. There were no menhirs. No grassy mound. The ground pitched under his feet as if the whole ridge were heaving—shifting in time from one epoch to another. It was a country of weird *orées*, he knew: edges between here and there...between one world and the next.

He felt it again, that shudder. Now there was something else as well: the cloying sweetness of horseflesh. And a stench: sweat and leather, perhaps.

Wake up...oh, wake up! It was his own voice, half-boy, half-man.

But he couldn't wake up.

The dream pulled him across the meadow to where the menhirs used to be.

The Knight's Gate.

"There's a confluence of energies up here, Charles."

Uncle?

"And music..."

"*Music?*"

"Of course! Arda's music lingers in the air here. The lyra, remember? She played it for her lover."

Something leaden dragged through the underbrush behind him. *Nearer. Louder.* Goodness, the weight of it! The sheer mass of a medieval warrior burdened by iron sword, wooden saddle, chain mail, helmet, and beneath him, an ailing charger.

How had the horse climbed the ridge?

Charles shivered in his sleep. Only Maugis and his magical steed could have done it. *They* could have reached the ridge in a single bound. It was some comfort to know that surely Maugis wouldn't have left behind the stink of a returning crusader.

He began to run. Teetering, tripping, he stopped himself just before plunging over the escarpment. He could feel the cold air now, rushing up from the river far below, and the vast, terrifying space.

There was a grunt behind him. A whinny.

Charles d'Outre-mer!

The voice resounded as if across centuries.

Charles held his breath. "Godfrey?" he mouthed.

Might the white bird have been a swan?

Without waiting for an answer, he launched himself over the edge and slithered down another vertical forest. The ancient oaks were wearing the mossy hides he recognized, shaggy and so very cool to the touch, like dead bears. His heart surged. Soon the bridge would be visible, and the lights of Villa Antioch!

But the forest had deceived him—led him into this trap. *How could a friend be so untrustworthy?* In sweaty terror he realized that he'd descended the wrong side of the ridge. There was no bridge on this side. No villa.

This is a land of mirrors, lad. Of dead ends. You need to have your wits about you.

He glimpsed the river now: the wrong side of the meander. Weeds were streaming like hair. The great pines on the bank rose as if from the water. Their sleepiness was deceptive; watchful.

He glanced up to where the edge of the ridge met the sky.

There was no horseman.

Relieved, he attempted to drag himself back up the steep pitch, but he could not. At each step he slipped backwards, his grip pulling away loose stones and rotten branches. The shaggy, ursine moss tore off in his hands.

"Charles!"

The voice had a viola's timbre.

He gasped; his heart weakened.

"Sylvana!" he cried.

He looked up: at the top of the escarpment was a tall, slender figure. There were no defining features. Not even a face. Just a mass of dark hair.

She seemed to have slipped down toward him, because suddenly she was close enough to hold out her walking stick.

"Grab it!" she yelled.

He reached up, but grasped only air.

"*Charles!*" she screamed.

With an agonized shout he lost his footing. Backwards he toppled, ever backwards...down, down, to where the sly river was waiting.

He shivered awake.

An eerie illumination filled the room. At first, drowsy, he thought it must have been the moon. But then he saw that it was still snowing. He opened the window: in the world outside, not a single landmark remained.

XXIV

Charles spent the weekends until Christmas at his boarding school, not returning to his father's house again until Christmas Eve. To his relief, Hugh announced that he'd be spending the holidays in the city moving his law firm into grander quarters. Fontaine & Milligan had outgrown its original office in just four months and found a taller, shinier building with an entire floor at its disposal. Hugh didn't ask his son to join them for the inaugural parties.

On the very day he came home, Charles trod through the snow to the chain link fence, scaled it and headed across Grace's yard. It was late afternoon and the light was already fading, though the little brick house shone with fairy lights like a boat on a weed-strewn sea.

"Charlie!" Grace had spotted him already and was standing on her porch in another blousy track suit—an orange one this time. She ushered Charles into her tiny doll's-house kitchen and wrapped her arms around him.

He clung to her as if she were long-lost kin. He hadn't spent more than a few hours in this woman's company. *How much time did it really take to make a deep connection?* Not much with Grace Holmes, apparently, although Charles had asked himself the same question many times about Sylvana and still didn't know the answer.

His lips sank into the soft pillow of Grace's cheek as he kissed her.

She reached up to touch his curls. "How handsome you are!" she said. "Such a gentleman!" She put the kettle on and laid a plate of brownies on the kitchen table.

Charles smiled sadly. He'd withdrawn into his books and lectures and closed himself into that world, not letting a single friend cross the threshold. His classmates had dismissed him as a remote moon in the teenage solar system, a description Charles actually found flattering. In fact, had it not been for the hectoring presence of his father, he could have stayed forever in that outer orbit, where the likes of Stephen de la

Fontaine and Godfrey of Bouillon could also be found, floating in historical half-lives.

"That came for you while you were away," Grace said, indicating the letter she'd placed next to the brownies. "From Belgium," she added with importance.

Charles stood at the kitchen table without taking off his coat, his attention riveted on the letter. He picked it up in slow motion and turned it over: the return address was not Villa Antioch, but a street in Brussels. Neither the handwriting, nor the street, were his aunt's.

"When did this come?" he asked quietly.

"Just this week," Grace said. "It's not from your uncle? Or your Aunt Ida?"

"No. I don't recognize the writing."

Charles's name (de la Fontaine), Grace Holmes's, and her address were all traced in tall loops and graceful arabesques, as if the writer hadn't heard that handwriting was a lost art.

"Tea or coffee?" said Grace, shuffling to the kettle in her red slippers.

"Oh, Mrs. Holmes...could I take a rain check?" Charles's American English was colloquial now, even if his accent still had soft European edges.

Grace turned to him, her eyes indulgent. "I understand, Charlie," she said with a wink. "You want to read the letter in private." She turned off the kettle, took a plastic bag from a drawer and put the brownies in it. "Here, take these home with you."

Charles flushed. He'd been very happy to see Grace again. But in truth, the main reason for his visit had been to check if she'd received any mail for him.

"There haven't been any lights on in your house," she said. "Is your father away?"

"Yes."

"For Christmas?"

"Yes."

"You'll have Christmas dinner with me, then!" Grace announced. "I'll expect you tomorrow around five."

Charles accepted, hugged her again and hurried home. He'd barely made it back to the house before he ripped the envelope open.

Cher Charles...

He gasped with delight. That the letter was in French rang a deep, neglected bell. That the handwriting was not Ida's rang a brighter, newer one. He went no farther than the granite-and-steel kitchen, as no one was at home to intrude on this moment. For how could he have waited any longer after he'd seen the signature?

XXV

*C*her Charles,

I hardly know where to begin. And my task is made more difficult by the fact that I hardly know you! But we shared something in the forest at Blancheron, didn't we? We made some sort of bond that still feels real. Do you think so, too?

I'm also writing on behalf of your uncle. He received your letter but is not really in a state of mind to answer it, so he asked me to write and explain.

As you might have heard, after you left Theodore stopped teaching. He was not dismissed, as some people think. He simply didn't have the heart anymore. He's continuing with his research, however. I ride my bike to Antioch on weekends to help him with his cataloging, filing, etc. I take him food, too, because he hasn't been looking after himself.

But before you feel envious of my attentions to your uncle (how did she know?), let me say that he experienced such deep sadness after you left. Une tristesse profonde. *There's a void in his life that cannot be filled. Certainly not by me. He left the faculty at the* lycée *abruptly. I was worried about him, and went to see him often. I'm a poor substitute for you, Charles, but at least I can distract him, and make him feel that his work has some value. He told me to tell you that he would never blame you for your departure. He knows how much you didn't want to leave—that you were forced to go. He also said that you should not attempt to come back until you are well away from your father's influence. This is very important, Theodore says. Because you see, Charles, your father is a criminal. I'm sorry to be so blunt, but there it is. You must not cross him in any way.*

Charles set the letter down on the granite counter. He stared at his hands, then at the floor. He glanced over at the coffee machine but couldn't conjure the healing presence of Ida. He tried to feel shock, or even surprise, but could not. For he'd known, of course. *Your father is a dangerous man…*

I don't feel I can talk in detail about these things, Sylvana continued. *Theodore will have to explain. Or your Aunt Ida. It's not right for me to involve myself in your family affairs. But I can tell you for sure that it has to do with ties to the Belgian antiques market. There was that nasty business about the dealer in Antwerp. You probably heard about it in the news: he was found dead not long ago under mysterious circumstances.*

Charles looked up again. This time he had no trouble conjuring the presence he dreaded the most—the one that rendered every space a zone of menace. He knew little about his father's involvement in the antiques market outside of the tasteless pieces with which he furnished his residences. He hadn't heard about the Antwerp dealer, either. How tactful, he thought, that Sylvana had implied Hugh's connection to the death without actually coming out and saying it.

I've enrolled at the Brussels Conservatory to study voice. Maybe that's a surprise to you. But I've always sung, and I want to give some beauty back to the world. I want to help people heal using their own voice. Theodore assured me he would be all right when I'm in Brussels studying. Anyway, I come back on weekends to see my mother, so I check on your uncle at the same time. Marcel Wauters at the inn in Rêve is bringing by his meals. Don't worry about him, Charles. He understands your situation. He will wait for you to come, no matter how long it might be.

I have some news! Remember how you mentioned that Arda might have hidden in a cave somewhere to escape punishment by the clergy? Well, I found something in the woods. I was climbing up the rise behind the spring. You remember it, surely. It's very steep. I followed a practically invisible path I'd never noticed before. Suddenly there seemed to be an opening in the rock face, behind a wall of vines and such. *Try as I might, I couldn't get through all the vegetation. I need to come back with a machete or something! But I'm sure it was a cave.*

I will close for now. I meant what I said at the pond, you know. You are straight and true, Charles d'Outre-mer. You are not like anyone I've ever met.

I hope you think of me from time to time. And I hope that you still have the crystal I gave you to remind you of the woods we both love.

Your friend of the forest,

Sylvana

XXVI

C *hère Sylvana,*

I was so very happy to receive your letter. It arrived at my neighbor's with no problem. I miss you. Let's keep using her address.

Charles let out a sigh and tore the page in two. He'd left the kitchen to retrieve pen and paper from his room so that he could answer Sylvana right away. She'd left no email address. But even if she had, it seemed only fitting that he should answer paper with paper.

He made himself comfortable by turning up the radiator under the granite counter and brewing an espresso. This would take quite a while, he reckoned.

There must be a better way to begin. The zeal to respond had been too great to resist but had muddled his thinking. Once he'd begun—and in considerable haste—he found himself wondering if Sylvana would have written at all had it not been for Theodore's prompting. Had his uncle regretted being so tight-lipped about the girl before Charles's departure? Had he rued thinking that a liaison with such a young woman might be too difficult for a sensitive boy to put behind him, which was perhaps the main reason Theodore had asked Sylvana to write: to assuage his own guilt?

Your friend of the forest...

No, thought Charles. Theodore had not prompted Sylvana to write those words. They were as guileless as she was, surely.

He took a fresh sheet of paper, decided against *I miss you* and *Let's keep using her address*, and deliberated.

Life hasn't been easy since I left Belgium...

Too self-pitying.

I look at your quartz crystal a lot...

Too pandering.

Charles poised his pen over the page and began writing again:

Thank you for telling me about Theodore. I didn't know those things.

Yes, that was it!

He reread Sylvana's letter, lingering over the words that pained him most—*une tristesse profonde*—because he'd wandered through the same depths that Theodore had and was roaming them still. *Why should I hide my pain?* he thought. If any soul could understand, it was Sylvana. And he knew that she would accept nothing less than total honesty.

The clock in the salon had long since chimed midnight by the time Charles looked up from the letter, his fervor spent. It was Christmas Day.

He'd held back nothing in his answer. Longing, anger and remorse roiled in successive waves, freely, each emotion sparking a memory that often didn't include Sylvana at all but rather an image from long before he'd met her. He described the sheltered spot between the standing stones on the Blancheron ridge, and the wooden stool in Theodore's study. He told her about a meteor shower he'd watched from the flat rock in the pond, so close that he was sure the trailing sparks would hiss in the water.

He was certain Sylvana would understand these memories in her own way, through her own bond with the forest. He had so little to go on when it came to knowing her. But with a lover's intimacy he knew every niche and cherished beauty of the landscape they shared. He could still imagine her standing in the ferns, the tiny ornaments of spring water glistening in her hair...the sweep of her pale hand through the air, like a wing. *What had she remembered of him?*

The more he wrote, the more his pain abated, and by the time he'd reached the end of his missive he felt that he'd brought everything he loved to this very kitchen, where the rich aroma of coffee seemed to have taken on the tang of moss and peat.

He ended with a lighter tone:

I'm delighted that you've enrolled at the conservatory. Might you have drawn inspiration from Arda? Please tell me more about this, and about your life now. And please wait for me to return before you go back and look for the cave!

I still have the crystal.

Of course I think of you.

Charles

XXVII

Charles got his wish to study *Beowulf* and Latin at Yale in the end. Forgotten Women of Medieval Europe, too. But the effort to disengage himself from his father's gravity had been just too great.

The day will come when you can stand up to him.

That day, alas, had not yet arrived.

He went to law school as Hugh had decreed; he became a partner in the firm (Fontaine & Fontaine now, Michael Milligan having been arrested for fraud). Acquiescence seemed so easy, so painless compared to the fortitude he would have had to have summoned to break free of his father's expectations. How much courage did it take to grab a walking stick and old leather satchel and spend one's life digging up history's secrets? Too much, as it turned out. Too much...

Charles simply assumed that the passion he'd once known as a young person was gravely ill and unable to be saved. A charlatan now occupied the hollow vessel that his true self had vacated. Fragments of his youth still lingered, however. At first he was unaware of them. But with time they sharpened, and the splinters they left in his soul would throb unexpectedly. He might be sitting alone in his office studying the piece of shale from the Blancheron ridge, and suddenly Theodore would be hovering at his shoulder. Or he'd take out the quartz crystal he always kept in his pocket and set it on his desk, its essence as clear and potent as the image of Sylvana. But the balm of memory could not dull the ache of loss. He'd abandoned his convictions; worse, he'd ignored the words of his own personal confessor, Grace Holmes: *You'll find your endeavor, Charlie. Just don't give up until you do.*

The word "endeavor" no longer figured in his vocabulary.

It was only through observing his father that Charles realized the extent of his own metamorphosis. What he had always dreaded—becoming like Hugh—had come to pass. Like him, Charles had succumbed to the path of wealth and status, a surprisingly easy road compared to the one his heart had been telling him to follow. *Despise pecuniary reward.* He'd flung those words at his father as a hot-headed boy, not realizing how difficult it would be to adhere to them himself. He observed his father as both a spectator and a participant, therefore, repelled by what he was witnessing as the former, and ashamed of his role as the latter.

Hugh Fontaine reveled in America's fascination with duplicity. It seemed extraordinary to him that someone with a criminal past could mask his transgressions so seamlessly in this new frontier. As it turned out, Americans were drawn to the European gentry even more than they were to true crime, so happily for Hugh, most people were blinded to his darker aspects.

Only belatedly did he realize that maybe he shouldn't have dropped the "ues" and "de la" from his name so hastily. These appendages, however creaky in European circles, disguised dubious behavior rather nicely here, even acting as tickets of entry. They caused a stir among the horsey socialites Hugh was courting, who themselves aspired to some kind of title—even a creaky one.

Still, what passed for aristocracy in America had shocked even Hugh at first. Naturally he'd expected the omnipotence of money. Just not the callous, overt embrace of it. He was bemused by the investiture into American nobility of names whose prominence rested solely on things like chicken farming, toothpaste and ketchup. The shock soon wore off, however. Hugh was a pragmatist above all else. Property, board rooms, private schools, season tickets to the Metropolitan Opera...this was the life he was after, and wasn't it enterprising for the early tycoons to have acquired it through selling unimaginable quantities of pickles or Coca Cola?

Now and then, he put the appendages back on his names just to turn heads, especially on invitation lists that might yield a catch. It was apparent that the women who interested him seemed far more attracted to Hugues de la Fontaine from Belgium (an intriguing place they couldn't locate on a map) than they were to Hugh Fontaine from

New York City. They kept asking him about his past; they loved his charming accent, and the way he never pronounced his "h's".

The ladies were persuasive, no doubt about it, especially in his bed. After they released him from their racehorse legs they inevitably steered the conversation toward Old Europe, and though he tried hard to contain it, the word "castle" did occasionally cross Hugh's lips. The women would light up like zealots then. *America is too new!* they gushed. They would tell him how much they loved history, and what perfect mistresses they would make for his château. He couldn't very well admit that the castle in question was just a few moss-covered stones on an overgrown ridge; or that the property was being babysat by an unhinged relative who spent his days poking about the fields and forests for broken tiles.

In due course, Charles took an office down the hall from his father. He had to traverse an acre of Oriental carpet to reach it, passing illuminated display cases filled with the antiques Hugh didn't have room for in his residences, and a mahogany reception area that served as a watchtower of sorts for all this Byzantine opulence. Certain imperial furnishings were missing: this was not Constantinople. But in their quicksilver deal-making and tainted promises—in the silk of their ties and the gold of their watches, Hugh's colleagues could easily have served as advisors to the emperor.

The law firm occupied the twenty-second floor of one of those buildings in Manhattan to which throngs of fellow clones streamed every day, and in which, as he approached the gleaming doors, Charles's own reflection revealed the same lukewarm soul he saw in everyone else. It had taken him years to understand that he was, in fact, no different from them. He'd long since left that remote orbit in which he'd been so happy, floating with his books and historical friends, and become locked in his father's, where he'd found nothing but an icy vacuum.

He never heard from Sylvana again.

XXVIII

"You've moved to the big city, then," Grace said flatly. They were standing at the chain link fence, their preferred conversation point on many occasions, but not since Charles had left for Yale and law school. He'd sought Grace out now as a gesture of courtesy—something that well-heeled young men did when it was necessary to be polite. Hugh was about to sell the Fairfield house and Charles thought he should look her up.

He'd just announced, with hubris he didn't feel, that he'd become a partner in his father's law firm and would be sharing Hugh's penthouse in New York City.

"I hope you've taken all those people from history with you," Grace said. "Stephen, Henri and the like. Charlemagne and Godfrey, too." She was wearing the fuchsia track suit from their first encounter on Thanksgiving eve over a decade ago.

"Oh, no, Mrs. Holmes!" Charles exclaimed, irritated.

"So you've lost interest in them?" she pressed him.

"It's not that..." Heat rushed to his cheeks as if he were the schoolboy Grace had discovered reading behind the garage, not a twenty-eight-year-old already set in his ways.

"I see," Grace said.

Charles glanced around. The rain-filled craters...the rusty nails and bedraggled trees...none of it had changed since his teenage years. Only the perception of them had.

Grave and pendulous, Grace studied her young friend. Her jowls notwithstanding, she resembled a woodland prophetess far more than she did a suburban widow who passed cookies over the fence. Charles feared what her "I see" would bring, and it did, indeed, bring it:

"You should at least take the books you were reading with you, Charlie," Grace said. "Surely your dad's new apartment is big enough." She lowered her voice for effect. "But it's probably not big enough for all the ideas you're passionate about, is it? At least, that you *were* passionate about. No apartment is that big!"

Her correction of the present tense stabbed at him. It was not an unfamiliar sensation. Splinters from his past left similar sharp pains, although now that he'd become a partner in his father's firm and deluded himself into thinking that he'd actually made this life choice himself, he would have thought that those juvenile twinges would have vanished.

Grace reached into the pocket of her track suit and pulled out an envelope with a return address of Villa Antioch.

"This came for you," she said.

Though Hugh's interdiction of mail from Belgium had long since lapsed, there'd been no letters anyway—not from Theodore, or from Ida. It was still a mystery why Sylvana hadn't answered his letter.

Charles stared at the envelope in shock. Then he ripped it open.

"From your uncle?" Grace asked.

"Yes."

Charles pulled out an index card with a photo glued to it: the two standing stones near the ruins of Blancheron. On the reverse side was written simply: *La Porte du Chevalier. N'oublie pas.* "The Knight's Gate. Don't forget."

It was a singular missive. *Had Theodore finally succumbed to dementia?*

Grace let Charles digest this communication, then said: "History is full of shadow-folk, isn't it?"

The comment unnerved him. "Shadow-folk?"

"Yes. People whose lives have entered ours somehow. They exist among us in a way you can't explain. You know this..." She let the comment hang on the air.

"Oh, I don't know, Mrs. Holmes," Charles scoffed, although he'd understood her perfectly.

"Those folk still have a lot to say," Grace said. Her gaze sharpened. "You still have that look in your eyes, Charlie. Like you can see the past or something. Who wouldn't want to use such a gift?"

Charles glanced over Grace's shoulder, and as usual his eyes fell on the family of plastic ducks by her porch. A thought briefly awakened—

something to do with how an ordinary woman with fuchsia track suit, copper-colored hair and plastic lawn ornaments could be so insightful on the subject of destiny.

"Your shadow-folk seem to have lived a long time ago," she said.

"Yes."

"But they can come to life again. Isn't that what a good historian does? Make them relevant?"

"Mrs. Holmes," Charles said with defiance. "I didn't choose medieval studies in the end. I chose law."

"And you're happy with that?" she said, just as defiant. "That's the problem with people," she continued. "They abandon their passions along the way, thinking that something better will come along..." She thought for moment. "I don't know...something like money. And then they wonder why they get so lost in life."

Charles had no answer; not even an emotion that could produce an answer. He stared at the ground. But as soon as Grace's red slippers entered his field of vision affection swelled in him, an emotion he hadn't felt since his adolescence.

He looked up at the soft, drooping face.

Grace smiled at him. "That look in your eyes doesn't lie, Charlie," she said. "Not to me, anyway."

Charles shuffled his feet. "I'll be going now, Mrs. Holmes," he said, and moved away from the fence.

"Stephen de la Fontaine was your relative," said Grace, raising her voice as he walked away. "Your kin. You owe it to yourself to know more about his story, don't you?'

Charles turned around. It seemed that Theodore himself was standing at the fence.

She's right, lad. When will you admit it?

XXIX

Y**ou'll** have to sell Blancheron for me, Charles. I don't have time to go to Belgium. Don't worry, you'll get your cut."

The death certificate lay on the desk where Hugh had tossed it.

Charles didn't have the heart to pick up the document. He felt suddenly immobile, as if every limb were tied to earth. From where he was standing, he could see the official stamp of the local Belgian administrator who'd processed the *décès,* and of course, the name.

Nom et prénom: de la Fontaine, Theodore Bohemond.

Charles reached for the certificate, surprised to notice the paper shaking in his hand. *Bohemond...* So Grandfather really had been quite the Crusade enthusiast! In one of those inappropriate trains of thought that emerges from shock, Charles considered that Theodore hadn't been anything like Bohemond of Taranto, who along with Godfrey of Bouillon and three other princes had led the armies of the First Crusade. Bohemond had towered over the tallest man; he'd been ruthless and conniving. Even his laugh had been a threat. While Theodore...

Charles swallowed hard.

Gentle, kindly Theodore...

"Well?" said Hugh, checking his watch.

Charles perused the rest of the document: *Lieu de décès*: Rêve-sur-Semois; *Date de décès...* He glanced across the desk at his father. "It says here that Theodore died six days ago. Is this the first you've heard of it?" His hands had gone cold. He was only able to take short, shallow breaths.

"Yes. Things move slowly over there."

Hugh, seated, smoothed his hands over the polished expanse of mahogany. The desk was big enough to stretch out on, and luxuriously empty for such a busy man of the world. (Charles sometimes wondered whether Hugh did, in fact, stretch out on it, and if so, with whom.) All around them, space yawned: a glossy expanse of hardwood floor punctuated by islands of beige carpet and leather seating arrangements. The Manhattan skyline gradually winked on in the twilight: the panorama Hugh had struggled so tirelessly to possess.

"As far as I know, Philippe Osselaer found Theo at the villa," Hugh continued. "He assumed it was a heart attack."

"Osselaer the notary?" Charles exclaimed. "He's still alive?"

"That's him."

"Christ, he seemed ancient decades ago!"

Hugh let out a laugh. "Osselaer was old when he was thirty. His father was your grandfather's notary. In fact, he's only a few years older than Theo: my age more or less. He always carried a torch for Ida, poor man. Probably still does."

Charles's mind made a quick detour to summer lunches at Villa Antioch: Theodore, the charmingly debonair host, a sweating bottle of Chardonnay in his hand; and Philippe Osselaer, his only guest, smiling wanly. Charles remembered the man's extreme slenderness. His face, meek and pinched, had inclined like a supplicant's. Osselaer had walked in a mincing way, his body skewed to one side as if skirting obstacles, an indelible image for a young boy. He'd humored Theodore and drunk too much, but in retrospect, the man had clearly been uncomfortable with such indulgence. To Charles, Osselaer had seemed about a hundred years old. And to think that he'd carried a flame for Ida!

"Was there any sort of inquest?" Charles asked.

"Inquest?" Hugh smirked. "Of course not! Why? Theo wasn't young. He drank too much. He was overweight. People die, Charles. *Point final.*"

Charles watched his father's smile fade to nothing, as if it had returned to the cold depths where it normally resided. But something lingered behind, caught in the churning wake. *Was it regret?*

"Does Ida know?" Charles asked. He wandered to the panoramic window, where the vast city offered him no comfort—nothing but a narcissist's indifference.

"I'm not in touch with Ida. I believe Osselaer contacted her."

"What about the funeral?"

"I've asked him to arrange it."

"And financial matters?"

Hugh regarded his son, bemused. "Theodore never owned anything in his life. He lived at Antioch free of charge, as you know. I left him a generous fund for maintenance."

The blatant lie drew Charles back from the window. He knew his father had long since emptied that fund.

"Other than that," Hugh went on, "he probably had some sort of state pension from his teaching job."

"But he quit years ago," said Charles. "Because of depression."

"Depression, my foot! He probably got tired of teaching and wangled disability payments."

"He was only seventy-one," Charles said tonelessly. "Was he ill?" It was a question that strangers asked—people who knew nothing about the circumstances. Not people who should have known better...who should have known if a loved one was ailing.

Charles stood at the center of his father's office and a chill filtered up from somewhere inside him, as if to remind him that with Theodore dead, the last embers of the passion he'd kept alive—passion for a life he'd never had the courage to pursue—had most certainly been extinguished, too.

What's happened to me? he wondered. *How did I end up selling my soul to the lowest bidder?*

He recalled the strange card Theodore had sent to him care of Grace Holmes, the last words Charles had received from his uncle.

The Knight's Gate. Don't forget...

What had he meant by that?

Hugh's voice brought him around. "Now, about Blancheron. If you leave next Tuesday, you'll arrive in Brussels on Wednesday morning and have plenty of time to get to Rêve for the funeral on Thursday at noon. Osselaer will help with the sale after that: the villa, castle and land. It shouldn't take more than a couple of weeks maximum."

Charles strayed to one of the leather islands and dropped into a chair, his heart numb. He knew it was useless to speak about Theodore's research—about the objects of historical value he'd found in the forests and meadows around Blancheron, and the dozens of papers and articles he'd authored. *What should be done with it all?* A shiver passed over Charles at the thought of the heron legend. He considered the parchment that his grandfather had translated—that had been miscataloged somewhere in the Library of European History; and his uncle's cryptic comment when they'd said good-bye at the statue on the Place Royale, something about a missing piece in Godfrey's story. *There's more information in the Biblothèque de l'Histoire, I'm convinced of it. I'll keep looking, I promise.*

Charles closed his eyes. In the peculiar lightness of grief, he was able to momentarily leave his father's office and hover over the Semois valley. He could see the Blancheron ridge clearly. He realized that even after nine hundred years, his family's roots still lived beneath all the shale and moss and peat. *How could anyone discard such a legacy?*

"Blancheron is just a pile of stones, Father," Charles said, his anger rising. "It's probably not worth selling. And anyway, why so soon?"

He knew at once how fruitless this was. One might as well have tried to convince Emperor Alexius that it was unfair to ask the crusading princes to hand over the territory they'd conquered.

"Of course it's rubble!" Hugh countered. "But a private buyer will be interested in such a piece of Belgian *patrimoine*. The Crusades and all that. Anyway, Antioch is part of the same package. The villa has some value, though it's probably gone to seed by now. I don't have the time or patience to be an absentee landlord any longer, especially when there are no occupants."

"But the estate has been in the family for nine centuries!" Charles exclaimed, all the while wondering when it was, exactly, that his father had finally crossed the line from avarice to cruelty. The notion that he'd ever imagined regret in Hugh's demeanor seemed preposterous.

"Forget that sentimental rubbish!" Hugh said. "Theodore's always conveniently ignored the fact that for over seven hundred years out of the nine hundred, the castle has been uninhabitable. I wouldn't call that a very useful family possession, would you? Anyway, Antioch is still livable. Although God knows what state it's in after Theo's been camping in it. I'm counting on you to see that the villa is spruced up and ready for sale. You'll have to go through Theodore's things. Throw away what you can. Give everything else to a local charity or something."

"There's a lifetime of research in that house!" Charles countered. "I don't suppose that Uncle left a will?"

"Osselaer would know if he had, but I doubt it. Theo was a dilettante, Charles. That's the sad truth of it. There are armies of medieval scholars better than he was."

Charles stood up and faced his father. "He mastered Greek and Latin," he said. "He could translate Old French, for heaven's sake! He was an excellent scholar. He knew what history means to *us*." Then, with a catch in this throat, Charles ventured to a place where he knew his father's pull was weakest: "I would have loved to have been what Theodore was."

XXX

He left Hugh's office, traversed the acre of Oriental carpet and nodded to the secretary in passing. Normally, he would have stopped at Denise's mahogany station to chat, but a state of emergency had announced itself, and though it was sounding from the far-off shadowland of childhood, the call could not be ignored. It was a call of rescue, he knew.

He'd barely shut the door and sought refuge behind his desk when the tears came, haltingly at first, then increasing in heat and volume until he lost control of them. He lay his head on his arms and sobbed as he'd never done before—even when, standing on the Place Royale, Theodore had taken his face in his weathered hands and implored him to seize his endeavor.

When he finally lifted his head, Manhattan was in full firmament, all its lights ablaze: veritable fairy dust to those working as high in a building as the Fontaines did. Here, on the twenty-second floor, there was no noise or car exhaust; no fear of not being able to find a place to sleep for the night. Just the cool glitter of money.

Oddly, the excess of illumination outside the window brought to mind the nocturnal forest and its complete lack of it: what it had been like to walk across the meadow on a moonless night with that curious, floating feeling of not being able to see one's feet, guided only by the gurgle of the river, and the scrape of rushes on the bank.

He rummaged through the bottom drawer of his desk and brought out the battered copy of Ralph of Caen and his grandfather's translation, and the gonfalon, rolled up and dusty, stuffed at the back of the drawer. He turned to the window and the soulless, alien world beyond it. *How perfectly it suited Hugh Fontaine!* he thought. A new emotion overcame him, quite unlike the grief he was feeling for Theodore: anguish that it was too late—that he wouldn't be able to change back from being the creature his father had created.

Charles was a partner in the firm now—a bonafide apostle of those twin gods, Lucre and Greed. He owned his own condominium on Central Park. He had his own personal servant and tailor. And the Ivy League women he dated...well, they were all classy females, no doubt about it, for whom "bookish" and "gentlemanly" were not necessarily the anachronisms they might have seemed to their less erudite sisters. But they were clones of Hugh's women nevertheless.

There were frequent trips to Paris, Dubai and Mauritius. Hugh kept an apartment in Bali and a chalet in Gstaad and gave Charles the keys. Only one place had been kept off the itinerary: the one that had never stopped aching.

Seize your endeavor, lad.

The shambling, charismatic Theodore seemed close enough to touch.

Why was I not more like him?

Charles got up from the desk. His eyes were dry now. *Blancheron...* Somewhere, a window had cracked open. Through it drifted the odors of sweet forest moss and wild carnations. Theodore's energy drifted in, too. *Hurry up, lad! I found more Roman coins under the bridge,* and Charles hurried, sliding around the villa's corners to his uncle's study, the tiles lusciously smooth and cool under his bare feet. Indeed, were he not facing a wall of law tomes and the double mahogany doors of his suite, he could have sworn that he wasn't in Manhattan at all, but in a place where stillness and beauty were the only currency.

He picked up the telephone. "Denise? Oh, good, you're still here. Do you have time to book a flight to Brussels for me? For tomorrow night. Not business class. Pardon me?" He paused. Then a feeble but convalescent resolve took hold. "No. Just one way."

Charles d'Outre-mer.

His breathing came quick and eager.

He called his father. "I'll need Osselaer's mobile number," he said, playing along with Hugh's plans for now. He mentioned nothing about a one-way ticket. "And a key to the villa, if you still have one. Oh, and could I have Ida's number as well?"

Charles collected his brief case and tucked the family gonfalon among his papers. He checked his suit pocket to make sure the quartz crystal was still there. He glanced around the room: something metallic lingered in the air. Stale coffee, perhaps. But it seemed fresher than that; bracing.

He lifted his coat off the rack. The staff and the purse—the pilgrim's traditional symbols—had long since been replaced by the suitcase and credit card. Nevertheless, he was travelling back from his own Outremer. And although the journey would be less arduous than walking the old Roman road from Jerusalem to Bouillon, whatever the pilgrimage, a first step had to be made.

Charles Fontaine's first step was to close the door of his office, lock it, and trap those twin gods inside.

PART THREE

Return

XXXI

S harl'..."

Neither spoke for a few moments: Charles, because he wasn't sure which language to answer in; Osselaer, because he was clearly too overcome to speak at all.

"I'm afraid that my French isn't as good as it should be," Charles ventured, in French.

"Ah, *Sharl'*... We can speak English if you want. Please accept my deepest condolences. Your uncle was a great man."

"Thank you. Yes, he was."

Charles wandered to the hotel window and looked out at the Gothic cathedral on the Grand Sablon in Brussels, a marvel of petrified lace. The thrumming of tires on cobblestones vibrated the window in its frame. *A great man.* Funny, he thought, how one could earn that appellation without even a trace of fame or fortune.

Osselaer went on to tell him about the funeral (to be held in the ancient stone chapel at Rêve-sur-Semois); the attendees (himself, Charles, Ida and maybe one or two others from the village); and the lunch afterwards at the inn on Rêve's main square.

Charles stirred at the familiar harmonic in Osselaer's voice. The man had dropped by the villa now and then during Charles's summers at Blancheron—indeed, he seemed to have been Theodore's only friend. They would have drinks in the study, and although Charles couldn't hear what they were saying through the closed door, their complicity had been rich and sonorous, carrying easily out into the hall like two cellos in duet.

"There's an office on Avenue Louise where you can rent a car," Osselaer went on. "You could take the train, but it's better not to attempt your uncle's Renault once you get down there."

Charles smiled. He remembered that car. Theodore used to bounce him around in it and scrape past village corners. He'd drive at high speed in low gear with no seat belts. The most distinguishing feature about Theodore's vehicle was that it had been so much like its owner.

"Monsieur Osselaer...Philippe..." There was no way to prepare the question so Charles just asked it: "What really happened?"

"I found him on the floor of the study," Osselaer said. As if to apologize for this bluntness, he backtracked:

"Theo called me a few days before he died, inviting me to lunch. He sounded worried—not like himself at all. He said he'd had an unexpected visitor the evening before and wanted to discuss it with me. I was working on an important sale and was only free two days later." Osselaer paused to clear his throat. "Maybe I could have calmed him down if I'd come sooner. Maybe this wouldn't have happened..."

"Who was the visitor?" Charles pressed him. "Did he say?"

"No. But I've known Theo all my life. We went to the same *primaire*. We studied history together at university. He hasn't had any visitors for years. I think you may have been the last one, Charles, come to think of it, and that was, hmmm...fifteen years ago?"

"Seventeen," Charles corrected him.

"Ah, seventeen. Well, the only people who stop by these days are myself and a housekeeper, who only comes once a week."

"And Sylvana Longfaye, I think, *n'est-ce pas?*" Charles said. The name felt foreign on his tongue. Indeed, it had been seventeen years since he'd uttered it, and then only to himself.

"Ah, yes, you're right. Sylvana." The name momentarily lifted Osselaer's tone. "A lovely young woman. She helped Theo with his research from time to time."

A flash of dark hair and pale skin lit a corner of Charles's memory and for a moment he was unable to speak.

"Theodore would have told me if he'd been expecting someone...*unusual*," Osselaer continued.

"Do you have a key?" Charles asked, the vision gone.

Osselaer sighed sadly. "Yes, but Theo never locked the door. You know the villa, Charles. It's in the middle of nowhere. The closest village is Rêve, and there's never been any trouble there. It's barely alive these days as it is. Most of the young people have moved to Liège or Brussels."

Charles considered what sort of visitor would have shocked the stalwart Theodore beyond what he could have handled. Someone with a purpose, who'd forced their way in. A frisson passed over him as he considered the various unearthly manifestations at Blancheron: things in the air that he himself had brushed against during his summers there. But Theodore knew those phenomena well—he'd lived among them all his life and never suffered any shock. A human interloper, however...

"I called an ambulance right away," Osselaer said. "They had to send to Bouillon for one. It was in vain, *hélas*. The coroner said your uncle had been dead for at least a day. There was no evidence of foul play...no injuries except for a bruise on the side of his head where he'd fallen."

"So you think the visit frightened him to the point of cardiac arrest?" Charles could barely mask his incredulity.

"Perhaps..."

It was a cautious, legal "perhaps". Charles knew them all too well. He said: "Was there any sign of a robbery?"

Osselaer hesitated. "Impossible to tell. You remember your uncle's study. It was complete chaos under the best of circumstances. There's no way to know if anything was taken."

"Yes, of course I remember," Charles said. He thought of the congenial mess that choked the study at Villa Antioch and just about every surface area in the house, including the staircases. Theodore probably still hadn't put Grandfather's documents into any sort of order. Charles let himself drift back to the sanctum of Theodore's study: the frog-creak of the leather chair...the battered behemoth of a desk.

Then he recalled the secret marvel of that desk. *Did Osselaer know about this?* The bottom left drawer was handsomely lined with green felt like all the others. But there was a small hole underneath the felt through which you could poke a pen or pencil to lift the false bottom. The distance between this false bottom and the real one was only a few inches or so, but it was enough to store a cache of papers one didn't want anyone to find.

The space had been empty on the occasion that Theodore had demonstrated this trick to his nephew. "Your grandfather took his research very seriously!" he'd laughed.

Had Theodore hidden something valuable in the drawer and someone had found out about it? It seemed unlikely...inconceivable, even. The hiding place was foolproof.

"I contacted..." Osselaer paused, as if mulling the choice of names. "Your aunt," he said delicately.

"I'm glad you did," said Charles, smiling at the notary's deference. "Ida and my father are estranged. Father wouldn't have bothered to contact her, even about something this important."

"Ah...*la pauvre*," Osselaer murmured. "So...she has no siblings now." His notarial tone resumed: "Your father is estranged from just about everyone in his native land, I think. He couldn't wait to leave Belgium and erase his past. Now he's in such a great hurry to sell up the family property. He would never have been in touch with me otherwise."

Charles looked idly out at the square. The mist had thickened into a light rain. At the bus stop in front of the hotel, people were folding their umbrellas one by one as they embarked with chorus-line timing.

"Father has never been that keen on the past," he said.

"That may have changed, Charles. He seems quite keen on it now."

It was an odd comment, and Charles could only imagine that Osselaer had meant to indicate Hugh's sharpened greed at the prospect of a sale.

"I'll call Ida right away," said Charles, lacking the stomach to discuss his father.

"Ah..." Osselaer said again. This time the tiny word was laden with tenderness. "Dear *Ide*. She was...*devastée*."

"Did she and Theodore see much of each other over the years?" Charles asked.

"I'm not sure. But they were close, that I can say...the closest of the siblings. They used to spend hours together in the woods around Antioch when they were growing up. Ida was Theodore's muse...his helper."

"What is she doing these days?" Charles asked.

"Oh, this and that." Osselaer's comment wafted vaguely. "She's a sort of patron of the arts, I would say."

"But I thought she didn't have much money."

"No, she doesn't. She's more a patron of the *spirit*. For musicians, mainly. Sometimes they come to rehearse at her place. She puts on an occasional chamber concert. But you remember your aunt, Charles, I think. She's always had the gifts of a mystic. She was wasted on that rogue of a husband!" Gentleman that he was, Osselaer still struggled to conceal his spite. "Thank God he's gone. At least he left her the house. She has practically no other material possessions."

Charles wondered if even the cracked sofa and tree-trunk coffee table had gone the way of Ida's other worldly belongings. Though not the piano, presumably. The three-legged fairytale beast must still be there for Ida's needy bohemians.

Charles thought again of those twin cellos in Theodore's study, one of them now gone, and the other with such sorrow in its tone. How uncanny that the memory of sound could weather the years so well.

They agreed to meet at eleven-thirty on Thursday morning in front of the chapel at Rêve for the funeral at noon.

Charles hung up and observed the square. The view was a confection of ornate façades, gables, turrets and above all, the graceful indulgence on the part of Beauty in a way that she couldn't indulge herself in New York. Charles, his aesthetic hammered into the clean, hard lines of the New World, could feel his edges softening already.

In a burst of courage he dialed his aunt.

Each ring summoned a memory.
White hands…
Dreaminess…
Gauze…
"Oui?"
"Auntie…?"
"Sharl'!"
A single thread had been offered.
He grasped it.

XXXII

The early fog would not disperse entirely, he realized. He'd walked to school often enough on such October mornings to know that Brussels would still not have lifted her veil by the time he walked home. And so he spent the three hours before his rendezvous with Ida wandering through a blurred, indistinct city.

Jet-lagged and grieving, he glided like an amnesiac pilgrim through streets he'd visited more often in dreams than in reality. *It's down here, surely, our old church. Was there always an engraving shop on that corner? What happened to the restaurant?*

He retraced the steps of his youth as best he could, trying to find the place they'd eaten *carbonnade* and frites after Mass. The brasserie was gone, but he kept staring up at the façade as if it were still there. He stopped dead at things that sparked a nerve: the *librairie* where Father used to buy his newspaper...the shudder underfoot as the tram lumbered past.

Tall and elegant, Charles Fontaine drew no attention in that fashionable part of Brussels. His cashmere coat and fine suede shoes, and the burgundy silk scarf with miniature fleurs-de-lys could all have belonged to one of the gallery owners or antiquarians from the neighborhood. His chestnut-blond curls would have turned a few heads, however, as well as his natural air of nobility. (*Never to be confused with an air of superiority, cheri,* Ida had told him, *of which you're incapable.*)

Any keen observer would have noticed something else, though. This seemingly confident man of the world had a slight slope to his shoulders and a longing in his eyes that betrayed a person who would have loved to have been someone else once, far from patrician constraints, had circumstances not forced him in another direction.

He wandered the perimeter of the little park of the Petit Sablon, where the yellow hands of chestnut leaves splayed over the cobbles. The ground exuded a moist gameyness, not from this year's autumn but from one still lying deep in the city's past...maybe even as deep as the marshy sands of thirteenth-century Brussels from which the Sablon had taken its name.

How far can we reach into the past, lad?

He stopped for coffee at Le Café du Sablon and slipped down the back streets to the Grand'Place, all the while avoiding where he wanted to go most. Besides Ida, there was only one other person in Brussels he wanted to see.

At last, tired and chilled through, he could ignore him no longer.

"Well, here we are," he said softly.

The statue seeped from the thick air. It was the sort of mist into which a horseman could have disappeared entirely had a young boy been observing him. A youthful imagination would have seen only an empty pedestal...would have trembled at the spark of hooves against stone.

But now the boy had disappeared and the horseman remained, still poised, it seemed, between Belgium and eternity; still undecided about whether to cross the square and head east to Jerusalem, or just forget the whole thing and go home to Bouillon.

Cashmere and chain mail, Charles mused. That's all we are now. Separated by nine centuries.

He waited for a break in the traffic and hurried across to the center of the square. Seventeen years had passed since the last time he'd done this, Theodore at his side. Now there didn't seem to be an inch of the Place Royale not touched by that beloved presence.

Seize your endeavor, whatever it might be. And for heaven's sake, persevere to the end of it!

Fragments of speech lingered and Charles listened to them now—to his dear, shambling mentor—and followed the steps they'd made together around the statue. Charles glanced up at Godfrey: at the frozen metal banner, and the hollow eyes in which a fire had once burned, and felt only emptiness.

A missing piece in his story...

Charles shivered. He adjusted the silk scarf higher on his neck and blew on his hands. *Had Theodore kept his promise to find that missing piece?* he wondered. Unease filled him. What if that missing piece were some kind of undocumented atrocity? Charles knew most of the documented ones. He'd studied the crusade chronicles, especially Ralph of Caen:

July, 1099. The Temple of Solomon:
The sword passed no one in peace. The sword tore up ribs, and necks, and cut through groins, backs and stomachs. The sanctuary was covered with vast quantities of blood. The doors, walls, seats, tables, columns, all were bloody. The walls were submerged knee high...

Godfrey of Bouillon had directed the battle from atop his rolling siege tower, a rickety contraption that was nevertheless a feat of engineering at the time. The nobles Tancred and Robert of Flanders had had to forage as far as Samaria for the logs and planks for this tower, which were carried back on camels...or by captive Muslims. An English ship happened to slip through the Egyptian blockade of Jaffa carrying crucial armaments and food, as well as ropes, nails and bolts for the siege machines. The heat was merciless. The sirocco blew without respite.

Godfrey, it was said, climbed from his siege tower onto the wall of the city, where he remained to direct the flow of combatants. *Did he stay on the wall?* This had been a crucial question for the young Charles. No one had ever answered it to his satisfaction. Had the duke joined the mayhem? *Had he?*

Charles remembered poring over the literature, searching for proof of Godfrey's depravity. He'd come across a quote by Albert of Aachen, one of the chroniclers who'd been a great admirer of the duke. It was not surprising that Albert had written that Godfrey, unable to stop the bloodbath, had abstained from participating.

"This seems unlikely, lad," Theodore had said. But Charles preferred to believe Albert when he'd written that the duke had taken off his chain mail, donned a woolen tunic and removed his shoes, and with three confidantes followed every station of the cross of the Via Dolorosa.

What was the real story? Now it seemed as distant as ever.

Charles leaned against the pedestal on the side of Godfrey's shield. It was a curious gesture for a grown man. But the diffident boy the man used to be had leaned here before, because in that spot, the knight's shield hid you from his probing eyes should he turn his head your way.

"Who are you?" Charles whispered.

He wasn't expecting Grace Holmes to pipe up just then:

He sounds like a hero and *a murderer, Charlie. Most heroes are, though, aren't they?*

There was a vibration: an approaching tram, perhaps.

A rank, greasy odor. *Soiled leather?*

For a second or two, it seemed that a hot, dry wind was blowing through the North Sea mist.

Charles felt a quaver in his chest—a fleeting lift. Then nothing.

XXXIII

Ida's gate was ajar. A faded *En panne* note flapped on the buzzer to indicate it was out of order. Perhaps none of this was surprising for a proprietor indifferent to material things.

Charles pushed open the gate and started up the gravel alley. The long, hedge-lined approach was just as he remembered, as was that peculiar phenomenon: once you'd reached the half-way point of the alley, the noise from the street no longer penetrated and the hedges themselves, twice the height of a person, seemed to gather around and usher you forward.

He stopped short before reaching the house.

Sounds were filtering down the alley: music notes, round and clear. Two long ones, four shorter ones, then a bright, joyful arc to complete the melody.

Charles thrust his hands into his coat pockets and tilted his face up to listen. Even though the tones obviously came from a piano, they were the slowest, most voluptuous piano notes he'd ever heard, as if someone were pouring warm oil, one drop at a time.

At once a baritone, rich and dusky, repeated the same melody, slowly, with a sad throb in each note. There was something willful about the voice; even a little wild.

The music stopped.

Charles ventured to the end of the alley.

The great weeping beech in front of Ida's house was taller than the roof now and obscured most of the façade. The trunk had widened over the years until it practically obscured one of the salon windows, which was open to the cold.

Charles slipped across the weed-filled lawn to the beech and peered around it into the salon. Whoever had been making the music had already left the room. Through the open window he noticed that the creamy sofa and tree-trunk coffee table were still there. He could even have counted the rings in the wood from where he was standing.

Charles drew back, his pulse erratic. He rested his cheek against the smooth gray bark of the beech. He'd forgotten the comfort offered by trees—their surprising empathy—and stayed in that position for as long as he could.

"Charles?" a woman called from the front door. "Are you there?"

Ida knew he'd be on time. She also knew to speak English so as not to embarrass him.

He stepped into view.

"Ah...my sweet knight!"

He bounded up the cascading steps to where Ida was standing.

"Why were you spying at my window?" she exclaimed. Wonderingly, she touched Charles's cheek, then kissed it. Her face was crinkled, grief-worn, but even more beautiful than he remembered. "My, my," she breathed as her nephew embraced her. "You're a little taller than I remember."

Charles closed his eyes at the sweet scent of orange blossom. How many times he'd imagined the fragrant, enveloping refuge...the silvery being at the heart of it!

"Aunt Ida," he said, grasping her shoulders and reveling in her gaze.

At that moment, someone slipped past them down the steps. The movement seemed without substance—more a trick of illumination than anything corporeal.

"Sylvana!" Ida summoned. "Come and meet my nephew."

But the woman in dark-green cape and black skirt had already reached the alley. How she'd crossed the unkempt lawn so quickly, especially in such long clothes, Charles had no idea.

"Sylvana?" he mouthed. *But how was it possible, here at Ida's?*

Dumbstruck, Charles wavered beside his aunt.

"That was Sylvana Longfaye," she said. Then: "Charles, are you all right? You look terribly pale."

He shook to life. "Yes, of course!" he said, seething inside. *I know who it was! What on earth is she doing here, anyway?* The boy-Charles seethed, too: *Why didn't she ever answer my letter?*

It didn't seem like the right moment to divulge all this to Ida.

"Come, cheri," she said, steering Charles through the door. She seemed to have forgotten the vision that had just disappeared down her alley.

She took his coat and led him into the salon. It hadn't escaped Charles's notice that Ida walked deliberately, her worn leather loafers bulging at the balls of her feet where more fashionable shoes had crippled her. Her loose dress, though pale-colored, was not as gauzy as he remembered.

He entered the place that memory had preserved. Honey-blond floor...creamy sofa...that unique tree-trunk table. Charles touched a key as he passed the piano, childishly wondering if it might have been one that Sylvana had just played. Seventeen years ago, she'd written that she was studying music in Brussels. *Was she one of the bohemians Ida had taken in?*

The china coffee pot was ready on the table.

He sat beside Ida on the sofa and watched her hands hover at their task. They seemed terribly thin, translucent enough to see the tributaries of blue veins threading under the skin. Her hair was still waist-length, lustrous as ice, falling in a single braid over one shoulder. The mystic in her was clearly in its ascendency. Charles fancied that her namesake, Ida of Lorraine, would have been proud to have lived on in this woman.

A mutual wordlessness governed the encounter at first. Seventeen years took some time to peel away, and as they did, no one seemed in any hurry to explain why there had been so many of them.

"It's terrible about Theodore," Charles attempted at last, taking the cup Ida offered him. He foundered in her sadness. It always amazed him how death, a passage even more profound than life itself, rarely inspired better words than these.

Ida held her cup to her lips and stared straight ahead. "Theo...he, well..."

Her nephew followed her gaze to the piano and trees beyond. The pines had edged closer to the house over the years and joined their branches to form a solid, brooding wall. He also noticed that the room he'd once considered the abode of an enchantress was in fact falling into disrepair. The walls were cracking and the sofa had yellowed. The floor was scuffed. The piano had crossed the fatal frontier between antique and wreck.

Charles shifted uncomfortably in his fine clothes. Thoughts of his own wealth stung his conscience: the marble atrium of his New York apartment and shellacked women who passed through it; the yacht that he and his father rented for the firm's trips to Mauritius. He felt depleted, as a zoo animal might feel after long years spent in the wrong habitat. He glanced at Ida: she rose above all this genteel shabbiness like a heron on a weedy pond, as if this were, indeed, her natural habitat. Her authenticity shone without guile. Charles could feel his constraints lighten and the door of his cage crack ajar.

"I spoke to Philippe Osselaer this morning," he said.

"Philippe..." Ida toyed with the word. "He's been so solicitous...so very kind."

She said nothing more about the event that had prompted such kindness. Like Charles she flitted around the subject of Theodore, who in any case seemed so present in Ida's salon that it was almost redundant to mention him.

Charles left Theodore alone for a moment.

"Philippe mentioned that you help musicians," he said.

"I let them use this space," Ida said. "Chamber groups. And singers like Sylvana. The piano's old, of course. But it still has a heart somewhere. I think that Sylvana is on some sort of quest to find it. She gets tones out of that old beast I've never heard before!"

"Auntie..." Charles began, fumbling. "You see, I've met Sylvana Longfaye before. At Blancheron."

Ida regarded him over her cup. "Why on earth didn't she say anything to you when she left?"

Charles looked away. "I'm not sure she noticed me," he said lamely. "Does she live in Brussels now?"

"Yes. She studied at the Brussels Conservatory and teaches voice. In a little apartment near the Trinity Church in Ixelles."

Charles thought of Sylvana's only letter. *I want to give some beauty back to the world.* Had his response gone astray—the letter he'd finished on Christmas morning all those years ago? Or had she decided that she couldn't continue a friendship with someone who lacked the courage of his convictions?

"She loves history," Ida continued. "Like you. She was Theo's student at the *lycée*. She helped him with his cataloging on weekends and brought him food."

"Yes, I know," Charles said, as if listening to the refrain of a familiar song.

"Still," Ida mulled, shaking her head. "It's strange that she didn't acknowledge you."

"Yes," Charles said. With bitterness he added, "Maybe her ignoring me has something to do with the life I chose to live."

"Maybe," Ida said bluntly, her regard pointed now. "A life that made you forget your own roots."

"Oh, Auntie," Charles moaned, locking glances with the beloved sibyl. "I'm so sorry about my silence...so very sorry."

Ida reached over and squeezed his hand. "Dear Charles," she sighed. "Hugues probably prohibited you from contacting your family. It would be just like him, too." She forced a brighter tone: "Never mind, you're here now. And what a gentleman you've become! *Tiens, tiens...* The first gentleman in the family for quite some time."

"But Theodore..."

"Yes, that's true. But Theo was more of a renegade than a gentleman. Like your grandfather, I suppose." The coffee seemed to have bolstered Ida. "Are you happy, cheri?" she asked. "Did you ever marry? Have you realized your dreams?"

A convenient "no" would have sufficed on all fronts, of course. As it was, saying nothing sufficed even more.

"I see," said Ida. "I know only that you followed your father into law, but not much else. Still, you're young. You don't have to give up on your dreams yet. It was medieval history, wasn't it? Like dear Theo..."

Charles let out a long, soft moan. "I don't know what happened to me," he said. "I never wanted to be a lawyer."

"Of course you didn't! But no one can cross Hugues without consequences...especially his son. You inherited your uncle's passions, thank heavens. Not your father's opportunism."

"I've thought of those summers at Blancheron all my life," Charles said. It was his first confession since he'd stood across the fence from Grace Holmes.

"Those summers will stay with you always," Ida assured him. She poured them both more coffee. "And the American ladies? They love Europeans, don't they?" She swept her gaze over her nephew in a queenly way. "You've become the perfect embodiment of the code of chivalry, you know," she laughed.

"Minus the military valor," he said, and laughed with her. Then, starkly: "Father didn't provide the greatest example on the female front, as you know."

"Oh, *Sharl'*. You'll never be like Hugues on any front. *Never*. Thank God."

They sat for some moments in silence, sipping their coffee and looking out at the pines. With all this talk of Hugh Fontaine, Charles could sense his father's density even from across the ocean. Its gravitational pull was intact. And why shouldn't it be? Charles had returned to Belgium on his father's personal errand, after all: to sell Blancheron as his proxy. Not to indulge in nostalgia.

He sensed that the moment had come.

"Philippe Osselaer told me it was Theodore's heart," Charles said.

Ida turned to him abruptly. Charles had expected to see affection at the mention of her brother. Perhaps deeper sorrow. But not this defiance. He held his breath at the sight of Ida, poised as she was, back rigid and chin raised, her braid draped over her shoulder like a royal accoutrement.

"Philippe knows better than to say that!" she exclaimed. "Someone threatened Theo, Charles. He told me so himself."

XXXIV

Charles stared at his aunt. "*Threatened* him? Theodore actually told you that?"

"Yes, he did. He came to see me last week, only two days before he died."

"That's when he'd had that visitor, according to Osselaer," Charles said under his breath. He recalled that the notary hadn't been free to see Theodore right away. In such dire circumstances, without his old friend to give him advice, Theodore had driven all the way to Brussels to confer with Ida, the trusted companion of his youth.

"Maybe you didn't know this, Charles," Ida went on, "but Theo gave up his research for many years."

Charles bowed his head. "Yes, I know," he said. "And I think it was partly to do with my departure. Sylvana wrote me a letter and said he was very depressed. *Une tristesse profonde,* she called it. She said there was a void in Theodore's life that couldn't be filled."

Ida smiled in spite of all this misfortune. "So she wrote you a letter, did she?"

"Yes. But just one. I poured my heart out in my answer but never heard from her again. Anyway, Sylvana's out of my league."

"The chivalric league, you mean?" Ida teased him.

Charles ignored her. "Sylvana is the one who's straight and true," he said glumly. "Not me."

Ida didn't respond, but Charles sensed that she'd understood.

At length she said: "That's true, Theo was depressed. But then something changed all that. Almost overnight, he went back to his research."

"Really?" Charles said. "But why?"

"Your father was suddenly keen to sell Blancheron. About six months ago, he gave Theo an ultimatum to move out."

"Father never told me about this!" Charles blurted. "I thought that Uncle's death prompted the sale." He felt disappointed that Osselaer hadn't mentioned Hugh's maneuvering...if indeed he'd known anything about it.

"It doesn't surprise me that Hugues told you nothing," said Ida. "He's a manipulator; and ruthless. He never reveals his methods until he has the prize in hand. The archetypical lawyer..." She tensed slightly and looked downwards: the gentlewoman's signal that her barb had misfired. She would never have aimed it at Charles, of course. But he could sense how sharp it would have been if she had.

He decided to push the conversation further: "Sylvana mentioned something in her letter about Father's ties to the Belgian antiques market," he said. It was as far as he felt he could go. Sylvana's comment regarding "that nasty business" about the Antwerp dealer who'd been found dead went unmentioned.

Ida placed her coffee cup on the table at the very epicenter of the tree rings and smoothed a hand slowly over the surface, saying nothing. Then she looked up at Charles.

"Theo got back to his work because he wanted to tie up loose ends," she said. "But then he came across something...something that fired him up again." She paused. "Something extraordinary."

An ember stirred in Charles. "Did Uncle ever show you Grandfather's translation of the heron legend?" he asked. The vow of secrecy he'd sworn to Theodore had dissolved.

Ida's eyes widened. "Why, yes!" she said. "He brought a copy of it the night he came here."

"He did?!" Charles exclaimed. "So you know about Stephen and Henri; you know that Stephen came back from Jerusalem with an olive wood box for Arda."

"Oh, Charles," Ida uttered. "I've always been fascinated with Arda, as you know. I was thrilled to read more about what happened to her."

A huge and liberating wave carried Charles aloft. At last he could speak to someone about the translation! His heart raced. His hands grew cool, then sweaty.

"Uncle gave me a copy before I left for America," he said breathlessly. "But he asked me not to tell anyone until Grandfather's translation could be authenticated. What did Uncle find? Why was he so fired up?"

In a rush of energy Charles got up to wander about the room, stopping by the piano to brush his fingertips along the keys.

"Theo found new information about the heron story in your grandfather's papers," said Ida.

Charles returned to her side at once. "What sort of information?"

"When we were growing up, your grandfather indicated there might have been an alternative ending to the story," Ida explained.

Charles held her gaze. "You mean there was more to the manuscript that Grandfather translated?" he said.

"Yes. But here's the strange thing: Grandfather spent countless hours with the original manuscript in the *Bibliothèque de l'Histoire Européenne*. He read Old French like the rest of us read the newspaper, so his task was relatively easy. But just when it seemed he'd come up with new information, he shut down his research. Stopped, just like that. It was odd, really. But then, he was a very odd man."

Considering that his grandfather had walked almost seven hundred kilometers from Antioch to Jerusalem wearing chain mail, Charles had to concur.

"Is that why Theo came to see you? Because he found out what Grandfather was concealing?"

By way of an answer, Ida got up and left the room. She came back a few moments later carrying a plain brown envelope. This she handed to Charles.

The envelope was sealed, and there was a bulge in one corner.

"Theo wanted me to send this to you in New York by special courier," Ida said. "Of course..." she stumbled. "He had no idea that you would be coming here in person. For his..." Another stumble. "I'm sorry, Charles. I should have sent it immediately. When Theo passed away so soon after he'd driven here to see me, I felt sure you would come."

Charles turned the envelope over, fingering the bulge. He couldn't help smiling at the person to whom it was addressed: *Charles d'Outremer*. He could even hear the voice that had spoken that name. He also heard the voice say:

Any story from the past offers you a thread. You must grasp that thread and pull it. Eventually, what comes to the surface is a revelation no one can ever predict...or even imagine.

"Who visited Uncle at the villa, Auntie?" Charles pressed her.

"The man didn't identify himself," she said. "Theo said that he offered him money for the information in that envelope. When Theo refused, the man threatened him, and said that he'd return. Then he left. But it wasn't the end of it, clearly. Poor Theo." Ida sipped some coffee to fortify herself.

"It all happened on the same evening Theo came here," she went on. "October 13th. He arrived well after midnight. What a state he was in! I begged him to stay the night. But he insisted on going back to Antioch after he'd brought me the envelope. The man honored his threat: he returned."

Ida's words faded to silence. She took a handkerchief from the pocket of her dress and dabbed at the corners of her eyes.

"Theo went home to his death," she said, drying a tear on her cheek.

"Osselaer told me that according to the coroner, Theo had a large contusion on his face," said Charles. "He said that Theodore had fallen in his study."

"Fallen!" Ida fumed. "He had the heart of an ox. Why would he fall unless he'd been struck?"

Charles gasped.

Ida met his stare. "Of course! There's no other explanation, Charles. The man must have come back to the villa that night. But the police from Bouillon refused to investigate."

Charles traced a ring in the coffee table with his forefinger. His heart withered at the thought of Theodore enduring physical harm.

"Theo didn't want me to know the details of what he'd discovered," Ida said. "Perhaps he thought it would upset me." She smiled ruefully. "Or maybe he didn't trust me to keep it to myself. He was always quite secretive about his research, you know."

Charles nodded. Theodore's riddles and deflections had indeed been an enduring part of his character.

"He didn't want *me* to know," said Ida with a lingering look at Charles. "But he wanted *you* to."

Charles caught his breath. He turned the envelope over again. The boy in him surged. *Theodore hadn't lost faith in him!*

They finished their coffee in silence. The salon had grown chilly and dim. The draining light jangled a nerve in Charles and he recalled that peculiar, sly nature of October afternoons in northern Europe: how they would descend only partially, and quite early, like a shade drawn halfway. Then, while you were hurrying about at the end of the day unawares, the shade would jerk down and leave you in the dark.

Jet-lag overcame him in the somber room. "I can't tell you how glad I am to see you again, Auntie," he said, getting to his feet. He took Ida's hands in his own and helped her up: it was like holding two ailing birds.

They agreed that he would come by at eight o'clock the following morning in his rental car to drive her to Rêve.

"Is Sylvana going to the funeral?" Charles asked, as casually as he could. "Can I drive her there as well?"

"She's taking the train tonight," said Ida. "Her mother still lives in the village and she'll stay with her."

Charles suggested to his aunt that perhaps she could take the train back to Brussels afterwards—maybe with Sylvana—as he was intending to stay at Villa Antioch for at least a week to put the house in order. He could give both of them a lift to the station in Libramont.

They embraced in the doorway. A whiff of orange blossom conjured the graceful, silver-white mystic Charles had left standing on the same spot seventeen years before.

Ida reached up and fingered one of his curls. "A bit of gray, I see!"

He sighed. "I'm getting old without ever having been young."

"There's nobility in you, Charles," she said, her eyes filling with tears again. "There always has been. I noticed it when you were a boy. Chivalry lives on in you, thank God! Then, shaking her head: "How could Hugues have produced such a son?"

XXXV

Charles set off down the alley. The hedges had trapped enough of the failing light between them to see one's exhale float out on the thickening air.

He took the tram back to the Sablon and stopped by Le Pain Quotidien for some hearty pea soup and a wedge of abbey bread. He ordered a glass of Merlot in honor of Theodore and placed his uncle's envelope beside his plate, lacking the courage to open it. Now, in the jagged aftermath of death, its contents weighed uneasily.

What had been so urgent to warrant a midnight drive to Brussels? Under the circumstances, perhaps the name of the addressee—Charles d'Outre-mer—should be considered more carefully. If indeed this was one of Theodore's riddles, then he was clearly indicating that Charles would need all the passion and resolve of the boy who'd left those things behind in the Ardennes.

Charles hurried back to his hotel room, unsealed the envelope and took out a handwritten letter of two pages.

The bulge turned out to be another, smaller envelope. This he tore open to find two keys: one modern and plain, and the other...

He examined the second key under the meager bulb of his bedside lamp. It had the aura of great age and was surprisingly heavy. The shaft was slender and rounded, a few inches long or so, with an open ring on one end. The metal was burnished—bronze, he guessed. He smoothed a finger along the shaft toward the key's bit, marveling at the irregularities left by the tool that had worked it. His heart caught: the bit had been forged in the design of the Jerusalem cross: the cross potent with four smaller crosses in its quadrants. The motif became the Crusaders' symbol in 1099.

It was also, he remembered, the coat of arms of Godfrey of Bouillon.

9 October

My dear Charles,

How to begin? It's been ages, I know. Hugues succeeded in keeping us apart after you left for America. I'll never forgive him for turning you away from me. Never. Then you grew up, and became a lawyer. Frankly, I didn't think we had much in common any more.

But these are sad excuses.

I was wrong to let our relationship drop, lad. At least I could have tried better. I suffered from depression and abandoned my work. Ida helped me through this period. And also Sylvana, who's a splendid young woman. But that's not why I'm writing to you.

You may know that for the past year or so, Hugues has been planning to sell Blancheron, including the villa, out from under me. He's in need of cash, it seems. Curious, isn't it, how the richer one is, the more money one needs? Anyway, I don't have to tell you what it would do to me to have to leave Antioch...what it would do to you, too, if I understand your love of your heritage correctly.

It's true that I didn't really think you had the commitment to become what you wanted to be. And I was right, it seems. Hugues got to you in the end. But there <u>was</u> a spark in you—I saw that. I like to think that I helped bring it alive. I hope to Christ it's still burning in you somewhere, lad, because you're the only one I can turn to now.

Your father's ambitions have been good for one thing: I've spent the past six months finally going through all my papers and the objects I've collected over the years. Enfin! Your grandfather's research, too. The place is even messier than it was before. Papers are everywhere now: in the study, the spare rooms, your turret room, the cellar. It's turned out to be an even greater undertaking than the First Crusade!

I came across a letter to your grandfather from Cédric Florus, a lovely gentleman and retired head of manuscripts at the Bibliothèque de l'Histoire Européenne, confirming a rendezvous to consult the original MS of the heron legend. Reading between the lines, it seems that Florus was confirming that Grandfather had possibly overlooked another ending to the legend. This was some years ago, and since then I understood that the MS had been miscataloged during a reorganization.

Two weeks ago, I went up to Brussels to see Paul Dujardin, current Head of Manuscripts. Apparently, the original MS of the heron legend has resurfaced. The text of the chanson de geste was bound in the same codex with two other Old French manuscripts from the early twelfth century and had apparently been overlooked. I wasn't prepared for what Dujardin told me: he said that in re-cataloging their collection, they discovered that a folio was missing from the heron manuscript. He showed me where someone had cut out a page at the end of the MS. In such cases, there's usually a heel of parchment that remains, and indeed there was one. Quite irregularly cut, too. No one had noticed it. The department had no idea when the folio disappeared, but Dujardin assumed it could have been years ago, even before Florus took the job.

I had deep suspicions when I went back to Antioch. You probably have them too after reading this. It took me several days to prove what I suspected: in a pile of papers on the floor of the study, covered in dust, I found an ancient folio. One side of it had been cut irregularly, just like the heel of the parchment in the library. Even more curious, it was in Latin, and not in the Old French of the rest of the heron manuscript. This astonished me. It meant that this part of the text was most probably written by a scribe in a monastery rather than a lay person writing in the French vernacular.

So now you know that your grandfather was a thief as well as a nutcase! If he'd made a translation, I didn't find it with the folio. I remember now that there was a point when he abruptly stopped his research—just didn't want to have anything more to do with it. I'm speculating this might have happened around the time he removed the parchment from the library. Why he did this, I can't say. But I'm certain it had to do with the contents: there was something in it he thought should remain hidden.

I've started my own translation, therefore. It's taking me some time. My Latin isn't what it used to be. Also, on the verso, the text becomes increasingly bunched together. This might have been to save parchment, as it was very expensive. In any case, the writing is almost *impossible to decipher at that point. But I can say with some certainty that the scribe was writing about events that took place in ca. 1103, because he mentions that they occurred three summers before the great comet. That would have been the comet that was visible in Europe during the early months of 1106.*

I'll finish this letter to you in a week or so once I get my head around the Latin.

Theodore had filled two sides of a sheet with his casual handwriting. Charles picked up the second sheet, expecting to find the continuation of the letter and details about the translation. Instead, he was aghast to find a note of just a few chaotic lines, dated October 12—the day before Theodore died.

Charles,

I'm leaving for Brussels at once. The folio, and what I managed to translate of it, are in the drawer of the desk. You know which one. It's safest there. The key to the drawer is in the envelope. Contact Cédric Florus in Brussels to finish the translation. He's one of the foremost specialists in medieval manuscripts in the world. And you can trust him. The other key was among your grandfather's papers. It's eleventh-century Byzantine. I'm fairly certain it's the key to the olive wood box.

I believe that your father knows something of these developments— that there could be something of great value in them. That's why he's suddenly so keen to sell Blancheron.

I saw it, lad. The bird. I went to the pond yesterday and there it was. It's always a sign. <u>Always</u>. I knew I couldn't delay sending you these things. Do whatever you can to hold on to Blancheron. It's your heritage, after all.

T. de la F.

PS I never told you Sylvana was my student because I thought, knowing you as I do, that it would have been even harder for you to leave if you'd known more about her. She's an extraordinary young woman. I'm sorry, lad.

Charles put the keys and letters back in the envelope, turned off the bedside lamp and stretched out on the bed without bothering to take off his clothes. He could barely lift his arms from exhaustion. In the few hours since he'd arrived from New York, he'd confronted the reality of Theodore's death, gotten lost in his old haunts, visited an indifferent Godfrey, made an emotional trek to Ida's and encountered the enigma that was Sylvana. And now this envelope from Theodore: this thread that his uncle was so urgently handing him.

XXXVI

Your turret room... Theodore always gave his nephew the highest room in Villa Antioch for the summer. *I need a decent sentry, lad!* And indeed, from the turret one could see in all four directions over the Semois dreamscape and beyond. Spiral stairs at the room's center led up even higher, to the very apex of the tower, where four miniature dormer windows were set in the roof. A flagpole extended from one of the dormers on which Theodore hung the family gonfalon. It was Charles's duty to put the banner out every morning, and bring it in at night.

Each day upon waking, he would turn around slowly in the square room, the oak boards rough against his bare feet, drinking in the four corners of Theodore's universe: the river and ridge beyond it; the river again, disappearing around a bend; the lawns and weeping beeches in front of the villa; and finally, at the last turn, the willow and old stone bridge. Then he would turn around once more, eyes closed this time, surprised at what lay caught in his inner vision: a glitter of light on the river, or rooks lifting in a black medley from the willow. He could easily people this universe, too: Henri, Count of Rêve, riding single-file over the bridge with his squire, Stephen de la Fontaine. And perhaps even the pale shadow of Arda herself, although the sound of her lyra always eluded him.

At night, the ancientness came. From which of the four directions it stole into the turret was never certain, but Charles felt it drift by his bed, and detected a slight hum in the floorboards as it retreated, as if it had come on horseback. He would fall asleep dreaming that the pedestal on the Place Royale was empty, its rider gone. *Gone where? Home to Bouillon?* In the hour before dawn all went calm, and it was the only time that Charles ever got any rest at Villa Antioch.

"What did people sound like back then, lad? What did they *smell* like?"

They were standing on the stone bridge one hot afternoon, leaning over the water, watching the river weed wrap itself, Godiva-like, around the glistening skin of the current. A breeze rose up and cooled their faces.

"Did you know that wise women used to gaze into river eddies for knowledge?" Theodore asked.

Charles shook his head.

Theodore laughed. "Ida used to try it when we were kids." He grew serious. "Actually, the movement of water is mesmerizing. It sharpens our intuition."

They crossed the bridge in silence on their way to the ridge, stopping in the meadow on the opposite side.

"Close your eyes, lad!" Theodore commanded.

"But Uncle!" Charles protested. It was one thing to turn in a circle in the turret room with his eyes shut, and quite another to walk blindly across a meadow.

"Try living through your other senses, Charles. Even just for a few minutes. You have the intuition to make discoveries this way."

Charles lifted his shuttered face to the sky. Gradually, his other senses sharpened. An isolated tone began to pierce the gurgle of river water. A blackbird's song turned around a cluster of throaty notes and he heard a woman's voice in them, as if it were an aria. Rotting meadow grass smelled sweet underfoot—something he'd never noticed before. It seemed that rain was pattering, but really it was dry leaves, crisp against the stones of the bridge.

Theodore squeezed his arm. "There," he said softly. "That's better. Listen. Smell. *Imagine.* People who lived here centuries ago lived in harmony with these things—in tempo with the universe. The modern world has lost this...to its peril."

Charles opened his eyes wide: his uncle was smiling at him.

"I'll take you out on a dark night soon," said Theodore. He grinned. "A *really* dark night. Then you'll know what I mean. Our ancestors called it "spirit listening". They listened to the grain in the fields...to the wind in the trees. They could interpret these things. We forgot how long ago. Alas."

"Wasn't it dangerous at night?" Charles asked.

"Maybe. But they trusted the forest."

Theodore nodded in the direction of the bridge before heading toward the ridge path.

"Have you never heard the horseman?" he asked.

"I...I don't think so," Charles faltered. He stood straight and rigid, as if he might hear him now.

"Most things that are truly extraordinary are invisible," Theodore said, stopping on the path. "Music, for instance. Or conviction."

"And ghosts," Charles offered.

"Call them what you will."

"Have *you* seen him?" Charles asked with a catch.

"The horseman?"

Charles nodded.

"You don't actually *see* such things, lad," said Theodore. "Not usually. You *sense* them." He laughed. "With that intuition of yours!"

"But have you *seen* him?" Charles insisted.

Theodore walked off down the path. "Maybe," he said.

They began the climb up the ridge. The day was hot and close and they were both perspiring heavily once they'd reached the menhirs at the end of the escarpment. Theodore dropped with a groan onto the soft earth between the stones and took a water bottle from his satchel, which he offered to Charles.

From their vantage point, far-off villages and farms seemed caught in the haze of a Renaissance painting. The river snaked through this ancient stronghold of Arduinna, past the rock on which fairies danced at midnight, and the cliffs where Maugis still practiced his shape-shifting.

"Why did Stephen build Blancheron in such an inaccessible place?" Charles asked.

"For protection, of course," Theodore said. "They were dangerous times."

"Who lived up here?"

"Besides Stephen? Oh, his squires, probably. Retainers and such. Now, Charles..."

And Charles braced himself for another quiz.

"Name at least six knightly skills that Stephen would have known," said Theodore. "It's an odd mix, remember."

"Oh, all right," Charles groaned, and recited: "Armed combat, horsemanship, dancing, backgammon, chess, presenting wine properly while kneeling, and..." He stalled, then lit up: "And how to carve meat!" He'd almost forgotten his favorite one.

"Very good, lad...very good."

Theodore took a wedge of chocolate from his satchel and gave the whole piece to his nephew.

"But Uncle...did a lady live up here with Stephen?" Charles asked, biting the chocolate.

"I don't know, lad. In the early 1100s Blancheron was just a set of stone defenses. More of a garrison, really."

"Maybe Stephen never married," said Charles. "Maybe he never got over his love for Arda."

"According to the legend, he didn't."

"He must have been very lonely." Charles glanced at the carnations fanning out over the grassy mound under the pines, as if tossed by hand, and vowed to remember their peppery scent—the scent of Theodore's kitchen...of contentment.

"He still had the sound of her music," Theodore said.

"Her music...?"

Theodore looked searchingly at Charles. "Music is gathered from the air, lad, where it has always existed. Arda's music remains on this wind." Theodore shambled off, stopping at the mound to gather carnations.

Charles bit his lip. A breeze pulled at his curls. Two magpies clamored over the escarpment with beaks locked and dropped out of sight. He closed his eyes, hoping that his sharpened senses would pick up a few stray notes of a lyra.

XXXVII

Ida barely spoke during the drive to Rêve. She didn't ask about Theodore's letter; she didn't even wonder how Charles was feeling after his first night in Belgium in almost two decades. He found his mind roaming, therefore. First to Sylvana and her abrupt exit from Ida's house. (*She must have realized who I'd become after I left Belgium.*) And then to Ida herself. He snatched sideways glances at his aunt as he drove, though she appeared to have retreated to a place so distant that she probably wouldn't have noticed if he'd stared directly at her.

Charles mulled over Ida's namesake—Ida of Lorraine, Godfrey's mother, who in her own way had cast a spell over history. The duke had left her behind in what is now Belgium, where she'd spread alms and peace while her son had set his sights on war. Charles glanced at his aunt again and his heart quickened. Words couldn't capture Aunt Ida. Certainly four walls never had. He'd always assumed she'd been made of a substance that could pass easily through solid matter.

It occurred to him that through her love of the forest, his aunt might embody an even deeper mysticism than her medieval namesake had been famous for: a connection to Nature and the universe that a Christian woman at the turn of the twelfth century—particularly a noblewoman pious enough to have been sanctified—would not have felt free to explore. A notion seized Charles. Had Ida of Lorraine ventured into the forests surrounding one of her abbeys—perhaps even wandered off alone, away from her retinue—to visit a peace-spot deep in the wilderness where she could meditate? Might she have crossed paths with a wise woman who frequented those sacred waters and stones?

Charles's skin tingled.

Might she have encountered Arda?

"We've passed Dinant," said Ida, as if Charles's thoughts had wakened her. "Do you remember the beginning of these hills, cheri?"

He tightened his grip on the wheel. *Of course he remembered!* His mind had already started down this familiar road even before leaving Brussels. Now, with the land folding abruptly into hills (always a surprise after the tabletop flatness of the rest of the country), he wondered how his ancestor had felt coming home to the Semois valley, caked with the dirt and sorrow of his journey.

Homecoming was not always unfettered joy, Charles was discovering. The heart brimmed and ached. No one ever returned home unchanged—particularly a warrior. Charles slipped into the skin of his ancestor. What scenes of carnage had tracked Stephen de la Fontaine home all the way from the parched plains of Outre-mer? What tortured cries had fractured his sleep for four thousand kilometers, and shadowed him through the immense forests of Europe until he could hardly bear them anymore? *Had he really been carrying Henri of Rêve's olive wood box back to Arda?*

Rêve-sur-Semois occupied the interior of a river meander. Like so many other Ardennes villages, a handful of stone houses clustered around an ancient chapel, the entire hamlet sheltering beneath the forested heights of the loop.

The Semois might have seemed moribund as it flowed through Rêve—indeed, swans were known to glide in the shallows—but every resident knew this was a deception. The river was very much alive, people would tell you; it had currents that slipped along on invisible errands, a phenomenon that lent the water a peculiar alertness. The swans never stayed for very long.

In the village itself, summer flower boxes had long since been taken in and drabness reigned: stone, slate, cobbles, all wreathed in river mist and weighed by dark-bellied clouds.

A palette befitting a requiem.

Charles parked on Rêve's main square in front of the Auberge du Chevalier, where Osselaer had arranged for lunch after the service. He helped Ida from the car and together they made their way across the cobblestones to the ancient church of St. Arda.

Osselaer was recognizable at once from across the square, standing before the stone edifice. The church bent towards the earth with such complicity, it was difficult to tell if it was coming or going. A giant yew leaned against the clerestory windows as if plotting how, in another hundred years or so, it might get in.

The notary was just a distilled version of what Charles remembered from years ago: balder, meeker, his mincing frame even slighter in a navy suit. But literally everything about Osselaer drew itself up to unexpected heights as soon as he'd spotted Ida.

"*Ide...*" The notary lifted her hand to his lips.

"*Bonjour*, Philippe," Ida mouthed inaudibly. Her head was draped in a black lace shawl that she held under her chin with a tight, bloodless hand.

Osselaer's gesture recalled a feature that Charles had forgotten about him: his courtliness. It was astonishing how such behavior could elevate the humblest of men. Not to the splendor of a Godfrey or a King Arthur, perhaps—one could hardly imagine Philippe Osselaer among the Nine Worthies of the world. *Or could one?* Charles observed the notary's gallantry and devotion more closely and reconsidered.

A priest emerged from the chapel and nodded to the little group, his hands clasped against his belly in a chubby orb. Charles nodded back, glancing through the dwarfish entrance at the altar: a baroque confection of white marble that still drew an occasional tourist.

Before the altar lay the simple wooden rectangle that was Theodore himself.

The sight of the casket struck a brutal chord in Charles. He swayed at Ida's side. A soul-ache flared. He asked Osselaer to attend to his aunt and dove around the side of the chapel to gather his wits.

There, another chord was struck.

XXXVIII

Beside the yew, contemplating the graveyard with her back to Charles, stood Sylvana Longfaye.

He didn't announce himself at first. *How could he? What could he possibly say to bridge a chasm of seventeen years?*

Sylvana hadn't perceived him. The same uncanny stillness enveloped her and affected Charles at once. He fell into her hush, as if observing a rare bird. His breathing slowed. The ache eased. He followed her gaze to the overgrown plot of leaning stones, where a fresh hole was waiting to receive Theodore.

"Sylvana?" Charles said at last, his voice failing. It crossed his mind that he'd uttered her name in the same way that he'd uttered *"Bonjour"* during their first encounter on the ridge.

She turned: he saw at once that she'd been weeping. Her tall, slender form appeared even taller and willowier in her long black skirt and habitual cape. Her hair was in somber harmony with the spreading mass of the yew. Charles marveled how the queenliness, which he'd last seen newly-minted in an adolescent girl knee-deep in ferns, had mellowed into this regal woman.

"Charles d'Outre-mer," she said, without a trace of irony. She gazed at him as if waiting for a reflection to settle in water. "So you've come home at last. And to such a sad occasion. I'm very sorry about your uncle."

Charles took a step toward her but could go no farther. In his charcoal-gray suit and cashmere overcoat, his silk scarf and fine suede shoes, he was not the man he thought merited doing what he so dearly would have liked to have done just then: take this forest vision in his arms and comfort her. No. He was, he knew, just a shallow imitation of the person he might have been: someone true to the ideals of his beloved uncle. He'd become a stranger even to himself, true to the ideals of a society obsessed with its own importance.

They regarded each other without speaking.

"How are you?" Charles asked lamely.

"As you see," she replied.

Charles wavered, uncertain what she meant. "Sylvana..." he began. "I...I wasn't sure if you ever received my letter."

Her smile had no warmth: "Really? *C'est curieux.* I wasn't sure if you'd ever received mine!" She swept her gaze over Charles. What he saw in her face then—in the doubt that darkened the changeable green eyes—left a wound deeper than any weapon.

It's obvious to her what I've become.

"I did receive your letter," he said. His cheeks flushed as if he were the youth she'd surprised at the pond. "Congratulations on your conservatory studies, by the way. Are you singing with an opera?"

Sylvana pushed a strand of hair from her face. "I don't perform," she answered. "As I mentioned in the letter, I want to help people heal using their own voice. I give lessons." She paused. "Mainly to the indigent."

The organ in the church began playing a hymn.

Charles said: "You also mentioned that you want to give back some beauty to the world."

Sylvana lifted her chin. Her eyes lightened. "You *did* read it," she said.

"I also answered it. You must believe that."

Her eyes widened. "You answered it?"

"Yes. With all my heart. I was sure you thought I'd sold myself to a life of greed and acquisition." Charles looked down at his feet. "I wouldn't blame you if you had." He stepped closer. "The letter must have gone astray."

Sylvana's regard softened. "Oh, Charles. I apologize for accusing you otherwise. I would have written again had I thought you were interested."

"Charles! Sylvana!" It was Osselaer, hurrying toward them. "Come, please! The service is about to begin."

XXXIX

They followed the notary around to the door, where Charles bowed to Sylvana for her to enter before him. She paused to savor this courtly gesture. He responded by searching in his coat pocket and taking out the piece of quartz. Without a word he lay this on his palm, as Sylvana had once done. She placed her hand over his, leaving it there until the crystal grew faintly warm.

They took seats in the front close to Theodore. From there, they could smell the lilies that the ladies of the parish had placed on the altar; and from there they might be lucky enough to witness (as far as anyone has ever been so lucky) death's mute barque setting off for a port no traveler has come back to describe.

The sweetness of the lilies couldn't mask the general mustiness of neglect, however, or the incense gone fruity with time. Charles had always found these odors oddly agreeable during the Masses he'd attended in Brussels—at least upon arriving, when one had the impression of entering the parlor of an aged relative while a gamey stew simmered somewhere out of sight. Inevitably, though, reality set in: unpadded chairs, and the morbid wave of cold lifting from the tiled floor directly up the pant leg. And of course, institutionalized guilt, which was without question the toughest part of the stew.

Charles rubbed his calves and smiled at the upward draft. He recalled how no matter how thick his socks, or however tightly he'd pressed against his relatives for warmth, he'd never been able to banish the cold from his ankles or understand how anyone could entertain any higher thoughts whatsoever—let alone feel something approaching rapture—when one's attention was drawn to one's feet.

In the tired tradition of European Catholics, Charles had been versed in the suffering of Christ. At one point in his young life, he could even recite the Stations of the Cross by heart (they were displayed in lurid detail in most cathedrals, after all). In theory, this knowledge should have made him more tolerant of the discomforts of hard chairs and cold ankles. But it hadn't. Instead he'd sat there shivering, seeking refuge in his own thoughts. It was the ideal occasion to indulge himself in this way, as no one seemed to mind his mental absence as long as his physical presence stayed in the chair. Perhaps they were all too busy trying to keep warm themselves to notice that Charles had found himself a phantom horse and gone off to join that bronze knight on the Place Royale.

Sylvana leaned in to him. "Theodore should be memorialized in the forest, not in a church," she whispered.

Charles reached for her hand. "He'll be near the yew," he said. "He'll be very happy to spend eternity there."

Mass began.

The priest raised his hands and then lowered them again, exerting himself in this manner several times. The theatrics had always amused Theodore. He would lean toward his nephew during family Mass, blue eyes twinkling: "I wish we could do that, too. At least he's keeping warm!"

The priest sprinkled holy water on the casket and began to chant, and as responsories grumbled through the ancient stones, Charles tried to imagine Theodore lying there in that box. The blue eyes may have been closed forever, but surely there was a faint smile fixed on his lips, perhaps even with a wry turn, as he enjoyed this final amusement before departing to...to...

A tremor crept over Charles.

I saw it, lad. The bird. I went to the pond yesterday and there it was. It's always a sign...

Charles had often felt something at the pond. The watchful air; the water-forest wavering beneath the surface. And most of all, that stillness. *Why had the bird appeared to Theodore?* he wondered, watching the priest perform his duties. *To guide him?* The tremor returned. *Or had Uncle discovered something that had brought this feathered bit of history out of hiding?* He suddenly rued having left the envelope with Theodore's letter and keys in his laptop bag and spent several anxious moments trying to remember if he'd locked the car.

The chapel door boomed softly.

Charles swiveled around. A man with a silver goatee slipped in and took a seat at the back of the nave. The baptismal font, carved from a single huge stone, obscured most of the visitor, although Charles perceived a dark-blue coat and the glint of something expensive. Even half-obscured, the man exuded arrogance.

"I know that man!" Sylvana hissed, grabbing Charles's arm. She'd gone eerily pale. "He followed me home once from your uncle's place. I was on my bicycle. He almost ran me off the road!"

Charles recoiled. "What did he want?"

The priest glanced up from his text and scowled.

He that believeth in me, though he were dead, yet shall he live...

"He got out of the car and asked me what I was doing at the villa," Sylvana whispered in Charles's ear. "Stupidly, I told him I was helping your uncle with his research. That led to all sorts of other questions."

"Like what?" Charles asked, feeling queasy. He glanced at the casket. The chapel's glacial draft seemed to intensify.

The souls of the righteous are in the hands of God, and no torment will ever touch them...

"The souls of the righteous, my foot!" Sylvana mouthed to Charles as the priest glowered at them. "That man is far from righteous. He wanted to know what documents I was cataloging."

"What?! Did you tell him anything?"

"Of course not! I went off on my bike and he followed me as far as the village. He was trying to intimidate me, obviously. But he didn't succeed."

Even though I walk through the darkest valley, I fear no evil...

If anyone could walk through the darkest valley and fear no evil it was Sylvana Longfaye, Charles thought. In fact, it sounded as if she'd already done so.

The door boomed again: the man had slipped out.

XL

Four pimply pallbearers in ill-fitting suits bore Theodore from the church.

Osselaer supported Ida by the elbow and steered her up the nave to the door. He seemed painfully aware that her spirit had been shackled—that this gracious mystic, who usually floated freely about in white, was now encased in black. Her delicate feet were no doubt frigid. Osselaer leaned against the lace shawl to say something in her ear and this seemed to cheer her.

Sylvana and Charles followed in silence. Marcel Wauters, proprietor of the Auberge du Chevalier, brought up the rear along with the two women who'd arranged the flowers at the altar.

Charles spotted the man at once. He was standing apart from the villagers who'd gathered on the square, the silver goatee admirably set off by a dark-blue Loden coat. He was tall, of muscular proportions, and as Charles watched he removed a leather glove to make a call on his mobile phone. A diamond flashed on his little finger.

"He's looking our way," Sylvana uttered as Charles steered her around the chapel toward the graveyard.

Theodore de la Fontaine had given no instructions for his funeral. Nevertheless, an unspoken understanding seemed to bind the mourners, to the effect that nothing was more profound than silence when one didn't know what to say, and so it was silence that guided them. Theodore surely wouldn't have minded, Charles thought. For although the words Sylvana had whispered in the church reflected what would have been Theodore's wish—to be memorialized in the forest— this quiet cradle of earth near the yew, with the hills looking down on him, was not a bad place to call home.

"I'm sure that Marcel can set an extra place for lunch," Charles said to Sylvana as the group headed off to the inn.

They paused under the yew.

"Thank you, but I'm going back to my mother's," she said. "I return to Brussels tomorrow."

"When can I see you?" Charles pressed, bereft at the thought that years might go by again until he did. But even as this emotion engulfed him, he was forced to look hard at reality: Sylvana Longfaye was still an enigma to him—a person whose substance owed more to his longing and imagination that it did to any concrete friendship.

Your friend of the forest.

He'd almost forgotten that she'd written those words.

"I don't know when," she answered. "Aren't you going back to America soon?"

There it was again: the doubt...the circumspection.

"I'd rather *come* back," Charles said. It was a singular comment, and surprised even him.

He studied the woman standing there, stately and distant. Suddenly she seemed little more than a stranger: a woman with dark hair and pale face who'd appeared in his life just that morning.

Then he looked down at the roots of the yew. In a miracle of regeneration, branches that had snaked down to earth had taken root themselves, so that even if other parts of the tree died, it would live on through this extraordinary life force. *The yew is eternal, lad. If that isn't a gateway to the spiritual, I don't know what is.*

"Sylvana..." Charles began. The ancientness of the tree suddenly made the morsel of time that had separated them trifling. *Seventeen years*. It was but a single afternoon for a yew. "I never thanked you for what you did for my uncle," he went on, gesturing toward the cemetery and Theodore's new lodging. "Looking in on him like that; helping with his research."

"You were always Theodore's dearest companion, Charles," Sylvana said. "He told me as much."

The viola tone seemed wrapped in velvet. She added: "Theodore's greatest wish was that you should continue his work."

"He said that to you?" Charles marveled. Then, with despair: "How could I have let my father keep me from him? That terrible sadness Theodore suffered..." His voice caught. "Sylvana, what happened to me?"

Even in one of those vibrant dreams before dawn, he never could have invented the choreography that followed. He'd imagined gathering this bewitching person in his arms, of course—so many times that one would have thought that reality, at long last, would have obliged. But Fate had a sly sense of irony, he knew. Sylvana Longfaye had been put in his path on the very eve of his departure, after all (appearing again at Theodore's own departure: a curious twist that Theodore himself would have found noteworthy).

So it shouldn't have been a surprise that it was she who pulled Charles against her...she who wrapped her arms around him and let him weep on her shoulder.

They stood like that for some time. Charles was aware only of the rough wool of Sylvana's cape, becoming gradually damp against his face; and of the fact that her silken neck smelled not of perfume or soap but of the sweet, fresh earthiness of the spring. As he calmed, these details ceded to a deeper impression: that the warmth of her body, singularly vital, must surely have been the warmth of body and soul combined.

At length she let him go. He stepped away to steady himself and Sylvana stood by without the slightest impatience, waiting.

Once he'd recovered, she dried his cheeks with the handkerchief she'd tucked up her sleeve at the funeral. Then she extracted a phone from her cape.

There was something surreal about this last gesture, as if an enchantress who usually rode about on unicorns had produced her car keys.

"Could I send you a message so you have my number?" she asked.

Charles took out his phone and gave her his number.

They'd exited the graveyard and were standing at the center of the village square, a cobbled expanse ringed by squat stone houses, the ancient chapel, a sheen of river, and Marcel's inn.

"You mentioned in your letter that you'd found a cave," Charles said.

"Yes!" Sylvana exclaimed. "I climbed the rocks behind the spring and found a path, barely wide enough for an animal to pass. I was holding on to the vegetation and suddenly there was nothing behind it. Just a void. It was definitely an entrance to something. But I was too timid to explore."

"I can't imagine anyone less timid than you," Charles said, and to his surprise, two pink circles colored her cheekbones.

He thought of Arda's flight from the village as described in his grandfather's translation:

She sought refuge in a cave beyond the spring.

"It could very well be Arda's cave!" he said.

"Oh, Charles..." It took Sylvana just an instant to pass a hand over his curls and kiss him on the cheek. "I would feel far less timid if we explored it together." To his delight she added: "I'll call you tomorrow about the cave."

"Wait!" he said, and dashed to his car parked at the edge of the square. He rummaged in his laptop bag and took out the envelope with the translation, leaving behind the smaller envelope with the two keys.

He hurried back to Sylvana and gave the translation to her.

"My uncle would want you to read this, I think," he said. He bent to kiss her cheek in return, but in an unplanned moment it fell on her lips.

XLI

L unch went on longer than Mass and burial combined.

Marcel Wauters had set aside the best table overlooking the square. *"La table de Monsieur le Professeur,"* he crowed. He'd planned a meal of *gibier* with braised chicory, and raspberry mousse for dessert—all favorites of Theodore's. The paunchy, balding innkeeper had always tolerated the mud-spattered boots on his polished floor, and the satchel crammed with forest treasures that Theodore dumped on the carefully laid table, because *Monsieur le Professeur* was such an authority on so many things, and one cannot argue with genius, *n'est-ce pas?*

No one spoke during the meal beyond the barest niceties. *The flowers were lovely... Theodore would have adored this lunch... Why is Father Boniface always so bad-tempered?*

"Who is that man, Philippe?" Charles asked from his seat at the window, for there he was again, the goateed poseur, leaning against a glossy BMW parked near the *auberge.*

The question constricted Osselaer on all the fronts that Ida had recently liberated. "I meant to introduce you, Charles," he said, not very convincingly. "That's Manfred Ames. The antiquities specialist."

"Manfred Ames...?"

Marcel arrived at that moment. "Was everything all right?" he oozed. "Ah, what a tragedy to lose the professor! I hope the lunch was worthy of him. You can pay at the bar when you're ready."

Osselaer got up at once to settle the bill. In a rush of indignation Charles followed him. "Just a minute," he said, touching Osselaer's elbow. "What do you mean by 'antiquities specialist', exactly? What is he doing here? Did you engage him?"

Osselaer shrank back, in obvious discomfort. The supplicant's face narrowed. "Your father did," he said.

Charles stared at him. "My father asked *me* to take care of these matters."

Osselaer sighed. "There's an enormous amount of work to be done with the sale of such an estate, Charles," he explained, regaining some traction. "Monsieur Ames is someone your father knows through his many contacts. Someone who can help appraise not only your uncle's artifacts, but also the villa. Even the castle ruins. Hugues expects me to show Ames the property this afternoon."

"His many contacts..." Charles echoed, wondering bitterly if those contacts had anything to do with the dealer who'd been found dead in Antwerp.

"Ames is well-known in the antiquities field," Osselaer offered, as if this might soften things.

"Blancheron shouldn't be sold," said Charles. "You know that, Philippe. The castle is our family heritage."

Do whatever you can to hold on to Blancheron.

Osselaer sighed. "Charles, such a castle is unmanageable these days. The coffers of the Belgian patrimony are tight. Your father will be much better off making a private sale." His voice quavered; his body sagged into something resembling a question mark. "I can help, of course. But I'm no expert on antiques...or medieval ruins, for that matter."

"So Father brought in someone who is," Charles concluded. "And you're working with him."

Osselaer said nothing. He bowed slightly in the direction of Ida, who was getting up from the table.

"Father asked *me* to go through those things," Charles exclaimed. "He said nothing about a third party." His palms were sweating now. Oddly, his courage suddenly swelled. "As the only representative of the family present—that is, if Ida will agree, and I'm sure she will—I intend to spend as much time at Villa Antioch as I need to put Theodore's affairs in order," he said. "I will certainly call on you for assistance, Philippe, in due course. But you can tell Monsieur Ames that there won't be any tour of the property this afternoon. I'll let you know when—or if—I need his services."

Charles glanced outside as they prepared to leave. Ames was watching the party exit the *auberge*. He pulled his mobile from his coat and made another call. The diamond on his hand flashed again. He nodded to the notary, his expression inscrutable, then got into his BMW and drove away.

"I assume you have a key to the villa?" Charles asked Osselaer as they returned to their cars.

Osselaer reached into his suit, drew out a key and handed it to Charles.

"Is this the only one?" Charles said.

Osselaer hesitated. "I think so." His voice held a tremor. He watched Ames's car turn left at the river and disappear from view.

XLII

Charles drove alone to Villa Antioch.

In a gallant gesture, Osselaer had offered to give Ida a lift back to Brussels even though he himself lived in Bouillon. "I won't hear of you taking the train," he'd tut-tutted, aghast at the very idea. "I'll take you home, then drive back to Bouillon this evening." He'd fussed over her like a lackey, concerned that her hands were cold, and that her lace shawl, though of course beautiful, could not possibly ward off the dangerous damp. Perhaps she might like another cup of coffee before setting off?

It would all have been more endearing had Charles felt he could trust the man. *What has Father concocted with Osselaer?* He drove slowly through the October half-light, mulling over the question. The fledgling confidence he'd experienced at the *auberge* had evaporated, and only the thought of Sylvana promising to call the next day staved off his growing emptiness.

The road followed the river until it made a turn and plunged into forest thick with old-growth pines, their obscurity lit here and there by a chestnut tree's autumn gold.

He missed the unmarked drive.

Charles turned the car around and spotted the plane tree his grandfather had planted at the villa's entrance. He'd forgotten about the tree's special feature: the little shrine to the Virgin Mary that the ladies of the Rêve parish had nailed to its patchwork trunk. Theodore invariably took it down again once they'd gone, and the ladies soon replaced it, Theodore denying all along that this irritating stand-off had had anything to do with any doctrinal dispute. *They're trespassing, lad!* he'd claimed with that infamous wink.

Charles turned into the drive and noticed that the shrine was intact. He smiled to himself: the ladies of Rêve had won. "Maybe it's for the best, Uncle," he whispered. "As you said yourself, you never know..."

The unpaved track to Villa Antioch had once been used as an access to the Roman bridge. Guy de la Fontaine had put up a *Passage Interdit* sign years ago to stop the practice, although most locals understood that he'd meant cars, not them, so occasional walkers could still be seen admiring the stone structure.

Charles stared ahead, his hands damp on the wheel. *Yes, there's the bend!* His pulse accelerated. He drove faster, for soon he'd reach the spot where you could see it all at once: house, bridge, willow, river. The boy-Charles had made a game of it, holding his breath in his uncle's Renault all the way from the plane tree to that magical spot, when he would gasp not so much for breath, but out of pure glee.

He slammed on the brakes.

House...bridge...willow...river...

There they were, the tenants of his young heart.

He got out of the car. A quartet of rooks rose from the willow and drifted toward the river like shreds of Ida's shawl. *A sign, perhaps,* Charles thought. He listened to their prehistoric language fade over the water.

Then he turned to the house.

Villa Antioch was a nineteenth-century confection of brick, stone and gable rising three stories high and topped by an imposing square turret. The rear of the house, where Charles had spent so many hours in his uncle's study and kitchen, looked onto a meadow dotted with centenarian beeches and ash trees and stretching to the river.

The villa's mullioned windows, tall as sentries, let in as much air around the edges as they did light, allowing drafts to scurry up and down every corridor and staircase. The side facing the river was even more generously endowed with glass: French doors leading to the terrace, and bay windows on the uppers floors. All this illumination— misty, opalescent, shot through with glints from the river—far outweighed the inconvenience of drafts.

Charles parked next to the rusting Renault. He glanced up at the turret with its tiny dormer windows: the flagpole was still there, though lacking its gonfalon, and for a moment he remembered what it had felt like to lean out and attach the banner. He could swear that the house was regarding him with compassion, as if he were a returning pilgrim. In one of those whims of memory a quote surfaced from Ralph of Caen, in which Prince Tancred struggled back from a particularly grueling and dangerous adventure:

Thus, after long labors, he returned home to Antioch.

XLIII

The front door was unlocked.

Charles paused, key in hand. Osselaer must have come by to check on things and forgotten to lock up, though this seemed unlikely.

He opened the door and a rush of air greeted him. The draft, strong and steady, seemed to be issuing from somewhere at the back of the house. He stepped onto the hall tiles: they felt gritty underfoot.

Charles glanced at the wide oak stairs and a memory overwhelmed him, of the chatty crick each step made as he'd climbed the seven flights to the turret room. He noticed that the ochre-leaf wallpaper was pulling away at the seams. In one spot, a whole strip hung in a desultory flap.

Light spilled uncharacteristically into the front hall: the door to Theodore's study was open.

Charles shrank in alarm. He'd never seen the room this way. Theodore had always shut himself inside or otherwise kept the study closed. There was something indecent about the open door, as if his uncle had been surprised in his underclothes.

He hurried in to find the door to the terrace wide open as well. *Osselaer must have left it ajar.* Papers lay strewn across the floor. *Probably the wind.* Charles closed the terrace door and surveyed the room.

It was obvious now that the place had been ransacked.

Even at the height of his research, Theodore had never been capable of such a mess. Incredibly, the twelfth-century ivory olifant, the most valuable object in the house, was still sitting on a pile of documents like a cheap paperweight. This couldn't have been an ordinary burglary.

Charles reached into his coat pocket for his phone, then put it away again. He'd call Osselaer after he'd had a look around himself.

He collected the books and papers from the floor, noting the back issues of the *Journal of Medieval History,* various scholarly articles on the Crusades in several languages, a dictionary of Old French and incongruously, a few Tintin comic books, and stacked everything on the leather sofa. He breathed in deeply and the river air revived him. But there was another tonic as well: Theodore's cedarwood cologne, forever immured in the place he'd inhabited for decades.

Charles pulled up his scarf in the unheated house and slumped onto the desk chair. *How should I proceed?* he wondered. *Call Osselaer? The police?* He examined the olifant, tracing the interlocking Moorish decorations and vines, turning the horn until he found the eagle and that lovely, sinuous deer. He swayed backwards, slowly, as Theodore had done, prolonging the frog chorus, threading his fingers behind his head like his mentor. Charles knew exactly how long Theodore could hold this position, for he'd sat on the hard stool for the same length of time, waiting for his next task.

Then he noticed the drawers.

He swung up abruptly: the two top ones were slightly open. In a panic he pulled them out: the contents were in complete disorder.

With cold fingers he examined the lower drawer...*the* drawer. He'd been avoiding it, he realized; avoiding what it was that Theodore said he'd hidden there. Charles bit his lip. *Was this the reason an imposter had come to the remote villa?* The incident had obviously terrified Theodore. Somehow, it had led to his death.

Only now did Charles remember that the key to the special drawer was in the envelope he'd left in the car. He wouldn't be needing it, however. For the lock had obviously been forced.

Charles rifled through the contents of the drawer. With a cry of relief he found the false bottom intact.

He sat up and took a long, slow breath. He remembered how to remove the bottom from the drawer. That wasn't the problem.

It was simply that he wasn't ready.

He wandered out onto the leaf-strewn terrace. The two chairs and little iron table with Delft tiles hadn't moved in seventeen years. The chink of glass against tile...Theodore shambling off to get the chocolates... All of this had only recently happened, it seemed.

Across the river, the ridge was already retreating into silhouette. Dusk would come early, Charles knew. He should have been using the waning light to look for footprints, or tire tracks on the drive—any clue to make sense of the break-in. But instead he found himself resuming something at the very moment he'd walked out on it.

Oh, we haven't changed, the landscape seemed to be saying. *We still flow, and rustle, and shift as we always have. Those rooks are descendants of the same family you knew. But you, Charles...whatever happened to* you?

It was not an unkind welcome, all things considered. His pulse warmed; he felt resolve stirring. But a task lay before him. *An endeavor.* And this would require the conviction of someone he still didn't believe he could ever be. A person of spirit...of courage. Someone who never abandoned their ideals, no matter what.

Someone like Theodore.

He balked.

Like Godfrey.

The first step awaited him in the study.

He went back inside and removed the false bottom from the drawer.

PART FOUR

The Parchment

XLIV

It was like pulling a living thing from the envelope. Like flesh. And of course, it was: the hide of a sheep or cow, soaked, scraped, dried and stretched, though it had been manipulated so many times over the centuries by human hands that Charles had the impression, on touching the folio for the first time, that the skin could have belonged to something closer to his own species.

He turned the page over: the surface was blanketed recto-verso with the most even, practiced Latin handwriting he'd ever seen, though illegible to all but the most expert scholars. The language in itself was unusual, as Theodore had indicated. *Why would a Latin folio be attached to a chanson de geste written in Old French?* He smiled as he ran his index finger down the jagged edge of parchment where it had been cut from the codex: his grandfather had been hasty with his scissors, it seemed. A sloppy hand, wielding a cheap instrument.

Charles knew something about old manuscripts. There were a few of them in his uncle's odd-ball collection. One summer, Theodore had held out a fragment of a fifteenth-century psalm to his young nephew. *Go ahead, lad. Touch it…smell it! I know they say you should use gloves, but to hell with it. Parchment is meant to be touched. Scribes were in constant contact with it. They breathed it all day long. Scratched it with their quill. Scraped it with their knife. Writing, like eating, was a two-handed operation back then, you know. Just think whose hand might have held this!*

Charles smiled, knowing exactly whose hand had last held this particular treasure.

He pulled the chain on the green banker's lamp, cleared a space on the desk and lay the folio in the spillway of light. Reverence overcame him. *This must be the alternative ending of the heron legend!* he thrilled: the document his grandfather had discovered—and stolen—from the Library of European History; the translation Theodore had been laboring over just before his death.

There were no illuminations on the parchment—no decorations of any kind. Punctuation was all but invisible, though neatly ruled lines had been scored directly into the surface by a knife or stylus. The bottom right edge of the page was darkened and scalloped from wear, giving the impression that it might be a palimpsest: a manuscript that had been scraped clean and reused several times. The ink had faded to a reddish-brown, like dried blood. Most probably iron-gall, Charles decided: a combination of ferrous sulphate and the galls found on oak leaves and twigs, all mixed together with wine, water or vinegar.

He combed the page for what he'd loved most as a boy: ink that had settled on the lower edges of the letters, revealing the steep slope of the scribe's desk. He lifted the parchment to his face and breathed deeply: whatever animal had worn this hide nine hundred years ago still left a trace.

He studied the folio until night came. A buffet of wind rattled the window now and then and leaves rasped across the terrace, but none of this disturbed his concentration. He remembered such moments from his youth: communion with an object from the past so intense, a gap seemed to open in time.

Charles smoothed the buckles and scores in the parchment and imagined his fingers brushing against other, long-dead ones. He let himself enter that corridor where history stole about in its soft leather shoes, lighting a taper here, adjusting a robe there. He glanced out at the terrace: nothing was visible now save a curl of iron railing and the usual bouillon of mist suspended over the lawns. The invisible, however, was everywhere.

If Theodore had been correct in dating the folio, it was older by over three hundred years than the fifteenth-century fragment he'd let Charles touch, and depending on the circumstances, it might last for hundreds more.

How far can we reach into the past, lad? Two centuries? Three? Come on, let's try for nine!

Charles removed the remaining contents of the envelope Theodore had hidden in the secret drawer: a sheet of unlined paper on which he'd written, by hand and in English, his partial translation of the Latin folio. He'd put certain words in parentheses that he'd been unsure of, or where there was an erasure in the original text.

Why were his notes in English? Charles examined the sloping, undisciplined handwriting. His fingers grew cool as he recalled the urgency in his uncle's letter. Soon it became clear: Theodore would have communicated with everyone else he knew in French. He must have directed this translation specifically to his nephew, therefore, whose French, he'd correctly surmised, would have grown slack.

Charles placed the parchment next to his uncle's translation and plunged into the world of Stephen de la Fontaine and Henri of Rêve:

These deeds occurred three summers before the great comet that appeared each evening for forty days from the first week of Lent. The ray that shone from it was very bright, like an immense column. The deeds took place in the years following the victory in Jerusalem by the Franks. It is a noble exercise to record events accurately, especially if they must describe a (erasure) whose heart was humble and virtuous, but whose soul was at a crossroads; who knew not whether to follow the path of the Gospels, or that of the sacred Earth. The world does not know that in great spiritual pain, he followed both.

Wind juddered the window frame and Charles looked up. A current of air lifted the edge of the parchment and chased a dust ball across the floor. He remembered Theodore mentioning the comet of 1106. The events described dated from 1103, therefore.

He closed his eyes. Instead of obscurity, he seemed to have stepped into the light; he'd exited history's corridor at its far end, where the soft leather shoes had led him. *How quickly one can traverse nine centuries!* He could hear the stamp of a hoof. Wood smoke laced the air. It all seemed strangely welcoming, and there was something else, too, pressing close. Fatigue, no doubt. *I'm so very tired. The trip from New York...the funeral.* Whatever it was seemed to cling to his body: probably just the overcoat he was still wearing in the frigid villa. Or perhaps...

Is this what chain mail feels like?

He shook off the heaviness and went back to the translation:

His faithful squire returned home to find the prophetess of the spring dead. This he learned from the mouth of the Moorish jongleur, that unwanted wretch, who said that a (lord) with splendid hand hunted the lady to her cave in the forest, defiled her, and cut her throat. He threw her precious instrument into the fire. The outcast, that Spaniard, found the poor lady in a lake of blood. There also, in the cold and somber dwelling, hidden away in rags, he found a babe...

Charles sat to attention.

A baby hadn't figured anywhere in the legend.

He got up and paced around the study. His tired mind spun outwards as he tried to recall the details of his grandfather's translation of the Old French, now in Sylvana's hands.

Stephen and Henri. Arda and Rodolfo.

These protagonists Charles knew.

But not a baby.

On impulse he rummaged through every drawer of the desk looking for anything else Theodore might have jotted down. He came across an unfinished essay on Roman coins; a few receipts from the Auberge du Chevalier; a bill from the Renault garage in Libramont—the typical miscellany of Theodore's life. But nothing that had to do with the legend.

Charles examined the parchment again. Clearly the Latin text picked up the story more or less where the Old French tale had left off: Stephen's return from the First Crusade. Charles recognized the Carolingian Miniscule script from his Latin tutorials—a tidy bit of pedantry, perhaps, but not very useful if you couldn't read it. The lower-case system of writing looked like opaque lacework to him now, with no evident beginning or end to the sentences. On closer inspection, the nicks and scrapes seemed linked to breaks in the text—spaces that had either been left blank, or overwritten.

He searched in vain for any proper name he might recognize, then recalled that in this system of Latin writing, proper names were not capitalized. In an odd sort of acceleration, the words became more and more crammed together as they went along, making it almost impossible to decipher one from the other until the verso resembled a mad dash to some sort of monastic finish line.

Charles peered at what at first glance looked like embellishments, but which he morosely identified as abbreviations: the squiggles, lines and dots used by scribes to denote missing letters. He would never be able to decode them himself.

He read the rest of what Theodore had managed to translate:

The Spaniard told the squire that he took the babe to the great abbey. (Valdoré?) There he knew the monks would give him charity. They took in the child, and for a time the bedraggled vagrant also, who ailed most cruelly from his woodland living. The Spaniard told the monks that the child had a distinguished father, a nobleman, who had lands and riches but who had died (erasure). He did not mention the boy's mother or her pagan ways, fearing that the monks would turn the child away. The noble son remained at the abbey until he was in his sixth year, when the squire heard the Spaniard's story and hastened to take the child into his custody.

The notes ended there.

Charles turned the parchment over, touching it with greater confidence now. His fingertips traced the scallops of wear along the turning edge. He smiled at a hole near the bottom of the page around which the writing flowed like water past a stone.

Those medieval beasts had ticks, lad! When you stretch their hides, every tiny prick becomes a hole.

After some time, Charles was able to decipher a few words with his dormant Latin. *Stella crinita:* "hairy star". *Of course, the comet!* Theodore had interpreted *valauri* as being "Valdoré". The abbey was a ruin now, but in its heyday, Valdoré had rivalled the greatest European abbeys in importance. Charles pinpointed *sibylla fontis*, which Theodore had translated as "prophetess of the spring", an unusually respectful appellation, it seemed, for someone the medieval church had considered a heretic. The name Arda was nowhere to be seen. But surely she was the mother of the baby; the woman of the "pagan ways". The Spaniard (*hispanus*) was no doubt Rodolfo, the itinerant *jongleur* of Grandfather's translation who'd probably migrated north from Moorish Spain. The faithful squire (*armiger fidelis*) was Stephen de la Fontaine himself, Charles surmised, whose noble master, Henri of Rêve, had entrusted him with the olive wood box to take back to Arda. And then that strange description, *splendida manu*: "with splendid hand".

Two men in love with the same woman. A common enough story. But the questions from Charles's youth plagued him now: *Where was the olive wood box? What did it contain?* And now a new one: *Who was this child?*

The baby must have been Henri's son, conceived before he'd headed off to Jerusalem. *A distinguished father; a nobleman...* Henri's squire, Stephen, would have hurried to reclaim the child from the abbey after he'd discovered this information.

Charles stared at the parchment and a few words caught his eye: *in familiam nomenque adoptavit...*

"Adopted in family and name..."

Theodore had evidently translated this as "taking the child into his custody". Perhaps this meant that Stephen had adopted the baby—the illegitimate child of his master, Henri of Rêve—and given it his own name: de la Fontaine. *Why?*

And why would someone ransack Theodore's study for this information?

Charles tucked the parchment back into the envelope along with Theodore's notes. His heart lifted at the thought of speaking with Sylvana the next day. He'd ring Osselaer in the morning and try to put things right with him. The notary had clearly been roped in by Hugh for some sort of shady agenda. Osselaer had been Theodore's oldest friend—perhaps his only one. They'd shared the same schooling; they'd spent endless hours discussing Theodore's research. *There's no one else I can trust with this,* Charles thought.

He turned off the desk lamp. Shivering, he reached under the desk and touched the radiator: cold as a church floor. He leaned back slowly and rested his head against the chair, eking out the familiar chorus, marveling at how even in his Latin translations Theodore's riddles lived on.

Soon Charles was drifting back down the time corridor. He'd never set foot in the Holy Land, though he'd travelled there countless times in his imagination. Thus he stepped easily into the dusty valley in Outremer where Henri of Rêve had been buried...where the earth underfoot had been fired in the kiln of an antique sun, and olive trees stood pallid as ghosts. A brackish stream stank, corrupted by rotting flesh. *How many pilgrims had perished of thirst here? Given birth in this very dust?*

There it was again, that heaviness...and such discomfort. It wasn't difficult to imagine how armor and chain mail must have scorched the flesh in that sun.

Charles put his head down on the desk.

He slept.

XLV

A soul was at a crossroads. *But whose soul?*

Why yours, of course! Seize your endeavor, Charles d'Outre-mer.
The voice was neither male nor female. Just an internal summons.

Charles answered the dream-tone:
The others are mustering already. You must tell them what to do,
Monseigneur, lest they stray. Which path will you follow? The path of
the Gospels, or that of the Earth?

Someone said:
They tried so hard to inspire peace with the Gospels, but people
never really followed them as they should. People have never figured
out how to stop fighting each other. Even that pious one, the Defender
of the Holy Sepulcher, took up arms and killed in the name of his god.
He was of two natures, the elusive Godfrey. It was just as Ralph of
Caen wrote: "In his eagerness for war, look to the father; in his
cultivation of God, behold the mother".

It was Charles's own dream-voice now:
I must find Arda. I must make sure she's safe. I'll be gone such a
long time overseas. Outre-mer... There will be danger at every turn.
Who knows if I'll make it back safely? Surely I'll find her at the pool.
But no, she's not there. I stand by the water, alone. A column of light
falls through an oculus in the trees. The water is pearly gray, like
quicksilver. Something brushes over it: a wing, reflected from the sky-
opening.
The nature-basilica is empty. There is no priestess. I wait. Is it
really she who can cleanse my soul? Or is it Walderic, my confessor?
No, no...he must not know that I've come here. There's so little time. I

must prepare myself...prepare my soul. August fifteenth tomorrow: the woods are already full of soldiers, noblemen, townspeople. Tomorrow, the olifant will sound. Tomorrow, I shall leave here, perhaps forever.

Oh, Arda... I must say good-bye.

I hear you playing. There's no other sound like it. A song from the Earth.

A song of warning.

"Consider what you are about to do," the music says. "God does not will it. Not an Earth god, anyway; not the Sacred Mother, who would claim no part in the destruction you are about to unleash."

I ignore the warning and stumble through the ferns after the sound. The cave would be impossible to find without your music.

There's no light inside. Just a low lament from the lyra. Then nothing.

I step through the entrance laden with doubt; with conscience.

Arda? Are you there?

The only sound now is the repeating note of the spring.

I'm falling, falling...into an embrace of impossible softness. Into swansdown. Into music itself.

How you manage to remove my mail shirt I cannot fathom.

The window juddered.

Charles lifted his head.

The dream let go of him gradually, so that when he opened his eyes and saw the outlines of a face at the window, he couldn't say for certain whether the vision was real, or something he'd seen in Arda's cave.

XLVI

He awoke the next morning on the settee in the salon without remembering how he'd gotten there. He'd slept in his coat: it was cold enough in the room that his breath hung on the air.

Charles gazed about at what appeared to be a garden seen through rice paper. Everything—carpet, drapes, armchairs, cushions—was floral but rubbed-out looking, as if it had aged in a medieval tapestry. Dark patches of humidity stained the fabrics. Theodore had never spent much time in this room, claiming that it was too formal for his liking. As a boy, Charles had poked his head into the salon from time to time, but its sad grandeur had kept him from entering.

The florals were a hold-over from his grandmother's time as mistress of this house. Charles tried to imagine the woman he'd never known, doing her best to make a home in the damp Belgian forest while her husband and son spent their time fiddling with chain mail and digging in the mud. Thank heavens the poor lady had had Ida for a counterweight!

The room faced the front of the house and Charles spotted the rental car. *Damn!* He'd left his bags in it. How stupid, given the break-in! He'd also left the envelope with the parchment on Theodore's desk and rushed to the study to make sure it was still there.

Then he remembered the face at the window.

He hesitated in the study doorway.

The dream returned—just shreds of it: pearly water; untamed music. And that unremitting heaviness.

He retrieved the envelope from the desk and glanced out at the miasma that still cloaked meadow and river. Gradually, he recalled more about that face. Surely he hadn't imagined it: wide forehead and cheeks; prominent eye sockets; swarthiness that didn't seem to have had anything to do with the prevailing darkness.

Had Theodore's intruder come back?

Charles hurried out to the car for his belongings. *Would the man keep coming back until he finally got his hands on what he was looking for?* He was heading down the passage to the kitchen when there was a knock at the front door.

It was Osselaer, tentative as always, a paper bag full of croissants in his hand. He'd parked some distance from the house, as if in deference to Charles's mourning.

"*Sharl'*..." he mumbled, avoiding eye contact. Behind him, the front lawns were a chaos of fallen branches and russet leaves after last night's wind.

The notary wore no coat over his blazer and no hat on his balding head. "I thought you might be hungry," he said, proffering the bag. "Theo never has much to eat around here."

"I'm delighted to see you!" Charles said, relieved not only by the food, but that he had a chance to make a fresh start with Osselaer. He hadn't eaten since lunch the previous day and was starving as well as frozen to the bone.

Osselaer kissed Charles on both cheeks. "*Ça va?* Are you managing?" His smile was disjointed, as if his face had been fashioned from remnants.

"Yes, fine, thank you," Charles said. "Just cold and hungry!"

Osselaer opened a door off the hall and disappeared down a flight of steps. "I'll put the heating back on," he called up. "October can be pretty chilly in these parts. The kitchen will be warmest."

Villa Antioch boasted a formal dining room that could have handled breakfast for a regiment, a stern and pretentious place. The humble galley kitchen, however...

Everything Charles loved about the room rushed to greet him: the scent of carnations; the cabinet where Theodore stored his cache of chocolate; that rickety table for two set against the window, where he and his uncle had taken all their meals when the weather didn't permit eating on the terrace. They'd sat either in lively discussion or in companionable silence, both perfectly acceptable forms of communication for two people who understood each other well, Theodore had said.

Charles motioned Osselaer to a seat while he busied himself with the espresso machine, the kitchen's only appliance except for a microwave.

They sipped their coffees and tore open their croissants, grateful for the ghost of heat in the radiator under the table.

"There's something about you, Charles," Osselaer said. His hallmark lean continued even in the sitting position, so that he appeared to be listening to his coffee. "Ida always said there was," he added, as if she were the final arbiter. "You're more of a European gentleman than an American one. A nobleman from another epoch, Ida said."

"She used to call me 'my sweet knight'," Charles said with nostalgia, wondering if Ida would ever use the term for Osselaer one day.

He hardly considered his own state worthy of a nobleman from any epoch. He was unwashed and unshaven, and he'd slept in his funeral wear, something that would have made his grandmother, in whose salon he'd done his sleeping, blush with embarrassment. He did notice that the notary's blue blazer had shiny discs of wear on the elbows and a sprinkle of dandruff on one shoulder, and took some comfort in these oversights.

Charles wiped condensation from one of the latticed panes and studied the river. The mist had lifted to reveal a stone arch of the bridge. He turned to Osselaer.

"Philippe, someone broke into the villa. When I arrived yesterday evening, Theodore's study door and the terrace door were open and his papers were everywhere. Do you have any idea who might have done this...or what they were after?"

Osselaer paled considerably. The effect on such a face was alarming.

"Are you all right?" Charles said. "Another coffee, perhaps?"

"No, thank you. I'm fine...fine." Osselaer produced a handkerchief from his blazer pocket and wiped his forehead. He smoothed a hand over his meager rows of hair. "Ah, Charles...Charles..." The man foundered pitifully. Repetition seemed his only lifeline. When he finally met Charles's gaze, it was with contrition.

And fear.

Charles balked. Osselaer had the appearance of a cornered animal.

"Do you think it was the same person who visited Theodore before he died?" Charles pressed him. Osselaer didn't possess sufficient guile to delude anyone for long.

The notary pushed a few crumbs together on his plate and said nothing.

"Theodore shared some of his recent findings with me in a letter he wrote just a few days before he died," said Charles, coaxing the man to react. "He shared his research with you from time to time, I think?"

Osselaer sipped his coffee, his skinny fingers laced tightly around the cup. He sighed. "I know about the parchment, if that's what you mean," he said. "Your uncle didn't keep much from me. He was terribly excited about it. The folio had been lost among your grandfather's papers for so many years. And *voilà*, there it was!"

"Did you take a look at it?"

Osselaer hesitated. "In passing. Theo suddenly became so secretive. He always shared any new research with me. But this time he seemed, well...so *worried.*"

This was, indeed, odd behavior for the expansive, bon-vivant Theodore, although it precisely matched the fugitive Theodore—the one who'd driven through the night to Brussels to give Ida the envelope he'd prepared for his nephew.

"He wasn't sure what to do with the parchment, frankly," Osselaer went on. "With what it contains, that is..."

"He didn't manage to translate all of it," Charles said.

"I know. But he did enough to realize that it might contain proof..."

"Proof?" Charles chafed at the frustration of not being able to read the manuscript himself except for a few paltry words. He'd stared its secrets in the face, just last night. But it had been a face behind a veil.

"Yes," said Osselaer. "Of the contents of the olive wood box. You know: the one that Stephen de la Fontaine brought back from the Holy Land on behalf of his master, Henri of Rêve."

"Yes, *yes!*" Charles jumped in. "And?"

"And proof of where the box is hidden."

Charles stared at him. "That information was not in the paragraphs Uncle managed to translate."

Osselaer pushed more crumbs around his plate.

Neither spoke for some time.

Charles had indulged himself during his medieval studies at Yale hunting down boxes and reliquaries in the Metropolitan Museum and imagining what they might have held: pieces of saints' bones; scraps of surcoat; a few links of chain mail; a remnant of a shoe that had touched Golgotha. He'd considered Bishop Walderic and that toenail of St. Simeon he'd carried about in a silver reliquary, and whether or not it had ever given him any real comfort. Despite all this, Charles had come no closer to what the olive wood box might have contained. But one thing had always seemed logical: Stephen had hidden it in the safest possible place at Blancheron.

Under a rock...in a crevasse...

In a cave.

Charles pieced together a passage from Grandfather's translation:

Take the box back to Arda, Stephen. If you cannot find her, then covet the box yourself. And hide the key in a separate place.

Charles pressed his foot against the laptop bag under the table. He'd tucked the envelope with the parchment next to Theodore's letter with the keys—one of which was eleventh-century and possibly the key to the olive wood box.

"Did you mention any of this to my father, by any chance?" Charles asked. *Osselaer must be the link,* he thought. Hugh Fontaine had displayed all the signs of a hound smelling blood on the air with this Blancheron sale.

Osselaer sighed again. "As you probably know, your father was putting pressure on Theo to move out."

"Yes, I know."

"Hugues can also be pretty ruthless at times."

"I know that, too."

"Well, you also know your Crusades, I think," Osselaer continued, trying to strike a lighter tone. "So you'll appreciate that Hugues has always conducted his affairs like a Seljuk Turk. You might remember that fearsome warrior: he circled the Franks in a swirling mass, unleashing hails of arrows. Then he feigned retreat on that fleet-footed pony of his. If you survived all that and made the mistake of going after him...well, he wheeled around in the saddle and took aim from there.

Personally, I think that Hugues has retreated for now. It's best to leave him alone for the moment and see what he chooses to do next."

Charles took another croissant from the bag.

"I'm sorry about the comparison," Philippe said, looking stricken. "It's a bit harsh, perhaps."

"Oh, it's very accurate," Charles said. "Only I tend to think of Father as more sedentary. Emperor Alexius, for instance. Wielding power from his throne rather than from a pony."

"*Sharl'...*" Osselaer said softly, stirring his coffee. "I was indeed the one who mentioned the parchment to your father. How could I know that the discovery would turn out to be that important?"

"How important?"

Osselaer studied the meadow. "Well..." he faltered. "It's obvious that whoever threatened Theodore and broke into the study was after the parchment."

Charles took the notary's cup and placed it under the coffee jet. Clearly Osselaer's kindness had a fatal flaw: he was liable to crumble at any time and do someone's bidding—like Hugh's—and then promptly confess to someone else—like Charles—what he'd just done.

"Philippe, there are several erasures in the parchment. Did Theodore mention these?"

"Yes. He thought they might have something to do with the child."

In the cold and somber dwelling, hidden away in rags, he found a babe...

"Why would those things be erased?"

Osselaer brushed a crumb from his blazer. "There's more in the parchment, Charles."

Silence descended.

After a few moments Charles asked: "How much does Ames know?"

"Your father engaged Ames to appraise the property and its contents," Osselaer said.

"Was that all he was engaged to do?"

Osselaer stiffened. "Charles, *nom de Dieu!* Are you suggesting that your father hired Ames to threaten Theodore—his own brother, no less—then to break in and seize the manuscript when that didn't work?!"

"Of course not," Charles said, knowing how perfectly capable his father was of such a thing.

"Hugues knows something of the real estate market in Europe," Osselaer said. "The Russians and Chinese have the deepest pockets these days when it comes to buying historic properties—especially if there's some intriguing tidbit associated with it."

"Intriguing tidbit?" Charles baited him.

Charles felt something stir...a current of air, perhaps. There were so many of them in the villa.

"Take the parchment to Cédric Florus in Brussels," said the notary. "At once," he added with urgency. "He's the retired head of manuscripts at the *Bibliothèque de l'Histoire*. He knew your grandfather and was a great friend of Theo's."

"Yes, Theodore told me to contact him," Charles said. "Apparently Florus is one of the world's leading experts in medieval manuscripts."

"He is. He'll be able to get to the bottom of what's in the MS. He'll know how to interpret it."

"Does Florus know that my grandfather stole it?"

Osselaer let out a pinched laugh. "Indeed he does. He was afraid he would lose his job over it if anyone else in the department found out."

"What if he confirms Theodore's hunch?" Charles asked. "That the manuscript holds a revelation?"

Osselaer didn't answer. He glanced at his watch and rose abruptly. "I have an appointment in Bouillon at eleven," he said. "We'll discuss it later." He produced Florus's number from his mobile and jotted it down on the croissant bag. "*Merci pour le café.*"

They'd arrived at uneven ground, it seemed. Charles realized he'd momentarily forgotten that the notary was in his father's employ—that the man was expected to obtain information and deliver it, like any other employee. Osselaer was just another vassal who'd pledged allegiance to Charles's father. The only possible bright spot was that Hugh was orchestrating everything from a distance, and may not have the leverage he thought he had. Emperor Alexius's influence had waned once the crusaders had packed up their belongings in Antioch and headed south to Jerusalem.

They proceeded single file along the narrow passage, Charles in the rear. He realized for the first time that the man's awkward pitch was caused by one leg being slightly shorter than the other.

XLVII

"M onsieur Florus? This is Charles Fontaine. Um, *de la Fontaine*. Theodore's nephew."

There was a long pause on the phone during which Charles, seated at his uncle's desk, watched a gray heron circle down to the river in a gliding arabesque.

At last Florus said: "Theo's nephew... *Mon Dieu*, I heard the terrible news. I'm so very, very sorry. He was a great friend of mine." Florus paused. "And despite what anyone says, a great medievalist."

"*Merci*," Charles said.

"You're American, I gather," said Florus, switching to English.

"Well, sort of."

"Ah..." Florus sounded bemused. "That's just the kind of thing dear Theo would have said! Your uncle was so...how should I say it? *Spécial*."

Charles's French was not so rusty as to have forgotten this rather uncomplimentary word, used for someone who is slightly odd; who lives on the fringes of society and is an embarrassment to their family. Which of course Theodore would have taken as a compliment.

Florus spoke with a British hum.

"Are you English, Monsieur?" Charles asked.

"Ha! No. Pure *bruxellois*. But I studied classics at Cambridge." He chuckled. The sound lifted Charles from all the heaviness of the past few days. "The accent clings like a fly to paper, *n'est-ce pas*?!"

Like honey to a spoon, more like, Charles thought. One could easily make the leap from the voice to a man of elegance and erudition. Someone who, like Theodore, stayed up late at night in search of historical truths; who during his time at Cambridge had developed a taste for reasoned debate, sherry, and that insult to every true Belgian: well-done meat.

"Monsieur Florus, I believe you know something about a Latin folio that was in my grandfather's possession."

Another chuckle. "Yes. And I know in whose possession it was before then!"

Charles hesitated. He hadn't expected Florus to make a game out of all this. "My uncle urged me to contact you on this matter," he went on. "I'd like to bring the manuscript by for you to examine, if I may. I know it's short notice, but would tomorrow suit you? I'll be driving back to Brussels in the morning."

Another, longer pause. "You mean you've found it?" Florus's voice was barely audible. All humor had vanished.

"Well, yes. Theodore came across it when he was going through my grandfather's papers. My father's planning to sell Blancheron and Theodore was preparing to move out."

"Ah. Poor Theo. He was a lowly tenant all his life."

"Have you actually studied the folio?" Charles asked.

"No. I knew that a folio had been misplaced during a reorganization, and..." Florus stumbled. "And that your grandfather might have, well...*found* it."

"You're aware, then, that it contains some information that doesn't appear in the Old French *chanson de geste* to which it was appended," said Charles.

"I'm aware of that, yes." Then, briskly: "Tomorrow would be fine. Can you come by my place, say around four o'clock? I make a very good cup of English tea!" His chuckle was brief this time.

Charles confirmed Florus's address and put his mobile in his laptop bag.

Then he climbed the seven flights of stairs to the turret room.

Each step creaked in welcome. Charles's own youthful lightness lingered in the sound as well as Theodore's heavy tread, which the boy had tried so hard to stay awake for even if sleep usually won in the end.

The older Charles had lost his lightness and had to pause often. The landings were piled with books and boxes and woodland artifacts, so he paused not only for breath, but also to appreciate these treasures, and conjure scenes from his youth in the ochre foliage of the wallpaper.

He entered the room as he always had, with eyes closed. It was such a childish thing to do, but the reward, he knew, would be great. He opened his eyes and gasped, not so much at the boundless view—a reward beyond measure—but at the boy who'd gasped every time he'd stepped into the room.

He glanced at the bed, just a thin mattress on slats. How many sleepless hours he'd spent on it! He would lie on his back and watch the stars wink on through the tower windows, and the moon increase in plumpness from the night before. And he would listen to the room itself, ever fearful that the floorboard near the foot of the bed would let out a squawk under some ghostly shoe. He trod on it now: the squawk hadn't changed.

With slow ritual Charles turned around at the center of the room, savoring each frame as it appeared to him: the river views, the willow, the bridge.

I saw it, lad...

He caught his breath: Theodore's words had slunk in unannounced.

He scanned the river for any flash of white. The gray heron he'd observed earlier had flown off. There was something about the view, though. It seemed suspended, as if caught between seasons, waiting patiently for the creeping mists, and bellowing stags, and the ducks flying in tight formation over the ridge to announce the start of autumn. Which was exactly how that evening had felt seventeen years ago.

XLVIII

Theodore had kept his promise to take his nephew into the forest on a really dark night, and so one weekend in autumn, Charles came down from Brussels to listen to the stags' rut: a frightening, ecstatic cacophony of roars emanating not just from the depths of the beast, but from the earliest primordial night.

At least, that's what he thought he'd come down for.

"Not too much, mind you," Theodore cautioned as Charles took a few sips of brandy from the flask his uncle carried in his satchel. "It's just to keep warm while we're out. And to build up your courage. We don't want any alcohol-induced visions, do we?"

It was mid-October. Moonless. Windless, too, although it had rained during the afternoon. A chill always infused the river valley at night, especially after a rain, and now the forest was like a stone cellar.

And very, very dark.

They crossed the bridge and turned left in the direction of the village.

"This isn't the way to the pond," Charles said, zipping up the over-sized oilskin his uncle had lent him. "I thought that's where you can hear the stags."

"Yes. We'll go there tomorrow. Tonight we're going to follow the Semois, then hike through the forest to a field across the river from Rêve. It's where local peasants gathered to leave for Jerusalem. 1096, lad! And believe me, where we're going, not much has changed."

"But it's so dark!" Charles exclaimed.

"That's the point!" Theodore laughed.

The river swept furtively along beside them as they walked. Century-old pines leaned close to the water—too close, their complicity unnatural, somehow. At times it was necessary to clamber over their roots, slippery and tangled and just a misstep from oblivion.

199

"We must not underestimate the vastness of forests in medieval Europe, lad," Theodore said, moving his satchel from one shoulder to the other. "They stretched right across whole countries. No one wanted to be caught in them at nightfall."

Charles stumbled along behind him, wondering if he should mention that they'd found themselves in exactly such a situation.

The path veered away from the river and Theodore struck off into deep woodland. Charles brought up the rear with some trepidation, knowing he would have to stay close to Theodore not to get lost. For it was clear that navigation through this ink-world would depend on the rush of the river and gentle thud of his uncle's boots, and on little else.

There must have been other sounds, of course. Night creatures in the underbrush, or an owl hooting overhead. But they couldn't possibly have drowned out the pumping of Charles's heart—or the footsteps he imagined trailing behind him.

He knew that these forests could conceal anyone and anything, even in daylight. *But by night...* Only a fool would try to get his bearings without a moon. Even the goddess Arduinna would have shunned such a night, the moon having been her alter-ego.

Who's abroad, then? Charles whispered to himself. He sucked in his breath. *Maugis.* He'd forgotten all about the Ardennes shape-shifter until then. *Oh, why did I have to think of him just now?*

The forest path widened somewhat and Theodore fell into a steady pace. Charles adopted the same rhythm behind him. The oilskin rasped with his stride and his boots had resonance on the peaty soil. His eyesight gradually sharpened, and soon he was able to pick out trunks and branches and even small stones underfoot.

"Godfrey would have hunted in these forests," Theodore said. He picked up his pace at a crossroads, where an eerie wash of starlight bathed the intersection.

"Which Godfrey?" Charles asked without thinking, only loud enough for the forest to hear. There were so many incarnations, after all. Godfrey of Bouillon was a shape-shifter himself of sorts: Swan-knight. Diplomat. Warrior. Worshipper.

Nightfarer... Was that one of his incarnations?

Charles stopped dead in the middle of the crossroads. *Had Godfrey ridden through here?* He drew the oilskin around him and shivered, combing the trees that crowded around. They appeared ashen in the starlight, as if ailing. *Maybe they knew something.*

"Hurry up, lad!" Theodore called from the gloom. "You don't want to linger at crossroads, remember."

Charles dashed to keep up. *How could he have forgotten Hecate?* The goddess of magic and witchcraft lurked at lonely intersections just like this one. They were places where two realms touched...where spirits could be summoned.

Where executions took place.

They walked for another twenty minutes or so until the forest abruptly ended.

"Here it is," Theodore said softly as Charles came up beside him. "The field."

Even in the darkness they could make out an expanse of meadow, flanked on three sides by a black mass of forest and on the fourth, by the river. The surrounding pines grazed the night sky like lances.

Theodore poked along the edge of the field, stepping high over vines and nettles. He beckoned Charles to a fallen log.

"Is this where the peasants of Rêve left on the First Crusade?" Charles asked, avoiding a patch of nettle and settling on the log. He glanced across the river at the village, where here and there a light betrayed an insomniac. It was past eleven o'clock and most country folk were well into their dreams by now.

"*Oui, exactement,*" said Theodore. "Our village had its own departure to Jerusalem. From this very spot. April, 1096. Peasants, beggars, women and children, poor knights. They shod oxen for the journey, as they didn't have money for horses. Most had no shoes. Imagine that: four thousand kilometers in bare feet."

Charles stared at the dormant field. Despite the brandy, he was already chilled through. The damp air insinuated itself into his collar and he pulled up the hood of the oilskin.

"The People's Crusade left a few months earlier than Godfrey and the other princes," Theodore said. "What a rag-tag bunch! More than fifteen thousand of them from northern France and Germany. Not at all what Pope Urban had had in mind when he'd preached Holy War from an outdoor scaffold in Clermont in 1095. Oh, no! He'd envisioned an orderly preparation. Nobles, well-trained soldiers.

"But it turned out that Urban had demonized the Muslim occupiers of Jerusalem so well that once the floodgates of zealotry were open, there was no closing them. Religious fervor ran amok. All sins would be forgiven. Pilgrims pinned crosses to themselves: silk and gold threads for the wealthy, cruder cloth for the poor. Godfrey's chaplain, Abbot Baldwin, dispensed with fabric altogether and had a cross branded into the flesh of his forehead—a practice apparently not that unusual."

"Gosh," said Charles.

"You remember Peter the Hermit, lad."

"Yes!" Charles exclaimed. "That strange preacher. He was filthy and smelled like fish."

"Oh, that didn't bother people back them! In fact, it was an asset. They were mesmerized by him; followed him everywhere. He preached Holy War and common folk thought he was divine. They even pulled hairs from his donkey for relics." Theodore laughed. "He could have sold mutton to a shepherd, that one. The people of Rêve were among his followers, you know."

"Really?"

"Yes. And he had a fabulous prop."

"What?" Charles asked, watching Theodore's breath float out over the blackberry vines.

"A parchment he claimed was a letter from God, fallen from heaven!"

"You're kidding!"

"No, I am not," Theodore said. He noticed Charles's teeth clacking and rummaged in his satchel for the brandy flask. "Here you go, lad. Just a sip. Your father would kill me. Anyway, as I was saying, Peter's so-called letter commanded him to raise an army, go to Jerusalem and battle the unbelievers."

"I heard that he might have been Godfrey's tutor," Charles ventured, emboldened by the alcohol.

"It's a strange thing, that."

"Do you think it's true, Uncle?"

"Well, the two personages couldn't have been more different: a peerless young noble and a vagabond zealot. Except their piety, of course. Maybe the young Godfrey could confide in him somehow."

It was an odd comment. *Confide about what?* Charles thought. His mind raced with the doubts and insecurities of a modern teenager: hardly an indication of how one of the Nine Worthies might have traversed adolescence.

He rubbed his hands together to warm them and studied the black wall of forest, which seemed to have locked away both the nobleman and the preacher with no intention of releasing them any time soon. How had the tutorials worked, exactly? Had Godfrey visited Peter in a hermit's cell somewhere in the wilderness to take instruction? It was a hypothesis as outlandish as the thought of the stinking preacher with bare, skinny ankles and soiled tunic being ushered into the ducal quarters at Bouillon Castle.

Theodore broke into this meditation. "You know, Charles, Peter the Hermit was backed up by some very bizarre events. Earthquakes, famine, pestilence and such. He would have considered them signs from heaven—portents of the Last Days."

"Wasn't there a huge meteorite shower?" Charles said.

"Yes, in the spring of 1095. The following February, the moon turned blood-red during an eclipse. Comets streaked across the sky and famine gripped the land. Oh, they were wondrous and terrible times! One of the chroniclers described torches of fire flying through the air—attested to by many witnesses. A woman claimed that a goose infused with the Holy Spirit would lead her to Jerusalem. Stablemen saw mounted warriors clash in the sky..."

Theodore suddenly broke off and grabbed Charles's leg.

"*Shhh!*" he hissed. "Look!"

XLIX

The wind stole in from the river and met them head-on: three gusts, like warnings. Then nothing.

Theodore glanced overhead. "Yes, indeed. We might see them tonight."

"What are we looking for, exactly?" Charles whispered. He looked up, surprised to see that the stars had been dimmed by the weather the wind had brought with it. He wondered how this change would have signaled to Theodore an opportunity to see them—whoever "they" might be.

"Look over there, lad," Theodore pointed. "Near the center of the field."

Charles peered at the place his uncle was indicating. Ground fog was starting to rise off the meadow.

"It's necessary to pick a spot like that and concentrate on it," Theodore said. His words were barely audible.

"But what are we looking for, Uncle?" Charles asked again, trembling.

"You must *become* history, lad," Theodore answered. "You must *feel* it. Now, think hard. It's 1096."

Charles sensed where his uncle was going with this. He concentrated on a grassy lump in the field and said nothing.

"You're Charles de la Fontaine, a peasant from Rêve," Theodore continued in a low voice. "You've toiled from dawn until dusk in the lord's fields all your life. You've never gone anywhere except perhaps a neighboring village—if you were adventurous. Everything you do is in the shadow of sin and damnation and the whim of an all-powerful church. You're superstitious; ignorant. The crops have failed. Your children are ill. Desperate, you make a pilgrimage to some wayside shrine containing a bone from the wrist of an obscure saint, but that doesn't help. A traveler tries to sell you a sliver of wood that he picked up from a merchant in Damascus, who said that his brother had bought it from a Turk in Constantinople, who claimed that it came from the True Cross. But you have no money to buy it.

"Then someone mentions Jerusalem: God's City. The navel of the world. Oh, what a magnificent journey it would be to liberate the tomb of Christ! To absolve all your sins and secure a place in paradise. Who wouldn't be tempted?"

Charles continued staring at the field. His heart ached for Theodore's downtrodden peasant—the poor man whose life he'd briefly entered. He felt something warm inside him where the cold had just been clamping down so hard.

"Should I still be looking at that space?" he asked. His voice caught. It didn't seem to belong to him.

"Of course!" Theodore said in a stage whisper. "Let the past coalesce."

They waited.

Nothing coalesced.

A creature rustled through the weeds; a bat dipped low over their heads.

Charles considered abandoning the project entirely when suddenly the meadow changed its aspect. Spellbound, he watched as the ground fog shifted. Wisps broke loose and began to drift.

At once a sound split the night in a long, painful rent.

Charles lifted an inch or two off the tree trunk.

"An olifant!" Theodore said gleefully. He glanced at his nephew: the boy was clearly shaken. "No, it's not, lad." He patted Charles's knee. "Don't worry. It's only a stag in rut."

But Charles wasn't so sure. Theodore's words had grown inexplicably faint and something else was taking their place. In the wake of the renting sound, the air seemed to lighten and separate. Charles found himself looking through this numinous gap at the meadow as it once was: a tableau from the past whose air he was now able to breathe.

The wisps of fog began to coalesce just as Theodore had predicted. Shapes formed with recognizable elements. Charles detected the bulk of an ox and a corner of the wagon it was pulling; he watched a man, weeping, say good-bye to his wife, who fell senseless to the ground. A monk glided barefoot toward the forest and dissolved into it. A cloaked arm broke through the vapors, brandishing a cross made of two sticks strapped together.

The stirring in Charles grew stronger. He felt hot, then cold again. "Uncle!" he gasped, suddenly terrified that someone he recognized might appear: Peter the Hermit, for example.

"I know, lad," Theodore said under his breath. "I know."

"Can you see it?" Charles breathed.

"My own version, yes."

They watched the pantomime of fog and air without speaking. In Charles's version, the weeping man lifted his wife from the grass, gently pried her hands from his tunic and walked away. He followed the path the monk had taken, stopping only once to look back. The ox and cart began to lumber off.

At length the shapes disappeared as quickly as they'd come. Whether the wind had snatched them, or the night sky, was impossible to tell.

Across the river, the last light in the village went out.

"Poor, stupid devils," Theodore muttered. He got up, stretched and slung the satchel over his shoulder.

"Why?" Charles said. He scanned the empty field. Everything he'd witnessed had vanished.

"They were going to their doom, that's why," Theodore said, picking his way back through the nettle. "All the people you just saw. They thought they were going to witness the dawn of the great New Jerusalem, but hunger and disease decimated them. They pillaged to survive. Then the Turks massacred them at Civetot."

Theodore lumbered along wearily, his usual bonhomie absent. "The greatest tragedy," he said, "is that most common men and women are lost to history. People who carried the sick and elderly on their backs; who gave birth in the desert and left their still-born babies in the dirt; who cooked up leather soles and animal hides to eat and drained blood from their precious donkeys and oxen to drink. Their names have been lost forever. It's up to you and me to fill in these peoples' stories, lad; to make connections. It's the only way that the historical record makes any sense to our own future."

Charles followed his uncle back to the forest path. He turned around to see if maybe, through some intervention, he might glimpse that weeping man again—perhaps even warn him of what was to come. But the field had closed in on itself. There was no fog. No movement of any kind.

Later he would consider that the very absence of these things was proof enough that they'd existed in the first place.

They proceeded in silence to the crossroads, where starlight had faded to a mere suggestion.

Theodore stopped briefly to catch his breath. He said: "Why have people never learned to keep God to themselves, in their own hearts, where the life of the spirit resides? Imagine what bloodshed could have been avoided if they had!"

L

It all happened in an instant.

One moment, Theodore was shambling ahead of Charles on the path, swinging his satchel. The next, the night seemed to have swallowed him whole.

"Uncle!" Even as he cried the word it occurred to Charles that he should be much louder...much bolder. But something held him back: a subconscious warning, perhaps, that the forest night reigned supreme and one wouldn't want to disturb any of its denizens. The prowlers of crossroads came to mind. Hecate sometimes had company of an evening: the devil himself, trotting at her side with his cloven clip-clop.

"*Uncle!*"

But Theodore was gone.

Charles struck off at a run, sweating in his oilskin. Beech, pine, oak...a gallery of stately witnesses leaned in toward him. They were not silent, though—no woodland ever is. *Why are you here, boy?* they seemed to be saying. *Don't you know what comes alive at night?* And then: *Perhaps this is a good time for you to find out...*

He remembered the two things he needed to navigate by: the river; and the thump of his uncle's boots. With one gone he must now look for the other. He stood still on the path and closed his eyes. It was Theodore himself who'd shown him how to discover things this way.

Sure enough, he heard it: the gurgle of a river eddy.

He left the path and plunged through the undergrowth. Soon the river's rush greeted him, and in the spaces between the crowding black trunks he could see shards of light glitter on the water, borrowed from the stars. He was not far from the village on the other side, he reckoned. Perhaps Rêve's swans were even dozing somewhere nearby.

"Uncle?" Charles called from the river's edge. "Where are you?" He fought back tears.

He sat on the bank's grassy lip and gazed at the river-forest wavering in the eddy—the world he imagined lived beneath the water's surface. *What things from the past had been caught there?*

Charles took a piece of stale chocolate from his pocket and gnawed on it. His heartbeat settled somewhat. To find his way back to Villa Antioch, all he had to do was to follow the river. He tried not to think of the misty field he'd just visited. Rather, he consoled himself with thoughts of the female sages who'd revered these woods and found peace in them—of Arda in particular, Rêve's pagan saint, who'd somehow managed to unite two world philosophies.

Theodore must have been worried, though. Neither of them had thought to take a phone into the forest. Mobile service was so spotty, anyway. Exhausted, Charles lay back on the grass. Soon his head filled with the comforting sound of his uncle's voice, not calling his name, oddly enough, but discussing the subject they both adored.

"History begs us to make leaps, Charles," Theodore was saying. "Like electricity jumping filaments in a light bulb. Such leaps follow the laws of nature. They really do. And you're rewarded with quite a bit of illumination in the end."

"We have to leap with people like Godfrey, don't we, Uncle?"

"Ah, yes...Godfrey."

"What was he like?" Charles asked eagerly.

"Well, we don't have much to go on. The best description I've read was written by the twelfth-century chronicler, William of Tyre. Let's see what I remember: 'Godfrey was a virtuous man, generous, upright and pious. Resolute in his words. Enemy of all evil. He detested the glories of this world, rare for a man of arms. He was benevolent and compassionate; very affable. He was also tall, strong and comely with light chestnut hair and beard.'"

"Was he really like that?" Charles pressed him.

Theodore laughed. "You have the instincts of a true researcher, lad! You have to prove your facts. Well, whenever I read Godfrey's story there always seems to be quite a lot missing. This fuels his myth, of course. People love an enigmatic hero. All of us have one side toward the light and one in shadow, don't we, lad? Godfrey never turned his shadowy side to the light, I suppose."

Charles got to his feet. He planned to pick his way over the roots and rocks along the bank until he rejoined the path they'd taken to the meadow.

He glanced at the water again before leaving and recoiled:

A face was looking back at him.

He leaned closer, heart pounding: the image bobbed and twisted on the eddy. *Was it his own?* He wasn't so sure. His pulse faltered: *the skinny hermit's?*

Charles stood very still and stared at the water. His breathing came in airless gulps. The eddy dimpled in a breeze and he couldn't be sure if the face was still there. He wheeled around, for the person must have been standing right behind him, leaning over his shoulder.

But there were only trees.

"Uncle!" he called once more, peering between the jostling trunks. "Are you there?"

Defeated, he sank back onto the bank. It had been such a long evening. Cold and startling, too. He watched the stars in their remote, icy palace and traced the Milky Way along its celestial river-bed. Before long, his eyelids grew heavy and closed.

"*Charles!*"

It was not the deep river-tone of a dream.

"There you are, *nom de Dieu!*" Theodore cried, blundering up. "What the hell happened?" He helped his nephew to his feet.

"Is there anyone behind you?" Charles said sleepily.

"Lad, it's me! You must have been dozing. Come on, we need to get you home. You've had quite an evening."

Charles was starting off after his uncle when something caught his attention: a tiny flash of white in the grass where he'd just been. He parted the blades and retrieved something so fine and soft, so weightless, it was more air than substance:

A feather of swansdown.

210

LI

Charles watched from the turret window as his young self crossed the stone bridge with his uncle and disappeared.

He glanced at his watch: the flight of memory had taken less than ten minutes. How pliable time was! You might endure an hour that seemed endless and unfulfilled, while in just a few minutes, without the slightest effort, you could leap from maturity to childhood—from the present moment to one centuries ago.

He was turning from the window when a movement caught his eye.

At first he assumed it was still his mind animating the view.

Then he noticed that a man had emerged from under the willow.

How long he'd been concealed by the drooping branches was impossible to say, as his beige raincoat blended so well with the dying leaves. He was hurrying across the bridge now. Seen from a distance, it was more of a scuttle than a run, as the man was short and squat. He tilted his head forward as he walked as if to gain speed, but his progress was impeded by the raincoat, which fell almost to his ankles.

He stopped at the far end of the bridge and turned around.

Charles drew back. His heart jumped.

Had he been spotted?

The stranger lingered for some moments, looking up at the house.

Charles stared out from the shadows of the room. Images flooded in: ghostly features at the study window...papers scattered across the floor. He glanced with relief at his laptop bag, which he'd carried up to the turret with him, although there was absolutely no indication that the man on the bridge had had anything to do with the break-in. Walkers occasionally strayed along the river this far.

This person did not appear to be sightseeing, however.

The man followed the base of the ridge until he found a gap in the trees and melted into it.

Charles grabbed his bag and burst out of the turret room. He took the stairs two at a time, the bag banging against his knee. He reached the front hall and rushed along the corridor to the terrace door, fumbling the lock and flinging it open.

He surveyed the meadow from the terrace railing. The panorama seemed unusually empty—maybe because it had so recently been populated by dream-folk. There was no sign of the intruder. Only the rooks betrayed some sort of disturbance. Having been dislodged from the willow by the man hiding beneath it, they were now returning to their perches one by one, like misshapen notes in a bleak melody.

Charles sighed and went inside. The forest was capable of swallowing so much: prophetesses and strange animals; hermits and sorcerers. Even entire armies.

To swallow a squat little man in a raincoat would have taken no effort at all.

It was early afternoon and Charles was ravenous. By some miracle, he discovered one remaining meal in the freezer made by Marcel Wauters. *Carbonnade:* a favorite of Theodore's.

He was just turning on the microwave when his phone rang.

Sylvana's name showed on his screen.

His pulse tripped. *She'd kept her promise to call!*

"Do you still want to go to the cave today?" she asked without a greeting.

Rather perfunctory, Charles thought. He said: "But aren't you going back to Brussels?"

"Later, around six this evening."

"I could give you a lift tomorrow morning," he suggested. "I have to go to Brussels anyway."

"I have lessons to teach in Brussels tomorrow morning."

"Ah. Of course."

"I can be at Antioch in about half an hour," she said, and hung up.

Charles warmed up his meal and sat at the rickety table at the kitchen window. Huge cumulus clouds with dark bellies hovered over the ridge. They changed by the minute in the wind, now sculpted into towering columns and pediments, now pulling asunder into puffy, light-filled valleys. The sky above Blancheron Castle was a realm that Charles knew well. In his youth, he'd constructed whole cities from these clouds, with marble and porphyry, gold and precious stones.

Today's sky would be like that, he thought, pleased that his excursion with Sylvana would be so honored. Then he remembered her mood over the phone and his pleasure soured.

He considered the one letter she'd written: she'd shared substantial things with him, about her plans for studying music and giving beauty back to the world; about her extraordinary discovery of the cave near the pond. She'd been solicitous and kind at Theodore's funeral. But now she seemed to have sensed the paradox that Charles had also detected: that they were two individuals who shared deep loves—for the forest, and for Theodore—but in fact hardly knew each other.

LII

She arrived on a bicycle.

Charles caught sight of her through the salon window and opened the front door before she rang. Sylvana had no helmet or reflecting jacket, just a backpack slung over her cape and her walking stick balanced across the bicycle basket. Her hair had burgeoned into a wild mass from the wind of her ride.

"I hope you don't mind," she said by way of a greeting, leaning the bike against the railing of the terrace. "This is where I used put it when I came to help Theodore."

"Of course I don't mind!" Charles said. "Would you like some coffee or something?"

Sylvana gave him a brief smile. "No, thank you. We should go before it gets too late." She glanced up at the sky. "I'm not sure this weather will hold."

"By the way," he said. "I can give you a lift to Libramont after our hike. You can leave the bicycle here if you want. Or I can drop it by your mother's."

Sylvana hesitated. "I'll manage on my own," she said. She took the terrace steps in two bounds and headed off to the woods.

Charles grabbed his laptop bag and Theodore's oilskin and sprinted after her.

They advanced briskly down the beech alley. Sylvana had the stride of a true walker and Charles delighted in matching his pace to hers. He savored this first excursion into his beloved forest since returning to Belgium, breathing in the richness of autumn—that savory potpourri that took months to blend, of things newborn, living and dying. Nature didn't distinguish between these phases as humans did, Charles mused. A pity, really, that we lacked the wisdom to even acknowledge this divine circle, let alone follow it at its own pace, with patience and love, reveling in the deep comfort that it had no beginning or end.

Sylvana said nothing as they walked. Her chin was lifted as if in deference to the trees, her profile remote. If companionable silence was as viable a form of communication as lively conversation, according to Theodore, it was soon apparent that the silence guiding this particular rendezvous was of a different sort. Wary and apprehensive came to mind. Indeed, as they advanced down the alley, the beeches seemed to be better company than Sylvana.

Finally she said: "How are you managing?"

"Well, I'm confused, to be honest," Charles said, his irritation rising. Sylvana seemed deliberately aloof.

She glanced at him as she walked. "Confused about...?"

"I just don't believe that Theodore died of natural causes."

Sylvana stopped in the middle of the alley and gave Charles her full attention. "What do you mean?"

He met her stare. "What I mean is, he was as sturdy as a bull, for one thing. And for another, he'd had a suspicious visitor on the night of his death."

"A visitor..." Sylvana breathed, contrite now. "But who?"

"I think it was the same person who broke into the villa last night and ransacked the study."

"*Mon Dieu!*"

"He was after the parchment, I'm fairly certain."

"Parchment?" The queenly regard softened further.

Charles looked at her in surprise. Theodore clearly hadn't said anything to her about the folio. "My uncle assumed it was an alternative ending of the heron legend," he said. "You know: the translation that I gave you yesterday. Theodore kept the folio in a secret place in his desk. It was safe there. I'm taking it to Cédric Florus tomorrow, the former head of manuscripts at the Library of European History."

Sylvana reached into her backpack and handed Charles the envelope he'd lent her. "It's quite a story," she said. "You must tell me what Florus has to say about it."

They struck off into dense woodland leading to the pond. Sylvana asked about Theodore's nocturnal visitor as they walked: whether he'd known him, and if there had been violence, ruing that she'd been in Brussels that day. *Was he after the parchment? What on earth does it contain?* They were the same questions Charles had asked himself many times and soon their unease began to loosen. When wordlessness once again seemed the best option, words were not missed this time, especially when the woods themselves were speaking incessantly, in the shiver of leaves, or a hawk's piercing cry.

A small clearing opened up and Sylvana stopped to poke the vegetation with her walking stick, lifting a blackberry vine and examining a stand of stinging nettle. Charles, who remembered her light-hearted explanation of the distaff and wondered to what other uses she could put her stick, hadn't considered this one. *Did she dowse for water, too?*

"There are many medicinal plants in this part of the woods," she said, talking more to the plants than to Charles. "I'll just be a minute," she added, her cape catching on a vine as she plucked a leaf from the long grass. This she handed to him.

"An afternoon snack!" she teased. "Try it."

He chewed on the leaf, which he recognized as plantain by its long parallel veins. It had a light mushroom aftertaste. "Theodore used to put this on my cuts," he said. "But he never said you could eat it!"

"It has many healing uses," said Sylvana, gathering more plantain and tucking it into her pocket. Then she handed Charles a heart-shaped leaf. "This is butterbur," she said. "It's best in spring, but you can try it." He did, surprised by the earthy, bitter taste. "It's used for migraine, hay fever, asthma," she said. "Lots of conditions. The roots are dug up in autumn."

"Where did you learn all this?" Charles marveled.

"Actually, from Ida," she smiled. At his astonishment, she explained: "You don't think I go to Ida's just for the piano, do you?" She laughed in counterpoint to the wrens squabbling in the pines. "Your aunt actually has a herb garden in Brussels with all sorts of medicinal plants. But alas, she's let it go. It's more of a jungle now."

Charles remembered this side of Ida: how much she appreciated the *idea* of something, but being a dreamer often lacked the practicality to implement it.

Sylvana broke into his thoughts. "You know, Charles, women used to chant when they picked plants. Yes, it's true! They were chants of respect...reverence. All that is lost. The chants, songs, words of wisdom, nature knowledge—none of it was written down by the clergy, and of course the local people were illiterate...Look!" she cried suddenly. She pointed with her stick to muddy patches in the grass. "The deer have been here."

Charles peered at the ground. "Did you know that when the two cleaves of a deer's hoof are together, they're walking?" he said. Sylvana shook her head, and Charles relished the fact that he could teach her something about the wilderness. "If the cleaves are a bit open," he went on, "they're trotting. And when they open up completely and there's a "V" on the ground, they're galloping."

"You learned that from Theodore, didn't you?" Sylvana said.

"Yes."

"Those deer were running," she remarked, pointing with her stick to "V" imprints in the mud. "Recently, too. Maybe someone spooked them while they were grazing."

A cool hand passed over Charles. *Had the man in the raincoat crossed this clearing?*

"Sylvana..." he began. He longed to confide in her about the stranger on the bridge...about the face at the study window. But his companion was mercurial. She might react strangely to news of a trespasser. *Why risk their fragile accord?*

They skirted the pond and began climbing the rocky outcrop to the spring. Sylvana took the lead, her boots skittering on the loose shale. Charles leaned into the steep, tangled vegetation and wondered who had climbed here before them. Arda, fleeing Walderic's men... Henri of Rêve, his heart more turbulent than armed pilgrimage.

And the descent... How difficult it would be to carry something heavy down this slope!

Rodolfo, bearing the murdered Arda from her cave...

They both heard the note at the same time: water purling around a single repeating tone. *A prehistoric sound*, Theodore said. *As old as Earth herself.*

They gained the natural platform at the spring. Charles smiled at his own surprise that the note hadn't changed. *What were seventeen years in the vastness of millennia?* He looked deep into Sylvana's eyes and navigated those changeable green pools, and he saw that she, too, had recognized the tone. Her steadfast gaze bolstered him.

He touched her cheek.

"You have a look in your eyes, Charles d'Outre-mer," she said. To his surprise, she placed her hand over his. "I noticed it before. Like you can see greater distances than most people."

He drew in his breath. "You sound like someone I knew in America," he said.

Sylvana hesitated. "A woman?"

He laughed. "Yes. Grace Holmes."

"Oh..."

Charles took the rash step of enveloping Sylvana in his arms. "Don't worry," he murmured, his nerves pulsing. "She was an older lady. Very wise. A seeress of the suburbs, you could say."

"You loved her, this Grace," Sylvana said. "I can tell."

"Yes, I did."

For a moment they stood next to the spring in tight embrace. Sylvana made no effort to extract herself—a singular development, Charles thought, considering her earlier remoteness. A chevron of ducks flew overhead and the two pilgrims listened to the doleful chorus fade away.

"You always had to draw water in solemn silence," Sylvana said, speaking from the depths of Charles's embrace. "It was sacred."

Charles stepped back. "The wisdom you talk about isn't lost, Sylvana." He gestured to the forest. "It lives here, in this green church."

"And we must keep it alive," she said.

They took turns kneeling on the mossy prie-dieu and sipping from the basin.

LIII

I t's here somewhere," Sylvana said.

They inched along a narrow ledge. A tangle of vines draped the rock face and they clung to them, trying not to look over the edge.

Charles parted the overgrowth where Sylvana was indicating.

At once he lost his balance and fell against the vines. It seemed that they were strong enough to hold him.

But they gave way.

"Charles!" Sylvana cried, and blundered after him through the opening. She helped him up from what appeared to be the floor of a cave.

They stood in the close, fetid space, their breathing shallow. An immense heaviness seemed to bear down on their shoulders.

"Do you feel it?" Sylvana whispered. Fear laced her words. She reached for Charles's hand and held it tight.

"It reminds me of the underground passage at Bouillon Castle," Charles muttered. "The same incredible weight."

"The weight of time," Sylvana muttered.

"The weight of *deeds*," he said. "How could anyone have lived here?" *Let alone a baby*, he thought, but said nothing to Sylvana. She would learn about it soon enough once Florus finished translating the parchment.

Did Arda actually give birth in this hovel?

Charles took out his phone and turned on the flashlight.

They both gasped: the cave extended deep into the side of the hill. The ceiling arched high into the shadows. The floor was a damp, matted layer of decaying leaves, fungi, animal droppings and mud, their redolence forever entombed.

"Look!" cried Charles, moving toward the wall. Two rough stones formed an altar of sorts on which someone had balanced a crude statue of the Virgin.

"It looks fairly recent," Sylvana said. "Marble, I'd say."

"Only two hundred years old instead of nine hundred?" Charles joked.

Sylvana smiled, but without humor. "It could be older than that," she said. "At some point, Arda's dwelling must have been discovered and the proselytizers moved in. Strange that they never left any votive offerings at the spring."

"If indeed Arda lived here at all."

"I've wandered through acres of forest around the pond and this is the only cave I've found," Sylvana said.

"Uncle wandered for decades and never found one," Charles added.

"According to your grandfather's translation, Rodolfo found Arda dead," Sylvana said. "In a cave. She'd been murdered. Then he buried her in the forest." She sighed. "We'll never know the truth, will we?"

"No," said Charles. He shone his flashlight deeper into the cave.

"To murder someone so close to a sacred spot would have been a sacrilege for the old beliefs," Sylvana said. "Like killing in a church."

"Yes." Charles drifted into the gloom.

A lord with splendid hand hunted the lady to her cave in the forest, defiled her, and cut her throat.

"Who do you think murdered her?" Sylvana pressed him.

Charles paused, his back to her. For a moment they both labored with their breathing in the airlessness.

He turned around. "Sylvana..." he began.

And he told her what Theodore had managed to translate of the alternative ending.

Most people would have left this sepulchral place by now. But Sylvana had been so moved by Charles's revelations that she burst into motion, scouring the cave for clues.

"Oh, Charles," she anguished, taking short, sharp breaths. "Imagine finding a baby in this hellhole! Please, shine the light over here."

Charles trained the beam on the pile of detritus she was probing with her stick. "What are we looking for, exactly?" he asked, sweat clinging to his shirt. "My phone doesn't have much battery left."

"I don't know...anything that might prove Arda was here."

"There isn't much that can last for nine hundred years," Charles reminded her.

"Her ceramic bowl, maybe," Sylvana said hopefully.

They spent a good hour turning the cave into an archaeological dig. The labor required every molecule of oxygen left in the space and they had to rest often.

At last Charles took Sylvana's arm. "Come," he said, pulling her gently. "You don't want to miss your train. In the words of the inimitable Theodore: 'Things are discovered only when the time is right.'"

Sylvana followed him to the cave entrance. "Your uncle was never wrong," she said. "Alas."

She bent to adjust her boot and gasped.

"What is it?" Charles said.

Sylvana prodded the ground with her walking stick. "There's something next to my boot!"

Charles shone the light where she was indicating.

With care she dislodged something from its bed.

They both let out a cry:

A dagger.

"Christ..." Charles mouthed, handing Sylvana his phone. He picked up the object and brushed it off. Rust had eaten at the iron blade but the hilt was in fine condition. "This could be bronze," he whispered, running his fingers over the grip. "And look at this!"

Sylvana held the flashlight over his hands. The cross guard was set with polished gems that winked awake after their long sleep.

"How old do you think it is?" Sylvana asked.

"It looks medieval to me," Charles said. "Maybe even from the 1100s." He indicated the gold interlocking pattern on the grip. "This is a Celtic design. It was often used in early Christian decorations." He lay the dagger across his palms. "This must have belonged to a rich man."

Sylvana caught her breath. "Arda's murder weapon?"

"Maybe."

Neither of them spoke as the scenario played out before them: *A man of rank and privilege clambered up the steep slope to the spring and discovered the cliff path. He found the cave and entered. There she was, the heathen enchantress he was looking for. He raped her. Then he slit her throat.*

"And the baby?" Sylvana whispered.

"It must have been sleeping...covered up."

"Rodolfo found them both, then. Arda's body...and her child."

"Yes."

"But a rich man would have had all sorts of flunkeys to do his dirty work, wouldn't he?"

"Not if it was a crime of passion," Charles said.

"How did he find her, do you think?"

"The cave may not have been so remote back then. Even though she tried to conceal herself, Arda was a healer, remember...a diviner. People from the village would have known where to go."

Charles photographed the dagger with his phone camera to show Cédric Florus when he went to see him the following day. Then he wrapped it in a handkerchief and put it away in his bag. They agreed that he should keep it in a safe place until Theodore's affairs were put in order. That meant the only safe place Charles knew: the secret compartment in his uncle's desk.

Together they inched their way back along the overgrown path and down the steep, slipping shale. The air glistened with the repeating note from the spring, but now they were too preoccupied to take notice. Charles paused at the bottom of the slope.

"I meant to tell you about the man I think might have ransacked Theodore's study," he said.

Sylvana regarded him quietly. "Oh?"

"I thought I saw him at the study window last night. And this morning, when I was visiting the turret room, I saw a man in a raincoat emerge from under the willow tree and cross the bridge."

"Not a tourist," Sylvana said.

"No."

"Where did he go?" There was a queer tone to her voice.

"Into the forest," he said. "He just vanished."

"What did he look like?"

"He was short, and pitched forward as he walked. His raincoat was long, almost to his ankles. Have you seen anyone like that around here?"

Sylvana glanced away. Her porcelain complexion, so recently flushed from her exertions, had gone pale.

"No, I haven't," she said, and strode off into the trees.

Sylvana didn't reappear. Disheartened, Charles resigned himself to her capriciousness and returned to the villa alone.

As he made his way back, he considered how people really did reflect their surroundings—sometimes to the point of *becoming* them. Theodore had achieved this over time, letting the wilderness pull at his hair and scuff his satchel, shape his boots and mold his spirit so that gradually, after many years, he started to resemble one of the forest's own. As for Sylvana...she seemed to have sprung from the woods fully formed, as perfectly adapted to her environment as any wild creature.

At once something darkened in Charles: the thought of his own father and *his* surroundings. How obvious it was now! Hugh Fontaine had become as hard-edged and unyielding as the cold steel of New York, just as Theodore had been softened and ruffled by Nature.

By the time Charles reached the pond the clouds had broken apart into fantastical shapes, gray at their base, edged with brilliance at their summits. They'd liberated a curious round space high over the water: a sort of basilica under which reigned a profound hush.

Charles stopped on the bank and looked up.

Something white gleamed in the heights of the dome. Just a flash. Nothing more.

Was it a trick of the air?

He held his breath.

Or had it lifted from the water?

There'd been no heron on the rock when he and Sylvana had passed on their way to the spring. And there certainly wasn't one there now. But as Charles observed the light spilling from the cloud-dome, it wasn't at all clear that a white feathered thing couldn't have risen up into the rays unperceived, and regained its kingdom in the sky.

PART FIVE

Awakening

LIV

He'd fully intended to call his father with his own version of events thus far, leaving out the break-in and any mention of the parchment. Hugh pre-empted him, however, on his drive to Brussels the following morning.

"Father, hello." Charles steered his rental car onto the verge of the E411 and turned off the engine. This would require all his wits.

"How's the sale progressing?" Hugh asked. His tone was chatty; vaguely warm.

"The funeral was only on Thursday. I need more time. And I'm exhausted."

"Surely you've spoken to Ames by now."

"Ames was at Rêve, yes," Charles hedged. He'd already suspected Ames's fealty to Hugh. *What, exactly, had the man promised to deliver? And how much had Hugh offered to pay him?*

"Good, good..." Hugh's words oiled their way over the international call, although Charles knew all too well that his father's pleasure usually came equipped with thorns.

"I assume that Osselaer has been in touch with you already," Charles said, amazed how anyone could not ask about his own brother's funeral...or how his sister was holding up. Even opportunism relied on basic niceties. Emperor Alexius himself, a many-faced ally at the best of times, had sugared every profitable relationship with courtesy.

"I spoke to Philippe this morning," said Hugh. "Apparently you're still going through Theodore's mess." He made no mention of a parchment.

"That's right. It might take some time. The house is packed with Uncle's things."

"A total chaos, I imagine. Did you find anything of value?"

"Well, there's the olifant," Charles said, deflecting comfortably now.

"Ah, yes. The olifant. Anything else?"

"No."

Silence ensued.

The car shuddered in the wake of a speeding truck.

"Did Ames give you any idea of a price for the property?" Hugh asked.

Charles faltered. Obviously Osselaer hadn't mentioned that Ames had been sidelined for the moment; or that there'd been an intruder at Villa Antioch.

"Listen, Charles," said Hugh. "Blancheron is going to be a major sale. Possibly of historic proportions."

"Oh?" Charles held the phone with a numb hand. The metal felt cold against his ear and he switched it to speaker.

"I'm relying on you..." Hugh said. His voice trailed, as if he'd been unwilling to say these words because they signaled weakness, but they'd overcome his defenses nonetheless.

Charles imagined his father in his office, strolling through the islands of expensive designer furniture. It seemed he could even hear the upper reaches of Manhattan through the airwaves: a quiet rush faintly punctuated by car horns, like a very distant army. He'd never understood how the heaving metropolis could appear at once so menacing and so benign.

"I need to make something absolutely clear," Hugh said, his defenses restored. "Do not do anything to interfere with this sale. Ames is responsible for assessing the things of historic value. Osselaer will draw up all the papers."

A tense, prickly pause.

"Charles?"

"Yes?"

"I cannot be responsible for what happens if you don't do this."

Charles said nothing. He surprised even himself by switching off his phone. The fact that he could do such a thing in the face of his father's threat encouraged him greatly. He recalled how Duke Godfrey, on passing through Constantinople with his army, had at first refused an audience with Alexius—let alone pledged him his allegiance—having had little faith in the emperor's honeyed promises.

Charles started the car and pulled back onto the highway. His encouragement was short-lived, however. For he knew that his father would succeed where he always had before, even if his son was an adult now: by giving Charles the illusion of freedom and extending his tether, only to yank him back into orbit when he'd strayed too far.

He arrived in Brussels by early afternoon and decided to drop by Ida's unannounced. Florus wasn't expecting him until four o'clock.

The day was gentle, sunny, with that early-autumn nostalgia that lures people to plazas and park benches around the city, deluding themselves that summer has not yet departed. Charles turned into Ida's street and parked the car some distance from the villa. Her gate was still out of order and he let himself in.

Once again, he could hear the piano before reaching the end of the alley; and once again, he slipped across the lawn to lean around the trunk of the weeping beech.

It was ridiculous, he knew, that a man of his age, dressed in a blazer, tie and cashmere overcoat and with "Ivy League" emblazoned on his forehead, should indulge in such behavior, but since arriving in Belgium he'd sensed that a singular endeavor was unfolding—an endeavor in the true, Grace-Holmes sense—and he shouldn't be too disturbed if bizarre situations happened to be part of his mission. He certainly shouldn't shirk them.

A man was seated at the piano.

Charles slumped against the tree in disappointment. He peered around again, considerably cheered to see Sylvana Longfaye herself sitting on the man's left, partially obscured from Charles's view.

It was clear that some sort of lesson was going on. Sylvana reached over to play a melody on the keyboard and the man tried to repeat it. Then she encouraged him to sing the same melody, which he did with an astonishingly rich baritone.

Charles straightened in surprise. He'd expected the voice to be as rough and unkempt as the man appeared to be. Disquieted, he left the tree and made his way up the cascading steps to Ida's front door. There he had to wait quite a while after ringing the bell.

This time it was Sylvana herself who opened the door.

"*Bonjour*," said Charles, his equilibrium askew. He hadn't expected this. *Had she given the student something to do in her absence?*

"Ida isn't very well today," Sylvana said, hanging Charles's coat on one of the hooks in the hall. "She's resting, but should be down in a few minutes. Are you on your way to see Florus?"

"Yes," he said. "Later this afternoon."

They stood face to face, both unsure how to proceed. Charles, brimming with things to say about Arda and the tragedy in the cave, said nothing. It already seemed as if a month had passed since they'd visited the cave together. Sylvana's hauteur left him with the impression that at best, their adventure had only briefly impacted her.

She seemed peaked; out of sorts. It was the first time Charles had seen Sylvana indoors, a foreign habitat for her, he realized. It was as if a forest creature had been captured between four walls and exhausted itself pacing. He eyed her long, dun-colored skirt and simple white blouse, and as before he was drawn irresistibly to her asceticism. He'd long since had his fill of posh females who used their looks as currency.

"Come to the kitchen," Sylvana said, and moved off soundlessly in soft-soled shoes. "I have to finish my lesson."

This last comment jerked Charles's thoughts back to the man in the salon, whom he'd completely forgotten. He followed Sylvana to the kitchen, passing by the graceful, arcing staircase on the left and salon entrance on the right, where he paused to steal a glance at the pupil.

The man had turned away from the keyboard and was writing something in a notebook, his back to Charles. His dark hair was cropped unevenly. His shirt seemed like a wrinkled sack. He was bent in earnest over the page and seemed unaware of his observer.

"One of your regular students?" Charles asked casually.

"Yes," Sylvana said. Her unease was palpable.

"He sings well for...for a..."

"For a vagrant, you mean?" she challenged him. "Such people are my pupils, Charles."

"Sylvana, I..."

"I'll go up to tell Ida you're here," she cut in, and hurried from the kitchen.

LV

Charles waited at the scrubbed table for a good thirty minutes, watching two crows preening in the lower branches of the pines and listening to the occasional piano chord from the salon. Regret filled him that he'd said what he had about Sylvana's student. He also rued that he hadn't brought Ida flowers. She would undoubtedly think that he'd picked up some boorish American habits during his absence.

She appeared in the doorway, as white in all her aspect as he'd ever seen her.

Charles jumped to his feet. "Auntie! I should have called first, I'm sorry."

She floated to him, feather-light. Her dressing gown, of heavy velour, disguised most of her frailty, but Charles recoiled at how thin she still seemed under the sash. Her hair fell to her waist in a lusterless ponytail.

They embraced.

"Poor, dear Theo," Ida whispered, wiping away a tear. "Ah, *Sharl'*... I miss him so."

Charles, who thought he'd mastered his grief, felt his eyes welling.

"Do you need anything?" he asked, taking his aunt by the shoulders and looking into her face. "Have you seen a doctor?"

"I never go to doctors," she snapped. "Anyway, I have Sylvana. And Philippe did some shopping for me after he brought me home from the funeral."

Ida moved to the stove and fired up the gas ring under the kettle.

I have Sylvana...

"Is Sylvana your housekeeper, then?" Charles asked, as innocently as he could. There would be a suitable moment to tell his aunt about their excursion to the cave, but this was not it.

Ida gave an incredulous chuckle. "Housekeeper? Oh, no! She just helps me out from time to time in exchange for using my piano. And she's become an expert in healing herbs."

"Ah, yes," Charles mumbled, recalling the earthy flavors of plantain and butterbur.

Said Ida: "I was just wandering through the streets about a year and a half ago when I heard her singing."

"On the street?"

"Of course not!" Ida seemed genuinely affronted. "Sylvana? She's not a common minstrel! Not at all. She's a kind of musical sybil, I would say."

The description arrested Charles. A memory flared. *The lyra throbbed and sighed and the girl sang aching melodies that echoed it.*

"There's a warren of streets near the Place du Châtelain, as you might remember," Ida continued, filtering coffee into a china pot. "And endless rows of those old Brussels townhouses. Many of them have barred windows just below pavement level where you can see into the basement—if you're nosey, like me. (And if you can see through all the dirt.) She was singing down there, in a house behind the church at the end of Rue du Bailli. The piano she was accompanying herself on was a relic, but it didn't matter. She was obviously connecting with a higher power. Her muse, perhaps."

Ida served them coffee and they sat side by side at the table, listening to the distant music. The usual synergy passed between them and Charles's equilibrium returned.

He was as transfixed by Ida's description of Sylvana and her music as he was by the image of his aunt trawling the gritty cobbled streets, undoubtedly clad in some flowing garment or other, looking more like a beggar than a member of the Belgian gentry. Hugh Fontaine had dismissed the entire class of them with some rare metaphorical prowess: "The aristocracy is a tangled root system, Charles, producing blooms that are prematurely old at birth, like your Aunt Ida. Oh, they're lovely, those sad blooms. But the petals are browning, and drop off at the slightest breeze."

At that moment Sylvana's pupil hurried past the kitchen window.

Ida lifted her coffee cup to him but he was furtive, grim-faced, and gave no indication that he'd seen her. He disappeared behind the pines in a matter of seconds.

"That was Raul," Ida said, more to her cup than to Charles. "Raul Mora." Something in her aspect had changed: a door had drifted shut.

"Why is he leaving through the back garden?" Charles asked.

Ida threaded her delicate fingers around her coffee cup. "*Sharl',*" she began. "I've known Raul for many years." Her words were measured; distant. "He's in difficulty. I knew that Sylvana would connect with him because of her intuition...because of her music. Most of her pupils are in difficulty, you know."

"Yes, I understand that now," Charles said, wishing that he'd understood it earlier.

"She seems to thrive on the challenge," Ida continued. "She's found a room for him in the building where she lives. I give him a bit of money for rent and food. He can be anonymous there." She looked out at the pines. "And safe."

"Safe?" Charles repeated.

"Yes," Ida said softly. "You see...he's wanted by the police."

Charles sat rigid. He had to suppress a guffaw. "You mean you're abetting a criminal?" he exclaimed. The thought was as outrageous as it was intriguing. Particularly when the criminal in question had such a fine baritone.

"Not abetting," said Ida. "I'm trying to rehabilitate him."

"But why? What has he done?"

"Oh, he started with petty thieving, that sort of thing. But then he became involved in bigger jobs: stealing artworks, mainly. Antiques. For a sophisticated ring."

Ida busied herself with the coffee pot, her hands as translucent as the porcelain. "And there's something else."

Charles followed the dance of her hands as he waited for her to continue. They might have grown more fragile over the years, but their beauty was intact.

Slowly, Ida set the pot back on the table. "Charles," she began. "Raul is wanted for murder."

"*What?*" Charles clacked his cup on the saucer. "I don't understand. Auntie, you're obviously in danger. And Sylvana..." Bile rose in his throat. He thought of that ravishing sibyl—of how her hands had been guiding a murderer's over the piano keys.

"Oh, I don't think he's guilty," Ida said. She sounded tired; irritated.

"What crime has he been accused of?" Charles asked tonelessly.

"An antiques dealer in Antwerp."

Charles froze. He could still recite Sylvana's letter by heart. How could he have forgotten the subtle way in which she'd implied his father's connection with the murder in Antwerp? She'd made no mention of Raul, however. *Did she know what he'd done?*

"I think that Raul was framed," Ida said. "He's not a murderer, Charles! The real culprit was even caught on a surveillance camera, for heaven's sake: he was much taller. With silver hair. Someone with connections turned the whole thing around to implicate Raul."

"Is Father involved somehow?" Charles said with the voice of an automaton.

Ida stared at him. "You know, then?"

"Well, let's just say that I wouldn't be surprised. A tall man with silver hair...might that have been Manfred Ames, Father's right-hand man in Brussels? The guy who turned up at the funeral?"

Ida said nothing. They sipped their coffee for a few minutes and listened to Sylvana sing a curious melody that rose to successively higher points, as if the singer were asking questions, and as the answers came, she sang her way closer and closer to the source.

"How on earth did you meet Raul?" Charles asked, not at all convinced that this feral man was *not* capable of murder.

"He simply turned up."

Charles studied her for any sign of guile, but in vain.

"I'd known his mother, you see, long ago," Ida explained. "She was of Spanish origin—her surname was Mora. She ran a restaurant near the Place du Châtelain. His father...well, that's another story. I met Raul when he was very young. He was abandoned by his parents early on and sent to a series of foster homes, *le pauvre*. In the last one, terrible things happened to him. Unspeakable things..."

Ida hesitated. In an attempt to lighten the mood, she said: "Raul reminds me of Beethoven, somehow." At Charles's bafflement she added: "Some say that Beethoven had Moorish origins, you know. Anyway, Raul certainly has his glower!"

Beethoven? The comparison seemed wanting on a number of fronts, not least the musical one.

"Charles," said Ida. "Even if Raul *is* guilty of something, how can someone with his experiences be blamed for breaking the law?"

And indeed, Charles began to wonder this himself. He also wondered why a single murder, perpetrated by someone who had been abused and framed, seemed so much more horrifying than uncountable atrocities. Jerusalem in 1099, for example. He stalled at these thoughts, unable to erase the sight of a miscreant's fingers brushing against those of a seeress.

"Life on the run has damaged him," Ida went on. "He speaks very little—just a few words. I knew that Sylvana of all people would be able to connect with him."

"A renegade, tamed by music..." Charles said this lightly but his heart was dark.

"Something like that," Ida said.

"Does Sylvana know his secrets?"

"I'm not sure what she knows."

"You didn't tell her?!"

"No."

Ida seemed unwilling to continue the conversation any further.

The music in the salon stopped. Sylvana closed the front door behind her without coming to the kitchen to say good-bye.

"Do come to the concert I'm organizing tomorrow evening, cheri," Ida said as Charles retrieved his coat in the hall. "It's a trio from the *conservatoire*. If we're lucky, Sylvana might sing as well. Seven-thirty."

Charles made no mention of the parchment he was carrying in his laptop bag, or the discovery in the cave. The revelation of Ida's musical outlaw had been disorienting to say the least. Nothing seemed to make any sense in the wider issue of Blancheron and its mysteries.

He hurried down the alley, not entirely certain what he had in mind.

LVI

Charles had never followed anyone anywhere. His personality precluded it, of course. Moreover, it wasn't something he'd even considered in the Connecticut suburbs where he'd spent his late teens. One had to have a car there, and he'd had no driver's license at the time, although even if he had, he would never have dreamed of using a car for what other boys were using them for: following girls in their own cars, at modest speeds, and eventually parking somewhere for an activity that had nothing to do with driving.

A middle-aged man, tracking a woman on foot...that was something else altogether. It had the worst of connotations, and Charles was fully aware of them as he tried to keep Sylvana in his sights.

He had her telephone number. *Why not just send her a message?* But no. There was something else going on here...something that felt off. Even though he'd shared secrets of his uncle's research—ventured with this woman to the fetid heart of his family's legend and even held her briefly in his arms—the enigma of Sylvana Longfaye persisted. *Was she, in fact, the sort of person one could never really know...or trust?*

Better to observe her from afar, he thought—to determine who, exactly, this Raul Mora might be, and what he meant to her.

The dark-green cape turned out to be a convenient moving landmark. The afternoon, however, was soft and mild, and wearing such a garment at striding speed would have been hot work. Sylvana soon removed it and slung it over her arm. Charles, sweating in his cashmere coat, kept his eyes trained on her white shirt instead.

The trek took them from Ida's rarified Uccle neighborhood to the bustling grime of Ixelles, two bordering districts of the city's nineteen. Charles knew many of these streets from his boyhood. The slightly rancid flavor of this part of town still lodged in the throat, just as he remembered. He dodged pedestrians and traffic as familiar details revived: stepped gables; mosaic friezes; exotic brickwork in red, black, white, and green; ornate stone, rounded and curled by master masons. Some of the splendor was gently crumbling. Much of it, thankfully, was still splendid.

Sylvana slowed her march as she reached the baroque Holy Trinity church. Charles hung back, gaining the square just as she was taking out her key. She disappeared into a house behind the church.

A tram thundered up, rounded the church and stopped. Charles crossed over the tracks to the hulking shoulder of the edifice and lingered in its shadow. His thoughts tumbled at random. *Why on earth should he conceal himself?* And then the grim reality: *If Sylvana was involved with Raul beyond being his teacher, why would anyone seek out the pain of confirming this?*

He studied Sylvana's house. At first glance, its promising mint green color stood out from the other shabby façades in the row. A closer look revealed that the paint was darkened by pollution, spattered by pigeon droppings and adorned with graffiti: *Encore ce soir!* "Once more tonight!" Rubbish sat uncollected at the front door. A vine, woody and leafless, curled around a downspout right up to the cornice.

Charles's gaze returned to street level, where he noticed the iron bars Ida had mentioned, and the filthy cellar window. *She may not come out again until tomorrow,* he thought morosely.

Then a woman began singing from the direction of the cellar. She explored the same melody that had drifted from Ida's salon, rising a little further at each repetition. The sound lent a glow to the fading afternoon, and it gave Charles such comfort that he knew he'd be able to stand there until tomorrow if necessary, listening to the church ring the hour with its toneless clang, and the 81 tram roll occasionally by. He took out his mobile and held it to his ear, just to appear busy. He didn't have the courage to actually call her.

The soft afternoon air turned to rain. Soon a steady dripping issued from the cornice and landed more or less where Charles was standing. He crouched down to peer through the bars: he could make out a simple kitchen table, a lumpen armchair, and the bulk of an upright piano. The scene was blurred by the dirt on the window and weakly illuminated by a bare bulb suspended from the ceiling. A pale rectangle on the far wall suggested the entrance to a room beyond.

Sylvana was standing next to the piano and facing this rectangle.

A figure darkened the entrance.

Raul.

Charles jerked away from the grill. *What was the man doing there?* Then he remembered Ida saying that he'd found a room in Sylvana's house. *But in the cellar? With her?* He peered in again, soiling the knee of his flannel trousers on the sidewalk. In the general gloom, the two actors were but shadow-players.

Raul entered and approached Sylvana. Her back was to the window, so it was only possible to infer one of two things: that they were staring at each other in silence; or that Sylvana was the speaker and Raul her rapt listener. For indeed he seemed rapt. As far as Charles could tell from this vantage point, the downward turn of Raul's mouth and his high, furrowed brow seemed to be permanent features, for even though the man seemed infused with ardor, he was still scowling.

Horrified, Charles watched him move suddenly toward Sylvana and take her face in his hands as if to kiss her. He had the compact burliness of a prize fighter.

Charles reached through the bars to rap on the window. He began yelling Sylvana's name but changed his mind at once: she'd stepped away from the man—just one step, but it had been enough to discourage him.

Raul dropped his hands to his side. But he tried again. He lifted one hand this time and Charles gasped. *He's going to strike her!* Sylvana's response was strange indeed: she sat down on the piano stool, a move that stopped Raul in his tracks. It was as if he'd stumbled upon a priestess about to commune with her oracle.

Raul exited the room at once.

Sylvana remained at the piano. She brought a hand to her cheek, though it was impossible to tell from the street whether it was a gesture of tenderness or indignation.

She glanced up.

Charles leapt to his feet. *Fool!* he berated himself, and moved off down the sidewalk. Someone jostled past him. Charles stepped aside and watched the figure recede: he was wearing a shapeless raincoat that fell to his ankles, and he bent forward as he stumped away.

Charles stopped dead.

He would have recognized the man's peculiar scuttle even from afar. For that was how he'd first seen him, from high in the turret room of Villa Antioch, looking down at the old stone bridge.

"Charles!" Sylvana was standing on her front step in her slippers. "Come in out of the rain."

LVII

She beckoned him into a hallway choked with cooking smells of the ages. On the right was a dwarfish door no higher than Charles's chest, which Sylvana opened. Steep stairs plunged directly into a cellar and she melted down them.

Her guest took a moment to glance at himself in the hall mirror: rain-flattened curls; skin indistinguishable from the porridge-colored walls. With the added touch of shadows under his eyes, Charles resembled a Latin scholar who hasn't left the library for weeks, trapped, perhaps, by the fourth declension. (Which was still preferable to looking like a lawyer, he thought with optimism.)

He stooped through the miniature door and felt his way down the stairs.

"In here!" Sylvana called.

Charles followed the voice across a dim hall to the parlor he'd viewed from the street.

"Why were you spying on me?" Sylvana demanded as he appeared at the door.

Charles had to adjust his bearings in the space, which he'd only seen from above. The parlor felt less stark than it had seemed from outside, although with the proprietress standing regal and defiant before him, it was hardly cozy.

"Sylvana, please listen," Charles said from the doorway. "When I asked you if you'd seen a man of Raul's description in the woods around Blancheron, you said you hadn't."

"Well it's true, I hadn't!" she exclaimed with indignation. She moved to the piano and gathered up a few red tulip petals that had fallen from a bouquet on the lid. She didn't invite Charles to come in.

"You must have recognized who I was talking about, though," said Charles. Then, hotly: "Why are you protecting him, Sylvana? He's dangerous." He immediately regretted this comment, as he had no idea what she knew about Raul.

"Is that why you were spying on me?" she responded, just as hotly.

Charles took a deep breath and entered the room. His heart caught as she regarded him. She might have been standing knee-deep in ferns, her hair complicit with the wind, with that abiding stillness he'd noticed the first time he'd set eyes on her. He ached that this extraordinary creature should be living in such penury.

"You once called me straight and true," he ventured.

"Yes," she said, glancing down at the linoleum floor.

"Well, then. It's in that spirit that I've come."

Sylvana looked at him as she had at Ida's, as if waiting for a reflection to settle. She seemed relieved when the image finally revealed itself. "Of course I accept that you've come in that spirit," she said at length. "Chivalry lives on in you, Charles. Somewhere," she added. In the room's scant illumination her eyes carried their own light.

She helped him out of his overcoat and lay it over the lumpen armchair, making no bother about the fact that the cashmere was damp. She briefly admired the burgundy silk scarf before draping it over the coat.

"Please, sit down," she said, beckoning him to the little chipped table against the wall. "We'll have some tea."

The feet of the chair stuck to the linoleum as Charles pulled it out. He set the laptop bag with the parchment he was bringing to Florus against the table leg.

Sylvana left the room.

Charles looked up at the window where he'd just been lurking. He could see the legs of passersby from this angle, and now and then an entire dog, and marveled at how ignorant they all were, hurrying by the hidden magic at their feet.

Sylvana returned carrying a tray with all the accoutrements of English tea, including a bone china tea pot and cups.

"Ida's cast-offs!" she smiled, and set to work with her tea-making. Charles reveled in her presence as she poured: the delicate skin and perfect oval face; the creases at the corners of her mouth; a curl that fell across her temple like a comma as she bent over the tea pot. The dun-colored skirt and white blouse were clothes one usually wears to not call attention to oneself. The irony, thought Charles, was that on Sylvana Longfaye, they emphasized her beauty to the point of practically shouting it.

Charles looked about the room as he sipped his tea.

"It's not much, I know," Sylvana said, observing him. She gave a laugh—a dismissive one, as if to say: *What are lodgings in the greater scheme of things?*

"You have a nice place," he said weakly.

She laughed again. "That's quite a compliment coming from someone of your background!"

He flinched. "The Belgian gentry, you mean?"

"Well, the American one, at any rate."

"You speak of wealth as though it's something to be ashamed of," said Charles, all the while secretly ashamed of it.

"It is," Sylvana affirmed.

Charles ran a nervous hand over his curls and glanced up at the bare light bulb. "What do you live from, then?" he challenged her. "Air?"

She glanced over at the piano. "Yes," she answered. "Music is air, after all."

They sipped tea quietly and watched the parade of legs pass by the window at the ceiling. An unresolved heaviness hung in the air.

"I know about Raul, if that's why you've come, Charles," Sylvana said, pre-empting him.

He set his cup down. "That he's wanted for murder, you mean?" The words had a brutal edge.

Sylvana played with her spoon. "He's not dangerous," she said. "You needn't worry about me."

"Should I worry that you're harboring a fugitive?" he pressed her, all the while thinking: *Should I worry that he's your lover?*

"The police will never find him here. He has a room upstairs at the back of the house and he's very careful when he comes and goes. He didn't do it, Charles. You must believe that."

"So why was he poking around Blancheron?" he said. "Did he ransack Theodore's study?"

Sylvana got up and wandered to the piano, a matter of only a few steps, but it was something to do. "I don't know," she said. "And that's the truth. But I do know Raul. There's darkness in him, it's true. Such damage. But music speaks to that."

Charles tried to read Sylvana's tone, her manner, even the way she held her teacup, looking for signals he might have missed. Was she really on a humanitarian mission with Raul? Was this wild man more in love with Sylvana than she with him? It had certainly seemed so from the scene Charles had witnessed through the window.

"Do you love him?" he asked precipitously.

"Yes," she answered at once.

Charles said nothing. He let the rest of his tea go cold.

Sylvana looked up at the window. "I love his essence," she explained. "Raul is the most guileless person I've ever met. He lives through his heart...by raw intuition. All his emotions are pure: grief, joy, fear. Like an animal." She hesitated. "Like music."

"Like music...?"

"Why, yes," she said, turning back to Charles. "Music is incapable of guile." Her cheeks flushed pale pink, like Blancheron carnations.

Charles reflected on this for a moment.

"Which makes your father particularly cruel, doesn't it?" Sylvana said, taking a step into this minefield. "Exploiting someone like Raul because it's easy to make criminals out of guileless people."

Charles stiffened. Her words sent bile coursing through him. She'd somehow discovered the link to his father. *How could I ever have thought she'd love me?* he wondered. *She was probably just being polite, saying I'm straight and true.* He looked at his watch. "I should be going to see Florus," he said, getting up from the table.

There was so much more to say, and waning courage with which to say it.

In the silence that followed, two crimson petals broke loose from a tulip and pattered over the piano lid.

Sylvana took Charles's coat and scarf from the chair. "Please let me know what Florus says about the parchment," she said, as if addressing a clerk in the library. "Will you tell him about the dagger?"

"Yes. I'll show him the photo of it." Charles picked up his bag. He felt himself slipping away from this encounter...from his woodland friend. With bitterness he indulged himself with her less appealing traits: her cool, moody detachment; her tendency to put distance between herself and the next person. *She's seen through me,* he thought. *She's seen that I cannot match her depths.*

Nevertheless, he moved closer to her and offered his plea:

"I'm not my father, Sylvana."

She helped him into his coat and gently draped the scarf around his neck. "I know," she said softly. "But I'm not sure that you do."

He covered her hand with his own before she could take it away and pressed it against his heart.

"Theodore said that sometimes you can hear Arda's music on the air at Blancheron," Sylvana said in a flight of improvisation.

Charles stared at her, disoriented. "Yes," he said. "The lyra."

"Have you ever heard it?"

"Maybe." He closed his eyes for a moment, remembering the curious scrape in the rook's call when it lifted from the willow. "Things live at Blancheron," he said quietly. "Unseen things."

"That's because they feel welcome there."

Charles put down his bag.

What had not been said in this conversation (Charles's inexorable slipping into love), and Sylvana's intuition (her uncanny awareness of what had not been said), ensured the inevitability of what came next, for it seemed utterly natural for Charles to gather Sylvana in his arms and kiss her with all the passion and conviction that Henri of Rêve must have reserved for his own sibyl when he'd visited her grotto.

LVIII

Within a few minutes of exiting Sylvana's cellar flat, Charles found himself standing before Cédric Florus's soaring *maison de maître*.

It was difficult to believe that two such contrasting dwellings could exist just a few blocks from each other. Then again, Brussels held her secrets close to her bosom. She housed a vast cross-section of humanity hidden away behind façades that were hardly ever what they seemed. Musical seeresses could live in the same neighborhood as famous medievalists, therefore, neither ever being aware of the other. (Suspected felons lived above their music teachers around here, too, which was even more surprising.)

A team of men must have been needed to heave Florus's massive front door into place. It was painted a lustrous forest green and punctuated with brass fittings of appropriate grandeur. No wayward vines climbed up the façade of this house. No graffiti defaced it. A handsome bay window jutted out on scrolled stone supports, and iron railings, recently buffed, wound in graceful arabesques. Everything oozed elegance and class.

As did the man who opened the door.

"Ah, Charles de la Fontaine, how lovely to meet you!" he effused. He extended his hand: it was smooth and dry, like vellum.

Of modest height, Cédric Florus was physically dwarfed by the door but not diminished in any other way. He stood erect and proud, his chin lifted as if he held some distant stronghold in his sights. His smile had a wry turn, poised between irreverence and warmth.

Charles returned the vigorous handshake. *How wonderful to hear his real name uttered aloud again!*

He followed his host into an entryway of pale gray marble, up several steps, and through double doors of beveled glass into a cavernous atrium typical of so many Brussels *maisons de maître*. A freshness lingered, as if someone had just mopped the marble floor. Charles glanced up the staircase and indeed a maid could be seen at the top of it, passing her cloth around a curl of railing.

He paused to admire a classical bust set on a pedestal.

"That's Horace, the patron of the establishment," Florus twinkled.

They entered a room that even the imagination could not easily have conjured. The grand dimensions and vast Oriental carpet...the archways and pediments and palms set on columns all gave the impression of an audience hall that existed only in opera or film. Opalescent light filtered through soaring courtyard windows to complete the stage set.

The contrast with Sylvana's cellar was overwhelming. For a moment Charles could only stand and gawk as he changed his bearings from grotto to palace. There was also the matter of disentangling his thoughts from other recent bearings: from the silken delights of Sylvana's lips, for example...from her exquisite neck, her hair, and the surging heat of an affinity he'd never known before.

All this, reluctantly, he managed to do.

A housemaid appeared at Charles's side as if by divination to take his coat and Florus motioned him to a comfortable wingback chair. The vast salon drew the gaze inevitably upward, and Charles was quite content to sit in the chair and crane his neck to study the huge plaster oval at the center of the ceiling, with its rosettes and leaves and cherubs.

"I was so sorry to miss Theo's funeral," Florus said, taking the chair on the other side of a little inlaid table. "He was my alter ego in a way. But as you know, Charles, he was a rogue scholar—someone you have to admire in secret if you have an orthodox position like I did."

Charles nodded, lamenting that someone with Theodore's genius would have had to have been admired in secret.

"I chose the path of standard academic dogma, alas," Florus continued. "Theo had the courage to think outside of all that. Academics loathe rebels like him. It's fatal to one's reputation even to get close to them."

Florus sat with his elbows perched on the armrests, fingertips touching, silver hair swept back and gleaming in the light from the courtyard windows. His air of distinction, and his Cambridge, tie-andtailcoat accent made it seem that Charles was being granted a formal audience. But a discreet glance at his host's quilted slippers, fraying at one toe, and the suede patches sewn onto the elbows of his sweater indicated a more relaxed sort of interview.

"My uncle thought very highly of you," Charles said, courting formality nonetheless.

Florus leaned his head back and laughed sadly. "Ah, Theo. We had such fun together. We used to have lunch every week at Carpe Diem. Do you know it?"

Charles shook his head.

"An off-beat sort of place near the Cinquantenaire where you can get a decent *carbonnade* for a reasonable price and chat for hours. I don't think there was a single medieval mystery we didn't attack, and even solve, over those lunches—especially when the wine was good!" Florus glanced at Charles. "Your uncle lived a life of genteel poverty, as you know. He never accepted any help."

The comment shocked Charles. The memories he guarded so zealously, of summers now impossibly distant, stirred to life. Theodore's poverty, genteel or not, had never crossed the mind of his young disciple. Living as he had in a villa called Antioch, surrounded by a forest full of medieval treasures, Theodore had seemed wealthy beyond measure.

"Now, I believe you've brought me something to look at," Florus said, all business now.

"Yes," said Charles, rummaging in his laptop bag. "You know the heron legend, I think, Monsieur."

"Cédric, please!" Florus said. "And yes, I know the Old French version in the *Bibliothèque de l'Histoire Européenne*. In fact, I know quite a bit of de la Fontaine family history from Theodore. But as I said on the phone, I have only passing acquaintance with the folio you brought with you—the one that your grandfather, um, *took home* with him. That is, the alternative ending of the legend."

Charles produced the envelope containing the parchment as well as Theodore's partial translation. Conscious of his host's scholarly reputation, he drew the parchment out as slowly and carefully as possible. It was a jolt, therefore, when Florus seized the manuscript without the slightest precaution. It was like watching someone roll a Fabergé egg across the floor.

"Ah, you're back at last," Florus crooned to the parchment, holding it up to the window. "My, my, what troubles you've caused, *ma belle!*" He examined the manuscript's nicks and stains with affection, as one might the face of an old friend, and giggled as he ran a finger down the jagged edge where it had been cut from the codex.

"You must have a pretty dim view of my grandfather," Charles said, "making off with such a treasure."

"Yes and no," said Florus. "Your grandfather acted from impulse; from *passion*. How many people do you know have walked from Antioch to Jerusalem wearing chain mail, for God's sake? And why, one might ask? I'll tell you why: because he wanted to *live* history, Charles! To feel it. Suffer it." Florus's energy easily filled the grand salon.

"Did he tell you about his journey?"

"Well, he did say that the Syrian police detained him, then let him go once they'd determined he wasn't a security threat. Then his blisters got so bad that he accepted a ride from a driver trucking oranges. But only for ten kilometers, mind you. He said he was sure that the pilgrims must have had far worse blisters."

Charles gaped. "He was barefoot?"

"Of course!"

Florus turned back to the parchment. "Your grandfather never intended to profit from the manuscript—certainly not to harm it in any way." He smiled. "It's a pity that he didn't have better scissors! Happily, he passed his qualities on to Theodore, which is what I so loved about your uncle." Florus gave Charles an appraising look, as if to see if the same qualities might have trickled down to him. "You look like a scholar yourself," he said with a hopeful note.

"I'm a lawyer," Charles responded. *How could he have called himself a historian in the presence of such a man?*

The words fell like a blow over the surroundings.

Florus swept his gaze over Charles's expensive clothes, and the luxurious brogues that seemed too new to have experienced much interesting walking. An "ah" of comprehension was all that was needed.

"I believe that Theodore died because of what's written on that page," Charles said.

The comment snapped Florus to attention. This time his "ah" was one of alarm.

"Here's the translation he made," Charles explained. "At least, as much as he could do before his..."

"Thank you," Florus said, relieving Charles of the dreaded word.

"And here's the letter he wrote to me."

Florus read Theodore's message. "*Tiens, tiens*," he muttered. "He really was in a hurry to write this down."

"He was in a terrible hurry to get it to *me*," Charles said, recounting how his uncle had been confronted by a visitor at Villa Antioch and driven to Ida's the same night, knowing that she would make sure Charles got the envelope.

Silence descended over the salon as Florus studied the parchment. Like all good scholars, his concentration was so intense, and his transport so complete, that he seemed to have left the room entirely.

Charles watched in admiration as the man stared down a certain word, and turned the folio over several times to find clues in another part of the document. Occasionally he consulted Theodore's translation and gave a knowing nod. He had the air of a sleepwalker exploring a realm invisible to everyone else. Charles would gladly have spent his life in such a trance.

"Iron gall ink, I would say," said Florus. "And a palimpsest...a partial one, anyway. There are several words and passages that have been rubbed out."

"Yes, I noticed that, too," Charles said, savoring the fact that for a few moments at least, his host was treating him as an equal.

"Hmm. This is a most curious folio for a *chanson de geste*," Florus continued. "Not only because it's in Latin. But because the heron legend in the library was written in the poetic meter typical of that genre. And this... Well, it was certainly penned by a scribe. At the Valdoré monastery, I would say, considering the locale. Most nobles in the late eleventh and early twelfth century were illiterate, as you undoubtedly know, Charles."

"I could find only one name in it," Charles said. "In lower case: *stephanus fontis.*"

Florus held the folio at arm's length. "The other names—Arda, Henri, Walderic, etc.—only appear in the Old French version, I would surmise," he said. "Ah, yes, here it is: 'Stephen of the Spring', or 'Stephen of the Source'. Stephen de la Fontaine, in other words. Your ancestor."

Said Charles: "The knight for whom Stephen acted as squire was not named in the Old French version. Grandfather assumed that he was Henri of Rêve."

"Indeed," said Florus. "It makes perfect sense. Henri was the most distinguished personage in the village."

He squinted at the parchment. "Hmm...there's no decoration of any kind." He laid the folio on his lap and gave Charles a leading look. "You know, I believe that this might have been intentional. It's in the style of a *chanson de geste*—no doubt about it. But someone didn't want to draw attention to it for some reason. They simply wanted to record an important piece of information."

Charles returned Florus's look and said nothing.

"The writing is so jammed together on the verso," said Florus.

"Yes, I know."

"Even a Latin scholar would have difficulty deciphering all the jumble toward the end of it. Perhaps the scribe—or the person who ordered his services—wanted to keep all the text to one folio. Maybe he thought that more than one folio would get lost. Hang on..."

Florus got up and wandered to the window. He held the parchment up to the light. Then, ignoring an interdiction all scholars were asked to abide by, he traced his index finger directly along the ink in a few places.

"Most of the erasures are targeted, it seems," he said. "Individual words have been rubbed out and overwritten. This word here, for example: *miles*—'knight'—is covering up an erasure. You can see a few vestiges of the original word. I agree with Theodore's translation of the passage: *It is a noble exercise to record events accurately, especially if they must describe a knight whose heart was humble and virtuous, but whose soul was at a crossroads.*"

"So you're saying that 'knight' was not the intended title for this man?"

"Correct. Now here's something interesting: 'with splendid hand'—*splendida manu*. Extraordinary. It comes after an erasure overwritten with the word *nobilis*, which your uncle translated as 'lord'. 'Nobleman' would have been more accurate, in my opinion. So we don't know whose splendid hand it was. Or who, as Theodore translated it, *hunted the lady to her cave in the forest, defiled her, and cut her throat.*"

Charles took out his phone and scrolled to the photo he'd taken of the dagger.

"I went up to the spring yesterday with Sylvana Longfaye...my uncle's assistant," he added somewhat apologetically. The title didn't seem worthy of Sylvana. "She claimed she'd found the entrance to a cave up there."

"Arda's cave?" Florus said, riveted.

"This is what we found in it." Charles passed him the phone.

Florus enlarged the photograph to examine the dagger's hilt. "*Nom de Dieu*," he muttered. "It's magnificent! These are precious stones. It belonged to a very wealthy individual, I would say."

Charles mustered his confidence and said: "I've thought about this, Cédric. Perhaps the 'splendid hand' referred to a 'jeweled hand': a wealthy person who was wearing a ring."

Florus rubbed his chin. "A nobleman could have worn such a thing."

"Or a church official," Charles said.

But before his host could comment, a most singular procession appeared.

LIX

The maid who'd taken Charles's coat emerged from a side door bearing a tray with a crystal sherry decanter, two crystal glasses and a bowl of salty nibbles. At her heels, with the indignity of a butler who's found himself trailing a servant, followed a portly, dour, resplendently colored rabbit.

Florus, at the window, ignored the procession. The rabbit, however, took a detour from the route to sniff his slipper.

The maid set the tray on the inlaid table and intentionally dropped a miniature pretzel on the carpet. The rabbit approached with some disdain, then began gnawing on it.

Florus thanked her and returned to his chair.

"This is Arnulf," Florus announced. He put the folio down—rather too close to the sherry, Charles thought—and gave the animal a vigorous scratching under one cheek. Arnulf immediately abandoned the treat and stretched out indulgently on his side, like a dog.

"Arnulf is the boss here," Florus said with a chuckle. "Like all pets, I believe. He's the spitting image of the first patriarch of Jerusalem, wouldn't you agree?"

"Arnulf of Chocques?" Charles laughed.

"That's him."

"Not a very flattering appellation, all things considered."

"No, it is not."

Theodore had always been somewhat bemused by Arnulf, chaplain to Robert of Normandy, one of the crusading princes. The cleric was a monument to ambition and opportunism. When a piece of the Holy Lance was discovered in Antioch, Arnulf debunked it, suspecting that his skepticism would catch the prevailing wind and bring him to prominence. When Jerusalem was conquered a year later, it was said that a chunk of wood from the True Cross lay concealed somewhere in the city. Sensing that the winds had changed, Arnulf seized on the cult

250

of this relic and widely promoted it (after torturing a few locals to find out where it was, that is).

The patriarch's long-eared namesake sat up, settled himself next to Florus's chair and embarked on an elaborate toilet, all the while keeping a wary eye on Charles.

"Of course," said Florus, "Arnulf of Chocques was an infamous womanizer, while my poor Arnulf here, *hélas*, leads a celibate existence. For a rabbit, it's rather like what being locked up in a monk's cell would have been for the patriarch. But let's push on with our work, shall we?"

Florus poured the sherry and slid the nibbles to Charles's side of the table. "I have to admit that I need more time to decipher this properly," he said. "From this brief perusal, I think your uncle did a fine job translating the first part. But all the tightly-packed lines on the verso— those are tricky." He took a sip of sherry and leaned down to give the rabbit a pat. "I'm intrigued by the mention of the child."

"Yes," Charles said. "Adopted by Stephen, apparently."

"Exactly: *In familiam nomenque adoptavit.*"

"The baby's father was 'a nobleman who had lands and riches, but had died...'" Florus said, reading from Theodore's translation. 'There's another erasure here: a gap after 'died'. Did you notice it?"

Charles shook his head.

"It looks as if a cause of death might have been omitted. In any case, I'd like to hold on to the folio for a day or two if I may. And also Theo's translation."

"Of course."

"I still have access to a scanner we use to detect text on erased parchment," Florus said. "It's an amazing machine: multi-spectral imaging that picks up traces of older writing on a palimpsest. Then I'll type the complete translation on the computer so you can actually read it!"

Florus got to his feet. "I'll make a PDF of the MS now and print out a copy for you." He gave a wry smile. "Technically, the folio is the property of the *Bibliothèque de l'Histoire Européenne*, so I'm afraid you'll have to part with it, Charles. Never mind. You can see it whenever you like. And anyway, I'm sure your grandfather would be relieved to know that it's finally going home!"

He exited the room via the small door where the maid and Arnulf had entered, leaving Charles alone with the patriarch of the house. Arnulf began a thorough cleaning of his ears, glaring at the visitor.

He was a suspicious creature, indeed. Entitled and arrogant. Charles's mind drifted to ancient Jerusalem as he recalled the other piece of Arnulf's story that had irked Theodore: namely his religious intolerance. The new patriarch had expulsed eastern Christian sects from the Church of the Holy Sepulcher: Armenians, Copts, Nestorians and Jacobites—fellow believers, as it were, who in one of history's cruel jokes soon discovered that they'd actually been better off under the Muslims.

The rabbit suddenly surged forward and began butting Charles's shoe. He was preparing to sink his teeth into the succulent leather when Florus returned.

"Now, now, Your Eminence," Florus chuckled, giving Arnulf a gentle shove with his foot. The rabbit took a gratuitous bite of Florus's slipper instead: clearly the cause of the fraying toe.

Florus handed two sheets of paper to Charles and returned to his chair. "That's the PDF of the recto and verso," he said. "I had a quick look at the text again while I was printing it."

He poured them both more sherry. "There's some curious business about a grave," he said.

Charles balked. "A *grave*? Arda's?"

"The 'prophetess of the spring' is mentioned in the same sentence, yes," said Florus. "And I infer from some obscure language that the grave might have been opened for some reason."

"*Opened?*"

"Indeed. And there's something else intriguing, two words that appear to be a place name: *porta ducis*. 'Duke's Gate'."

"Christ!" Charles exclaimed. "The Duke's Gate...that must be what Theodore used to call 'the Knight's Gate'. The locals call it *la Porte du Chevalier*. Do you know what that is?"

Florus said "no", which he clearly didn't often do when asked if he knew something.

"It's at the opposite end of the Blancheron ridge from the castle," Charles went on, "where the cliff drops down to the Semois valley.

According to legend, it's where Blancheron knights went to meditate. I used to go there all the time with my uncle. He claimed there was a confluence of energies there. That Arda's music lingered somewhere."

"Quite the romantic, that Theodore!" Florus said.

"Is the *porta ducis* described as part of the ridge?" Charles asked.

"I'll know more when I've studied the text."

"Oh, I almost forgot." Charles pulled the smaller envelope from his bag and extracted the bronze key. This he handed to Florus. "Theodore believes this is the key to the olive wood box that Stephen de la Fontaine brought back from the Holy Land."

"The cross potent…" Florus marveled, bringing the key up close to his face. "A fine object. Perhaps the olive wood box was a reliquary of some sort. Jerusalem and Constantinople were awash with relics."

"It was Godfrey of Bouillon's coat of arms."

"Yes, yes, so it was," Florus said. "But the symbol was used more generally around 1100. Particularly for a reliquary. A lovely key." He handed it back to Charles. "But not much use without the lock, I'm afraid. It's quite small, so my guess would be that it was for a coffer of modest proportions."

Florus glanced around the room, suddenly misty-eyed. "It always amazes me how everything suddenly quickens in the presence of such an object," he sighed. "The room. The air… Your uncle thought that one literally touched the past when touching such things."

"Yes, I know," Charles said. He could even hear Theodore say it: *We must have physical contact with the past to understand it, lad. Would you prefer to read a boring biography of Godfrey, or touch his rusted spurs?*

A tiny, eager flame awakened in him.

They parted in amiable fashion. Florus gave Charles a warm embrace and promised to call him the minute he had more information.

Charles turned up his collar against the damp and headed off. The afternoon had already seeped away and street lights were winking on. He glanced up and down Rue Paul Emile Janson, one of those forgotten Brussels neighborhoods that hadn't changed in a hundred years. You could round a corner and suddenly slip through time to a street where towering mansions regarded the street dolefully, forgotten ballroom beauties with heavy eyelids and lace at their busts, still waiting to dance.

A man was lingering on the corner Rue de Livourne. It was a curious street, misleadingly sedate, as its nightlife could be slick. Here the houses might have had the appearance of ballroom beauties, but in fact they were hoydens with coarser intentions.

Charles slowed his steps. *A bit early to be trawling*, he thought, observing the lingerer.

No sooner had he made this observation than the man launched himself around the corner, head jutting forward. The hem of his raincoat was the last thing to slip from view.

LX

Charles had some practice as a tracker now, though the labyrinth of Ixelles streets was daunting by dark. Raul plunged down an ill-lit backwater and he followed him.

I should abandon this stupidity, Charles thought, all the while keeping his eyes on his quarry and forging ahead. *I must confirm the link between Raul and the intruder in Theodore's study.* He had no desire to find himself alone at Villa Antioch again, at night, with a prowler outside who already knew how to get in.

These thoughts took his mind off the route he was following, and thus it was with some astonishment that Charles realized where the man had led him:

Ida's villa.

They were now on her street. The lights were brighter here and cast a cool, operating-room blue over the neighborhood. There was no traffic. No noise. Only a solitary dog-walker, tarrying some distance away.

Charles abandoned all caution and followed Raul right to Ida's gate.

The man wheeled around to confront him.

Charles reared back. Though he towered over the gnome-like figure, it was clear even through the shapeless coat that the man would win any fight he chose to pick. His face caught the streetlight and Charles contracted. There was no doubt about it now: this was the man he'd seen outside Theodore's window. The high forehead and deep eye sockets...the downward turn to the lips...

Charles took another step backward. Neither spoke.

Raul glowered, and precipitated himself to within inches of Charles, his fists lifted. It was a skillful feint, for it immobilized his pursuer. Then he turned, pushed the gate open and slipped up the alley.

Charles sagged, breathless. He grasped his phone: he had to warn Ida at once—alert her that this was the man who'd trespassed at

Blancheron...that he'd likely ransacked the study and was involved in Theodore's death.

"*Oui?*"

"Auntie!"

"Ah, *Sharl'*. How was your meeting today?" She sounded relaxed. Content, even.

"Is someone there with you?"

"Yes! Don't worry, cheri, I'm not alone: Raul just came by. We're having tea."

"Auntie, listen: Raul has been following me. He turned up near Cédric Florus's place today. And I definitely saw him on the bridge at Blancheron yesterday. I'm certain it was he who broke into Theodore's study. He was probably *hired* to do it." Charles paused for breath, bewildered by Ida's lack of response. "Auntie, don't you see? This man hasn't changed his spots. Despite all your efforts...and Sylvana's."

"Charles, *je t'en prie*, calm down." Impatience laced Ida's voice, a singular emotion for someone who's just been warned about the dangerous brute in her kitchen. "There are many things you don't know," she went on. "Things I promised Hugues I would not divulge."

Charles's hands turned to ice. "How exactly is Father involved?"

Ida sighed. "He has a very long reach, as you know," she said, her voice darkening.

Charles wandered off toward his car. It seemed that days had passed since he'd left it there for his earlier visit to Ida. He sat in it for a few moments, the phone still pressed to his ear.

"Yes, I know," was all he could manage. He rolled down the window and breathed in deeply. The soupy air had a spice to it, of wet, decaying leaves in the gardens nearby.

Hugh's reach was long, indeed—made even longer through the complicity of Osselaer and Ames and now, apparently, Ida. *What was she concealing for Father?* Charles's heart shrank as he imagined Hugh holding money out to his own sister. He'd counted on the family's wayward bohemian accepting it in exchange for whatever she'd promised to do. Nobody could escape the lure of the paper god, after all.

Charles had never known an instance when someone had refused Hugh's money. Why would Ida? In a moment of clear-headedness, he realized that a lucrative sale of the castle hinged on the parchment and what it might reveal. Ames...Osselaer...Raul: all of them made up the vanguard of Hugh's campaign. Raul was the one who got his hands dirty; the expendable one.

And Ida was Raul's keeper.

How much did she know?

Charles let out a long, faltering sigh. *Sylvana.* He could only hope that she had nothing to do with this besides being Raul's teacher. *Please let it be so*, he anguished. Anything else would have been unthinkable.

He took the quartz crystal from his pocket and lifted it up until it caught the street lighting. The facets glinted as he turned it. The tiny feathery forest within came to life. *Who was I back then?* he wondered, holding the cold stone against his cheek. *On that day in the forest when she'd laid this on my palm?*

Charles shivered in the unheated car. Grace Holmes had known who he was back then.

You still have that look in your eyes, Charlie. Like you can see the past or something.

Was it possible that by some miracle he hadn't really changed?

"*Sharl'*, are you still there?" Ida asked.

"Yes," he said, putting the crystal back into his pocket. Energized, he asked: "What does Father want with Raul?"

"That's what I cannot tell you," she answered. With greater warmth she added: "Please don't ask me any more questions, cheri." She hesitated. "And don't be in too much of a hurry to judge."

"I'll speak to you later," he said, and hung up. He was gripped by the same sour fear that had plagued him during that snowy Thanksgiving in Connecticut. And like then, his father had everything to do with it. Indeed, so overwhelming was Hugh's presence that even from a distance of almost six thousand kilometers, he seemed in perfect control of Blancheron and its destiny.

The yoke had begun to chafe.

LXI

Cold and hungry, Charles drove back to the Sablon.
He overshot the turning behind the cathedral and found himself on the Place Royale instead. The unlit statue of Godfrey was just a wedge of negative space in the gloaming. Only a corner of his banner and the horse's raised hoof were visible. *Or had he imagined them?* Charles drove too fast around the statue, his hands tight on the wheel. The city was shrouded in humidity. One couldn't have said for certain if Godfrey had been there at all.

He found parking near his hotel and headed across the square to a restaurant with candles in the windows. He parted the heavy curtains inside the door, smiling at the fug within. He'd never known an American restaurant to exude the centuries from its walls like those of his native city.

"*Bonsoir,* Monsieur," said the waiter in floor-length white apron, and seated Charles at a table overlooking the square.

An old-fashioned stove crackled nearby and soon warmed him through. Brass plates and engravings of old Brussels decorated the walls. Pieces of leather harness hung from exposed beams along with an ancient ploughshare.

Charles closed his eyes and listened to the genteel chink and murmur of fellow diners. The combination of leather, wood and fire lured him to another epoch.

The waiter returned with a pitcher of red wine and basket of bread. Charles opened his eyes: the movement had set the candle on his table sashaying, a dance he remembered fondly from Theodore's study. He watched the flame, and as he used to do as a boy, tried to predict from where the next draft would come, and in which direction the flame would bow.

"*Le stoemp maison,* Monsieur," the waiter said, appearing again at his elbow. He served Charles a fragrant concoction of mashed potatoes, root vegetables, cream, bacon and spices. It was a classic Belgian peasant dish, dressed up slightly for the big city.

Charles tucked into his dinner with gusto. The fragrance of thyme, bay and bacon bewitched him, and as usual with such alchemy, his thoughts loosened and strayed. He poured himself a second glass of wine, gazed up at the ancient ploughshare and listened to what Cédric Florus had said just that afternoon: *It always amazes me how everything suddenly quickens in the presence of such an object. The room. The air. Your uncle thought that one literally touched the past when touching such things.*

Charles drifted to medieval Rêve-sur-Semois—to the visions he'd seen with Theodore in that cold, dark field. He sipped the wine until his thoughts drifted far enough to study his own daydream:

People were gathered outside a squalid little inn where a man and his wife were too sick to make the journey. There was weeping. Beseeching. A rider stopped by, curious. He seemed far wealthier than the others; well-dressed. Someone to whom everyone else bowed. The nobleman dismounted his palfrey and handed the reins to his squire. Then, to the surprise of all, he threw back the hood of his cloak, inclined his head and entered the inn.

Charles stiffened: all the candles in the restaurant windows had jerked in unison. *Had someone opened the door?* A chill crept over him. He knew he'd been the last one to enter.

He stared at the candle on the table. *It puts you in the right century, lad!* Charles had never quite understood how this process worked, exactly. Now it was dawning on him that history, unlike the legal profession, existed more outside of books than it did pinned neatly on their pages. *Isn't that what Theodore had been trying to tell him all along?*

"You have to *read* history, of course, lad," he'd said. "Just like musicians have to practice their scales. But you'll never truly understand it if you cannot touch a stone someone else touched, or walk a battlefield, or light a candle without feeling a presence beside you."

The air in the restaurant felt suddenly denser. Charles pushed his wine glass away. *How foolish to drink so much, considering how tired he was!* He rubbed his eyes and looked up. The heavy curtain at the door billowed slightly into the room.

The waiter wandered to the door. "Windy tonight," he muttered, and twitched the curtains together. He leaned over a windowsill and glanced around the square. "*Comme c'est étrange,*" he said. He turned to Charles's table and refilled his glass. "Did you hear it, Monsieur?"

"Hear what?" Charles reached for his glass with a cool hand.

"A horse," said the waiter.

"No," Charles whispered.

"Oh, well. It must be the mounted police on some kind of exercise."

"I wouldn't think so," said Charles, his hands frigid now. "They don't ride at night."

LXII

No, *no*, lad! Concentrate, for God's sake. *Accidit per id temporis quiddam inopinabile sine exemplo casus.* Try it again."

Charles shifted on the wooden stool. He'd already spent several hours on it, and although sitting shoulder to shoulder with Uncle Theodore at his great desk was the highest honor he could imagine, his hips were beginning to ache. The rain hadn't stopped all afternoon, which was the main reason why they were stuck inside translating Ralph of Caen.

"'It happened that by these times...'"

"'At this time', lad! *Temporis*...genitive singular!"

"Why the genitive?"

"It's an expression! Now, please. Continue."

It crossed Charles's mind that maybe Theodore himself didn't know why the genitive singular was used in that instance. It was disquieting, to say the least, that his uncle actually might not know something. Anyway, it was not the first time they'd embarked on this particular chapter of the *Gesta Tancredi*. Ralph of Caen's grammatical challenges were already too familiar. The scene itself, however, was so strange that it captured the young boy's attention each time he tackled it, regardless of how often the genitive tripped him up.

It involved a dinner.

June, 1098. The crusaders had spent eight months camped outside Antioch trying to wrest the city from Muslim hands. Without a victory there, they would not be able to advance to Jerusalem. But a most brutal irony unfolded once they'd finally captured Antioch: they found themselves besieged within its walls. Not only was the enemy still ensconced in the mountain citadel just above the city, raining arrows down on the Christians, but Kerbogha, that fearsome Atabeg of Mosul, was even then mustering his immense army on the plains nearby.

The usual absurdities of war, Theodore liked to say.

And not exactly the opportune moment for a dinner party.

"This scene was actually sewn into the original manuscript of the *Gesta*, lad," said Theodore. "Just between the part where Tancred reenters Antioch after his vigil at a garrison tower, and the description of Kerbogha's 400,000 mounted troops, threatening death and slavery to all inside."

"I heard that troop numbers were often exaggerated," Charles said.

"Yes, yes, you're right," Theodore humored him. "But let's get to the story, shall we?"

"Who sewed it into the manuscript?" Charles asked. "Did they really have time for a banquet just then?"

"No one knows who put it there. Medieval manuscripts were rarely signed. And no, they didn't have time for dining. But they did have time for soothsaying," Theodore added leadingly. "It's a scene of portent, Charles, as surely you must know by now."

Indeed, Charles had tackled the Latin enough times to know the gist of the story fairly well: Bohemond of Taranto, that prince with the threatening laugh, had summoned two counts to dinner at the palace of Antioch, which he now occupied. Robert of Flanders sat to his right, and Eustace of Boulogne, Godfrey's brother, to his left. After dinner, Bohemond brandished a knife, which disquieted Robert. It was a time of joy, he said to his host. Not of anxiety.

"I am preparing a little game," Bohemond told him. He indicated a large candle on the table—thicker than all the others burning around it. "I shall cut this candle in two with a single stroke."

This seemed like a silly game to the counts.

"In that case," Robert said, humoring his host, "do what you have boasted. If you succeed, I will give you my jerkin as a mark of your strength. If you fail, you shall give me your own."

Bohemond nodded. He drew his sword and easily sliced the column of wax in two. Everyone around was stupefied, because the part of the candle that had fallen off continued to burn. Moreover, the remaining stump suddenly burst into flame without anyone lighting it.

The news spread fast. A great many people were in the palace at the time and they rushed from every corner to witness this astonishing event. Even Bohemond himself was taken aback. However, as the crowd watched, the flame that had miraculously come to life went out. A gasp united the witnesses. Everyone understood what this augured: tragedy. For if both burning parts had remained in tandem and perished together, a long lineage of succession would have been assured that would have lasted until the end of time.

But because the new fire had come to life and just as quickly disappeared, soothsayers promised hope for future offspring, but their early death, as well. This did, indeed, come to pass. Bohemond the Younger, who eventually came to rule Antioch, died fighting in Cilicia in 1130.

"Do you think that's what it meant, Uncle?" Charles asked. "An early death for Bohemond's son?"

"Perhaps," said Theodore. He picked up the ivory olifant and toyed with it idly, as one might a cheap trinket. "Sometimes a story comes down to us—like this one about Bohemond and the candle—and we're stumped in the face of it. It extends a hand to us—implores us to make a connection; to interpret it through the long lens of history. But we just cannot. It's heartbreaking, isn't it, our inability to understand so much of what's been handed down to us?"

Theodore turned the olifant over with greater attention. "It's even more frustrating to hold physical evidence of that time—like this olifant—and still know nothing about the exact circumstances in which it was used." He gave his nephew a penetrating look. "How do you imagine our own stories will fare in nine hundred years' time, lad?" he asked.

"I don't know," Charles muttered. He couldn't imagine anyone ever being interested in his own story—let alone after nine hundred years.

"No better than the candle tale, I should think," Theodore answered for him. "And probably much worse. It's funny, but in crazier moments I think that this scene was sewn into the *Gesta* parchment where it was—in the midst of all the horrors of the Antioch siege—to indicate that the crusaders should have turned around and gone home when they had a chance. They were fleeing in droves by that point in the campaign anyway. Even the nobles were deserting. Peter the Hermit himself slunk off into the night. They'd been reduced to eating boiled shoe soles, for God's sake."

The notion galvanized Theodore: "Once they captured Antioch and got trapped inside, things got even worse," he said. "There weren't any shoes to boil. Imagine starving to death and being shot at by Turks at the same time!" He shook his head. "And to think that similar scenes are playing out all over the world at this very moment. Just different actors." He smiled at Charles. "And different shoes."

In a dramatic gesture, Theodore blew out the candle on his desk. "A little flame," he intoned, "and whether or not it lived or died. Sometimes that's all our ancestors needed to read the world around them. It's not surprising that Ralph quotes Virgil at that point:

'Should the fates show such a thing to the land,
They will not permit them to endure for long.'"

"He quoted Virgil a lot," Charles said. It was a bold attempt to impress his uncle, for one never knew if Theodore would reward scholarship, or chastise presumption.

"Oh, he loved those classical authors, old Ralph did!" Theodore said. "He borrows from them all over the place: Virgil, Horace, Roman mythology, Lucan. He was educated at the cathedral school at Caen. You think his image or metaphor is original, only to find out that it's not his at all. Now..." Theodore tapped his finger loudly on the page. "Where is the word for fate here?"

"*Fata*," Charles said.

"Of course. Good. Nominative plural. *Fates*. Meaning?"

"Pardon me?"

"What does it mean, really? *The Fates*?"

"Um...well...it means..."

"Destiny, Charles! Fortune. *Chance!* Use your head! Doesn't it strike you as odd that people who are waging war in the name of Christ are still wedded to so-called pagan interpretations of the world? Oh, they see a lot of angels and other Christian visions along the way, to be sure. But then, as you remember, when the pilgrims were struggling across the bleak plains of Anatolia, Ralph says things like: 'Fortune turned its slippery favor from the supporters of Christ to the supporters of

Mahomet', or: 'Matters are transformed by the will of fate.' He didn't say: 'By the will of God'."

Charles squirmed on the stool, thoroughly miserable now.

"*Mon Dieu!*" Theodore exclaimed with uncharacteristic venom. "What's happened to your classical education? I suspect that my brother's been squeezing it out of you with all that math and science."

Charles stared at the floor. He burned as if with fever. In an instant he'd leapt from the stool and fled the study, careening off the wall of the corridor and dashing up the seven flights of stairs to the turret without stopping, two steps at a time.

It took an hour for Theodore to cajole him back down.

"Please, Charles," he called from the bottom stair on which he was slumped, blue eyes mournful. "I'm sorry. Really I am. Come down. We'll have some chocolate."

It was Theodore's answer to just about every predicament. For cases like this—which were rare—he kept a tin of the coffee creams he knew Charles couldn't resist.

They met up in the kitchen, took their seats at the table and munched in silence.

The rift healed at once.

Charles pressed his nose against a mullioned pane and studied the vista. The rain had stopped, leaving mist trailing over the river like boatless sails. The rooks had deserted the willow. The only beating heart in this still life was a gray heron poised on the bank, but even he seemed to have been borrowed from some obscure tapestry.

"We're surrounded by signs, lad," Theodore said at length, softly, as the scar was still tender. "Just look outside."

Charles rubbed his breath from the glass. "The heron..." he speculated.

"Yes, of course. Though perhaps he has no message for us today. The right moment has to appear for a sign to have effect."

"He's not the white one, anyway."

"No, he's not. But he keeps watch, and reminds us that the white one is not too far away. The white heron is the symbol."

"Of what?"

"Well…" Theodore examined a chocolate before popping it into his mouth. "Of natural wisdom."

"You said that the White Heron legend is more real than some of the others."

"Did I?" A remoteness came over Theodore.

"Yes. Anyway, it must be true," Charles said. "We're descended from Stephen de la Fontaine. That's pretty real."

"Yes. But bloodlines are difficult to confirm, lad. One can never really say for sure…"

Charles stared out into the twilight. The ridge was just a featureless battlement crenellated with pines. "I wish our world still had all that magic in it," he murmured.

"Ah, magic…" Theodore's voice was both warm and sad. "Don't you worry, lad: magic is all around us. And why should we miss out on it just because of the dull imaginations of so-called experts?"

"We should ignore the scientists, then!" Charles blurted.

"No, lad, we shouldn't," Theodore said, smiling indulgently. "That would make us ignoramuses. Anyway, even science can't explain why signs appear *when* they do; or why they affect someone in a particular way. That, I'm afraid, is up to someone with intuition: a seer (or a seeress, of course). Not a scientist."

Charles regarded his uncle with expectation, as though such a seer were indeed at hand, sitting across the table from him nibbling chocolate.

"The old beliefs still linger here, don't they, Uncle?" he said.

"It would be foolish to think otherwise, wouldn't it?"

The comment unnerved Charles. It was a few moments before he could ask: "Do ghosts?"

Theodore cocked his head at his nephew. "You mean the horseman who crosses the bridge?"

"Maybe," Charles faltered. "You said it could be Stephen de la Fontaine."

Theodore arched his eyebrows. "Or someone else, perhaps," he said coyly.

"Uncle!" Charles protested. "Who are you talking about?"

"The one who never came home."

LXIII

W e're closing soon, Monsieur," the waiter said, snuffing out the candles with a napkin. "Shall I bring the bill?"

Charles emerged from his reverie. He looked about the restaurant: all the other diners had left. The fire in the stove was out and the room had lost its village cheer. Despite the rich meal he felt strangely empty; apprehensive.

He paid the bill and crossed the Sablon through torpid air. It was past ten o'clock. Most night life had moved down to the Grand'Place, or up to the bars and clubs around Avenue Louise. The cathedral presided over the evening's business as it had for more than eight centuries of evenings (give or take a few), with that forbearance immured in stone monuments built to make it to eternity, but obliged to tolerate car exhaust and pigeon droppings along the way.

"A letter came for you while you were out, Monsieur," the hotel receptionist called across the lobby as Charles headed for the elevator. He hurried over and handed him a rather thick envelope addressed simply to "Monsieur C. Fontaine." Ida's name and address appeared on the back of the envelope in small, embossed cursive.

"Madame de la Fontaine delivered this herself?" Charles said, incredulous. Why would Ida, who didn't drive, leave her villa at ten in the evening, presumably by taxi, to deposit a letter at Charles's hotel? Stranger still was why she felt she had to write at all instead of ringing him.

"A gentleman delivered it," said the clerk. "About half an hour ago."

"A gentleman?" This was even less plausible. "Did he give his name?"

"No, Monsieur. He didn't say a word. He just put the letter on the desk and left at once."

Charles lingered at the reception. "Was he...a tall man?"

"Quite the opposite, I must say," the receptionist said, obviously uncomfortable with this bit of personal commentary.

"*Un costaud?*" Charles pressed him, using the expression for a solidly-built person.

The man shuffled some papers. "Monsieur, please excuse me. I have some work to do. *Je vous souhaite une bonne nuit.*"

Charles drifted from the desk. Funny how clear an answer could be by not giving it.

Raul...tracking his every step.

The hotel lobby was deserted. The usual array of unappealing designer furniture dotted the space, but one maroon chair seemed comfortable and Charles took it. He'd summoned the courage to open Ida's letter, but somehow just couldn't do so in the solitude of his room.

"Would you like a *tisane*, Monsieur?" a bellboy asked.

"Brandy, maybe," Charles said, unfolding several pages covered with Ida's elegant script. His courage wouldn't go very far on herbal tea.

My dear Charles,

I began this letter to you long ago, when you were still at university. I was so impatient to tell you these things. But then I realized it would have been unfair to you. Hugues took you to America for you to have a new life, and even though I didn't agree with what he did, removing you from your roots and pushing you down a road where, quite honestly, I don't believe you've found happiness, I knew that I didn't have the right to interfere with your upbringing. Hugues wanted the best for you in his own way.

But now dear Theo is gone. When he brought me that envelope in the middle of the night to give to you and I saw what a state he was in, I knew that what I'd always feared had come to pass: that Hugues had found out valuable information about Blancheron and intended to profit from it. I suspect that Theo passed his findings quite innocently to Philippe Osselaer, who naïvely relayed it to Hugues. Poor Philippe! He could never keep a secret, even as a child. But there you have it. Philippe's a wonderful man. You must never think otherwise. Hugues has been abusing his good nature, and his loyalty to the family, to get what he wants.

The bellboy crossed the lobby with a tray and placed it on the table next to Charles: a snifter with a generous amount of brandy, and a tiny bowl of peanuts. Charles nodded his thanks, and for several minutes lost himself in the heady vapors of the glass.

I don't know what Theo told you in his letter. I don't even want to know. I learned from an early age to speak as little as possible about the family. I suppose that I've never gotten over that need for secrecy. Your grandfather was generally considered to be an embarrassment—for Hugues in particular. Your poor grandmother pretended otherwise all her life, bless her. As children we were ridiculed at the lycée in Bouillon. "Medieval orphans", they called us. "Maugis's brats". That sort of thing. Hugues suffered most from this indignity. He was the only one of us who could physically challenge the bullies, and he did. He paid a hefty price in the end: his humanity suffered gravely. He never missed an opportunity to belittle me...worse, to belittle my relationship with Theo. He must have been counting the years until he could escape to the New World and leave everything behind!

I clung to Theo and cherished our time together. But I learned to keep family lore to myself. This wasn't so difficult, really. The heron story in particular seemed very strange to me...scary, even. Maybe because there was always the unspoken understanding that much of it was true. I was afraid of Arda: that I might run into her somewhere near the pond, or up on the ridge when Theo and I went exploring. It bothered me that we could never find her cave.

But I've strayed from my course.

I wanted to tell you about Raul. I don't know of any indirect way to say this, so forgive me if I use the direct one. You see, Charles, when you called me today to warn me about him, how could you possibly have known that Raul Mora was my nephew?

Charles lowered the letter.

He reached for the snifter, gulping the brandy as if it were emergency medicine.

His pulse hammered in his ears

I'm related to the raincoated man.

The room tilted around him.

His mind made that curious detour that so often follows news brutally imparted: a sort of instant recharting of the route already taken, and what it might have looked like had none of this occurred. *Would he still be in New York living a half-life?* In a further bending of brain tissue he thought of Rodolfo, and how Stephen de la Fontaine had surprised what he thought had been a dangerous beast in the cave, only to realize that the monster was human, and had been unfailingly loyal to Arda.

But there was something even more daunting than the news that Raul was his cousin: the fact that Theodore must have been Raul's father.

He read on.

LXIV

I realize that you've probably interpreted my words as meaning that Raul is Theo's child, Ida wrote. *This is not the case. Sadly, neither Theo nor I ever had children. Dear Charles, you must know, and I'll tell you myself: Raul is your father's son. He is, therefore, your half-brother.*

Hugues met a Spanish woman several years before he took you to America. She ran a restaurant near Place Flagey, a little Catalan place that's gone now. The affair didn't last long. Raul was born shortly afterwards. (Your father didn't seem to think much of his children's mothers, did he?) Anyway, years later, when you were already in high school, I received word from your father that Raul had surfaced at some sort of state foster home, and would I be willing to take him in. He was about ten years old at the time. You can imagine my shock! This was the first I'd heard of the boy. I thought it an extraordinary imposition on Hugues's part and I refused. I've regretted it ever since.

For when Raul was sixteen, he turned up at my door. What a wild, hunted thing he was by then! I was appalled. Hardly a day goes by that I don't wonder if he would have turned out differently had I taken him in when Hugues asked me to. (Perhaps there was a shred of humanity in Hugues after all, seeking care for his son.) I couldn't refuse Raul again, of course. Perhaps you think this was a rash decision, Charles. Even dangerous. You've seen yourself what he's like.

I was very fearful at first, believe me. I couldn't call Hugues, of course. He was in New York by then and had severed all ties. But something deep inside the boy spoke to me. His eyes, if you look closely, don't have violence in them. He hardly said a word, even then. But he always made intense eye contact, as if this were his lifeline. I couldn't very well reject my own nephew, could I? When Sylvana met him and I saw how he responded to her, I knew that music could help him enormously. But just a few months after he arrived, he disappeared again for many weeks. This would be his pattern of behavior for the next twelve years. (He's twenty-eight now.)

Oh, Charles. I can't possibly imagine what's going through your head. What you must think of your father, let alone this unknown brother. Or of me, for that matter. But there's more I must tell you. Please, keep reading. But try to do so with an open heart.

"Monsieur, are you all right?" The bellboy was hovering near Charles's chair, uncertain. Something about this guest obviously required either immediate attention or complete privacy, and it was unclear which to provide.

Charles looked up, his face white. "Yes, I'm fine, thank you. But I wouldn't mind another brandy."

"*Oui, bien sûr,*" said the bellboy, relieved to have a task.

Hugues got back in touch after he learned that Raul had contacted me. Your father suddenly had a plan for the boy. Oh, it all seemed benign at first. Maybe Hugues had changed! The thought heartened me greatly. I knew that he was investing in European antiques from afar. He needed someone to let him know which auctions were worthwhile, what was being sold, that sort of thing. One can do these things on the internet these days, of course. But Hugues needed...what's that expression Americans use? "Boots on the ground", I think it is. I didn't know about Manfred Ames then. I just thought that Hugues was training Raul to be those boots. That he was finally looking out for him. Raul barely had any education. (He'd gone to school only until fifteen.) But he was smart and able. Naïvely, I thought that he would even begin to prosper having his father's attention.

The boy was very dubious socially, it's true. But I'd developed an affection for him and could only see progress. He was my blood relative, after all. The son I never had. Hugues sent me money, saying that I should give some of it to Raul and keep the rest for my trouble. It wasn't much, mind you! You know your father, Charles: money is his answer to everything. "Just keep an eye on that damned Spaniard," he told me. "He needs supervision." Which should have been a warning that Hugues hadn't changed. But during all the weeks when I didn't see Raul, I just assumed he was under the aegis of someone else who was grooming him for Hugues's projects.

How wrong I was! When he was twenty-three, Raul turned up in prison for breaking into an auction house in Antwerp. He spent four years behind bars. Among the objects he stole was a Stradivarius viola—one of only ten that are known to exist. They say it was worth over 40 million Euros. I should have realized then that Manfred Ames was the man Hugues had employed for the genteel part of his enterprise. Raul, on the other hand, was his grunt. His serf.

Then I heard news reports of the murder in Antwerp. Soon Raul's description turned up in the press. The police were looking for him everywhere. I took him in, Charles. So you were right: I was abetting a felon—if indeed Raul is one.

How Hugues didn't get his wings clipped on that occasion I'll never know. But he and his cohorts escaped unscathed. Perhaps Belgian law doesn't reach as far as Manhattan. At first I felt certain that Raul was protecting his father by not exposing him. But later I reconsidered. You see, I'd met Ames by then. I realized that he, in fact, was the most dangerous element in this whole affair, not Raul. Ames most likely killed that man in Antwerp.

Raul's life is in danger, Charles. I fear that you, too, must watch your step. Your father is determined to get his hands on Theo's discovery...on the information in that envelope he gave you. By force, if necessary. He will then demand a fortune for Blancheron. He sent you to Brussels to pursue his scheme. He's using you...just as he uses everyone. I believe that Ames was the person who assaulted Theo in his study on the night he died. And I have no doubt that Hugues has set Raul on your trail. But Ames is the one to fear. Raul is capable of much dirty work, it's true. But I don't believe he's evil. Please consider the likelihood that Hugues is monitoring everything you do while you're here in Belgium. And please: don't let Theo's envelope out of your sight.

The second brandy arrived. This time it was less a warming soporific than an agent of alarm. *Raul was his half-brother; he was doing the bidding of their shared father.* The revelation had only been heightened by alcohol.

Charles folded Ida's letter into the envelope and tucked it in his blazer pocket. Then he thrust an arm into his coat, grabbed his laptop bag and headed for the door. *Air. Movement. Answers.* He was desperate for all three.

"Put the brandies on my bill, please," he called to the receptionist, and strode out into the night.

LXV

H e walked briskly past the quaint art and tea shops dotting the square and turned the corner onto Rue de la Regence. He hadn't intended to visit Godfrey, though he could hardly ignore him, the statue being on his route.

Everyone had spies during the battle for Nicaea. This errant thought did not seem incongruous to Charles. *The Franks spied on the Turks.* He warmed to the subject. *The Turks spied on the Franks. Emperor Alexius spied on everyone.* Not incongruous at all, in fact. Charles himself was a target: of spies paid for by his own father, no less. He swung the laptop bag over his shoulder and marched ever faster, trying in vain to outpace this realization.

The crusaders had taken Nicaea, their biggest prize between Constantinople and Antioch, with a wily combination of blockade and various modern war machines, such as catapults and battering rams. Kilij Arslan still commanded the city—the dreaded Seljuk strongman who'd decimated the People's Crusade the previous year.

The point of all this now, thought Charles, as the Royal Museum of Fine Arts hove into view on his left, was that human deception had hardly changed in nine hundred years. Arslan's spies had infiltrated the crusaders' camp to find out their battle plans. One spy was killed. The other, threatened with torture, confessed that Arslan was planning a pre-emptive dawn attack from the steep hills south of Nicaea. The news shocked the Franks and galvanized them into action.

Charles pulled up his scarf and smiled wryly. He was a gentleman, not a warrior. If his father had sent spies to track him, he couldn't very well resort to medieval methods to make them reveal their plans. There were only two things he could do: avoid them; or confront them in a considerably more genteel manner than a Frankish crusader might.

He paused on the corner of the Place Royale. Streetlamps bled into the thick air. A single taxi barreled past. A tram retreated with its sad, metallic wail. Otherwise, Godfrey rode alone.

So many emotions were speeding, diverting, colliding. Charles barely had a chance to identify them as they careened past, but among them he was surprised to spot jealousy: of Raul and the affection he enjoyed from both Ida and Sylvana. And relief: that according to Ida, Theodore had been assaulted not by this dark horse-turned-relative, but by Hugh's personal operator, Manfred Ames.

Charles pressed his hand against his blazer pocket. Ida's letter contained more information about his family than he'd learned in a lifetime. *And now, a brother.*

He crossed the empty square to the statue and looked up at about where, in the gloom, the rider's resolute heart would have been. He fancied that if you traversed the vacuum of time and burrowed into all that bronze, you might find a stalwart, beating marvel. Though Godfrey's most intimate secrets had never made it out through the weight of time and metal, on contemplating the statue through the haze, Charles considered that perhaps one or two of them might not have been lost.

A story like this—any story from the past—offers you a thread. You must grasp that thread and pull it. Eventually, what comes to the surface is a surprise no one can ever predict...or even imagine.

This seemed like a good time to tug on it.

Stephen and Henri had come and gone from the forests around Rêve and left their stories of Arda behind.

Had Godfrey encountered her, too?

The thread moved slightly.

Charles left the square and headed back past the museum.

He didn't sense the shadow until it was upon him.

A dark patch of stealth crossed the street toward the museum and brushed Charles from behind. The shadow was quick as well as deft: within seconds it had taken possession of the laptop bag.

Charles lashed out at his attacker, but too late.

This man was not compact. Certainly not feral. Even through the North Sea blur it was clear that he was statuesque; urbane. He glanced back at Charles as he slipped away. His goatee lay like a wedge of silver over the collar of his dark-blue coat. He had the bemused air of a victor so superior to the vanquished, he could pause for a few seconds to savor his success.

"Ames!" Charles growled.

Rue de Ruysbroeck pitched down to a dog-leg turn below the museum and the man took it. He rounded the corner with finesse, as if leaving the stage. His right hand swung out behind him and the diamond sparked in the lamplight.

"*Ames!*" Charles shouted, springing into pursuit. He lurched down the cobbled way. The stones propelled him unevenly, like the surface of the bridge at Blancheron, and combined with the lingering effects of the brandy made forward motion difficult.

Charles halted at the dog-leg turn, breathing heavily. He stared down the alley through the fog of his own exhale: there was no trace of the man. The city had enveloped him.

He straggled back up the cobbled way. The theft of the laptop had been bad enough, but there'd been even worse losses: Florus's photocopy of the Latin parchment; the ancient bronze key; the key to the desk drawer at Villa Antioch, and Theodore's letter to Charles alerting him to the folio he'd discovered. It was little consolation that his childhood companions—the family gonfalon and Ralph of Caen— were still at the hotel in his duffle bag.

LXVI

Charles collapsed on the hotel bed. There seemed no point in filing a report with the police when he knew perfectly well who'd stolen the bag and why. Anyway, the police were notoriously slow in their investigations. Far more important was to find out how, exactly, Hugues intended to use this new development and thwart him somehow. All hinged on the results of Florus's analysis—on how valuable the parchment really was.

As he lay there coming to terms with Raul's identity, Charles detected a chink of light in his father's well-laid plan: Raul himself. It would take a hardened criminal indeed not to be softened by Ida's tenderness—or healed by a sibyl like Sylvana. Hugues had been able to buy Raul's allegiance until now, but he hadn't counted on the revelation of bloodline.

Do whatever you can to hold on to Blancheron.

He slept restlessly that night, like the castle itself.

She must be here! I can see the lyra on the fallen beech. She's set it down for a moment. But where is she? Something's wrong. I can feel it on the air, just as Theodore said you could.

Is that her voice calling from the ridge?

I'm climbing, but at each step I slide backwards over dead, sopping leaves. They pull away from the hillside like skin from a rotting carcass. It's difficult to breathe: my chest is burning.

Someone's climbing in front of me. Theodore! That's his satchel swinging out behind him. But no...it's not him. It's not a bag at all, but the edge of a robe. The hem is sodden from the underbrush. A hand—white, fleshy—clutches at the fabric. An enormous sapphire ring gleams blue like Theodore's eyes.

"Walderic..." Charles muttered in his sleep. "Where are you going?"

I see her now, at the far end of the meadow near the Duke's Gate. A cold wind is blowing. She must be freezing to death in that flimsy tunic. I'll never catch up to Walderic now.

"Darling..." Charles whispered.

He's almost upon her. His robe fans out like some angel of death. Arda is waving frantically: to me, it seems. Yes...to me!

"Darling, I'm here!"

She's holding something in her hand. But Walderic is upon her. She screams and resists. She screams again. He throws her to the ground.

"Arda!"

Walderic's pale hand is visible even from across the meadow. He's pressing her down against the cold, wet grass. He lifts an arm to the sky. Something glints in his hand.
He drops his arm suddenly, heavy as a blacksmith's hammer.
A hollow moan escapes her. I can hear a name in that animal sound. Again and again she calls it. But it's not my name.
"Godefroid...Godefroid..." I hear her crying.
Walderic turns his back on the dying girl. He does not see her raise her hand from the grass. She wants me to see what she's holding:
A small box.

The phone jerked him awake.
"Charles!"
There was only one person who could convey authority, disdain and menace in that single word.
"Father. It's the middle of the night here."
"I'm concerned that the sale is not moving ahead as it should."

Charles lifted himself on one elbow and looked at the bedside clock: 3:36. "Concerned enough to have me followed?" he asked. His pulse accelerated. Suddenly one image of his father eclipsed all the others: the way he'd tossed his brother's death certificate on the desk like rubbish.

"What are you implying?" Hugh said.

Charles sat up in bed. A fleeting glimpse of that Thanksgiving audience crossed his mind: the formal salon, and his father's crushing presence; the deceptive purity of the snow. How strange, he thought, that his father's tone had not altered a bit since then. Stranger still, his own voice was practically unrecognizable as he said: "What do you hope to gain by having your people follow me, Father? By having them assault and rob me?"

Silence.

Charles got out of bed and wandered to the window. The cathedral dozed in the half-sleep of great age.

"Listen to me, Charles," Hugh said, unease creeping into his voice. "I strongly suggest that you follow whatever course Manfred Ames sets out for Blancheron."

"Are we talking about the same Ames who mugged me last night?" Charles retorted. "So *he's* in charge of my inheritance now?"

"He's more experienced than you are at assessing antiquities."

"He's damned lucky I didn't call the police!"

Another silence. Then: "That would be extremely ill-advised."

Charles glanced across the square at the restaurant where he'd dined. The windows were dark; the candles extinguished.

"I wondered when you were going to come out and threaten me, Father," Charles said. "Especially since you have no difficulty threatening your other son."

The words were as devastating as Seljuk arrows. Charles even briefly regretted resorting to this tactic, as the usual hesitation that Hugh exhibited before speaking now seemed longer than any of the others: perhaps even suggesting, at long last, a breath of humanity.

Hugh deflected the arrows, however, using what had always worked for Emperor Alexius: bait.

"It looks as if Blancheron could go for several million now," he said, emerging from the suspended moment. "Your cut will be more than generous, Charles. More than generous..."

Ames obviously hadn't had the photocopy translated yet. *Father must be improvising*, Charles thought. *He has no proof that a stunning revelation about Blancheron is imminent.*

If Charles had had to define a specific moment in his life when he finally, definitively grew up, this would have been it.

The day will come when you can stand up to him.

He smiled. "That day has arrived, Uncle," he whispered to himself.

To Hugh he said, without a trace of guilt or fear: "It may come as a surprise to you, Father, but I'm not interested in your money." The tiny flame that had come to life at Florus's was burning nicely now. "In fact, I was never interested in your money. Or your lousy, mercenary firm. I hereby renounce my position in Fontaine and Fontaine, effective immediately. And I'll have nothing more to do with the Blancheron sale." He summoned all the resolve that Grace Holmes had once detected in him: "Or with you, for that matter."

LXVII

"Auntie," he whispered in Ida's doorway, as concert guests gathered behind him. "When can we discuss your letter?"

She took his face in her hands and kissed his cheek. "It's not me you need to talk to, *Sharl'*," she breathed in his ear. "You know that now."

"But..."

Ida smiled over her nephew's shoulder at the person behind him, exhibiting the talent for simultaneous welcome and dismissal that the European gentry possess from birth. She squeezed his hand as he entered, however, in private appreciation of his being there.

It was the first time Charles had ever seen Ida's piano open. There was something slightly risqué about the instrument exposing its aging innards like that, especially in a room with so few other distractions. For indeed, even though a performance was about to take place, only a handful of folding chairs had been placed at random around the spacious floor.

Charles took a chair next to the sofa. Two of Ida's friends, even bonier than she, obviously needed the extra padding and he indicated the sofa to them. They nodded their thanks in a sideways, bird-like manner. The window through which Charles had first heard Sylvana was behind them, and the memory of her singing spread over him like warm oil.

Would she be singing tonight? Ida hadn't been certain that she would. Charles glanced around. *Where was she, anyway?* This question was moot, he knew, for it seemed that Sylvana's presence could be felt without actually seeing it.

Ida floated in, a silvery wraith. She welcomed the little gathering and said something about the piece that was about to be played: the Brahms Piano Trio No. 1 for violin, cello and piano. Then the musicians entered to a smattering of applause.

Charles held his breath: Sylvana had entered behind the three performers. She carried the score of the Brahms and walked solemnly, not acknowledging anyone. It was clear that she'd be turning pages for the pianist and was trying to be as invisible as she could, which of course would have been impossible for her anywhere, let alone in public. She was dressed in black with her hair fastened in a bun, the whole effect lending her skin a nocturnal glow. She set the score on the piano and took the chair next to the keyboard.

The two string players took their time adjusting stands, tightening bows, exchanging a few quips, tuning. In the general shuffle, Sylvana sat straight-backed and motionless. Her hands rested in her lap and her calm spread over the room. *The stillness of the heron*, thought Charles.

The concert began.

Gone were the dreary family coffees; gone the barbed politeness, and the counting of tree rings just to escape it all. The room had changed utterly, gripped in a spell. If someone had asked Charles later about the color of the violinist's hair, whether or not the cellist had been wearing glasses, or even if the players had been male or female, he would have had trouble answering.

Sylvana glanced at Charles just once. He knew the importance of the page-turner from the galas he'd attended with his father at Lincoln Center. With complex music like Brahms she would have to be glued to the score.

Charles met her glance, and to his relief saw empathy. He was sure she'd sensed it, too. Their fledgling history could hardly have been more unusual. *A funeral...a cave...a medieval dagger and parchment.* Not the usual components of early-stage romance. But as the pianist began the first poignant melody, Charles dearly hoped that they would be more than enough to carry him forward in Sylvana's company.

At times the music was so difficult that the players seemed to wrestle with their instruments. As they ventured heroically into dense territory, the piece nevertheless demanded that they sublimate all physical difficulties, and this, miraculously, they managed to do, finally slipping their earthly bonds to achieve rapture. It seemed to Charles that as in any transfiguration, this was only possible if one had absolute faith that it could be done. At that moment he understood how pilgrims had managed to walk four thousand kilometers without shoes.

The first movement ended with a swell of arpeggios and crisp final chords. The musicians remained motionless, hands in the air. The audience froze with them, as technically, this silence was still part of the music.

Finally the room came to life and the strings tuned softly for the next movement.

Sylvana turned the page.

The music continued with the same pull between heaven and earth. The precise, repeated notes of the scherzo gave way to the sublime adagio: a conversation between saints.

The trio launched into the turbulent finale and Charles let out the breath he didn't know he'd been holding.

He turned around to look outside and his heart contracted:

Raul.

The man was leaning against the weeping beech not two meters from the salon window. He was positioned exactly where Charles had been just a few days before, his hand resting on the trunk in the same spot.

Charles swiveled back to the room. The scene that had just enchanted him was in remnants. He was hardly aware of Sylvana. The surging final movement of the Brahms washed blandly over him.

He turned to the window again. Though half hidden by the tree, it was obvious that Raul was poised for flight. His whole aspect bristled. *But his face...*

Charles stared at the man. He could do this without detection, for it was clear that the essence of Raul had been transported and only his body was present. The same stormy features that had bled through the gloom at Theodore's study window, and shone like an autopsy under the lamp on Ida's street, had smoothed out; reconfigured.

Charles turned back to the salon, his breathing uneven. He glanced over at Ida, sandwiched between her friends on the sofa. She gave him the briefest nod, as if signaling a bid in an auction house, and he took this as the clearest of signs. He got up to leave just in time to see the renegade dart away.

Charles circled around the villa to intercept Raul. Applause erupted from the house, followed by the relaxed chatter after a spell has been broken. The front door opened and someone stepped out for a smoke.

He passed the disarray of Ida's garden: roses with blight; broken pots; a tilting birdbath. One of the tangled beds must have been the herb garden Sylvana had mentioned.

He rounded the back of the house and stopped in surprise at the pines: they'd grown into huge, pointy-capped sorcerers. Then he noticed what they were sheltering: Raul was crouching at the base of one of the trees near the salon window. He'd been caught in mid-flight, it seemed, by the promise of more beauty, for inside, Sylvana was preparing to sing.

Charles stayed where he was. Suddenly he could see how important music was to this troubled soul...this brother. As the piano sounded a few chords and Ida's audience settled back into place, he wondered how much Sylvana was affecting his own trajectory. *Had she nourished his ailing resolve without him even realizing it?*

She began singing.

LXVIII

"Raul," Charles said softly, approaching with caution. "Please, may I speak with you?" His French sounded stilted; insincere.

Raul seemed not to have heard him. He was still crouched under the pine, tracing a finger through its dead needles, listening. The voice issuing from Ida's salon no longer appeared to be music, but rather pure emotion distilled from sound. And the sound itself...well, no one could have sworn that it was being produced by human means, so closely was it allied to the purling of water and the wind's phantom bow.

"Raul..." Charles said again.

This time the man leapt up, coiled and at the ready. He glared at Charles. Furrows returned to his brow. Under the tent of pine boughs Charles could still see the pockmarked skin, rubbery and mask-like.

"No closer!" Raul warned. He plunged a hand into his raincoat pocket and Charles backed off a few paces. Only now did he consider that the man could be armed.

Does he know that we share a father? Charles wondered. Ida hadn't indicated this in her letter. He himself hadn't the slightest notion about filial relationships. But this one, newly-found, happened to be unfolding within earshot of a singing enchantress, so even if a fugitive criminal were involved there could be no room for fear.

"My father is Hugh Fontaine," Charles declared.

"He sent you..." Raul stumbled. "The bastard! What does he want?" Though he was primed for flight, Charles's news seemed to have paralyzed him.

"No, it's not that!" Charles said in a stage whisper, ever-conscious of the music playing nearby. "He didn't send me. I know that Father has forced you into working for him...I know from Ida that you're not guilty of murder. Raul, please. I can help you."

Raul stared at him like an animal a heartbeat from doom.

287

Sylvana's voice traced a long, slow arc of surpassing beauty before returning gently to earth. The piano played a final chord. There was silence. Then the salon exploded with clapping and cheers.

"We are brothers," Charles said, emboldened by Sylvana's presence. "We can resolve this together. Blancheron is your patrimony, too," he added unconvincingly. He stopped short of asking Raul to abandon his allegiance to Hugh.

The music seemed to have touched Raul differently, however: "You are rich, like him," he growled.

Charles balked. *Despise pecuniary reward.* Hadn't he once thrown that item of chivalry at his father?

Raul seemed tuned to an excruciating pitch. Even under the shapeless coat it was clear that his whole body was drawn tight enough to snap. His hand bulged in his pocket. With awful rancor he spat the words: "You *are* him."

Charles paled. It was a terrible accusation.

But it was the truth: Hugh had manufactured a clone. Why did Charles even pretend that he was any different from his father? With mounting desperation he tried to engage his brother—to at least make eye contact. *His eyes, if you look closely, don't have violence in them.* But Raul's gaze was shaded by heavy brows and too turbid to fathom.

Soul... The word had been there all along, Charles realized, waiting for him to notice it. *Why, despite his hardships, did Raul seem in tune with his deepest source?*

At once the man swirled around and scuttled from the pine grove. His raincoat caught on a low branch, snapped it off and sailed free.

Charles stood there rooted, listening to his own inner turmoil. *So many clamoring voices.* Among them, rising through the din, he wasn't at all surprised to hear Grace Holmes's. She'd always been there for him in some form, after all. As he tarried under the pines, ripe for another infusion of Grace's insight, Charles realized for the first time how little he knew about the woman over the fence in Connecticut. He'd never asked her who she was. A widow? A divorcee? A mother? With the wallowing selfishness of the young, he'd only been aware of his own universe. And yet he couldn't help but wonder now what she would have advised him to do.

Was there a certain wisdom bestowed on those with shapeless track suits, copper-colored hair and plastic ducks? Was wisdom, in fact, attracted to such humble means? The answer must surely have been "yes". Because true wisdom had no artifice, Charles was discovering. It also was not dependent on wealth for its richness.

He stared through the window into Ida's salon and began to piece together one of Grace's nuggets—one he should have taken note of long ago. For she'd clearly been talking about him when she'd said:

"That's the problem with people, Charlie. They abandon their passions along the way, thinking that something better will come along. Something like money. And then they wonder why they get so lost in life."

The comment had surfaced with a startling vision of the woman who had uttered it. Resolute. Frank. Guileless. A woman who could have led her own army of pacifists if suburbia hadn't condemned her to its shallow comforts. Which made Charles regret that the crusading experience had been documented by well-heeled churchmen, and not by the Grace Holmeses of the twelfth century.

He was skirting the blighted roses when his phone rang.

"Charles!" It was Florus. "Where are you?"

"At Ida's. Why?"

"You told me to call the minute I knew anything."

"Is something the matter?"

"Well..." Florus hesitated. "I don't know about that. But I can certainly tell you that a great matter is at hand."

Charles regarded the jungle that was Ida's herb garden, the phone pressed to his ear.

"By the way, your father called me just now," Florus said.

"*Father?*" Charles recoiled, then remembered Florus saying that he'd met Hugh once. His fingers went cold. "You mean he's gotten to you, too?"

"No one gets to me, Charles," Florus snapped. He paused. "But he did threaten me."

Charles stood rigid. "What do you mean?"

"Well, it was quite unambiguous. He said he'd send someone to my house (his words) if I colluded with you regarding the Blancheron sale."

"Send someone to your house..." Charles echoed. His mind lurched picturing the thug his father probably had in mind for this task. *Raul.* "It's not an empty threat, Cédric," he said.

"Empty or not, I don't care a damn," Florus huffed. "Hugues is convinced the parchment contains something earth-shattering."

"Is he right?"

"I would say so! I'll pick you up at the corner of Ida's street and Rue Edith Cavell," Florus said briskly. "Ten minutes."

LXIX

Florus turned up in an antique MG of peerless British Racing Green, its convertible roof ill-fitting. It was just beginning to rain as Charles folded himself into the passenger seat.

"We have to be careful," Florus said, suede gloves gripping the leather-covered wheel. He shot a glance in the rearview mirror, satisfied that no one was following them.

Charles studied the interior of the miniature car with admiration. It must have been at least forty years old. The dashboard was of rosy wood, the gauges had the look of precision watches, and everywhere leather wafted and cricked. As the car bucked around turns and trembled impatiently at traffic lights, Charles mused that it was the perfect palfrey for this *chevalier*.

"My laptop bag was stolen last night," he said. "Right in front of the museum. Thank God my wallet and passport were in my pocket."

"You have to be careful in central Brussels these days," came the response.

Charles glared at Florus. "Cédric, the copy you made of the parchment was in that bag!"

"That's of no consequence. I mean, I'm sorry about your bag, of course. But one cannot scan a photocopy for overwritten text. If someone was after the manuscript, it's the missing text, and what it might imply, that they'd be looking for."

Irritated, Charles added: "The bronze key was also in the bag."

"Ah," said Florus. "That *is* a loss. There's no box, however. At least, not yet."

"What do you mean by that?"

The medievalist floored his antiquated motor. "Because I think I know where it is."

Charles lost all track of where they were going. He probably could have found his way around this part of Brussels by day. But not at night, with the amnesia of long absence. No landmark or intersection seemed familiar. Before long, they'd left all lights and traffic behind and entered what Charles assumed was the Forêt de Soignes—a vast reserve of towering beeches that bordered southern Brussels.

Florus swerved onto a broad, unlit avenue and after a few kilometers turned off into a parking area for walkers.

He cut the engine and doused the lights. They sat for a moment without speaking.

The car faced a looming black wall. Gradually, through some indistinct light source, the forest made itself known: a tree's ghostly torso...a shiver in the leaves. The slender ribbon of a foot path darkened the underbrush. The Forêt de Soignes had once been the royal hunting preserve of the Habsburgs, and some of the tallest beeches were almost two centuries old. Charles recalled one of Theodore's quips: "They're grandiose, all right. But they're shallow and acidic—like some family members."

The clouds parted briefly, and in the weak moonlight the beeches emerged as phantom clerics in gray robes. They stood as if in obeisance, and indeed, farther down the footpath, Charles could make out a giant among them: a tree of immense height and breadth facing its fellows as Pope Urban must have faced the Council of Clermont in 1095, when he'd preached holy war. The sermon had been outdoors, after all. Well-dressed clerics and nobles had attended, but also simpler folk—ragged, like the edges of this woodland.

Florus broke the silence. "The police don't patrol this part of the forest very often," he said, adding: "Although it's not the police I'm worried about."

"You know about Manfred Ames, then," Charles offered. He didn't mention Raul, as his emotions had veered strangely from fear to protection on that front.

"I know that your father has his bloodhounds on the scent."

"Yes," Charles agreed. "So...are you and I colluding, then?"

Florus chuckled. "I hope so!" He turned on a small lamp that he'd obviously had fitted to the car's dashboard. The forest outside plunged back into anonymity. The light glanced handsomely on Florus's silver hair, and more unflatteringly on deep lines in his face. The man was clearly exhausted.

"I scanned most of the parchment," Florus said, reaching behind Charles's seat to produce a worn calfskin document case.

"Most of it?"

"Yes. I have to use the scanner once more for certain details. I may be able to do that later tonight."

"But..."

"Charles, please listen. I didn't get to the lab until late yesterday evening, then was up most of the night translating. I thought I'd begin by showing you some of the passages and words that are, in my opinion, key to understanding what's going on here. Then you can take a look at the whole translation yourself. Multi-spectral imaging can be used to read erased text these days—even if the parchment is damaged or the erasure is deep."

Charles could barely contain his anticipation. "Was Theodore on the right track with his translation?"

"Oh, Theo did an admirable job!" Florus enthused. "But the bulk of information is on the verso. All that condensed script is very difficult to read. I thought that I'd first explain the erasures I deciphered from the scanner, then let you have a look at my translation, which I've typed out."

"Great!"

"Before all that, though," said Florus, echoing Theodore's delight in the professorial role, "I'd like to mention a few oddities about this document...about your family's legend."

"All right." Charles concealed his impatience.

"The folio is unusual in several respects," Florus began. "It was written in Latin as an ending for a *chanson de geste* that was penned in Old French; it's in a combination of prose and poetry, which is more reminiscent of a crusader chronicle than a *chanson de geste*, and indeed dates from the second decade of the twelfth century, which is more in line with other crusader documents than with the French epic genre. *The Song of Roland* is the only *chanson* from around that period. I suspect this folio was penned by a churchman at Valdoré."

"And then nine centuries later, someone removed it," Charles joked.

"Indeed!" Florus laughed. "What strikes me most is that this is chiefly a document of return: that is, the events that surrounded Stephen de la Fontaine's *return* from the Holy Land—not what he did there. Which in itself is remarkable and exceptionally interesting. You see, Charles, as you know, most crusaders—knights, infantry, peasants, hangers-on—didn't return home. If you did, the person you used to be before going had little in common with the person who came back. Even your own village had trouble recognizing you. Scholars tend to skip over the actual coming home part."

Coming home...

Charles rolled down his window and combed the obscurity outside. Night had cloaked the trees but he could still feel them there, the whole congregation, observing him. He could smell the centuries they harbored under each root...in the veins of every leaf.

He could smell the land of his birth.

"Everyone likes to get on their high horse and argue about the morals of people heading off on crusade," Florus continued. "But no one wants to discuss the sorry sight of thousands creeping back, exhausted, diseased, starving. They weren't carrying any treasure home with them. That's a common misconception. Mostly they just brought back palm fronds. The more enterprising ones picked up relics along the way: a single hair from Christ's beard; a shred of the Virgin Mary's tunic; slivers of the Cross and the Holy Lance and enough bones to rebuild the same saint many times over."

"Not such a glorious undertaking," Charles said.

"No. And those who deserted were especially reviled. Stephen de Blois, for example. Theo told you about him, surely: his charming letters to his wife, Adela, daughter of William the Conqueror, are an important part of the literature. But instead of a warm welcome, Stephen faced Adela's open condemnation for deserting. Many of these 'failed' crusaders endured such public shame for their supposed cowardice that they departed on crusade again in 1101 to make up for it. It was a disastrous campaign. Many who'd survived the First Crusade would die this time around—including poor Stephen de Blois. Let's hope it made Adela happy."

Florus fingered the leather document case. "If you think about it, Charles," he said, "what difference did it really make to the daily lives of the majority of Europe's citizens if Jerusalem was in the hands of the Muslims or the Christians? Ideologically, maybe. But when fields lie fallow and fruit rots on the trees...when the women, children and elderly who stay behind are left in the protection of landlords and churchmen who have the power to abuse them and frequently do, who cares about ideology? Most simple people struggled cruelly in the absence of so much of the population—particularly their menfolk. The only modern analogy I can think of (and there surely will be more in due course, knowing human history) is Britain after the First World War, when the better part of a whole generation of young men was wiped out."

Homecoming was indeed a grim business, Charles thought, remembering a line from Theodore's translation: *His faithful squire returned home to find the prophetess of the spring dead.*

And that had been only the beginning of Stephen de la Fontaine's drama.

LXX

"Now, let's take a look."

Florus produced the parchment from the case as well as several pages of handwritten notes and a typed text. He balanced the manuscript on the gear shift for Charles to see it more easily and trained the lamp on it. Charles rolled up his window to protect the parchment. It was a futile gesture: moisture was finding its way into the old car through a multitude of gaps.

"Here's what I found," Florus said.

Charles bent over the document.

"We've already discussed the phrase *in familiam nomenque adoptavit*," Florus began. "It's clear that Stephen de la Fontaine did, indeed, adopt Arda's baby and give it his own name."

"De la Fontaine," murmured Charles. He lay his fingertips on the folio's scalloped corner where the hide had been blackened by so many fingers turning it. Once again, he thrilled at that skin-on-skin pleasure; at the thought that maybe Stephen himself had rested his hand on that very spot.

Said Florus: "As you know, he's the only person mentioned by name in the MS: *stephanus fontis*. 'Stephen of the Spring'."

"So you're saying that my family's bloodline originates in this adopted baby," Charles said. "Or did we hail from children Stephen sired himself through a later marriage?"

"I'll get to that," Florus said. He traced his finger along a line of text that Theodore had already translated. "Here, the word *miles*—which Theo translated as 'knight'—has evidently replaced another word, but I haven't been able to retrieve the erased text yet."

Florus drew his fingertips lightly down the page as a blind person might read Braille. He stopped at the word *nobilis*. "This word—which your uncle translated as 'lord'—is shorter than the word that was erased. Actually, two words."

"Two words?" Unable to restrain himself, Charles placed his own finger next to Florus's to sense the lost traces of ink the parchment was hiding.

"Yes," said Florus. "*Eximietatem suum.*"

Charles said nothing, humbled by his own ignorance.

"It's a title," Florus prompted. "'His Excellence.' Thus it reads:

'His faithful squire returned home to find the prophetess of the spring dead. This he learned from the mouth of the Moorish jongleur, that unwanted wretch, who said that His Excellence with splendid hand hunted the lady to her cave in the forest, defiled her, and cut her throat.'"

Charles sucked in his breath. "A high church official, then."

"Exactly. Likely a bishop."

"So it was Walderic who raped and murdered Arda!"

"It would seem so, yes. And most probably with that dagger you found in the cave."

Charles trembled. For a moment the feel of the dagger lying across his palms eclipsed all else. *The last person to have touched it had likely been the murderer.* "He must have abused Arda when she was his servant, then," he said, his voice robotic. "The baby was his. He was trying to destroy all evidence of this. Thank God that Arda managed to hide her child!"

"Let's proceed," said Florus. His manner was clipped; efficient. "I want to give you a sense of the whole document. Now, still in Theo's translation, there's a gap in the text where the Spaniard—the Moorish outcast—takes the baby to the abbey of Valdoré: *The Spaniard told the monks that the child had a most distinguished father, a nobleman, who had lands and riches but had died* (erasure). You'll remember that I suspected a cause of death in this erasure."

"Yes," said Charles.

"Well, in fact, it's the name of a place. And quite a place, too: he died in Jerusalem....*in hierosolyme.*"

"*Mon Dieu!*" Charles exclaimed. "Henri of Rêve, Stephen's master, died in Jerusalem." He thought for a moment. "We know that he fell in love with Arda before leaving on crusade, according to the Old French legend. So Stephen's master was the baby's father, then. Not Walderic."

"It would seem so thus far." Florus maintained his impartial tone. "Now, some intriguing words occur in my part of the translation: '*sepulchrum*', for one, which of course is a grave. Notably, it's described as the grave of a heretic—and a female heretic at that: *sepulchrum haereticae*."

"Arda…" The name caught on Charles's breath. His heart surged. "Does it say where the grave is? According to Theodore, no one has ever found it."

"Yes, it does."

Charles could barely contain his impatience.

"It's not far from the Blancheron ruins," Florus went on: "Do you remember that yesterday I mentioned something about the grave having been opened?"

Charles nodded. In a rush of excitement, he seized the parchment (Florus seemed inordinately casual about such things) and began searching for the verb *aperire* in whatever form his woeful Latin might recognize it. Here it was: *Sepulchrum aperuit*.

"'He opened the tomb!'" Charles exclaimed, his sails momentarily inflated with this tricky past tense. He looked up at Florus and flushed: clearly the past tense was hardly the most compelling part of this phrase. He whispered: "Who opened it, then?"

"Stephen himself, apparently," Florus said. "Whether he had help from the Spaniard—from Rodolfo, as the old French *chanson* called him—I'm not sure. It does not say '*we* opened the grave'. But the purpose is clear: according to his master's dying wish, Stephen had been instructed to give a small box to Arda, even if he had to open her grave to do it. Since loyalty was one of the great virtues of chivalry, this was the only way he could have fulfilled that wish literally."

Charles leaned back in his seat, suddenly light-headed. "A small box…"

"Yes. Here is the passage." Florus indicated the reddish-brown letters. "*Capsula ligni olivae*: a small box of wood from the olive tree."

"The olive wood box," Charles mouthed. "It's my family's most enduring mystery. All we have left is the key." He stopped himself in the face of another awkward past tense. "Well, that is, we *had* the key. Until I was mugged last night. Does it say what was in the box?"

"It's a curious thing, that," said Florus. "According to the folio, it seems that the box contained only a lock of hair—*cincinnus*: a curl, more accurately. And some seeds."

"*Seeds?*"

"Yes: *seminae.*"

"You mean Stephen opened the box before burying it with Arda?" said Charles.

Florus grinned. "Maybe human curiosity trumped the code of chivalry in the end!" He continued: "Charles, you wondered about whether or not Stephen had married—whether your line can be traced to Stephen's own offspring, or to the child he adopted."

"Yes! And...?"

"Toward the end of the verso, the text uses the word *miles* again, but this time in a different context: in reference to the building of Blancheron. The castle was apparently built and occupied by a *miles solitarius*—a solitary knight. (Remember that Stephen left as a squire but came home as a knight himself.) He lived alone, in other words. I interpret this as meaning he was celibate. Unmarried. Clearly the adoption was intended to give his own highly respectable name to what in fact was the illegitimate offspring of his master and a forest girl."

Florus turned on the headlights. "Now, please take a few minutes to digest all this. I'll go for a short stroll. Let's hope the battery doesn't give out!"

He got out of the car and started down the footpath. The headlights carved an illuminated nave through the beeches, and Florus, with his silver hair and proud walk, lacked only a long vestment to fit perfectly into the scene.

Charles began as Florus had suggested, by rereading Theodore's translation. The erasures for which Florus hadn't yet deciphered the underlying text had been left in parentheses.

These deeds occurred three summers before the great comet that appeared each evening for forty days from the first week of Lent. The ray was very bright, like an immense beam. The deeds took place in the years immediately following the victory in Jerusalem by the Franks. It is a noble exercise to record events accurately, especially if they must describe a (erasure) whose heart was humble and virtuous, but whose soul was at a crossroads; who knew not whether to follow the path of the Gospels, or that of the Earth. The world does not know that in great spiritual pain, he followed both.

His faithful squire returned home to find the prophetess of the spring dead. This he learned from the mouth of the Spaniard, that unwanted wretch, who said that His Excellence with splendid hand hunted the lady to her cave in the forest, defiled her, and cut her throat. He threw her precious instrument into the fire. The outcast, that foreigner, found the poor lady there in a lake of blood. There also, in the cold and somber dwelling, hidden away in rags, he found a babe.

The Spaniard told the squire, Stephen of the Source, that he took the baby to the great abbey. There he knew the monks would give him charity. They took in the child, and for a time the bedraggled vagrant also, who ailed most cruelly from his woodland living. The Spaniard told the monks that the child had a most distinguished father, a nobleman, who had lands and riches, but had died in Jerusalem. He did not mention the boy's mother, or her pagan ways, fearing that the monks would turn the child away, or even accuse the Spaniard himself of her murder. The noble son remained at the abbey until he was in his sixth year, when the squire heard the Spaniard's story, and hastened to take the child into his custody.

Then began Florus's effort:

The wondrous beam of light traversed the heavens, and one evening it appeared as if this beam was forking into many rays. The knight understood this was a sign that he must labor, and build a noble seat for the noble child he had adopted. But his hope became soured by fear. The knight feared for this child...the progeny of his own beloved master and the forest woman, whom he also had loved. He lamented, and languished in his fear. His Excellence had many powerful allies. He could snuff out the life of the child, or of anyone who knew his story, as the wind stirs from its lair and, even while still dozing, extinguishes a taper. But Stephen had fought the barbarians in Nicaea, and Antioch, and Jerusalem. He knew that fear can give one wings, even as now, after returning from the holy wars, he walked upon fires buried beneath treacherous ashes.

His master, that great warrior asleep for eternity so near the rock of Calvary, had been the sum of all things: a noble hero whose name was fashioned by his honesty, by his deeds, by his virtues. As guardian of his child, Stephen was prepared to lay down his very soul, even if his own ardor for the prophetess, the child's earth-mother, had never been quenched.

Stephen's ancestors held the land on the inside and outside of a coil of the snake-river. His family had earned praise far beyond the borders of the region. Stephen's brothers had found glory in the campaign against pagan Sicily. Though Mars had cheated some in battle, he had bestowed his favors on others, and thus Stephen, like his brothers, returned home from his exploits safely, to adulation.

But the tidings delivered by the outcast jongleur severed Stephen from his family forever. He retreated to the high rock spur above the snake-river. Here he was determined to build a domain for the noble orphan. Here, protected by the river, and cliffs, and ravines, he knew he could build a refuge for this adopted son and keep him safe from all enemies. But first, his obligations weighed heavily. Before he could lay the first stones, Stephen had a task to fulfill.

The Spaniard led the knight up the mountain of the clinging forests. Hidden in his garments, against his heart, Stephen carried the small box of wood from the olive tree, and the bronze key with princely shape. The loyal friend of the child's mother, that Moorish jongleur, had buried her under the sky where the herons flew. It was where she had gone with her nobleman. And so they climbed, and the knight felt that he was leaving behind a vale of tears and entering a mountain of joy, for at last he could fulfill his master's wishes and return the box to the prophetess of the spring.

The Spaniard led him to a grove of pines near the Duke's Gate. He indicated a rise in the ground. Then he turned away, as the knight was overcome with emotion. The Spaniard, also, could not conceal his bereavement. The grave was rounded like a boat's hull, covered with soft grass and the needles of pines. Stephen carried with him a mattock, and with this tool he began to dig into the grave of the heretic woman.

He dug for some time, as the earth was full of stones, but at last his tool encountered something besides dirt and rock. The knight stopped, soaked from his labors. He knelt, and with the tears coursing down his cheeks he gathered his spirits and peered into the void. With reverence, he reached in to touch the shrouded corpse.

At once he trembled in awe. A sound took on life, and lingered. A strange light filled the sky. With it came a wind, of the sort he remembered from the plains of Persia. He knew not whether this was the power of heaven speaking, or the will of Earth, that ancient mother, whose beloved daughter lay at his feet. He knew that the grave should never have been opened. But his loyalty to his master was greater than his fear of Christian hellfire. Greater even than the ire of an older god.

The sky and the wind had spoken. He knew what to do.

He extracted the olive wood box wrapped in waxed cloth from his surcoat, and the key from a hidden pocket. Quickly he surveyed the meadow, and the dark pines. There was no one. The Spaniard had vanished. Stephen begged forgiveness, then with faint heart he inserted the key into the lock and opened the box. Surprise overcame him. He had expected a jewel; a golden talisman; at least a piece of folded parchment on which a scribe had written words of love on behalf of Stephen's dying master.

Instead, the little coffer contained only a curl of hair and a clutch of dry seeds. He left the curl where it lay, though he would have loved to have kept it for himself. The seeds he poured into his palm and lay on a flat stone. Then he locked the box, wrapped it in its cloth and put the key back into its secret pocket. This he placed in the grave on the stilled heart of the woman who lay there. He gazed at her form just once.

Though nature had taken the woman back to her bosom, and by now relieved her of her fleshly bonds, Stephen could make out broad cheekbones under the shroud, and the outline of her arms. His heart quickened. He remembered her beauty; her music and vivid spirit. Like one possessed, he returned the earth to its hole, as he was eager to keep his memories of the living woman, and forget as quickly as possible what he had just seen.

He then took the seeds and scattered them over the mound. They were the seeds of the pale pink carnations that grew wild in Jerusalem.

With the help of the sturdy Spaniard the building commenced. Though this renegade was not a follower of Christ, the knight found in him a strong and honest worker, and other citizens also helped to construct a castle high above the snake-river, across the windy meadow from the Duke's Gate. The labor was long and heavy, but Stephen had helped to prepare the sieges of Antioch and Jerusalem so he was robust. Here, moreover, the strength in his heart was greater even than when he was serving his Christian god in foreign lands. At last he could fly his banner from the highest tower, and thus lay claim to the seat that could now be bestowed upon his adopted son, who took his name, and on all his descendants in perpetuity.

The solitary knight kept only a small retinue of servants and guards. But even so, until the boy reached manhood, the knight passed his days and nights in vigil on that remote rock, for in his heart he would always be keeping watch on behalf of his beloved master. He descended through the clinging forests only to bathe in the river from time to time, and visit the grove with its holy pool, where the prophetess, whose home was now in the sky, occasionally sent her emissary to greet him: a white heron.

Stephen died an old man in that castle on the lonely ridge. The boy grew to possess the virtues, broad chest and handsome curls of his blood-father, (erasure), and he strode into the world proud to bear the name of the man who had adopted him.

Charles lowered the page with the adagio of a sleepwalker. He gazed out at the bright nave that the headlights cast through the beeches. He could make out a figure some way off, though to his tired eyes it wasn't apparent whether he was approaching or receding.

Clinging forests...snake-river...heron.

The tremor within him was constant now and Charles no longer doubted its provenance.

Coming home.

The sweet, peppery nutmeg of Theodore's carnations filled his memory.

Could flowers really reseed themselves for nine centuries?

LXXII

Florus drifted toward the car. He climbed into the MG in a single practiced movement and said softly: "Now you understand a bit more about your heritage."

Charles put a hand to his mouth and shut his eyes. A tear dropped onto the parchment with a raw slap. Florus squeezed his forearm and gently took the folio.

They sat without speaking.

"Why did Stephen sever ties with his family?" Charles asked abruptly. He rubbed his eyes, exhausted.

"His adoption of an illegitimate child would have caused too much scandal," Florus said. "Especially a child of the very knight he'd served as squire—a local nobleman known to everyone in the Rêve region—and a pagan outcast. We can't even imagine the extent of such a scandal today. A Christian and a heretic... Well, I suppose there are some places in America where this would still cause a scandal!"

"But loyalty meant even more to Stephen than that," Charles said.

"Yes, indeed," Florus conceded. "Loyalty, and heritage: Stephen obviously meant for the boy to inherit everything: his name and social standing; his property and land."

"Heritage..." Charles echoed.

Florus placed the parchment on an outstretched palm and pressed the other palm on top, as if to trap it. "Something of great importance must have compelled someone to write this, Charles," he said. "I surmise that Stephen, on taking custody of the child, asked a clergyman at Valdoré to draw up this document. The clergyman must have been both sympathetic and discreet. There were all those scandalous bits: the clear reference to a bishop. To a pagan grave. And of course, a bastard child. But reputations were at risk. Someone must have had second thoughts about putting the information in writing." He gave Charles a long look. "Why else the erasures?"

"Would Stephen have kept the parchment at Blancheron?" Charles asked.

"It would have been far better taken care of in the abbey's scriptorium. What we *do* know is that someone felt it important not to destroy the parchment completely, as it contained information of value."

"You mean documenting Stephen's return from Jerusalem, building Blancheron and the like," Charles said.

"I mean," said Florus, holding the parchment up to the light. "Documenting facts. This folio feels like documented truth to me."

A tingle passed through Charles and he said nothing. Suddenly he was sitting in Theodore's kitchen again, eating chocolate hearts and discussing the power of signs and legends.

"The manuscript deals with some very specific things," Florus continued. "An adoption; a grave; a reliquary; an identifiable place."

"Pink carnations."

"Yes: *seminae dianthuum*."

"And a noble father," Charles said. "Henri of Rêve. Grandfather was fairly certain of this."

"Yes."

"It does reveal quite a few things, doesn't it?" Charles went on. "We know that the olive wood box was buried with Arda; that it certainly didn't contain anything of great value. Whoever stole the photocopy must have made at least a rudimentary translation by now. They'll be disappointed, I fear."

"That there's no obvious treasure?"

"Of course!"

Florus's gaze narrowed. "One man's junk is another man's treasure," he said.

Charles looked at him.

"I'm talking about that long erasure at the end of the verso," Florus explained.

"Ah, yes."

"It's odd to find such a long gap in a medieval manuscript," Florus said, tucking the documents back into the leather case.

"Cédric," said Charles. "When you called earlier, you said something about a great matter."

"Indeed." Florus put on his seatbelt and reached for the ignition. Instead of looking vaguely past Charles at that distant stronghold he was so fond of, he locked his gaze on his companion and said: "I must verify it. I'm going back to the lab tonight."

Florus drove back to the city at reckless speed.

"Go to Blancheron immediately, Charles," he said. "Tonight. You should also alert the police in Bouillon."

"The *police?* Why?"

"Because you should expect trespassers at the villa."

Charles balked. "Looking for the original parchment, you mean?"

"Perhaps." Florus hesitated. "Though I think that if they've made a translation of the photocopy by now, it's more likely they'll be looking for the grave."

Charles gaped, incredulous. "The *grave?* You mean my father's sending his henchmen to dig on the ridge? But you said there's no treasure there—nothing of real value."

"If the parchment is to be believed, the box is in the grave and Ames now has the key. They may think that the contents are, in fact, of value." Florus stopped himself from saying more.

"It's my father's private property, after all," Charles said. "He has a right to dig where he likes."

"One could argue that. But it's also your inheritance. Hugues asked you to help manage the sale, didn't he? That includes the land on the ridge."

Charles could hardly admit that he'd just cut off all contact with his father and quit his job. Florus also seemed to have handily forgotten that he'd been threatened himself. As he considered these bleak realities, Charles only hoped that he hadn't also cut the threads of courage he would need to continue this endeavor to its end.

The MG burbled around the cobbled corners of Ixelles and Charles watched the old-world façades pass by in the lamplight. He'd initially asked Florus to drop him off at the Sablon where his rental car was parked. But suddenly risk sparked, then flared, and not knowing why, exactly, he changed his mind and asked to be let off at Sylvana's place instead.

PART SIX

Pilgrim

LXXIII

There was no light in the cellar flat.

It was almost midnight. The concert must have finished well before ten, Charles reckoned. Ida would probably have served drinks, after which the musicians had straggled home to their digs. Sylvana should have been back by now.

He peered through the bars at the cellar window. The dim outlines of the little parlor seemed robbed of their stage lighting, as if a scene had played out there—one of the more important ones of his life, Charles realized—and now the theatre had gone dark. Even the vase of tulips, still visible in the shadows, looked staged, with a semi-circle of petals lying artistically on the piano lid.

Charles took out his phone to call Sylvana: she'd turned hers off. Then he called Ida. He had to wait for many rings, during which he kept looking down into the subterranean abode of the only woman who'd ever breached the defenses of his heart. He reenacted the scene in his mind: Sylvana's defiant stance upon his arrival, and her gradual acquiescence; the universal olive branch offered by tea; their sharing of deep concerns such as Raul, Blancheron, wealth, music. And finally...

The entwining of arms.

He shied at this last memory. She'd spoken of her love for Raul, after all; she'd challenged Charles about his patrician lifestyle. And yet... If two trees had been fused together in the embrace he'd shared with Sylvana, no one would ever have been able to separate them.

"Charles?"

He'd almost forgotten about his phone.

"Auntie!"

"It's after midnight. Why are you calling at this hour? Are you all right?"

"I'm at Sylvana's."

"Ah, I see..." came the leading remark.

"It's not what you think!" Charles said with pique. "She's not here, anyway. I'm wondering if you know where she might be."

Ida hesitated. "*C'est curieux.* She left my place right after the concert, at 21:30 or so." Another pause. "Did you see Raul, cheri?" she said.

"Yes. In your garden. He wasn't very...forthcoming." It was the only way Charles's tired mind could describe the encounter with his half-brother. "Does Sylvana stay out late sometimes?" he asked.

"She might have gone home with a friend from the conservatory," was all Ida could offer.

This seemed unlikely, somehow. *What has happened to her?*

Charles said nothing to his aunt about going down to Blancheron immediately, in the middle of the night, as Florus had advised him to do. She would find out soon enough.

"*Bonne nuit,*" he said, and hung up.

He set off on foot to recover his car at the Sablon, weighed by the twin specters of Florus's urgency, and Sylvana's absence.

The drive to the Ardennes seemed far longer this time. Tinged with foreboding. Charles missed Ida's company in the car, even if they'd driven to Theodore's funeral mostly in silence. *Theodore... What would he have advised at this juncture?*

A funeral was obviously an ending, Charles thought. *But might it also be a beginning?* Not for the deceased, of course. (Although many believed that a new life did, indeed, begin at that point.) But a beginning for *him*...for Charles de la Fontaine. *A beginning of what?* he wondered. *Of life as a failed heir?* That didn't matter. *As a failed historian?* The idea sickened him. *But wait!* He was not yet forty: he could continue his studies if he put his mind to them. He could become a professor. A researcher. Surely there was a bright side to having severed ties with his father and quit the profession he hated. At last he would have the freedom to do what he'd always wanted. Grace Holmes would certainly have approved. And if that freedom resembled the threadbare life Theodore had led, so much the better.

"Oh, Uncle," Charles whispered, driving too fast down the empty highway. He considered—he hoped—that the realm his uncle currently inhabited was closer than one might imagine...perhaps even as close as the air at his shoulder. The possibility lifted his spirits considerably. It suggested that his uncle's wisdom had not been lost; that it might, in fact, come in handy tonight.

He passed Dinant, a picturesque town on the banks of the river Meuse. It was famous for an imposing needle of rock said to have been the work of the magic horse Bayard, whose giant hoof had separated the rock from the valley cliffs as he'd flown by. The magician Maugis often figured with Bayard in those stories. He often rode him, too.

Charles shivered.

Perhaps along this very route.

The lonely highway stretched ahead. A dark rise in the land was perceptible against the wash of night sky: the ridges and valleys of the Ardennes, the land of margins, where legends lay awake under the earth, and shadowy creatures roamed the stones and waters as if they still had complete sovereignty.

I saw it, lad. The bird. I went to the pond yesterday and there it was. It's always a sign. <u>Always</u>.

Charles swerved briefly out of his lane. *The white heron. Blanc héron.* It wasn't by chance that Stephen de la Fontaine had given the castle that name.

He tightened his grip on the steering wheel. *I must prepare myself,* he thought, suddenly wondering what, exactly, he was going to do once he arrived at Antioch. Florus had warned him about trespassers at the villa—that he should alert the police in Bouillon. Ames had clearly been nosing about the property.

Charles considered the refinement of his attacker in the Rue Royale—the stealth with which he'd accomplished his deed. Unfortunately, history usually attributed violence to those who looked like Raul, not like Ames. Discreet evil was not so easily pinned down. Men who wore silver goatees and Loden coats and dealt in antiquities were gentlemen, and usually exempt from any other label even when they trailed a stench. Which was why, Charles thought, the Antwerp murder had been pinned so handily on his own half-brother.

Might Raul have already received an order to go down to the Ardennes as soon as possible and await further instructions? If so, how would he get there? There were no trains at this hour. Raul probably had little money. With Hugh applying pressure from his distant throne, maybe Ames had had to swallow his pride and give the renegade a lift in his BMW.

Charles stabbed at the frites he'd bought before leaving Brussels with a little plastic fork. They were cold and soggy by now, but along with a bar of chocolate were a passable snack. It was as if everything were happening to someone else, somehow, and he was simply the chauffeur, happy to wait in the car and eat frites while deeds transpired without him. The only truly pressing thing was to find out what had happened to Sylvana.

Then another voice entered his head.

"History is full of shadow-folk." (Grace Holmes again, that sage of suburbia.) "Heroes and heroines of the past still have a lot to say. Not everyone can hear them. But you can, Charlie. You can…"

Yes, I can hear them, Grace, he whispered aloud. *Stephen. Arda. Henri. But I can't figure out what they're trying to tell me!*

Charles exited the highway and started down the series of long, deserted roads leading to Rêve-sur-Semois. A storm was gathering and the car shuddered in random gusts, now and then lurching into the oncoming lane.

Illumination was scant and fleeting. A moon rode high on shredded clouds, only to be engulfed by them again. The headlights picked up the eyes of a fox, then a hare: tiny braziers in the night that reminded travelers where they were, exactly; that while daylight revealed the squalid doings of man, a country night was still firmly in the hands of the Earth and her devotees. *Careful,* the creatures were saying. *Arduinna is abroad tonight. You are entering the source of all things: Nature. It is she who is true divinity.*

Theodore and Ida had understood this, Charles thought. But Sylvana actually seemed to *live* it. Perhaps that was why she seemed so unapproachable at times: it was simply because she existed on a higher plane.

Charles considered Raul's roughness—a piece of clay the sculptor had discarded and Sylvana had picked up, seeing the potential in it. *Was that true love?* he wondered as he skirted Rêve along the river road.

He suddenly felt overcome by Sylvana's presence: the light in her eyes...that preternatural stillness. And her voice, of course: the viola-tones, each one humming with vitality. *Your friend of the forest.* She'd written those words seventeen years ago. *Were they still true?*

To eschew unfairness, meanness and deceit. It was part of the code of chivalry. *Chivalry lives on in you,* Sylvana had said. Charles's blood chilled at the notion that in her most private thoughts, she might not believe this; that she might actually suspect him of being one of Hugh's accomplices, and that was the reason she'd disappeared after the concert.

His foot jerked on the brake. The car slowed. There were no markings on these rural roads and one could end up in a ditch, or worse. But the real driving issue was the tears that blurred his eyes and trailed down his cheeks. It was no wonder that once again he missed the turn-off to Villa Antioch.

LXXIV

He crept back along the road until his high beams glanced off the shrine nailed to the plane tree. Maybe this happened often to returning pilgrims, he thought: they forgot the landscape of their homeland.

Charles pulled into the drive and stopped the car.

Coming home.

He doused the lights and imagined himself traversing this inky landscape on foot, dehydrated, in pain from countless blisters and unhealed wounds, forced to desert out of fear and exhaustion. *Deus vult...* Was this really what God had willed? Why had so little been written about the return of pilgrims from crusade, anyway? An answer came to Charles now: perhaps because the return, largely avoided by historians, had been the most difficult part to describe; perhaps because in the long light of history, the killing itself, as monstrous as it must have seemed to the thousands who'd engaged in it, had in fact been easier to bear than confronting oneself afterwards.

Charles turned on the headlights:

A figure darted into the trees.

He gripped the wheel, spellbound.

A figure in a cloak and hood.

The wind sharpened. Dead leaves performed their macabre dance in the beams.

A curious recognition overcame Charles. Nothing appeared unusual about this scene: not the darkness, or the country silence. Not even the figure, for it seemed to have strode directly out of his own thoughts, as if it had been inhabiting them for quite some time. Breathless, he followed those thoughts where they were leading him: *It was probably just a novitiate from Valdoré, late for Mass. Or maybe one of the charcoal dwellers from the deeper woods...*

His hands turned damp and cold on the wheel. *It's the twenty-first century, for God's sake!* It was the reproach that Theodore had occasionally slung at him when he'd lost his way in the past.

He doused the headlights again and got out of the car. He'd stopped at the beginning of the villa drive, near the place where a tangle of vines marked the way to the great oak. It wasn't really an access—one had to know about it. To navigate by night, one had to know it intimately.

The person had gone that way.

Instinct seized him and he plunged into the forest after the figure. It seemed he was making the noise of an ox and he halted several times to listen for the intruder. The wind was rushing from treetop to treetop now, but here, on the ground, there was no sound in the underbrush. The person had been moving rapidly: perhaps they'd already left this part of the woods.

Charles arrived at the oak's clearing. The opening in the trees was so remarkable, so unexpected, it was as if the forest itself had singled out this spot. The oak stood in dead calm, untouched by the wind.

He placed his hands on the ridged bark. Seventeen years ago, bereft, he'd perceived the leviathan pulse deep inside the tree. But now there was nothing. He pressed his cheek against the trunk, trying in vain to summon the energy he'd detected there before. Maybe the life force had finally ebbed away.

He remembered those barefoot peasants passing through the grove on their way to Outre-mer, the fire of faith in their eyes. For them this tree had been part god, part Earth mother. *Had they returned by the same route?* Charles closed his eyes and came home with them, not in cashmere and silk but in torn linen and soiled leggings, the soles of his feet bloodied and calloused.

He'd been lucky at first: he'd found a bony nag early on in Constantinople, but it had collapsed and died underneath him. People had taken pity on him, given him transport in their wagons where, to his chagrin, he'd shared an honored place beside toothless crones and pregnant women. They didn't know he was a deserter; he didn't tell them that his deep shoulder wound had happened fleeing Jerusalem, not scaling its wall. And while it was true that in his legging he'd been carrying a splinter of the True Lance—a sure-fire guarantee of passage—he'd traded this relic at the first opportunity. For the bony nag, as it happened.

"You shouldn't have come."

For a moment it seemed that the tree was speaking.

Charles turned: at the edge of the clearing he perceived a slender, darker patch of shadow. The voice itself seemed to have issued from a source with no solid matter at all.

The clouds opened briefly and the figure stepped into the starlight. Very little was visible except a long cape and walking stick.

"Sylvana," he mouthed, pulling himself into the present day.

"It's not safe for you here," she said. "Your father has his spies everywhere."

"You should have stayed in Brussels!" Charles exclaimed. "How did you get here, anyway?"

"I hitchhiked. Raul didn't come home last night, Charles," she said. Her voice quavered. "I fear he's in great trouble. I'm sure that your father has set a task for him. A dangerous one. Here at Blancheron. Something that must be done before Florus weighs in with his findings and others get involved."

"The parchment, you mean."

"Yes."

"Do you think Raul is around here somewhere?"

"I showed him where the oak is. Hardly anyone knows how to find it. He understands he's safe here, if he needs shelter."

"Sylvana..." Charles stepped toward her. "There's something I have to tell you before we go any further."

She stood her ground and squared her shoulders. "Yes?"

"I learned last night that Raul is my half-brother," he said. "My father's child by a Spanish woman in Brussels."

Sylvana remained motionless. When she spoke again, it was more out of anger than from shock. "Then your father's villainy is even worse than I thought." Bitterness poisoned her words. "Not only has he been exploiting a guileless person…but his own son!"

To Charles's surprise, she came over to him and lay a hand on his cheek. "How sad for you, Charles, to learn that about your father."

"What I've been learning is that there's no limit to his villainy," Charles moaned.

They embraced. It was more a gesture of solidarity than of passion.

"Do you know what Raul has been ordered to do?" Sylvana asked at length, pulling away.

"I think his task might be on the ridge."

"On the *ridge*?!"

"Yes. But I'll tell you more when we get to the house. Come on! I'll park the car where it can't be seen and we'll approach on foot."

Charles took Sylvana's hand and together they felt their way back through the thick brush. Charles eased the car into the trees until it was invisible from the drive. Then they squared themselves against the tempest.

Wind and rain battered them at every step. They tried to keep close to the trees in case a trespasser should spot them, but in truth they could barely navigate in the maelstrom and blundered ahead blindly. Branches thrashed overhead as if to remind them that human free will was utterly useless in all of this.

"It's just a squall," Sylvana said, covering her head with her hood. Charles had no such covering and his curls were soon drenched. There would be more squalls during the night, he knew. Ever stronger ones, interspersed with moonlight: a typical Ardennes spectacle. He carried his duffel bag against his chest as ballast.

A shoulder of the villa rose up on their left. Above it, the turret's black pyramid reared against a scudding sky.

"Hurry!" Charles shouted, and grabbed Sylvana's arm. "Let's get inside!"

They ran to the front terrace, the wind nipping at their heels.

"Charles!" Sylvana hissed, pulling him back. "There's someone inside!"

He'd seen the curtain shift at the window.

"Come on," he said, unfazed. "We can't stay out here."

The front door was locked. They stood there, hearts pounding, as Charles rummaged for the key in his pocket.

"Maybe we should go around to the back," Sylvana urged, "and wait there until we know more."

"I won't let my father's bloodhounds intimidate me," Charles said, his pique rising.

He unlocked the door and pushed it open.

At first the hall offered its usual greeting: the cool, faded tiles...the loftiness of a forgotten era. In the gloaming, Charles spotted the telephone on its table, and the coat stand beside it.

There was a draft.

An alien shuffle.

"Someone's here!" Charles blurted. He put a protective arm around Sylvana.

LXXV

The moon broke free and light spilled down the kitchen corridor into the hall. A shadow burgeoned grotesquely.

Broad.

Imposing.

Especially for such a slight man.

"Philippe!" Charles gasped. He pulled Sylvana against him in relief.

"Charles! Oh, thank God it's you!" The notary crept apologetically into the hall.

"What on earth are you doing here?" Charles said. He introduced Sylvana, forgetting that the two of them had met when she'd come to the villa to help Theodore.

"I'm keeping watch," Osselaer answered with some importance. He greeted Sylvana with a tilted bow.

"But how did you get here?" Charles pressed him, suddenly uncertain about Osselaer. "Where's your car?"

"I took a taxi from Bouillon," Osselaer said, obviously pleased with his initiative. "I didn't want anyone to think the house was occupied."

"And you're keeping watch for…"

"Ah, *Sharl'*, *Sharl'*…" Osselaer shook his head sadly.

Charles exhaled with relief. The notary must have changed his allegiance! He was clearly protecting the villa from the intruders Florus had warned would turn up.

Hugh's bloodhounds.

"What a fool I was to think that your father was anything like Theodore," Osselaer said. "Or like your grandfather, for that matter. I took over your family's affairs when my own father retired as their notary. I never imagined what that would entail." He shuffled his feet. "Now I know."

"But what did you intend to do if you ran into Ames and his cohorts?" said Charles.

"Ames?"

"Come now, Philippe! Ida told me all about Manfred Ames—how he's been using Raul." Charles stopped short of accusing Ames of murder. "And using *you*."

The idea of the gentle, misshapen notary confronting Hugh's forces was preposterous, of course. But Charles observed Osselaer now and saw that there was defiance in the little man. His pinched face jutted at a superior angle. His remaining strands of hair, usually so carefully combed, protruded with such abandon that he must have been out patrolling in the wind. And Charles had never seen him without a tie before.

Osselaer puffed slightly. "No one is using me anymore," he said. He shared a wan smile with Sylvana. Then he regarded Charles. "Why are *you* here?"

They all stood in silence.

Do whatever you can to hold on to Blancheron.

"I'm here for one reason only," Charles said. "To honor Theodore's wishes."

The three of them looked through the open study door at Theodore's desk chair and green banker's lamp; at the ivory olifant, and half-melted candle on its brass stand. The squall had passed and everything was visible in a wash of moonlight, about as clear a sign as one could hope for in a land of signs. Even Theodore himself seemed present. He'd been gone only a short time, after all—so short that a frisson passed over the little assembly, as if he might return at any moment to retrieve something he'd forgotten and offer them a tip or two.

"Perhaps you would both appreciate a warm drink," Osselaer said. "Mademoiselle?" He invited Sylvana with another sideways bow.

The trio headed down the corridor to the kitchen. The moon's reprieve had been short-lived. Rain was striking the mullioned panes in giant fistfuls now. Gusts howled along the back terrace. Osselaer fetched a third chair from the dining room and got to work at the espresso machine.

"We'll have to operate in the dark," he said. "We dare not turn on any lights."

Charles hesitated as he entered the kitchen. He shared a long, inquiring look with Sylvana. She'd noticed it, too, he was sure: the air was laden with peppery nutmeg. The scent was so immediate, so strong, that he glanced around for the jar of wild carnations. Theodore had been dead for over two weeks, but even before then...well... *He wouldn't have been collecting flowers in October, would he?*

"Thank you for keeping an eye on the house, Philippe," Charles said, which greatly heartened Osselaer. The notary served the espressos and wedged himself between Charles and Sylvana at the rickety table.

"Ames stole my laptop bag with the photocopy of the parchment Florus made for me," said Charles.

"And?" Osselaer responded.

"Florus showed me the full translation of the lost ending of the heron legend," Charles explained. "Just last night. Ames must have a translation by now, too. Not everything...not the scanned parts. But enough to muster his thugs to help him."

"Maybe just one thug," Sylvana added quietly.

Charles clasped her hand. "Yes," he said. "Raul."

"Arda is buried on the ridge," Charles went on. "The olive wood box is apparently in her grave. Ames will no doubt be heading there, though presumably not until the weather clears."

"Raul will be with him!" Sylvana cried. "Oh, Charles, what is your father orchestrating?"

"I've broken all contact with my father," Charles said with a note of triumph. "Anyway, Ames is in charge here. We can't stop him. We can only try to negotiate with him."

"*Negotiate?*" Philippe said. He lined up his strands of hair with nervous fingers.

"You knew about the parchment, didn't you?" Charles pressed the notary. He glanced at Sylvana. She was cleaning the condensation from a window pane with her sleeve, lost in thought. She hadn't touched her coffee.

Said Osselaer: "Theo had some inkling that there was more to the parchment than met the eye. But he didn't know what to do about it. Just before he died, he suspected that your father had a motive for selling Blancheron." Osselaer shifted uncomfortably on his chair. "To my eternal regret, it was I who mentioned to Hugues that there might be something of historical value in the parchment."

"*Alors...*" said Charles. "The real coup is the fact that the Fontaine family are blood relations of Stephen's knight—Henri of Rêve—and not of Stephen himself. That's hardly explosive information, is it? Or worth much money."

Osselaer hesitated. "No," he said. He watched Sylvana as she traced a finger over the windowpane. "Didn't Florus tell you any more than that?"

"He said he has to scan a few more things," Charles said.

"Ah." Osselaer got up and put his cup in the sink.

The wind mounted a direct assault on the window and Sylvana drew back, alarmed. The storm was as random as it was violent and they all froze, bracing for another attack.

A gaping silence filled the kitchen.

Charles broke it with: "All this horrible subterfuge just for an old box with seeds and hair!"

"Indeed..." Osselaer said meditatively. "But Ames clearly thinks differently. Anyway, no one will be able to climb up to the ridge until the weather improves."

Charles listened to the wind's operatic rising and falling. There were so many voices in storms, he mused. Ancient ones. Imagined ones.

And Theodore's: *Seize your endeavor, lad.*

"Philippe," Charles said, his pulse quickening. "Do you ever handle estate sales for anonymous buyers?"

Osselaer pulled himself up. His gaze sharpened. "Of course," he said. "Especially if they involve a lot of money."

"And what if they don't," said Charles. "I mean, what if there really *were* a bombshell to do with Blancheron, but there was a sale before it became public. The estate would command a much lower price, wouldn't it? What if the potential buyer wanted to remain anonymous?"

"The potential buyer being *you*, you mean," Osselaer said. He didn't seem surprised.

Charles smiled at the notary. "What would Blancheron be worth in that case?"

Now it was Osselaer who smiled: "Oh, I reckon you'd probably get more for that ivory olifant."

Was it madness or inspiration, Charles wondered, to buy back one's own inheritance? Or was he, like any good knight, simply persevering to the end of the enterprise he'd begun?

LXXVI

It was 2:30 in the morning. They agreed to make their way up to the ridge at first light. According to the forecast, the storm would have abated by then. They'd bring a shovel, and make sure that at least one of them had a working phone in case they had to call the police. (Not that the *commissariat* in Bouillon would be of much help.)

It was assumed they'd be looking for Arda's grave. But what if Ames had gotten there first? Or he turned violent? And how would they extricate Raul from Ames's grip—if they managed to find him at all? No one could answer these questions. Nor did anyone want to admit that the excursion to the ridge daunted them, for even if the storm were to ease, the climb would still be treacherous.

"Wouldn't it be better to wait for the police and go up with them?" Osselaer asked, his new-found confidence waning.

"I plan to go up to the ridge at dawn no matter what," Charles said. "No police. Not yet, anyway. I just hope that you'll both join me."

The other two nodded their assent.

Osselaer insisted he would be fine sleeping on the settee in the salon, where he'd already spent two nights, and that he'd cook them some eggs just before daybreak.

"Why not get some sleep in my uncle's room?" Charles said to Sylvana. "We still have a few hours before dawn."

She agreed, and hung her cape and walking stick on a hook in the kitchen corridor. Underneath the cape she'd been carrying a small backpack: her only personal item. Charles marveled that she was still wearing her long black ensemble from the concert—that somehow she'd managed not only to hitchhike from Brussels in it, but brave the path to the old oak and back. She'd added a white sweater for warmth, baggy and worn and obviously second-hand, although lace at the neck and wrists hung like plumage, indicating a more illustrious past.

He picked up his duffel bag and led her up the first two flights of stairs. Each step creaked to life, and without thinking Charles ran his fingertips along the knobs on the wallpaper. Piles of Theodore's books and documents lined their way. He breathed in the moldy air, amazed that the scent of carnations lingered even up here. He paused and set down his bag. There was something else, as well.

"Do you smell that?" he asked Sylvana.

"The carnations?" she asked.

"Yes. But there's another thing I can't identify."

She took a deep breath. "It's quite heavy, isn't it? Dense. Well, it's not surprising, with all these old books."

"I suppose that's it," he said. He opened a door off the landing. "This is Theodore's room. You'll be comfortable here."

Sylvana gave him an unreadable look. "Do you mind if I see the turret?" she asked. "I've never gone up there."

She followed Charles up five more flights to the turret room. Out of habit, he pushed the door open with his eyes closed. This time, of course, there was nothing but blackness outside the windows when he opened them again.

Melancholy filled him. The curious heaviness he'd noticed on the stairs seemed stronger here, and had a slight tang. Perhaps the turret had been shut for too long. Theodore's housekeeper rarely climbed this high, if ever.

Charles crossed the room, treading on the squeaky board at the foot of the bed.

"So this is where the magic lives," Sylvana said, entering the room. Her voice was barely audible above the storm. She wandered over to the spiral staircase at the turret's center and looked up at the rafters. "That's the highest point, isn't it?"

"Yes," said Charles, and he told her how he used to climb up to put the gonfalon out every morning, and climb up again to take it in at night. It was tucked away in his bag now, he said. But maybe one day, if he could save Blancheron, it would fly again.

"Have you spoken to your father?" Sylvana asked abruptly.

Charles wasn't prepared for her bluntness—or for his father. He felt as if he'd allowed a rare and beautiful bird into his private chamber, only to deal with its ungainly flap.

"'I hope I never speak to my father again!" he exclaimed. It was a childish outburst, he knew. Indignation burned his cheeks.

Sylvana gently explained: "I asked because if we knew more about his plans, we might have a better idea where Raul is."

"I have no idea about his plans," Charles said. "Anyway, it's too late for me and my father. I can't believe that I stayed loyal to him for so long." He hoped that Sylvana realized he was speaking the truth—that he'd convinced her once and for all that he wasn't the slick bourgeois clone of Hugh Fontaine that she might still believe him to be. "Raul is my brother," he went on. "I'll do everything I can to find him. I promise."

But he knew he couldn't promise this. Raul was his father's drudge. He'd already been nosing around Blancheron on Hugh's orders. How could Charles forget that face at the window...or the figure emerging from the willow? Raul had obviously been on a mission. Maybe he'd already scouted the ridge for any sign of a grave. If Ames had given Raul a lift from Brussels last night, he'd probably dumped him in an obscure part of the forest—left him to make his own way through the seething storm. The night was pure Maugis. Had Raul even found the old oak in the maelstrom? Was he sheltering somewhere else? *In a cave, perhaps?*

No, Charles couldn't keep his promise that Raul would be safe.

At all times speak the truth. The chivalric code rose up and stung him like nettles.

LXXVII

They stood on opposite sides of the big square room, listening to the storm. Gust followed gust. Moan followed thud. During breaks in the mayhem, sickly moonlight fell from the little dormer window where the gonfalon used to fly. It was impossible to see anything outside, so they glanced variously at the floorboards; the bare, narrow mattress; the Latin dictionary on an otherwise empty bookcase; and finally, inevitably, at each other.

"How are you going to do it?" Sylvana asked softly. "To hold on to your heritage?"

He smiled. "I have an idea," he said. The windows shook in the wind and an eddy passed through the room. He smiled again, but privately, as he'd remembered the turret drafts cooling his cheek, and for a few seconds he'd become the boy who'd once slept here.

Sylvana perceived this, and slipped up to his side. "It's just as you described, Charles. There's so much in the air here."

"Yes," he said. "When I was young, I thought I could hear things pass by my bed at night."

"You must have been terrified!"

"Oh, they weren't malicious things," he explained, remembering the ancientness that made its home in the humid, redolent Semois valley. Then, quietly: "In fact, they were my friends. But most people are unnerved by things they can't see, aren't they?"

Sylvana let out a brief, melodious laugh and drifted back to the spiral staircase. "Not musicians. We spend our lives with invisible friends."

Charles bowed slightly, embarrassed. "Of course. I wasn't thinking." He paused. "Historians do, too, you know," he said. He cringed at this artifice. *Was he including himself in that category?*

"Theodore said that you're a wonderful historian, Charles," Sylvana said, reading his distress. "That you have the gift of putting yourself in the place of historical figures. Of feeling what they felt."

Her words opened a sonorous space in his heart. Maybe not quite as sonorous as other words might have. *I love you, Charles*, for instance, although he knew better than to ever hope for that. But the fact that she considered him a historian at all was an honor indeed.

"You know, Sylvana," Charles said. He gave the narrow mattress the briefest glimpse. "We should get some sleep before going up to the ridge." His pause was longer than he'd intended. "There's a duvet on Theodore's bed."

"Ah," Sylvana mused. "You want to preserve my honor. How nice to meet a man from another epoch! Well, there *was* a knight in your family tree, wasn't there?"

He was on the verge of telling her what Cédric Florus had just discovered: that the true knight in his family had not been Stephen de la Fontaine, as had always been assumed, but Stephen's master, Henri of Rêve, who'd died in Jerusalem, but this was hardly the moment to discuss his medieval roots. He was fairly certain that Sylvana didn't want to discuss them, either.

The storm had weakened. A longer silence filled the room. Sylvana stood very straight and still, her gaze serene. The clouds dispersed and her white sweater glowed uncannily in the moonlight.

"I know so little about you, Sylvana," Charles said. "But though it's little, it seems...well...infinite."

"Infinite..." she repeated, incredulous.

"Yes. And now I realize why that is: because everything I know about you, I know through the forest."

Charles let out a shuddering breath. He covered the short distance between them as if they'd been the last faltering steps of an unimaginably long journey. Sylvana held out her arms, the lace at her wrists weightless as feathers.

She took his hand, snatched up her lyra and led him up through steep forest to an escarpment overlooking the river. It was a sacred spot, she told him. They sheltered between two stone pillars, and there she played and sang for him. He declared his love for her that day...

Charles did manage to get some sleep that night. But rather than dreaming about the cashmere softness of Sylvana—her hot breath in his ear, and the perfect harmony of their limbs on the meager mattress—he dreamt instead about a battle scene from Ralph of Caen:

Soldiers were rushing from one of the gates of Jerusalem. Five of them attacked Tancred, who was observing the city from the Mount of Olives. Tancred took on all five with his lion-like roar and god-like spear. Two of the attackers remained unharmed, but Morta, one of the three fates whose task was to mark the death of mortals by cutting the threads of their lives, was displeased. She snipped at their threads. But as the men retreated, the threads, though frayed, became whole again. This was an astonishing piece of good fortune that had always impressed the young Charles.

He stirred in his sleep, wondering if Fortune would favor him like that, too: if she could possibly make his tattered threads whole. It was impossible to stir on such a small bed without being reminded of the other presence there: another sort of Fortune—her sister, perhaps—who had already gathered his damaged threads and pressed them tenderly to her soul. Whether they would heal there, and become whole again, he couldn't possibly say. There was one other soul who might have been able to tell him, had she lived in his time: the woodland one, who'd preached peace to a reluctant crusader.

Charles awoke to a pulse of light.

He rolled over: Sylvana was gone.

The beam trembled at the turret window, then probed the room randomly.

He sat up: the storm had passed and the moon had set.

Tires crunched on the gravel drive.

LXXVIII

The pounding was audible even in the turret.

Charles dressed in an instant and descended the seven flights as if Tancred himself were pursuing him down the Mount of Olives.

Osselaer was already at the door, woeful in his undershirt. "Your uncle should have kept a gun," he muttered.

Charles stood barefoot on the hall tiles. Fear clamped down on him. *Where was Sylvana?* It was as if she'd vanished into the ferns of Blancheron.

He'd not yet emerged from his surrender to her.

Falling, falling...into an embrace of impossible softness. Into swansdown. Into music itself.

He therefore lacked the presence of mind to wonder why his father's goons would bother to knock at all. Or why, for that matter, there'd been a familiar warble to the car's sound. A smile gradually overtook him: he should have recognized that bucking old palfrey.

"It's all right, Philippe," Charles said, and opened the door.

"Cédric!" cried Osselaer. "It's four-thirty in the morning!"

"I'd hoped to get here sooner," said Florus, and without delay swept into the house.

Cédric Florus was one of those people who occupied a space far greater than their physical stature. But though he might have seemed confined in a hallway like Theodore's, it was obvious to everyone that even a vast arena couldn't have contained the magnitude of why he was there.

Osselaer took Florus's suede car coat and recovered his own trousers and blazer from the salon. Charles led the men into the study. It seemed the appropriate place, somehow. Florus radiated gravity and portent, and if Theodore himself had been hosting this nocturnal gathering, surely he would have ushered his colleagues into his sanctum.

Sylvana appeared at the study door. She'd given no greeting. Her form barely breached the hall shadows. No one but Charles had even detected her there, and for a private moment he basked in the transcendent beauties into which she'd just guided him. He stared at her, fused to her presence, for even had she been completely invisible, he still would have felt the searing emotion in her gaze, locked on him alone.

Charles introduced Sylvana briefly to Florus but she declined to come in.

"I'll make some coffee," she said, and went off to the kitchen.

Without ceremony, Florus cleared some space on Theodore's desk and turned on the banker's lamp. He slid the ivory olifant to one side, opened his document case and lay out the parchment alongside his translation.

"I was going to telephone," he said, sitting in Theodore's chair. "But things were moving too swiftly."

Charles took a place next to him on his boyhood stool. Osselaer perched on the edge of the desk.

The storm had exhausted itself. The Semois dreamscape lay dormant around the villa. Only the men's breathing was audible, and the distant chink of cups in the kitchen.

"My suspicions were correct," Florus said. Then, chattily: "Are you planning on going up to the ridge?"

Charles glanced at Osselaer. "Yes," they said in unison.

"I'm going with you," Florus announced.

The two men fixed their laser attention on their visitor.

"As I mentioned, Charles," Florus continued, "the manuscript is short on some details, but has many that are unusual for a *chanson de geste*: an adoption; a grave..." He rubbed a palm over the parchment. "And a particular item: the olive wood box." He indicated a little huddle of red-brown letters. "*Capsula ligni olivae.*"

He went on: "Stephen de la Fontaine was given a specific task by his master: to give the box to the woman known variously as the 'prophetess of the spring', or 'pagan woman', or simply 'Arda' in the Old French *chanson*."

As if answering to these appellations, Sylvana padded in with four coffees on a tray and some plain dark chocolate and placed this on the desk, as far from the parchment as she could. The lace at her wrists swept back and forth as she moved, of the same antique white as the olifant. She took her own cup to the leather sofa and listened from the back of the study.

Florus thanked her with a little bow of respect, as if to acknowledge that the tradition of sibyls had not been lost in this corner of the Ardennes.

"Remember," he resumed, turning so that Sylvana was part of the discussion, "that at the time, relics of any sort from the Holy Land were more valuable than gold. Bones, teeth, hair…"

"Toenails," Charles smiled, with a nod to St. Simeon.

"Exactly. So even though according to the parchment the box contained just a curl of hair and some seeds, hardly valuable in themselves, we must assume that they nevertheless carried great importance."

"Also according to the parchment," Charles added, "Stephen scattered the seeds over Arda's grave."

Florus asked: "Charles, what did your uncle tell you about the man who gave Stephen the box?" The scholar was casually sipping his coffee directly over the document.

Charles hesitated. Florus's demeanor had changed.

"He said that Stephen's master was a member of the nobility around here," Charles explained. "That he was in the retinue of Godfrey of Bouillon and often dined at Bouillon castle with his squire. Grandfather always assumed that he was a local aristocrat: Henri of Rêve."

Florus's fingers tarried on the blackened edge of the parchment, as if to add his own prints to the nine centuries of fingers that had turned it.

"Yes," he said vaguely. "He was, indeed, noble." The chair let out a creak as he leaned back in it. "As you remember, there were two erasures that I had to verify. The first, on the recto, had been overwritten with '*miles*'." Florus tapped his index finger on the spot. "Which your uncle translated as 'knight'".

Florus looked at the two men and glanced back at Sylvana. The desk chair gave a faint crick.

"The scanner revealed that the erased text was in fact *dux*," he said. He got to his feet.

Charles and Osselaer stood up as well. "Duke," they murmured in unison. Sylvana tip-toed up to join them.

"Yes," said Florus. "Stephen's master was a duke."

No one moved or spoke.

Florus turned the parchment over with a crisp flourish. "The second erasure is even more fascinating," he said, indicating the blank space at the very bottom of the verso where the gap seemed eerily long. "First of all, because it's a modern erasure."

Charles clacked his cup on the saucer. "*What?*"

"Yes. You'll surely notice that the scraping off of text is somehow brighter and cleaner than the older erasures. And the fact that the gap was not overwritten like all the others is certainly noteworthy. Space was at a premium back then, as you know. It's very rare to find such a long blank area in medieval writing."

Charles bent over the parchment. Osselaer leaned closer. Sylvana squeezed between them.

"It *is* a rather long erasure, isn't it?" Charles said. He reviewed Florus's translation:

Stephen died an old man in that castle on the lonely ridge. The boy grew to possess the virtues, broad chest and handsome curls of his blood-father, (erasure).

"Who do you think did it?" Charles asked faintly.

"Your grandfather," Florus said.

"My *grandfather* erased it?!"

"Indeed. He was just as intent on hiding certain things as the anonymous scribe. Happily, the scanner could still detect the hidden text under the medieval overwriting as well as under the new erasure."

Florus stared out at the terrace. "It's odd," he said, "but the medieval erasure was overwritten with the same text that the scribe had rubbed out initially—which your grandfather then rubbed out again.

"So the same text was erased *twice*?" Charles exclaimed.

"Yes. It seems that the scribe had scraped the words out, but couldn't bring himself to replace them with anything else (my interpretation), so reinserted them." He paused. "You see, the words were simply too monumental...sacrosanct, even."

The little group held its collective breath.

Then, in a monotone made graver by its Cambridge sounding board, Florus said: "Charles, your grandfather rubbed out the words *advocatus sancti sepulchri*."

Defender of the Holy Sepulcher.

Charles paled. He couldn't breathe. He moved rapidly to the French doors and threw them open for air. The knight whom Stephen de la Fontaine had served as squire—whom he had watched die in slow agony in Jerusalem in 1100—had lived in the castle just up the river from Blancheron. There had been only one Defender of the Holy Sepulcher in crusader history:

Godfrey of Bouillon.

LXXIX

The clues were there all along," Florus said at the kitchen table, tucking into Osselaer's scrambled eggs. "It made no sense that Stephen's knight was never identified by name—either in the Old French *chanson* or in the Latin folio. Or that there appeared to be two personages all along: Henri of Rêve, and the shadowy Godfrey."

Florus ate with gusto: medieval sleuthing had clearly sharpened his appetite.

Osselaer only picked at his food and Sylvana slipped upstairs, saying she wasn't hungry.

And Charles...

How strange that Florus hadn't actually come out and said it:

Godfrey of Bouillon was your ancestor.

Charles considered the sobering possibility that Theodore had suspected it all along.

The past is alive. In you.

Would his uncle even have said those words, and repeated them with such solemnity, had he not had an inkling himself?

Charles pushed his plate away. It sickened him to think how his father would exploit this revelation. He could barely digest it himself. He turned to the window, where a wan face stared back at him framed by chestnut-blond curls.

"But why did Grandfather rub out that reference to Godfrey?" Charles asked, even though he suspected the answer.

"Because of the implications," said Florus. "He clearly didn't want the information to become public. Oh, he could have made himself a rich man, that's for sure. But you never knew your grandfather, Charles. He was eccentric, not greedy. He didn't want Blancheron to become some sort of crusader theme park. Because that's exactly what would have happened."

"Yes, you're right," said Charles. "These days, all kinds of people with an agenda would descend on Blancheron."

Florus shook his head in amazement. "The legendary Godfrey of Bouillon...the famous celibate and peerless Christian, falling in love with a heretic and fathering her child. Just imagine! Nine centuries of received dogma would have teetered and fallen once people found out. Not a pretty sight, I assure you: academia collapsing under its own weight." He chortled. "I'd give anything to witness such a thing!"

Florus slapped some more butter on his toast. "Good God, how could I have missed those clues? The *porta ducis*...the Duke's Gate. Godfrey himself must have gone up there with Arda. *He's* the one for whom it was named." Florus munched his toast meditatively. "And one clue was hiding in plain sight."

The others waited, expectant.

"In Guy de la Fontaine's translation of the *chanson*," Florus explained, "there's a passage describing the death of Stephen's knight that's practically lifted from Albert of Aachen's crusade chronicle." Florus rifled through his papers and produced the passage in question:

"'Four of his companions were with him: some took his feet onto their laps; others supported his head so that he could lean back his upper body. Some indeed were weeping over him with very great grief and lamentation, because they were very afraid of being forsaken in this long exile.'"

Florus put down the paper. "Albert was describing the death of Godfrey. The folio left out one thing, though. The original reads: 'They were afraid of being forsaken *by so great a prince* in this long exile.'"

Charles felt suddenly light-headed. He moved his gaze to the ridge, where the pine armies were mustering in the incipient dawn. *I should eat something*, he thought. Soon they'd be making their way up the steep approach to Blancheron. It would be slippery after the storm. Dangerous. They would look for Arda's grave. Confront Ames. Learn of Raul's fate.

But although these trials loomed, a strange sadness enveloped Charles. He was overcome by the thought of Blancheron's shadow-neighbor languishing in Outre-mer, knowing he would soon die far from his native land...from his beloved Arda. Thousands had already perished. Many had fled. *Where had Godfrey's mind been during all that?* Charles wondered. Had the duke's thoughts, feverish, strayed back to the forests of his youth...to the comforting beliefs of these ancient hills?

And so this strong, comely warrior, who consorted with bishops and kings and who normally would have been seeking marriage into a family whose estates he could join to his own, could think only of the forest girl.

Charles unlatched the kitchen window and breathed in the air his famous ancestor had once breathed. *How many times had Godfrey slipped away into the forest to see his lover?* Had he invented hunting excursions to foil suspicion? Visits to the clerics at Valdoré? Imagination broke all restraints and Charles could see his ancestor clearly now, escaping his obligations and making his way to the remote pond; waiting for Arda on the heron's rock, or finding her there already, stirring the dense, humid air with her melodies. From there they would have climbed up the ridge to a place where they knew no one would discover them...the place that would become known as the Duke's Gate, a name given by someone who had, in fact, discovered what those two prehistoric stones had witnessed.

Charles smiled at a memory: his boy-self telling Grace Holmes over the fence in Connecticut that in Godfrey's milieu, it would have been unthinkable for such a lord not to have found a suitable wife.

Finally, after seventeen years, he understood her response: "Well, then. Maybe he found an unsuitable one, and couldn't marry her."

"Are you all right, Charles?" Florus asked.

"Yes," he said. "Just a bit overwhelmed."

"I don't doubt it!"

"Are you sure you don't want some eggs?" Osselaer asked, still manning the stove.

"I'm all right, thanks, Philippe," said Charles. "Cédric, could I see your translation again?"

Florus produced it from his case.

Charles found what he was looking for and read the paragraph aloud:

...that great warrior asleep for eternity so near the rock of Calvary had been the sum of all things: a noble hero whose name was fashioned by his honesty, by his family, by his virtues.

Charles and Florus stared at each other, complicit. A shared energy seized them and in a single voice they announced:

"The rock of Calvary!"

"It's the biggest clue of all!" Florus exclaimed. "Not to mention all those superlatives."

"Yes, of course!" Charles said, secretly happy that even a great scholar like Florus could have missed such a thing. Like all good students of the Crusades, Charles knew that Godfrey of Bouillon had been buried at the site of Christ's crucifixion.

"I'll take those eggs now, Philippe," he said, suddenly hungry.

"I think that Stephen himself asked the monks at Valdoré to draw up the parchment," said Florus, as Charles devoured his breakfast. "He wanted posterity to know about the child's real bloodline: that the child wasn't his own, let alone Walderic's or even Rodolfo's. But..."

"But...?" Charles prompted him.

"He also wanted to save the reputation of a great hero. Think of it, Charles: the baby—your ancestor—was the son of the most pious Defender of the Holy Sepulcher and a pagan forest woman. God knows what the Church would have done had the news gotten out. So Stephen adopted the baby, gave him his name and brought him up in obscurity."

"Hence the erasures."

"Yes. Someone at the abbey probably had had second thoughts about putting such a scandal in writing. He overwrote the more obvious references...as well as any mention that their very own Bishop Walderic was a murderer!"

"Finally, though," mused Charles, "some diligent soul wrote *advocatus sancti sepulchri* back in."

Florus smiled. "Until your grandfather got his hands on it!"

Osselaer collected the breakfast dishes from the table. "We should get ready," he said. There was surprising conviction in his tone.

Florus got up from the table. "Indeed!" he said. "We must find the box."

"But what will the contents prove?" Charles asked, exasperated.

"DNA, Charles," Florus said patiently. "DNA..."

Charles stared at him, dumbfounded that he'd overlooked such a thing.

Florus retrieved his coat in the corridor. "Of course, testing the hair in the box only proves that your family is related to the hair's owner," said Florus. "Not the actual identity of that person. To prove scientifically that the curl was really Godfrey's, you would have to analyze the bones of his poor mother, Saint Ida of Lorraine, whose reliquary is with the Benedictines in Bayeux. I'm pretty sure that the French wouldn't give us permission to do that. The grave of his father, Eustace II, is unknown."

"Maybe it would be best not to ask the French," Osselaer offered.

"I agree," said Florus.

"But the proof is in the parchment anyway, isn't it?" Charles asked. "It's all been documented." He chose a battered oilskin from Theodore's collection in the corridor: the one he'd worn for their nocturnal excursion to the field.

"Of course it's proof!" said Florus. "But only for people like us: for scholars. These days, everything has to be scientifically proven."

"Would the translator working for Ames and my father have caught the references to Godfrey?" Charles asked.

"They only have a photocopy. They wouldn't have been able to read the erasures. Therefore, the words 'Duke' and 'Defender of the Holy Sepulcher' would have remained illegible to them."

They drifted into the hall. Sylvana was already waiting at the door in her long cape and sturdy shoes, holding her walking stick. Her expression was grave. She drew Charles aside. "Are you all right?" she asked. "You look positively ashen." She lay a hand on his forehead. "You're starting a fever."

"I'm all right," he lied. A wave of heat rose in him, followed by a cool sweat. Sylvana's hand felt like balm.

She reached into her backpack and took out a honeyed lozenge. "Suck on this," she said. "It's full of medicinal herbs."

They filed out into the half-light. Charles picked up the shovel Osselaer had found in the cellar and locked the door behind them, already feeling stronger from Sylvana's lozenge. *Or was it the memory of what had happened in the turret room?*

There was something else, too.

As he searched the pocket of the oilskin for a handkerchief, he pulled out a crushed white feather. It took him some moments to realize what this was: the swansdown he'd found on the grassy riverbank all those years ago.

LXXX

The storm had left behind a silent water-world. Meadow, rock, forest…all were sodden and inert. Remnants of fog hung over everything like the aftermath of creation.

They crossed the bridge in single file without speaking. Charles, Sylvana, Florus, Osselaer. *Rich, poor, scholarly, hapless.* A comprehensive representation of any pilgrimage, Charles thought. His mind roamed with the approaching fever and he considered that something wondrous happened to people with a shared mission. Labels no longer fit them, it seemed, so that Osselaer the Hapless had turned out to be a patrolman and an organizer, and quite a decent cook. He'd even brought a thermos of tea for them to share on the ridge. Florus, unlike any scholar Charles had ever known at Yale, was striding along like a seasoned mountain man (his city shoes and suede car coat notwithstanding). And Sylvana…well, she surpassed all labels anyway. Her hauteur had returned and she rose, heron-like, above all the drama around her.

For himself, Charles reserved judgment. His uncle would have been proud of his resolve. But his physical strength was not what he'd hoped it would be. The shovel he was carrying felt as heavy as an ox's yoke and with his usual courtliness, Osselaer offered to take it.

It dawned on Charles that he'd never embarked on any project with so few creature comforts. Hugh Fontaine had made sure that the life he'd manufactured for himself and his son followed America's worst credo: *More. Easy. Fast.* Caught inexorably in Hugh's orbit, Charles had followed this credo to the letter, never doing anything without good clothes and food, elite transportation, and of course, several credit cards.

None of this would have done him any good now.

He found the entry in the trees leading to the ridge. That is, his intuition found it. For there was nothing at all to indicate that this was the place to begin the climb.

Memory was fickle, Charles knew, but also charitable, it seemed. Because what it offered him now was comfort: Theodore's swinging satchel; his bright gaze piercing the gloom. Charles thrilled that the boy who had followed his uncle up this ridge, and the adult doing so now, were not so very different after all. He grasped a branch and leaned out over the precipice, just to feel the familiar vertigo again and spot a glint of river. *It's all here*, he thought: the twisting trees...the tuneful chink of shale.

They scrabbled their way up the clinging forests of Stephen's story. Beneath them lay his snake-river, unfathomable as ever. *How could Rodolfo have carried Arda's body up through this?* How many times had he set her down so he could rest, his heart torn asunder by the waxen shell she'd left behind? What devotion—what *love*—to bury her near the stones that would bear the title of her famous lover.

"We must all be as quiet as possible," Florus said sotto voce. Sweat gleamed on his forehead. "Ames could be anywhere." They were the words of a Cambridge medievalist, not a sleuth. Even as he spoke, his foot snapped a twig and let loose a volley of scree.

Charles nodded, and gestured upward to the next safe rock. He grasped Sylvana's hand to help her over a loose patch of shale. His confidence inexplicably soared. In that soaking, somber forest, his feet were finding their way as if he'd only recently passed here. Perhaps it was the final surge before sickness caught hold of him.

They gained the ridge. The little band huddled together to catch their breath and quell their fears. From here, they could see the chimney of Blancheron Castle poking from its mossy tomb, and to their right, the meadow draped in fog. Beyond, at the far end of the ridge, the two menhirs darkened the air like totems.

Osselaer took out the thermos and they passed around a cup of steaming tea. No one spoke. Only their breathing was audible— Charles's in particular, coarse and watery. A magpie joined in from the ruins with its own grating mutter.

"We have to cross the meadow," Charles said softly. "The grave is near the standing stones."

The loyal friend of the child's mother, that Moorish jongleur, had buried her under the sky where the herons flew. And so they climbed, and the knight felt that he was leaving behind a vale of tears and entering a mountain of joy, for at last he could fulfill his master's wishes, and return the box to the prophetess of the spring.

Charles said: "If we keep to the trees we'll be safer..." But his words were cut short.

They'd all heard it:

The sound of spade against rock.

They stared at each other and Charles put a finger to his lips.

Another sharp chink.

"Ames has beaten us to it, I'm afraid," Osselaer whispered, tight-faced.

"Shall we confront him?" Florus mouthed. His suede coat and city shoes were damp and soiled. He'd carried the document case with the parchment under his arm should anyone have attempted to break into the villa while they were gone.

"I'll have to confront him," Charles said, keeping his voice low. The fog, he knew, played all kinds of tricks with acoustics. "I'll try to negotiate with him for the box."

No one was convinced...least of all Charles. He'd already been assaulted by Ames. As if that weren't enough, the man's ruthlessness had been confirmed in writing by Ida, who wasn't the sort of person to even mention the word "murder", let alone accuse someone of it without certitude.

Osselaer glanced around at the uninviting vista. "Can't we negotiate in a more civilized setting?" he grumbled.

"The digging seems to have stopped," Florus said. "Maybe he's gone."

"It could have been Raul," said Sylvana. "Oh, Charles..."

He put his arm around her. "We shall face this together," he said, and held her close. They were his own words, but they carried echoes of his mentors. *Theodore...Ida...Grace...* He leaned his cheek against Sylvana's hair. Over her shoulder he could see the exact place in the ferns where she'd first appeared to him, proud and remote, in complete harmony with the earth beneath her feet.

He waved a hand to the others. "Let's go," he said.

LXXXI

The intrepid party started off toward the Duke's Gate. The meadow was shrouded; bleak. Whatever "mountain of joy" Stephen had described in the manuscript had been subsumed by the centuries.

They kept close to the pines, slowed by countless dips and hillocks in the ground. Nameless creatures, disturbed in their lairs, scrabbled away under the leaves. Here and there, remnants of the castle protruded from the grass where Stephen's men had laid them nine hundred years before.

Keeping to this route, they would arrive near the mound that Charles suspected was Arda's final resting place: the raised shoulder of earth where carnations had always grown.

Had Uncle known all along that Arda was buried there? It was strange that Charles had never asked him why the ground rose in that spot; or why wild carnations still grew over it as if strewn by hand.

He then took the seeds and scattered them over the mound. They were the seeds of the pale pink carnations that grew wild in Jerusalem.

Charles halted under the pines and the three others stopped some distance behind him. He could see it from here, the gentle rise unlike any other on the ridge. Whoever was digging seemed to have gone.

Charles picked his way over the sopping grass to the grave. The trio, uneasy, followed.

"There's no one here," Sylvana said under her breath. A rook chattered at the sound of her voice and wheeled up from the pines.

They stood in a line at the side of the mound and stared: the earth had been freshly turned.

Charles glanced across the meadow. The fog was thick and close to the ground, but even so, one could have spotted a dark shape in it—a movement, at least. But there was nothing.

"We're too late," Florus said, brushing moisture from his sleeves. "The grave has clearly been opened. He must have found the box...if indeed it was here at all."

"We have to make sure," said Charles, feeling as irrational as he sounded. His throat was beginning to hurt. He seized the shovel from Osselaer and started digging into the loose earth.

"Charles, please." Sylvana put a hand on his shoulder. "Leave her in peace."

But his heart carried the loyalty and determination of Stephen's. He dug with passion—with despair—as the others looked bleakly on.

The earth was heavy after the storm and sweat dripped down his back. But he could no sooner have stopped himself than if he'd been limping up the drive to Villa Antioch after limping for four thousand kilometers, and someone had told him to stop just before you could see the house, and river, and willow all at once.

Charles set down the shovel: he'd struck something that didn't seem to be rock. The earth was paler in that spot. Something grayish was lying just beneath the surface.

With the tears coursing down his cheeks, he gathered his spirits and peered into the void.

They all pressed around him.

Charles kneeled down and reached in.

The grave was shallow: it wasn't difficult to touch its contents. Gingerly, he patted his hand along the delicate bones lying under the loose earth. He gasped as his fingers brushed against the bulge at one end of the pit: *Arda's skull.* But even as he leaned over her mortal remains, Charles couldn't help but wonder what had happened to the rest of her—to her true essence. He knew by heart the instructions that Stephen had carried home from his dying knight...from the man they now knew to have been Godfrey. *Tell her that I swear before God she will find me again, no matter who her own god may be.*

Charles sat up on his heels, his head spinning. *Had she, in fact, found him?*

"There's no box," Sylvana whispered. She put a hand on Charles's shoulder. "Leave her be."

But he leaned back into the hole. He ran his fingers lightly down the bone at Arda's side until he felt a collection of smaller ones, clumped together like a mini ossuary.

Charles caught his breath.

Her hand.

He pulled away. As he did his fingertips encountered a small object. He smoothed the dirt away and removed the thing from the grave: a hardened, black, arced piece of wood with notches in it.

He stood up, faint. The others crowded around and stared at what lay on his palm.

"Charles..." Florus gasped.

"I know," Charles said. "The lyra." He recognized the bridge of a stringed instrument, and the notches that had held the strings in place.

"Carbonized," Florus muttered. "It never would have survived otherwise." Then he intoned: "Walderic..."

He threw her precious instrument into the fire.

Tears shone on Charles's cheeks. His nerves sparked at the feel of the blackened wood. *Now you can really touch the past, lad!*

"Rodolfo must have collected the remnants of Arda's lyra from the ashes in the cave and buried them with her," said Florus.

"Yes," Charles murmured. He glanced overhead. The thick air had begun to lift and flush with the dawn. He remembered waiting with his uncle for the cracks to appear in the clouds over Blancheron...for the sky to shine with the beauty of porphyry, marble, gold and precious stones. The most elusive of these wonders had been sound—the lingering notes of the lyra that could still be heard on the ridge, it was said, although Charles had never met anyone who'd actually heard them. He listened now, as Stephen had.

He knew not whether this was the power of heaven speaking, or the will of the Earth, that ancient mother, whose beloved daughter lay at his feet.

The little group continued staring at the object on Charles palm. No one noticed the shape emerging from the fog.

LXXXII

The figure coalesced into Manfred Ames. The man stepped toward them as casually as if he'd been crossing a street. His dark-blue overcoat was draped over his shoulders and in his hands he held a small bundle of cloth.

"Is this what you're after?" Ames asked. His voice had no tone.

He drew near and unwrapped the object, holding it out as a Magi would an offering. The diamond on his little finger flashed in the feeble dawn light.

The pilgrims held their breath.

The box had the air of a time-traveler. Scarred, darkened, it had crossed so many centuries that it no longer looked real...or even plausible.

Florus approached Ames and gasped. "It's in remarkable condition!" and "You're in possession of a stolen antiquity!" followed each other rapidly, probably not in the order he'd intended.

"It was wrapped in waxed cloth," Ames said, ignoring the second comment. "As you know, that's what preserved it so well." His goatee gleamed in the watery light. A half-smile played at the corners of his mouth, as if this were simply a congenial exchange between seller and buyer.

Ames produced a small key from his coat pocket. "Presumably the lock still works," he said pleasantly. "They were made to last."

Charles slumped against Osselaer. The fever had taken hold now— or perhaps it was the rankness of the grave that had overcome him. His color drained as he watched Ames fit the key into the lock of the olive wood box.

Just imagine if you could actually touch something that had been Godfrey's.

Charles knew what was in that box. *How could anyone possibly disturb it?* The notion weighed on him like time itself. It was only a curl of human hair. But that curl was powerful indeed, for there was nothing else left of the mortal Godfrey of Bouillon: his tomb in Jerusalem had been sacked, his remains scattered. Suddenly history seemed *too* close. Charles could feel it not only breathing at his neck, but tracing a cold finger down his spine.

He stood there, frozen. *Best to leave it alone*, he thought. The curl had been meant for Arda, after all. Stephen had done his best to return it to her on behalf of his master, carrying it in his surcoat across an entire continent. Now Ames had pillaged it from her grave, probably using Raul as his grunt. *How could Charles de la Fontaine, Godfrey's own descendant, allow this to happen?*

Trembling, he slipped the bridge of Arda's lyra into his pocket. He knew what he should do. Defying the ache in his limbs and the shock of all these revelations, Charles drew himself up as best he could and confronted Ames.

"The parchment's a forgery," he said. The fog lent his voice a dull echo.

No one moved. A mantilla of mist inclined over Arda's grave like a mourner.

"It's a hoax," Charles blundered on. He knew how he must have appeared to the others: mud smeared over his trousers and jacket; curls hanging in sodden semi-circles. His eyes glittered, and his voice was thick and slurred.

Ames glared at Charles, his fingers still on the bronze key. He hadn't yet turned it in the lock. "Your grandfather stole the parchment from the Library of European History decades ago," he said coolly. "It's certainly authentic. I have the photocopy, as you know. But as your father's representative, I'm entitled to see the original."

"My grandfather was an eccentric," Charles countered. "An oddball. Everyone knows that. You can't walk from Antioch to Jerusalem in the hot sun wearing chain mail and *not* be daft." A mysterious wind filled his sails and he careened ahead, rudderless. "Grandfather was also talented," Charles went on. "He could fabricate medieval folios and make them look like the real thing. Anyway, the heel left in the library codex where the folio was supposedly cut out doesn't match the jagged edge of the parchment."

What lies! The words hammered in Charles's head until he could hardly bear it. His flimsy story didn't even make any sense to him. *Why would someone have removed the folio in the first place if it hadn't contained anything important?* He stopped to catch his breath. He didn't have the heart to look at Sylvana or Osselaer, let alone Florus, who must have been suffering some sort of academic melt-down just then.

He'd underestimated Florus, however.

"Charles is right," said the scholar. He smoothed his hair back into a silvery wave and seemed utterly at ease again, his elegance restored. He took the document case from under his arm and pulled out the parchment. "This is a modern confection," he announced, waving the manuscript at Ames. "No doubt about it. It's brilliant work, though. It almost had *me* fooled."

"Cédric..." Charles stammered, but Florus held up his hand and continued: "I am quite prepared to formally discredit this manuscript, Manfred. I doubt that anyone will disagree with me." He seemed to be thoroughly enjoying himself now. To make sure his message wasn't lost, he added: "I'm afraid that Blancheron will never have the sensational cachet you hoped for now."

It was an extraordinary move. Perilous. Charles reeled more from Florus's theatrics than from the fever. Here was one of the world's greatest medievalists, prepared to compromise his reputation— perhaps ruin it forever—by discrediting an authentic manuscript. Charles never imagined that Florus would have backed this deranged scheme.

Ames struggled to remain calm. Everyone in the antiquities business knew Cédric Florus. His word was gold. People would listen even if he'd cast doubt on the Bayeux Tapestry.

At once Sylvana cried out.

Another figure had materialized from the fog. He kept well behind Ames, but his long raincoat was visible, as was the spade in his hand.

"*Raul!*" Sylvana yelled, launching herself toward him.

But Charles restrained her. Raul had dropped the spade and was creeping up behind Ames like a fox. No one—not even Ames—seemed to have predicted his next move. All they knew was that Raul had vanished into the fog as imperceptibly as he'd appeared.

And that the box was gone.

There was a collective gasp.

"Raul!" Sylvana cried again.

Ames melted back into the fog in pursuit. Sylvana slipped from Charles's grasp and dashed after the two shadows.

"Sylvana!" Charles shouted, and attempted to follow her. Cédric grabbed his arm to stop him. Raul was heading for the steepest side of the river loop—the vertical forest that appeared in nightmares, and tricked the tired, disoriented walker. One wrong step and you would plunge down to the river, swift and swollen from the rains.

"Please, Cédric," Charles said. He felt his will buckle. "Call her back! It's far too dangerous on that side of the ridge."

But Osselaer had already gone after her.

The sky had lightened and turned the fog to gauze. The figures of Raul and Ames moved as silhouettes behind a screen, blundering forward, perilously close to the edge.

Sylvana's silhouette foundered along behind them. Her long skirt hampered her, and several times she was brought to her knees in the deep grass. By the time Osselaer reached her, she was inconsolable. She screamed at the gallant notary as he tried to dissuade her. He pulled at her arm, tugging her back from the edge.

"Let me go!" she cried. "Please...let me go..." Sobbing, she collapsed at Osselaer's feet, and her moans rose up to join all the anguish that had ever unfolded on that ridge. *Raul! Oh, Raul...*

LXXXIII

"Come," Florus said, steering Charles gently by the elbow. "You're very ill. We must get you home. Philippe will close the grave and accompany Sylvana back down. And don't worry about Raul: it seems he knows this land intimately. He can take care of himself."

"Home..." Charles whispered.

"I think we can assume that Ames was fooled by your magnificent dare," Florus added. "If so, he'll give up and leave Raul alone."

Magnificent dare... Charles mouthed the words as he stumbled along beside Florus. He'd never dared in his life—certainly not with magnificence. *Had it really been daring?* he wondered. He'd left Sylvana on her knees in the meadow. He'd abandoned his new-found brother to the jaws of a killer. These were the hallmarks of a coward.

"The box," Charles rasped, his throat raw. "The box..."

"The box is out of our hands, I'm afraid," Florus said. "We can't prove that Ames took it. We can only *disprove* what it's supposed to contain."

"But Cédric, what about your reputation? Your body of work?"

Florus smiled as he led Charles around a stand of nettle. "Sometimes it's necessary to crash and burn to make a point," he said. He seemed entirely comfortable with this concept—even bemused by it. "You see, Charles, I'm not any less of a misfit than your grandfather and uncle were. I live alone with a misanthropic rabbit called Arnulf; I have a tendency to talk to my manuscripts; I was perfectly aware that your grandfather stole that parchment and yet never brought it to the attention of the *Bibliothèque de l'Histoire*. So there you have it. Perhaps I shall enjoy an enhanced reputation through infamy."

As Florus guided him back across the meadow, Charles perceived other witnesses to this drama. The dawn clouds, of course, rose-lit, with porticos and boudoirs and thrones. But also human apparitions clad in silks and fine linen, pressing all around him. Resplendent white horses, too, mustering at the edges of his delirium.

And one other onlooker: someone who didn't possess silks or fine linens, but a fuchsia track suit and cheap red slippers.

"You said that I'd find my endeavor, Mrs. Holmes," Charles muttered. "You said that I just had to persevere until I did..."

"Charles?" Florus said, steadying his patient. "What are you saying?"

"Well, I did persevere!" Charles exclaimed. "I found it, Mrs. Holmes. I found my endeavor! Thank you...oh, thank you..."

"Charles...?"

At once a cry rent the ridge.

"Someone must have fallen!" exclaimed Florus.

The two men peered through the lifting fog. The forms of Osselaer and Sylvana were visible making their way back across the meadow. They'd stopped, too, at the cry. Osselaer gripped Sylvana again to hold her back, but she seemed to have lost her fight. She stood gazing at the place where Raul and Ames had disappeared.

"Raul is fit and strong, Charles," Florus said quietly. "It was most likely Ames. Indeed, let us hope that it was."

Charles clung to his thoughts, shreds though they were. He hoped fervently that Florus was right. But he also knew that once the rotten leaves gave way and the shale peeled off underfoot, nothing could stop you from sliding down the far side of the ridge. Until the river stopped you, that is—the sly, ever-watchful river.

"There's nothing we can do now," Florus said, and steered Charles past the castle ruins to the lip of the descent.

For a sick man and a city man, the way down was daunting. Vertigo seized them both. The descent could only be done safely by choosing a tree, skittering down into it, embracing the trunk and then choosing the next one, over and over again. Every third tree or so, Charles had to sit on his heels on the slipping shale to catch his breath, and Florus would seize the shoulder of his oilskin from behind to keep him from pitching forward.

It took them an hour and a half to reach the bridge. Osselaer and Sylvana had found another route down and were waiting for them there. They rushed up to support Charles on either side. Florus brought up the rear carrying the shovel, a relief after half-carrying Charles.

It hadn't escaped any of them that their mission to find the olive wood box had been a failure—perhaps even a disaster, pending any news of Raul. If Ames had recovered the box, there might still be a way for Hugh Fontaine to capitalize on the notoriety of Blancheron.

Charles turned his face upwards: the dampness soothed his burning cheeks. He closed his eyes: how redolent it was! His senses sharpened, just as Theodore had taught him. He detected the peaty tang of the riverbank, and the water's crystal-green freshness—the savors of his childhood. Something else was folded into these odors, too, he noticed, as if it had been caught there for a very long time and begun to rust.

There's a horseman who passes by here sometimes. Haven't you ever heard him?

Charles stopped dead. A shiver coursed through him: something flinty had struck a stone on the bridge. *The clack of Sylvana's walking stick?* The humid air played with sound, he knew, making it sharper and hollower and tricking the mind. There was no telling what it might have been.

He fainted.

LXXXIV

T here, there, my sweet knight..."

"Ida?"

"No, it's Sylvana."

He opened his eyes long enough to notice the tattered lace at her wrists as she settled him onto the leather sofa in the study. *Such light hands...strong, too. They could heal, and play music. Her very essence was distilled in them.*

There'd been no question of climbing any stairs. Theodore's bedroom was out of bounds, therefore. No one had proposed the salon, either, which might have been more comfortable but was certainly less cheery. Sylvana had made up the sofa in the study, therefore, and with the help of Florus and Osselaer carried the patient into his favorite room. The aging leather creaked agreeably as Charles sank onto it, a sound that would accompany his every toss and turn over many days.

"Please, I'm all right," he mumbled, moaning with pain whenever his skin touched anything at all—even the flannel pajamas Theodore had worn to chamois softness.

His three friends hovered around the sofa, uncertain. They proffered the herbal tea and fruit juice they'd found in the kitchen, and ransacked Theodore's bathroom for a couple of expired aspirins. Florus made a show of driving into Rêve, where Marcel Wauters admired the vintage MG and donated a container of stinging nettle soup—one of his specialties, he said, and excellent for restoring health. Then, sadly: "It was one of Theodore's great favorites."

"Call a doctor," Sylvana beseeched Osselaer as the first evening wore on. Charles had already perspired through his sheets.

"No doctor," the patient hissed.

Sylvana leaned over him. "Your fever is very high."

357

Charles was not too sick to notice the little comma of hair straying across her cheek, or the illumination she brought to his pillow. "I want to be here," he murmured. "With you, and Theodore, and Godfrey."

That cemented the decision. Osselaer picked up the hall telephone and interrupted Dr. Francois Roche's after-dinner liqueur in Bouillon.

As a young assistant, Roche had treated Charles's grandfather, Guy de la Fontaine. He'd been summoned to the villa by Madame de la Fontaine when the old man had returned home from what the lady had called "a strange excursion abroad". The doctor, his medical degree only a few years old at the time, had not yet had any experience treating sores on the back and shoulders brought on by wearing chain mail in the hot sun, but he'd acted as if this had been a common complaint, and as a result Grandfather had treated Roche with a deference the doctor had never forgotten (although Grandmother had tried hard to forget the whole sorry episode).

"It seems like a bad flu to me," Roche said, casting a dubious look around the sick room. He sniffed the air: there was the usual dust and mildew from all the books and papers, but there was a sweetness, too...with a singular, peppery edge.

Sylvana drew Roche into the corridor. "Doctor, he's been talking as if his dead uncle is still here," she whispered. "And someone else, too..." She hesitated.

"Also dead?"

"Yes. But Charles doesn't seem to think so."

Roche nodded knowingly. "Don't worry," he said. "It's normal to hallucinate with such a high fever. I'll take a blood sample just to be certain it's nothing more serious."

Blood... What was left of it after nine centuries, anyway? Charles's thoughts drifted to the olive wood box—to the curl that had journeyed all the way from Outre-mer and lain in the grave of its beloved since the early twelfth century. How odd that this miniscule piece of a human should be more compelling than the centuries of lore, legend, glory and controversy that Godfrey of Bouillon had left behind.

Raul... The name surfaced with throbbing remorse. *Was he even still alive?* Surely the recovery of one's own missing brother was more important than recovering a tiny piece of Godfrey. He *is* a piece of Godfrey. *Like me.*

He must have spoken Raul's name aloud, for he heard Sylvana say: "They haven't found him yet, Charles." She sounded bereft—a shocking thing to hear in the voice of a sibyl. "Ames is gone, too." Those words clapped shut like a door.

Charles's fever abated temporarily after Roche left. Painkillers took his attention off his joints long enough for him to appreciate Sylvana's comings and goings and the ministrations of those wondrous hands. They also induced a pleasant, buoyant feeling, allowing his thoughts to float off on their longest tether. There they collided with Aunt Ida and Grace Holmes, adrift and welcoming. As he observed them from his sick bed, Charles wondered how two equally wise women could have been so widely separated by geography and circumstance.

He slipped even further along the tether—deeper in time, it seemed—for he spotted St. Arda and St. Ida in their medieval ether, two wise women even more drastically separated than the first two, not only because one was in rough, stained linen and the other in fine wool, but because their sainthoods had been so differently bestowed: one a peasant sage—a pagan in an unmarked grave; the other a wealthy noblewoman beatified by the Church, her relics reposing at Bayeux. This is where it got interesting, to paraphrase Theodore. Because no one would ever have been able to prove that the powers of one woman, guided by the Earth-matriarch, had been any less potent and spiritual than the miracles performed by the other, guided by her patriarch god.

"Charles?" Sylvana whispered. "Shall I read to you while your fever's down?"

"Yes, please," he said, taking the opportunity to clasp her hand as she pressed a cool cloth to his forehead.

He asked her to read from Albert of Aachen. It was perhaps odd for a sick individual to seek comfort in a crusade chronicle. But far from being the dour experience one would have supposed, Albert was bracing company, and also the most empathetic of the chroniclers. Particularly when he wrote about Godfrey's brush with death.

LXXXV

The Frankish crusaders, having made it through the moonscape of waterless gorges in the Mountains of the Sultan in August, 1097, descended to rest in the beautiful, fertile valley of Pisidia, in present-day Turkey.

"'Duke Godfrey and the other nobles pitched their tents all over the delightful meadowlands...'" Sylvana looked up from the book. "Is this where you want me to begin?"

Charles nodded. He flattened himself against the back of the sofa so that she could sit on the edge of it, pressing agreeably against his legs.

"I'll pick and choose, shall I?" Sylvana said. "It's a long text. All right?"

"All right, my love," Charles whispered.

It was a response Sylvana clearly hadn't been expecting. She blushed and turned away, a detail that the patient, rallying somewhat, had noticed.

"'Finding a woodland most suitable for hunting,'" Albert continued (by way of Sylvana), "'they took up bow and quiver, girded on their swords and went into the forests near the mountains to see if anything would appear which they would be able to shoot and chase with their cunning young hounds. Each on his own path to ambush the wild beasts, Duke Godfrey saw that a bear of most enormous and frightful appearance had seized a helpless pilgrim out gathering twigs.

"'The duke, as he was accustomed and ready to help his Christian comrades at all times of misfortune, hastily drew his sword, vigorously spurred his horse and swooped down upon the wretched man. When the bear saw the horse and its rider bearing down on it at a gallop, it met the duke face to face at no less speed, opened its jaws to tear his throat and unsheathed its sharp claws to rip him to pieces. The duke was keenly provoked and violently angry, and with the point of his sword turned toward it, he approached the brute in a rash and blind attack.

"'But the beast suddenly drove its curved claws into the duke's tunic, brought him down to the ground and embraced him in its forepaws, and wasted no time before tearing his throat with his teeth. The duke therefore, in great distress, remembering his many distinguished exploits and lamenting that he who had up to now escaped splendidly from all danger was now to be choked by this bloodthirsty beast in an ignoble death, recovered his strength. Seizing the sword, which had got entangled with his own legs in the sudden fall from his horse and the struggle with the frenzied wild beast...'"

Sylvana put the book down. "Honestly, Charles. Don't you want me to read you something a bit more restful?"

"Please, continue!" he huffed.

"Oh, all right. Let's see...here we are: '...he held the sword by the hilt and aimed swiftly at the beast's throat, but mutilated the calf and sinews of his own leg with a serious cut. But nevertheless, although an unstaunchable stream of blood poured forth, he did not yield to the hostile brute.

"'A man called Husechin, who had heard the great shout of the poor peasant delivered from the bear, rode at speed to the assistance of the duke. He attacked the terrifying wild beast, and together with the duke pierced its liver and ribs. The duke for the first time began to lose heart because of the pain of his wound, the excessive loss of blood. Everyone rushed together to the place where the brave champion and man of wisdom was brought wounded. Laying him on a litter, the chiefs of the army brought him down into the camp with great lamentation and grief of the men and wailing of the women, summoning the most skilled doctors to heal him. The wild beast they divided among them, saying that they had never seen anything like it in size.'"

Sylvana crept from the sofa and put the book back on the shelf, for astonishingly, Charles had fallen asleep. What she didn't know was that in fact he'd wandered off, and far at that: he'd found himself in Pisidia, pressing into Godfrey's tent with the crush of lamenting pilgrims, as doctors tried to stop the bleeding of his hero and squires brought water and fresh cloths to aid this noblest of men. Charles caught sight of the grievous injury and had to back out of the tent, queasy, before he'd had a chance to gaze on the face of the injured one.

He lingered outside the tent, listening to the panic within and occasional moan of the patient. Surely such pain would have brought on a spectacular kaleidoscope of visions, he thought: fancies, dreams, regrets; surely Godfrey's suffering had spirited him back to Bouillon, to the forests and rivers of his youth...to the mists and lonely ridges of his birthright. *To Arda...*

"Sylvana?" Charles asked when he woke up. "Could you light the candle on my uncle's desk?"

That evening, his fever returned with a vengeance.

LXXXVI

He tossed on the creaking sofa and watched shadows flit through his delirium. Sylvana's had the faintest glimmer—a will-o'-the-wisp above the pond. That glimmer led him along a path at once ancient and fresh. He knew this trail—every step of it—for it was leading him to a familiar source: to the very heart of his journey. In all his ramblings across remote escarpments and haunted groves, he'd resisted the route closest to hand, assuming it would be the most difficult of all. But he'd been wrong. For when one could resist no more, it turned out that the path that led inward was the easiest one.

Forest... Charles whispered the word in English, with the refreshing "s" still intact. Somehow the sound brought Theodore to his side: *Europe was covered with forests, lad—a whole continent of them. The sheer vastness...well, we have no idea. Only remnants are left. But they can still enchant us,* n'est-ce pas? *They* must *enchant us. Or we risk losing our souls.*

Charles smiled through his fever. He remembered that he'd once considered disappearing into the forests around Blancheron to avoid the move to America. A boy of sixteen, at a crossroads, ready to bolt. But obedience had embedded itself. His father had seen to that. Through intimidation. But also through the withering slander of everything that Charles had loved. No wonder it had taken him seventeen years to set foot in the Ardennes again.

Blancheron... All those unexplained stirrings. Even as a boy he'd been aware of them. He'd always kept a wary eye out whenever he'd trailed home after Theodore. *But for what?* He'd never known. For Peter the Hermit, maybe, that ragged, reeking proselytizer. Or one of Walderic's henchmen, lurking behind a rock with a knife. The idea of spotting the white heron had filled him with trepidation. *What if it was really someone else?* White animals were not entirely of this world, after all.

He sighed. *So many souls in the forest...*

But it hadn't been the prospect of deranged hermits, or bandits, or white birds that had frightened the young Charles, he realized now. Because here he was, a man in his thirties, finally admitting to himself that one soul in particular had disturbed him far more than the others.

Who was Godfrey, really?

Charles opened his eyes and watched Sylvana fill his glass with fresh water. Beyond her he glimpsed the candle she'd lit on the desk at his request. The lacey cuff of her sweater brushed his cheek as she changed the cloth on his forehead.

Sylvana slipped from the room and closed the door.

The candle shimmied and buckled.

Puts you in the right century, lad.

He felt a warm, heavy presence.

There was breathing, too. Measured and coarse.

Charles.

The presence knew his name.

LXXXVII

He turned a burning cheek on the pillow and caught sight of the wooden stool. How many hours he'd spent on that hard, unforgiving piece of furniture! The thought heartened him, for he'd known true happiness there. With a rasp he breathed in the mélange that was Theodore: musty tomes; cedarwood; carnations—better than any drug.

He lifted his head:

The stool was occupied.

This didn't seem odd, somehow. Dr. Roche had said he might hallucinate with such a high fever. *But would a hallucination sit on a stool?*

Charles fell back on the pillow. It had taken him only a few seconds to memorize his visitor: beige woolen tights; an ochre tunic draped over a linen shirt; thick beard, broad shoulders and frank regard. He hadn't bothered to glance at the man's hair, for he assumed it was like his own.

"Monseigneur," he whispered. *My lord.* "May I call you that?"

"Of course."

Charles lay still. The response frightened him. *Maybe I should ask Sylvana to call Dr. Roche.*

But instead he said: "Can you stay for a moment?" Suddenly his anxiety had less to do with the vision on the stool and everything to do with the possibility that this revenant (if that's what it was) might vanish, never to return.

"I have plenty of time," came the reply.

A door must have closed somewhere. Or perhaps the visitor had changed position. For a wave of peppery nutmeg drifted over Charles.

"I'm sorry that I can't be more welcoming," Charles said.

"I'm very sorry you are so ill."

The voice that Charles had tried so hard to imagine as a boy was in fact more complex than he would have thought: grave yet warm; lush, like a bank of ferns; deep, like night.

His fear vanished. Indeed, he wondered how he could have felt it in the first place. They were, after all, very old friends.

"Do you think much about Outre-mer...about what happened there?" Charles asked, as if resuming an old conversation.

"One has a lot of time to think over nine centuries."

In all his meditations, Charles had never considered that his shadow-friend might have a sense of humor.

"You were the least self-serving of the Latin princes, I think," Charles said, wavering. *Why weren't we ever prepared for such moments?* (Not that such moments happened very often.) He attempted: "I always assumed that you rode above all the misery of the campaign on a sort of elevated byway. In fact, you rode beside the lowliest peasants, didn't you?"

Charles stopped speaking. He listened for any sound in the vicinity of the stool: there was none. "Dr. Roche..." he moaned softly.

But the visitor spoke again:

"There were no elevated byways, as you call them, Charles," he said. "Only struggle and privation. The simple, ordinary pilgrims are the ones etched in my memory. Drinking blood and urine. Chewing thistles. All the illness and pain. None of it destroyed their will, though." A pause, and then: "Riches cannot feed our resolve, can they?"

"No," said Charles.

"We have to find it within ourselves somewhere."

"Yes."

"No matter what our circumstances."

Charles nodded, his head throbbing.

"I tried to help where I could," the man said. "My mother taught me humility and charity, it's true. But it was she who was the saint...not I."

"But Monseigneur..."

"Charles, I was as bellicose as all the others. The stories you've read are mostly true: I participated in the slaughter. I cut someone in two. I rode into Antioch after battles like all the others in my company, with heads hanging from my saddle. Does that shock you?"

"Well…" Charles hesitated. He'd known about those things, of course. He faltered, and in his weakened condition grasped at a familiar guide:

People are messy and unreliable, lad. They don't fit neatly into books. Especially the famous ones. The myth of heroes completely obscures their humanity. But then again, maybe that's a good thing. I mean, do you really want to know if Godfrey had decaying teeth or flat feet? Or how he must have stank by the time he reached Jerusalem?

Charles considered these words, thinking that Theodore should have added: *Or how severed heads had swung from his saddle.*

"There was the code of chivalry, as you know," said the visitor, cutting into Theodore's lesson. "And then there was the reality of being a knight. They were quite different."

"Yes," said Charles. He shut his eyes, as even the evening light was hurting them. He did not, in fact, want to know about his visitor's teeth or feet…or about severed heads, for that matter.

He listened to the man shift on the stool, perhaps out of discomfort (he was quite a quite a robust individual); or perhaps from the mental weight with which fame burdened humble people. Even so, it was difficult to reconcile such humility with the temper that must have surged when required: for manning a siege tower and breaching a defense…for swinging a sword hard enough to cut someone in half.

The guest let out a cough: a watery sensation Charles felt in his own lungs, followed by a sour, metallic taste.

There was movement at the door: Sylvana slipped in to refill Charles's glass and tip-toed out again. *How rude, he thought, not to acknowledge his guest.*

"Would you like some water, my lord?" Charles asked, gesturing to the glass.

"No, thank you. You are very kind, though, offering hospitality in the midst of your pain."

"I'm sure you did the same after your own illness."

"Ah, you *have* been reading!"

They fell silent for a while and an agreeable camaraderie filled the study. Charles, not knowing whether to let himself fall asleep again or keep himself awake, settled on a pleasant drowsiness between the two into which a few pointed thoughts nevertheless made inroads.

After some time he asked: "Is there really such a thing as just war, Monseigneur?"

More silence.

Finally the visitor said: "The idea of killing sanctioned by God—*Deus vult*... Well, it seemed most unholy to me. We were taught to hate; whipped into a frenzy of rage and revenge. One cannot kill if one doesn't hate, you know. What god would sanction that?"

"It was part of the general violence of your age, though, wasn't it?" said Charles.

"And your age isn't violent?" the man retorted. A stern note had crept into the lush baritone. "Heads are still being severed in Outre-mer, aren't they? Violence and discord abounds. War is raging everywhere. An infinity of hate and revenge keeps the killing alive."

Charles lay still and watched the shadows cast by the candle dance across the wall. There was nothing to add or refute. The man was right, of course. *He must feel so desolate that bloodshed has only thrived since his time.*

He'd perceived a hesitation in his guest that didn't appear to have anything to do with the subject at hand: a tight, coiled aspect one would expect in a superb hunter and warrior, but that this time, away from the hunt, seemed to embody long-suppressed disclosure.

Charles could sense the man's turmoil. He tried to raise himself on the sofa but the throbbing in his head was just too great. As it happened, he didn't have to ask his most pressing question—the one he'd harbored since boyhood and had finally mustered the courage to ask.

"The woman I loved did not follow my god," said the guest, pre-empting Charles. Though spoken softly, the words had torn through the tiny opening that had been made for their exit and now careened around the room, irretrievable. "She followed the ways of the Earth," he breathed.

The admission, and its wrenching delivery, filled Charles with unexpected joy.

"Charles..." the visitor began. And as if he were making the confession he'd never been able to make to a priest, he told him about Arda.

LXXXVIII

He started with his own mother.

"Ida of Lorraine had the most wondrous, mystical vision of the world," said Charles's guest. "She believed it was a true marriage between creator and creation: the purest of harmonies. We lived amidst such arbitrary cruelty and oppression so it was remarkable that she still thought this. She was a Christian in the deepest, best sense. Had she known what Holy War truly entailed, she would have called her sons home at once. I'm sure of it."

There was that shifting sound again; the coarse, measured breathing.

"My mother taught me how to listen to the voice of God," the man continued. "But..."

Charles lifted his head to glimpse his interlocutor: there had been such distress in his tone.

"But?" Charles prompted him, never dreaming that the man would complete the sentence the way he did.

"I'm not sure that I've ever heard the voice of God," he said.

"But sir!"

At all times speak the truth.

Charles had no doubt that the man's word could be trusted. *But how was such an admission possible from this famous Christian?* "What did you do?" he asked with a quaver.

Far from balking at the question, the man seemed to embrace it.

"I rode incognito to a village called Rêve-sur-Semois," he said, with both relief and eagerness. "They told me to seek out a woman who lived near a pool deep in the woods. I did this, and encountered a strange person indeed. Her religion was one of peace; of oneness with Nature and the cosmos.

"I didn't speak to her at first," he went on. "She was sitting on a rock in the pool and I just listened to her play her instrument: a lyra. There

370

were frequent visitors who sought her counsel. It was some time before I had the courage to do this, too. You see, Charles…"

"Yes?"

"She wasn't…well…*Christian*. I never could have talked to anyone about her. Certainly not my mother. The old beliefs of the forest, and the seeresses who guarded them…they were mercilessly snuffed out by the Church. The only person who knew about Arda was my squire, Stephen de la Fontaine."

Charles turned on the sofa and groaned softly. *Did the visitor know about Stephen's own love for the forest girl?* He sipped some water, his nerves frayed.

Did the man know about the child? That is was his?

"It's *your* blood, Monseigneur," Charles muttered. "*Your* blood." But the words did not breach the vapors of the sick room.

Charles reveled in his visitor's descriptions of Arda's forest pool—of the Semois valley as it used to be: impenetrable forests that could swallow whole armies; a universe of rock, marshland, birdcalls, springs, all of which had been compromised or exploited in recent times. He rode at the elbow of this strange interloper telling a story that Charles already knew. He listened to the sound of the lyra that had drawn two men irrevocably toward their destiny. How easy it was to imagine the wail of that exotic instrument: the longing that was not human, or angelic, but something trapped between the two.

And the girl herself…

Hers was not the description of physical beauty or clichéd romance one would expect from a medieval lover, but of respect…of awe. "Arda was a healer," the man said. "A diviner." He spoke deliberately; with tenderness. "She carried the wisdom of the ancients." He thought for a moment. "The stillness of the heron." Then he said: "To believe in the sanctity of the Earth is humanity's only way forward. Remember that, Charles. Please, remember it."

Charles's heart began to race. He could feel his fever spiking. *Could a Christian hero say such a thing?*

"But really," the guest continued, "everything Arda needed to say, she said through her music."

"Through her music..." Charles echoed.

There was a pause; a profound hush, as if the man were searching for something so ephemeral, the only way to capture it was to imprint it on the soul, and he wasn't sure that he'd done this completely.

An outrageous thought occurred to Charles: that he might somehow summon the strength to get off the sofa, make it to the corridor and retrieve the blackened piece of lyra from the pocket of Theodore's oilskin. In his current condition, this seemed impossible. He also feared that were he to do this, his guest might be gone when he came back.

Nevertheless, he pulled himself up, struggled to his feet, swayed for some moments and shuffled to the door. *How strange that the man hasn't offered to help me*, he thought.

No one was around. Sylvana must have been resting upstairs. His legs teetered underneath him as he crossed the hall to the kitchen corridor, but the tiles felt delightfully cool against his bare feet and the sensation propelled him forward.

Charles retrieved the carbonized fragment and struggled back across the hall. He stopped at the door of the study, heartbroken:

The stool was empty.

"Monseigneur," Charles moaned, leaning against the door frame. He managed to get to the desk, where he set the piece of lyra next to the ivory olifant. By then the room was spinning. Somehow he made it back to the sofa and collapsed onto the creaking leather. He fell asleep at once.

It was the hot, lurid sleep of the sickbed.

He leapt up to the ridge as easily as an enchanter, to the place where the menhirs loomed like judges. *The lyra lingers in the air here.* Indeed, it lingered now. The player seemed to be asking questions of the instrument, and at each answer, dared to ask more, playing her way closer and closer to the source. *Maybe she knows where my visitor has gone,* Charles murmured. *Maybe he isn't so very far away.* As if in answer, there was that same rasping sound; the sour, metallic taste. *Why did they call you the Swan Knight?* Charles asked, for he'd felt the presence again. *Why couldn't anyone know your name?*

Ah, that, said the grave baritone. *It's an appealing legend. But there was another bird, too...*

LXXXIX

"You've been sleeping for almost twenty-four hours," Sylvana said, helping Charles to sit up. She offered him some water. "Did you know that you talk in your sleep?"

"No, I didn't," he said. "How long have I spent on this sofa?"

"Five days. You should try to get up."

Sylvana put Theodore's slippers on his feet and his dressing gown around his shoulders and steadied him as he got up. Together they inched their way to the hall, where they stopped to rest. Charles had avoided glancing at the empty stool. In his blurred state, he couldn't quite remember why he'd been tempted to look there at all.

"Is the olifant still on the desk?" he asked Sylvana in confusion.

She stalled. "Why on earth are you asking me that?" She sounded worried, as if her patient had suffered a relapse.

"Please, could you go and check?"

Sylvana looked at the desk from the door. "Yes, it's there."

"Is there anything next to it?" Charles asked, his voice trembling.

To humor him, Sylvana went over to the desk.

"No," she said. "There's nothing next to it. Now let's go to the kitchen and have some of Marcel's nettle soup."

She guided him to the kitchen past the coats hanging in the corridor. Charles had only a faint recollection of making the reckless trip to the coats from his sickbed. Not too faint, however, for he stopped again to search the pockets of Theodore's oilskin.

They were empty.

What had happened to the piece of lyra?

He paused. "I'll be all right," he said, gesturing for Sylvana to go ahead.

He searched the pockets again, this time in the hope that he might remember what had happened at the grave—whether he'd really taken

374

the charred bit of wood, or whether he'd imagined it along with everything else he'd obviously been imagining in the miasma of illness.

There was no sign of the object.

"Come," Sylvana said from the kitchen. "The soup will do you good."

They shared the simple meal, and Sylvana filled him in on what had been happening while he was ill.

Florus had gone back to Brussels for a conference, taking Osselaer with him, who wanted to deliver all the breaking news to Ida personally. Florus would stay in Brussels, but Osselaer was due back at Rêve at any time.

Charles reached for Sylvana's hand and clasped it as tightly as his depleted strength would allow. He balked: exhaustion had ravaged her. Her skin had gone alarmingly gray and her eyes, those vibrant forest pools, were dull and lifeless.

"What about Raul?" he said, fearing her answer.

"Nothing yet," she said. "The Bouillon police have been searching up and down the river. You would think they would have found a...a..." Her voice caught.

"But darling, that's good news!"

For a moment, Sylvana paused to savor Charles's endearment and touch his cheek.

"As long as they haven't found a body," he said, "there's hope."

"Yes, maybe," Sylvana said, unconvinced. "Also, your mobile has been ringing a lot. I hope you don't mind, but I've been checking it to see if there might be some news about Raul."

"And...?"

"And it was always your father."

A chill burrowed into Charles. "My father? What did he want?"

He knew, of course, what Hugh wanted: to take control of a situation that had gone horribly awry. The chill deepened as he asked: "Where is he? Do you know?

"No."

"He didn't come back to Brussels, did he?" Even as he said this, Charles knew how unlikely this was, as whatever had gone wrong with Hugh's Blancheron scheme would certainly have been overshadowed by the criminal issues waiting for him as soon as he set foot in Belgium.

Sylvana enfolded his hand in both of hers. "What does it matter, Charles?" she said. "He can't harm you now." She gave him a cryptic smile. "You're part of the swan's story, you know," she said. "An appealing legend. But there was another bird, too."

Charles stared at her. His light-headedness returned. *Had she been listening at the study door?* The words had been his own, surely. The fever had made him talk in his sleep.

But he remembered the baritone that had uttered them: *it had not been his own.*

At that moment, the front door opened and Osselaer called out a greeting.

The notary appeared in the kitchen brandishing a file of papers. A smile creased the narrow face.

"Forms for your purchase of Blancheron, Monsieur de la Fontaine!" he crowed. "Anonymous, of course. Hugues is already aware that a buyer is interested. After everything that's happened, he had no choice but to accept a far lower offer than he'd hoped for. The only way he'll find out it's you is if he comes to Blancheron himself one day, which is unlikely."

Sylvana leapt up, helped Osselaer out of his coat and offered him tea, making Charles wonder how many times she'd reenacted such rituals over the past several days, always in the service of someone else.

"Cédric has a conference in Brussels, apparently?" Charles said.

"Well...let's just say that he has business to attend to."

"Regarding the parchment?"

Osselaer stalled. "Regarding a journalist he contacted about the whole sorry business."

"A journalist?" said Sylvana.

Looks were exchanged around the kitchen table.

"Cédric seems to think that he can pre-empt Ames," Osselaer said.

More looks exchanged.

"In the press, that is," Osselaer elaborated. "In an article in *Europe Weekly* that's coming out tomorrow." He inflated slightly, adding:

"Cédric let me drive his MG down from Brussels today. He'll take the train when he comes back to Rêve on Friday."

They all fell silent over their soup and tea.

At length Osselaer said: "By the way, I'm glad to see that the gonfalon is finally flying again. I'm just surprised that you made it up all those stairs, Charles!"

Charles stared at him. "I could barely make it to the kitchen," he said. He glanced at Sylvana. "Did you hang up the banner?"

She shook her head.

They turned their attention to Osselaer.

"Well, it's there, I assure you!" he said. "It's just odd that the window was open. Generally, whoever puts the banner out closes it afterwards."

POSTSCRIPT

*E**urope Weekly*, 1 November
Brussels Edition

Blancheron Castle, situated in the Belgian province of Luxembourg near the village of Rêve-sur-Semois and dating from the first half of the twelfth century, was recently put on the market by its current owner, Hugh Fontaine, a resident of the American state of Connecticut. Fontaine's ancestors, the de la Fontaine family, have had unbroken ownership of Blancheron since its construction began in around 1107. The castle itself is in ruined condition, but the estate also comprises a large nineteenth-century villa and considerable lands.

New explosive claims have emerged that the de la Fontaine family is descended from a child fathered by the legendary Godfrey of Bouillon (ca. 1060 – 1100), Duke of Lower Lorraine, former owner of Bouillon Castle in the Belgian Ardennes and a leader of the First Crusade. The information came to light in a twelfth-century parchment that was found at the villa on the Blancheron estate. Cédric Florus, renowned scholar of medieval history and retired Head of Manuscripts at the Library of European History in Brussels, has studied the parchment in question and conclusively pronounced it to be a hoax. This will no doubt disappoint Fontaine and his heirs, as clearly the sale was timed to coincide with the breaking news of the parchment's revelations. The list price of the estate has already plummeted drastically.

Interested buyers were flocking from as far away as Russia and China when prominent antiquarian, Manfred Ames, leaked the news that Godfrey, famously celibate and a pious Christian, had fathered a child with a local woman considered to be a heretic before his departure to the Holy Land in August, 1097. The bogus parchment also claims that the child was raised at Blancheron Castle by one of Godfrey's squires, Stephen de la Fontaine, who adopted him and gave him his name. Not a single chronicle of the period—or any reputable historian of the Crusades—makes mention of this sensational claim.

In other news from the Ardennes, a critically injured man was found on the bank of the Semois River near Rêve-sur-Semois on Monday. His identity is still unknown. He had in his possession an antique wooden box estimated to be hundreds of years old. Investigators have learned that the box was stolen from the Blancheron estate and the man was attempting to return it. He is expected to survive.

A NOTE TO THE READER

*T*he *Heron Legacy* is a work of fiction inspired by history: a story through which historical events, personages, places and documents have been woven alongside their fictional counterparts. Blancheron Castle, Villa Antioch and the village of Rêve-sur-Semois are invented locales in the Belgian Ardennes, although the enterprising explorer is sure to find actual ruins, houses and villages on the Semois River that could have served as models for these places.

Details of the First Crusade, as well descriptions of both the present-day and medieval Ardennes, have been rendered as faithfully as possible. All text from Albert of Aachen's chronicle is quoted from the Susan B. Edgington translation. The excerpts from Ralph of Caen are taken from the Bernard S. Bachrach and David S. Bachrach translation. Thank you to these distinguished scholars.

Godfrey of Bouillon is an imposing historical figure whose story nevertheless contains many shadowy elements. It is into these shadows that the author's imagination felt free to roam.

ACKNOWLEDGMENTS

No book is seaworthy without the support, advice, insight and deft pen of an editor, and for all those things I am so grateful to you, Jones Hayden.

Then, intrepid, the book sets sail, and owes much to the courageous early readers who have kept the story on its course. Mark Cackler, Rosemary Clayton, Miriam van Dixhoorn, Shelley Hanson, Barbara Kieffer, Mary Pat Lease, Art Oller, Kathy Parsons, Maggie Robinson: heartfelt thanks to you all!

Dr. Michiel Verweij, professor of Latin at KU Leuven and specialist in medieval manuscripts at the Royal Library of Belgium: thank you for taking time from your distinguished research to venture into the fancies of fiction, tempering this novelist's love of invention with some expert advice on Latin usage and medieval parchments.

To my family, whose love and encouragement keep me afloat and help me find words on the air of my little room, I can only say: "I could not find those words without you." And to Peter, champion rower: "Your steady hand on the oar makes everything possible."

LEONA FRANCOMBE is the author of
The Heron Legacy, The Universe in 3/4 Time: A Novel of Old Europe
(shortlisted for the Eric Hoffer Award Grand Prize), *The Sage of
Waterloo, Madame Ernestine und die Entdeckung der Liebe* and
numerous essays and short stories. Her discovery of a medieval ruin in
a remote part of the Ardennes Forest inspired *The Heron Legacy*.

Leona is also a pianist and composer. She lives in Belgium with her
family.

For more information please visit:
www.leonafrancombe.com

Printed in Great Britain
by Amazon

58883633R00219